The
True
Sources
of the
Nile

The True Sources of the Nile

A Novel

SARAH STONE

Doubleday

New York London Toronto Sydney Auckland

PUBLISHED BY DOUBLEDAY
a division of Random House, Inc.
1540 Broadway, New York, New York 10036

DOUBLEDAY and the portrayal of an anchor with a dolphin
are trademarks of Doubleday, a division of Random House, Inc.

Book design by Caroline Cunningham

Library of Congress Cataloging-in-Publication Data
Stone, Sarah, 1961–
The true sources of the Nile / by Sarah Stone.— 1st ed.
p. cm.
1. Women human rights workers—Fiction.   2. Cancer—Patients—
Family relationships—Fiction.   3. Tutsi (African people)—Fiction.
4. Mothers and daughters—Fiction.   5. Americans—Burundi—Fiction.
6. Burundi—Fiction.   I. Title.
PS3619.T68 T7 2002
813'.6—dc21   2001037293

ISBN 0-385-50301-6

May 2002

First Edition
10   9   8   7   6   5   4   3   2   1

For Andrea Barrett

A Note About the Names

Presidents Major Pierre Buyoya and Melchior Ndadaye, as well as Pontien Karibwami and Gilles Bimazubute, who were president and vice president of the National Assembly when Melchior Ndadaye was president, are actual historical figures. The rest of the characters in this novel are fictional and bear no relation to any actual persons, living or dead. For Kirundi speakers, or those who know Burundian culture well, it will be apparent that the names I have used are arbitrary, which is never the case among the real-life Burundians. If these characters were real people, their names might reflect not only their ethnicity and clan, but historical events, religious backgrounds, the circumstances surrounding their births, their parents' states of mind at the time of their birth, their parents' worries or hopes for them, and so on.

I wanted to be clear that this is a work of fiction and not a history. More realistic names would identify these imagined people too closely with locales or family groupings. Jean-Pierre and his family are invented, and therefore of no actual Ganwa clan.

All human beings are born free and equal in dignity and rights. They are endowed with reason and conscience and should act towards one another in a spirit of brotherhood.

—Article 1, Universal Declaration of Human Rights

Man is altogether desire, say the Upanishads.

—Robert Hass, *Human Wishes*

The
True
Sources
of the
Nile

One

It began as an ordinary lunchtime. Every business and government office in Burundi had shut down for two or three hours, and Jean-Pierre came to join me. We'd already disappeared into the bedroom while Deo, my housekeeper, finished making lunch. The sound of his disapproving hymns, floating back from the kitchen, had continued all through our lovemaking. Now we sat on my porch, gorging ourselves on Nile perch lapped in palm oil and surrounded by green bananas baked until they were soft, fat, sticky with oil. Though it wasn't raining just then, it had been earlier, and the clouds were thick and spectacular overhead, massed above the black mountains of Zaire as they rose up across the lake, the light and water harmonizing in dense, luminous grays.

We picked through our rice, casually, sorting for little rocks, and Jean-Pierre said to me, in his rich Kirundi-accented French, "I have such a surprise for you."

"A surprise?"

"Don't make any arrangements for the weekend. Friday, after work, look for my driver. What would you say to being away from other people for a few days?"

"I'd say, yes, *please*. Should I bring anything?"

"I will have what you need. Deo and I have an understanding. But don't try to get anything out of him. He doesn't know the whole story." He crossed his arms. I had his smiles memorized: this private, ironic smile, full of secrets; his official smile, judicious, formal—lips narrowed, teeth covered; and a reckless, teeth-baring grin, a smile that made me crazy with desire.

The neighbors' dogs, all eight of them, began to bark (how I wanted to poison them! Sometimes, when I slept alone and they kept me awake with their barking and howling, I would imagine how I'd do it, though I'd always been an animal lover before). Outside, on the broken pavement of the road, a tank rumbled by. But it was only one, and Jean-Pierre paid it no attention, so I knew it didn't mean much. My house wasn't that far from the military installation.

We had stopped eating. I wanted to go back to bed, but not to overdo it, to lose the chance of spending the night together. "Shall we take a walk?"

"You have read my mind. Again." He grinned, and I grinned back. An awareness of the way two very different creatures could function as one. He reached out and took my hand.

My house was only ten minutes by foot from Lake Tanganyika, though there was no time of day when I could safely walk to the lake by myself. The streets were half-deserted; all the stores and stands were closed for the midday break. We passed the Musée Vivante, with its re-creation of a traditional housing compound, and an adjoining reptile park. The park had an old crocodile in a shallow pond, glass cages full of mambas, and one indifferent king snake who'd been flown out from California to live on a branch and a pile of rocks. He was taken out and shown to frightened tourists and children who couldn't tell a poisonous snake from a harmless one.

"I want to see the bats," I said, and Jean-Pierre, courteous and obliging, turned around. We walked toward the Ministry of Education and the fruit bats.

The earth was unbearably red. Banana trees, jacaranda, and papayas crowded the mud-streaked, potholed roads, luscious and terrible. The saddest place in the world, this piece of central Africa, site of a terrible history—German and Belgian colonization, the breaking of Ruanda-Urundi into two countries: Rwanda and Burundi. Coup after coup. And, most of all, the struggles between Tutsi and Hutu: power grabs, betrayals, death, people fleeing to Zaire. But Burundi felt more and more like home to me. The leaves and blossoms shone jade, emerald, rose, and vermilion against silver and ebony trunks. I inhaled the smells of wet earth, of diesel fuel from the truck rumbling past, of Jean-Pierre beside me, sharp and familiar. He was sweating, and the smell of his skin aroused me, uselessly.

As we walked, we told each other stories about our mornings. Jean-Pierre was a government official at the Ministry of the Interior, a kind of internal affairs bureau. He maneuvered fluently in Burundi's local, trade, and colonial languages—Kirundi, Kiswahili, and French—and with difficulty in English. Apart from English, I had only my rapid but awkward French and a little Kiswahili, so we always talked in French, with Kiswahili words thrown in.

Now Jean-Pierre told me about a colleague who hadn't been available when urgent papers needed to be signed (all signatures in Burundi have to be gathered in the proper order), and then it had been discovered that someone had seen him in the Bally store in the morning, and someone else in the afternoon—this subminister had spent an entire day picking out shoes. I was laughing helplessly, my hands over my eyes. The bracelet Jean-Pierre had given me for my birthday, heavy, hammered-gold links, fell forward against my face. He looked at me, and then he stopped talking. I often didn't know how to interpret his silences.

"What are you thinking?" I hadn't meant to ask. We'd been

lovers for six months; he was the first man who had ever made me think, for more than two weeks, *marriage, children.*

He shook his head with a half-smile of refusal. I had a brief moment of missing the self I had been before I knew him, my brisk energy, my effectiveness and decision. I looked at him again, trying to see him as I might after twenty years of marriage, and then as I might if I were a stranger passing him in the street.

After a moment he said, slowly, "What you were asking earlier. About my family." He had introduced me to a couple of his sisters, reluctantly, as a friend. I went along with the fiction, which they may or may not have believed, but it didn't seem very loyal or noble of him. After struggling with myself for weeks, I had said something today, when we were getting dressed again. I'd brought out what was on my mind, that he was ashamed of me, and his evident surprise had reassured me, but he hadn't really replied.

Now, though, he said, "You have so much life in you. So much bravery. You do not think, If I move my rook, in four moves, the bishop will check my king." He frowned and touched my arm, as close as he would come to caressing me in public. "Before you, I was half alive. But when your leg is asleep, and it comes back to life, there is also pain, isn't there?"

"Not for long, not if you move around and get the circulation going again."

"For my family also, there will be some pain. They think already that I should not have spent so much time at the Sorbonne." I started to object, but he said, suddenly deciding, "Soon, then, I will tell them. Do not worry." He touched my cheek, briefly, smiling. "You have your Mary-at-the-foot-of-the-Cross look. But it is unnecessary." He had said to me, more than once, that my long, oval face and round eyes made me look like a fifteenth-century Italian Madonna. I actually thought I looked a little stupid, a little surprised, most of the time. Two years earlier, on my thirty-fifth birthday, I had chopped off all my hair in an attempt to look worldly. It hadn't worked, and I was growing it out again.

Jean-Pierre said, "The bats," and we walked across the gravel of the parking lot, stopping halfway, standing back from the two great trees, fifty feet tall and so thick with bats that the trees themselves seemed to be shimmering, moving. The ground was limed with guano, and the trees' foliage had disappeared under the weight of bats clinging to bats, a dozen deep. In the evening, clumps of bats would fall away, detaching themselves, skimming out into the sky, uttering squeaking cries as they flew. Even in the daytime, an endless chittering hum of high-pitched squeaks came from the restless sleepers where they clung.

I felt myself being looked at, and turned to see Jean-Pierre watching me, smiling. He lifted up an arm and pointed at one fascinating set of shapes; I had the sense, again, of *seeing in tandem*, of being half of a two-part unit of perception and analysis.

I turned my head as we walked away, watching the bats until the last possible minute, both charmed and unnerved. Around us stood small groups of tourists or visitors, fascinated by that great huddling mass which could break loose at any time, the bats beautiful, but also creatures out of a nightmare.

On the way home, Jean-Pierre said, "I can drive you back to your work if you like. Perhaps we'll have dinner at Chez Laurent."

Knowing I'd see him again that day filled me with happiness which lifted me up, like helium, almost onto my tiptoes so that my feet bounced along under me.

The houses around us, great square fortresses of buildings, bars on the windows, crouched behind guarded fences or hedges. I smiled at the guards, many of whom knew me by sight, and they smiled back, some nervously. A teenage boy on a bicycle labored past us, so loaded down with green bananas that his bike wobbled.

Then we reached my house. Deo stood on the front steps,

waving frantically. "A woman speaking English. Crying." And, no, he had no idea who she was.

I ran inside, but the connection had been cut. The call had to have been from the U.S.—anyone in Burundi would have had enough Swahili or French to at least leave a message. I dialed my younger sister, Lizzie, but she wasn't home, and neither was Mom. Then I tried my older sister, Margaret, thinking that it was useless, but she answered at once. "Good. I thought he hadn't understood me."

"It *was* you, then."

"Annie," she said, her voice dramatic. "I think you had better sit down for this," which frightened me, of course, and gave me a sense of forboding, but also a flicker of annoyance. I thought it was just like Margaret to use this clumsy and melodramatic phrasing, to insist on the drama of something that would need no insistence, that would be bad enough on its own. "It's about Mom," she said. "She goes in for surgery tomorrow."

"What's wrong?"

"A malignancy in her larynx. We don't know how bad it is. But it could be. They operate tomorrow. How soon can you get here?"

I had a shocked feeling of recognition, of the expected. So many of my friends had had to do this already. But I didn't believe it yet. I covered the receiver and said to Jean-Pierre, "My mother is very ill." He ran his hand up my back, squeezing my shoulder. If I hadn't known him so well, I wouldn't even have seen the quick glance at his other wrist, the little shifting of his shirtsleeve that uncovered his Rolex. I was furious with him, but also with myself because I too was thinking about my own schedule, my work, Jean-Pierre, my life in Burundi. His sister Christine was getting married the weekend after the approaching one, and he had finally invited me to come, although as part of a group that included several other Americans, not singled out in any way. And then there was his mysterious surprise for Friday.

I said to Margaret, "Meg, I am so sorry. I'll call her. But I can't come home. We have the first elections in Burundi's history, the first elections with more than one candidate, coming up next week. Anything could happen. Democracy. Civil war. I have work I have to do."

"Annie, you haven't taken it in yet. And you're not the clearest thinker at the best of times. I'll be at the hospital today, home tonight. You can call me with your flight information." I could picture her in her glossy kitchen, too full of energy to sit down, even when talking on the phone. At forty-two, only five years older than me, eight years older than Lizzie, she had settled into a matronly middle-age, her face age-spotted and wrinkled from time out in the family orchards, her manner a hard shell of bossiness, brisk purpose. When I didn't answer, she said fiercely, "You'll have to stop being the international expert now, jet-setting around with your friends and telling the Third World what to do about itself. I'm afraid we still don't have any *servants* here. And your *mother* needs you."

"I'll call you later," I said and hung up, tipping my head back to try to take in more air, pulling my shirt front away with sweating fingers.

I said to Jean-Pierre, "Elections. And Janvier Barantandikiye and Jacques Nahimana at least being considered for release from prison." It had taken eight months of hard work to get even to this point: months of research, pursuing officials, attending polite dinners, negotiating for the gentle pressures and assistance of World Watch/Africa and Amnesty, pleading for the inevitably low-key help of the State Department. Hours in the waiting areas of dusty government buildings, day after day after day. I thought *FreeAfrica!* finally might be about to effect Barantandikiye and Nahimana's releases. Men who could be very important Hutu leaders. The religious prisoners, the Jehovah's Witnesses and Seventh-Day Adventists, had largely been released, but not the political prisoners. Since *FreeAfrica!* had only three employees, my American boss, Jack, his

African assistant, Charles, and me, we couldn't spare anyone. And what about my investigations into certain disappearances, into the stories of bodies in the Ruzizi up in Cibitoke province? "I can't leave Jack to ruin this."

I shouldn't have said even this much. Barantandikiye and Nahimana were imprisoned for belonging to FRODEBU, the illegal, mostly Hutu opposition party. UPRONA, the government party, was Jean-Pierre's, of course. He came from the ruling class, his family a part of one of Burundi's royal dynasties, so his sympathies, of course, lay with the Tutsi. We talked about the details of my job sometimes, but the purposes behind it as little as possible, even though Jean-Pierre had indicated to me sympathy with the idea of a more open government, of a real democracy.

"What is your mother ill with?"

"Cancer," I said, and burst into tears without warning. My mother's sharp little remarks, the smile when she had made them. The world without her, inconceivable. "I can't go. I can't not go. She might be dying." I heard in my voice a stagy theatricality, like Margaret's.

Jean-Pierre put his arms around me, and I burrowed into him, my head under his chin. What if I left and he came to believe while I was gone that we had been caught in a kind of erotic madness, that he should be breaking it off with this alien American woman? I didn't know if I had had time yet to prove to him that I could fit permanently into his life. And what if my feelings about him changed, what if I saw him differently, away from his actual presence? I also felt what I could hardly acknowledge, a cowardly desire to get out of Burundi, to escape the suffocating atmosphere of fear and suspicion.

The borders with Tanzania and Rwanda were closed. Tutsi soldiers with locked-down faces and scary eyes (they were scared themselves, but you looked into those eyes and you could see what they'd already done in their lives, what they were prepared for) stood all along the streets, bayonets mounted. Rolls of barbed wire appeared in the night, steel tumbleweeds, blocking the roads. Checkpoints. When we drove, we moved at the soldiers' pace, white foreigners silently impatient, Burundians terrified. The soldiers turned minibuses full of Hutus into the streets, examining them one by one, making a production over their *cartes d'identités*, their papers. The Hutus submitted absolutely, shaking. If I stayed, would I be staying for the elections, or because of my fear of breaking the enchantment Jean-Pierre and I had together? If I left, would I be going because of my longing to see, and my duty toward, my mother, or would I be running away from the tension of Burundian life?

/ / /

On the way to the airport two days later we had to produce our papers five times, although when the soldiers saw Jean-Pierre's, they gave a kind of bow and made smiling jokes in Kirundi. More than one of the embassy people had said to me that the HIV-positive rate in the army was over 90 percent, and that all of them knew this.

I put my hand into my pocket, touching the little silver cross which had been my grandmother's, my father's mother's, which I'd taken from my father's bedside table hours before his funeral. I don't know when or how my grandmother had acquired it, but it was at least a hundred years old, almost black with tarnish. She had attended church every Sunday; my father stopped when he left home and never went back to it, but when she died, my father brought her cross back from the funeral and took to carrying it with him. After his death, my mother had asked all of us where the cross had gone—fixating on the small loss. She, like me, had remembered him turning it over in his fingers, rubbing the silver beading. It had become my good luck charm, but now I would have to give it to her.

As we got close to the airport, I could see the lake, gray and silver. A skin of red, eroded dirt spread out from the shoreline. Two cormorants, uttering painful-sounding cries, rose in an arc over the

Black and White, a notorious nightclub which looked only dusty and sad in the daytime. One old Renault was parked in the dirt of the nightclub lot. The car had been stripped months before and was rusting where it stood. I checked again for ticket, passport, shot card, while Jean-Pierre drove along the clean straight lines of the Ulvira road, passing Africans on foot or bicycles, the women in brightly dressed groups, the men eyeing us in suspicion or with longing for Jean-Pierre's old Suzuki.

"You might talk to your family while I'm gone?" I tried this out in my primitive Swahili. I wanted to move away from the colonial French used by the Greeks, Belgians, and Indians who ran the port and the shipping, the stores, and the import businesses—although everyone in Burundi used Swahili as easily as French.

Jean-Pierre patted my leg but didn't answer. "We've learned to hide what we think and feel," he'd said to me once.

And, after all, I hadn't told my family about him either. That was another thing we had in common, families who kept important things private. I remembered my mother carefully sealing money from the sale of her eggs and chickens into an old, postmarked envelope, hiding it among the tape, paper clips, notepaper, and stamps in her bureau drawer. My father was outside, preparing for another disappointing apple harvest. I'd walked in on my mother without warning—I was about six and still hoping that I could somehow surprise her into warmth, into holding me on her lap and stroking my hair. My mother hadn't had time or patience for the imaginary or time-wasting, for the luxuries of games and cuddling.

She was obviously dismayed, but she smiled. "You don't understand yet, but you will. And for now, it will be something only you and I know." She blew me a kiss. I would have agreed to anything which would yoke her to me more firmly. My father, Margaret, Lizzie would all be outside our secret, and her attention would be on me, not on them, not on her chickens, apple trees, patchwork, baking, dishes, laundry.

Now tears ran down my cheeks and the sides of my nose. Without looking away from the road, Jean-Pierre reached one hand down to touch my knee. "You have the eyes of a cow, Ah-na," he said softly—a great Burundian compliment, and an old joke between us.

I wiped my face. Jean-Pierre moved his hand to my thigh and left it there, comforting me as he drove. Both of his own parents were dead, though I didn't know what they had died of; that seemed to be one of many taboo subjects about his childhood. But he understood my fears. There was no safe spot to pull over along this road, no way for him to stop and hold me. If we stopped, we would be set upon by bandits with rocks or maybe iron bars. But I was no longer crying—the feeling of his hand on my thigh started the heat that spread in all directions, the ferocious hunger for him.

He said formally, though also somewhat ironically, "This I have not seen for myself, I have heard it told by my ancestors," the traditional indication that he was beginning a story from Burundi's history and lore. I nodded, concentrating. He went on, "When the very first of our kings, Ntare I, was old, a drought fell over the land. The sun burned terribly, the crops failed, and so the people went for help to the soothsayers, who revealed, after some deliberation and fear for their own lives, that because the king was old and withered, because he had lived past his time, drought had seized the country. All the people were afraid to tell the king the truth, that it was time for him to die, but when he heard the decree of the soothsayers, he said that he would do what he must to save his country, and if he could preserve his people then he would die without regrets. He spent the evening with friends, eating and drinking, then went to sleep stretched out on a bed with a bowl of water underneath. His loyal retainers, following his orders, set fire to his home. The king slept deeply and without stirring as the palace burned. The fire was extinguished at dawn by the falling of the rain." Jean-Pierre concluded, also according to the traditional formula, "And that is what I have had to tell: let there now be peace."

We were silent for a moment, out of respect for the story. Then he added, "Of course, there are many stories about Ntare I, many versions, most of them fantastic. But this one makes its point: in doing our duty, we find tranquillity. You are right to go home, Ah-na."

We were quiet again, and then I asked, "Jean-Pierre, when you think of 'home,' is it your family? Or a particular place and the memories of that place? What did you miss most when you were at school? Or when you're in France or Belgium?"

He considered this. The open, engaging upper half of his face, his compact forehead and nose, gave him a boyish look when he was laughing. When he was serious, though, the way his long jaw and round chin pushed forward could make him appear stubborn, even when he was just being thoughtful. "My first instinct is to say my sisters and brothers, my elders, my friends. Or bananas in palm oil. Or the gray light after rain. But perhaps, most of all, it is the sense of what I am here, the way in which I am a part of a structure and my place and tasks are clear. In Europe, I am only another African. I become visible merely as a representative of a culture, a symbol of immigration in Paris, and so on."

"Almost the opposite for me. Because in the U.S., I'm just another American."

"So this may have to do with the smallness of Burundi. Another characteristic, for me, of home. It is all *known*. Nothing here can be unfamiliar."

Before Jean-Pierre, I had been someone who thought about the practicalities of work, first public health, then human rights. Also, what I was going to eat next, what I had to do that day, whether the pothole I had just driven over had damaged the car, little practical matters. I wanted to say to someone, *He makes me think about the world. How did I get into my midthirties without ever really thinking about what anything meant?* But there was no one I could say this to. My best friend in Burundi, Zoë, had gone to Malaysia. If it hadn't been for Jean-Pierre and my human rights work, I would have followed her. Then there was Christine, Jean-Pierre's younger sister, but that friendship was still no more than a hope, based on a couple of ambiguous encounters.

I put my hand above his knee, squeezing a little, trying to make a joke of my need, "You won't forget me while I'm gone, will you? You'll still be here when I get back?"

"It is an experiment," he said. "Perhaps I will be here. Or perhaps I will perish of loneliness. I do not talk to others the way I talk to you."

"You read my mind. Again." I smiled, but he was looking sad and didn't answer.

/   /   /

The airport was a series of white domes like a row of duck egg tops. A dome for waiting, for greetings and good-byes, its spiral staircase and stretches of floor crammed with people; a dome for ticketing and the paperwork and bureaucracy of departure; a dome for baggage and customs and the paperwork and bureaucracy of arrival. Throughout the airport, voices rose up and echoed back at each other, so that there always seemed to be a minor crisis in progress.

Jean-Pierre and I came in through a glass door in a wall of glass doors. The army major (same rank, theoretically, as President Major Pierre Buyoya) in charge of airport security acknowledged us and we went up to him to exchange courtesies.

"A small country," Jean-Pierre had said to me. "Everyone knows everyone." We were on social, reception-going terms with a number of them, but this man—all the army high-ups—frightened me. The coldness of their faces. The remote eyes. No one with a military history could be clear of implications, not in Burundi. How many of them were personally responsible for the deaths of hundreds, maybe thousands, of Hutus? How many had used their bayonets or machetes on the relatives of the people all around them? I used to wonder what the high-ups had to tell themselves about what it meant and who they were.

Unfortunately, my boss, Jack, was waiting in the terminal with a few Greek and American acquaintances, including the kind American administrative officer who'd helped me get out in a hurry, a clucking, detail-ridden man worn down—though he can't have been much older than I was—by bureaucracy, tropical heat and diseases, and the cautious, secretive, and ingrown State Department culture. Jack hadn't planned to come; he'd said he had too much work to do, his tone implying that since I was indulging myself with my mother's cancer, he had to carry the weight for both of us. At the sight of him, my body stiffened.

I said my hellos, then went into the ticketing area, checked my bags, filled out a series of different-colored forms. Jean-Pierre and the rest had to wait in the main dome; I could see them through the glass. What was Jack saying to them?

When I had finished, I went back out. The administrative officer said, "All the formalities accomplished, then?" and a Greek acquaintance put one arm around my shoulder. "Perhaps your mother will be better soon," she suggested. "You have great medical advances in the United States."

Jack cleared his throat. Tall, thin, lecherous, he had a grin that said he knew something you didn't—it seemed to come up out of his throat and take over his face, very unpleasant. "First time home, isn't it? Since you've been here."

"It's not a vacation." I was always defensive with him.

"I predict you are going to be one royal pain in the ass. But, hey, let the folks know what it's like out here. You just go on and do some good, honey, that's your job."

And yours too, I wanted to say. But he used to talk bitterly about the United States Agency for International Development—their huge houses, their swimming pools, their pension plans. He was still hoping to get in, to escape the hand-to-mouth life of private voluntary organizations.

"Just kidding," he said, giving me his wolf-smile.

There was an awkward pause. I could see everyone wanted to reassure me, and I wanted to help out, but couldn't think of what to say. At the souvenir kiosk, a woman in elaborate braids, looped and arranged down to her shoulders, yawned, leaning on the counter among the Burundian coffee and tea sealed into red, green, and silver packets, the pointed baskets. The airport was crowded with people, the strong smells of bodies.

Finally, I said, "Take care of yourselves here, please." We shook hands all around. The Americans hugged me, Jack for an instant too long, and then, at the last moment, so did Jean-Pierre, a little stiffly.

"*Kwa heri*," he said. Farewell.

I gave the customary answer. "*Kwa heri ya kuonana*"—Farewell until we see each other again—then had to pinch myself, hard, on the soft underflesh of my forearm, concentrating on that little, sharp, physical pain.

Jean-Pierre watched me with his grave, impenetrable look, his gray suit hardly wrinkled despite the heat and hour. He had a presence like a stone figure in the oldest collection of a museum: so imploded, so powerful, that everything else in the room just faded away, became meaningless. I had a panic-stricken thought that I wouldn't be able to leave him after all, but then they announced the last call for my flight, and the administrative officer gave me a small, friendly poke on the arm. "I'll be back in three weeks," I said. "No time at all." I turned and ran out to the tarmac.

Two

I arrived in San Francisco two and a half days later, after four flights and too much time in different airports.

Margaret met me at the airport with her children: Susan, thirteen, scarily thin, with a closed, private look and a way of smiling secretively at her feet, and Bobby, four, hiding behind his mother's legs and waving a pirate sword at me, his face and body still showing the last traces of the round deliciousness of babyhood.

Margaret had aged visibly in the last couple of years. I had always thought her the best-looking of the three of us, handsome and mournful. She had the family's long, oval face and flat cheeks, but her dark hair and large dark eyes gave her, even now, a romantic look that had nothing to do with her real nature. "Well," she said. "You certainly took your time getting here."

"The plane was late, Meg. Surely you can't hold that against me?" And then, getting hold of myself, I asked, "How is Mom?"

"Little pitchers," Margaret said, waving at the children. Susan, red with annoyance, turned and started toward the car.

On the two-hour drive, I had a feeling of unreality, of having been plunged into a world I thought I had escaped. Apple trees up and down the Gravenstein highway were just coming into bloom—rows of feathery white blossoms, spooky in the darkness.

In the living room of our mother's old house, Lizzie slept in a chair, curled around a book. Her long blond braid trailed over one shoulder, showing her ears, now sporting nine earrings between them. Her face, which awake had a pointed, foxy quality, had gone soft and childlike in sleep. When we came into the room, she opened her eyes and jumped to her feet. "Annie!" A whispered shout. She threw her arms around me and we rocked back and forth.

I was embarrassed by how dirty I was from the days of travel, how badly I smelled. "Please tell me what's going on with Mom." I looked at Margaret, who hadn't particularly wanted to hug me herself, but who now had the stiff look that sometimes came over her when she watched Lizzie and me together. I felt the usual guilt/resentment. "I'm pretty torqued that I didn't even know this was happening."

Margaret and Lizzie exchanged glances. Now they were the allies. And then Lizzie's face remembered something that made her unhappy. She turned away from Margaret and said to me, "Let's put your bags in your room." On the way, she said, "We're both being careful in front of the children. Mom doesn't want us to tell them how bad it is. So we've said she'll be better after the treatments. But. She had sore throats for months; the doctors thought it was an infection in her tonsils, so they kept giving her antibiotics. Then they decided she had a growth, and they'd just take it out. Mom didn't want to worry you. The chances of this being malignant were so small."

"What do her doctors say?"

"They can't talk to us without her permission, and she says she won't be talked over, as if she were a child. You know how she hates for people to fuss. But one night, when I was sitting up with her, she whispered that they've given her, if she does the whole chemo course, three months to two years. She's marked 'Terminal.'

She saw it on the charts. All she can buy herself is, maybe, a little time."

We put our arms around each other, clinging. Lizzie buried her still-silky head in my shoulder. She'd been my baby, and I no longer resented her annoyingly winsome little tricks—what stayed with me was the desire to protect her.

Margaret, coming through the door, surprised us, and we jumped apart, as if we were the lovers, she the spouse.

"Lizzie was just telling me what's going on with Mom." I tried to stop myself from blushing by an effort of will.

"It would surprise her too much to see you in the middle of the night, but she'll probably be awake around eight," said Margaret, her face reproachful and punishing. *Why don't you love me the way you love each other?* her expression asked.

/   /   /

Around seven the next morning, Lizzie set out plates—pancakes, eggs on top or at the side, according to each child's passionate particularities, with little soy sausages, pale at the edges and smelling suspiciously vegetable. Bobby pretended to feed some to his toy dinosaurs, and Aurora, Lizzie's three-year-old, imitated him. She had the same enchanting, willful quality as her mother, a fey otherworldliness. Margaret had gone off to her job as a bookkeeper—she was still working three days a week. Her husband, Jerry, a paper goods salesman, was off on a business trip.

I was still shaking off my dreams—the antimalarials I took, chloroquine and paludrine, gave me restless, vivid nights and a leaden taste in my mouth in the morning. The kitchen looked both familiar and strange to me: the jar of dusty artificial roses; Grandma Eleanor's old chest of drawers with a lace cloth thrown over it; Margaret's barbecue potato chips, beef jerky, and fat-free doughnuts on the refrigerator; Lizzie's isoflavone soy protein powder and vitamins next to the blender; and the children's toy fire trucks and Barbie dolls scattered across the floor, the dolls in ball dresses with their hair frizzed out, missing shoes or arms.

I said to Lizzie, "So you were going to tell me what you're doing these days." Our first chance to be alone together, I would tell her about Jean-Pierre, but I didn't want to talk about him in front of the others, not yet.

Susan pushed the food around on her plate, trying to disguise how little she actually ate. "Aunt Lizzie does a combination of past-life regression therapy and reiki. It's really cool. I wish we learned it in school. I wish we learned *anything* in school."

On the floor, Aurora held two dolls over her head, somersaulting them in the air. My pancakes and sausages were growing on me, more different flavors and textures than I expect from a breakfast. "In Burundi, only a minority from the ruling ethnic group get to go to school at all. Everyone else winds up selling pineapples and eggs at street stands, doing manual labor, driving taxis and minibuses. Ninety percent of the labor is agricultural. The minimum wage is about eighty cents a day."

Susan hid some pancake under a napkin. "That's Africa, Aunt Annie. Here the taxi drivers are all immigrants or Ph.D.'s in philosophy. So what are we going to school *for*? $X + y$ times $x - y$. I mean, could anything be more useless?"

Bobby got down from the table and began to run around the room as if accomplishing some urgent task. He skidded into a cabinet, bounced off, and kept running.

I said, "I'm going up to see if Mom's awake." But when I opened the door to her room and tiptoed in, she was still in the hard sleep that follows a bad night, her breathing loud enough for me to hear—not a snore but a small, whistling groan. I could see, in the muffled light, purple shadows under her eyes, the puffy flesh of her face. I'd thought she'd be thinner, but she had a bloated look, like a drowned woman.

On her bedside table sat the kidney-shaped blue pan from the hospital, a handheld bell, used tissues, and a pile of thrillers and romances. *Love's Wildest Adventure.* On the cover, a redhead in a clinging nightgown with an orchid in her hair ran from the powerful man in a vaguely military jacket and boots behind her, as he caught her in his arms. I had a moment of fierce desire for Jean-Pierre. The knowledge that I was being absurd did nothing to change the delicious feeling of sinking into my body. I picked up the book.

> The Twelfth Earl of Devon strode into the room and flung down his riding crop. His mama, thin and faded, though elegantly dressed, laid down her needlework, and his sisters, engaged in poking the dying morning-room fire, turned to look at him in surprise.

My mother had never had much time for reading, but when she did read it was biography, history, daily-life accounts of other centuries and countries. The romances were something new for her, though Lizzie and I had read dozens of them in our teens.

My mother sighed, turning onto her side, small gray curls falling forward onto her cheek, the flowered coverlet twisting around her. She had cabbage roses everywhere in her room—on the armchair and footstool, decorating the mats of the framed nineteenth-century advertisements for Sebastopol Gravenstein apples or Fairy soap, crawling up the curtains.

She opened her eyes then, giving a small gasp. Bending over her, I gave her a kiss on the cheek. I thought, *I love you,* but couldn't say it aloud. I might as well have said, *I know that you're dying.* Instead I sat down and touched her shoulder with one finger.

She whispered, "You took your time."

"The planes took their time. I got here as soon as anyone told me."

"Huh." She closed her eyes, then opened them, looking me over.

"Prosperous." A faint whisper. Code. She'd always said, when someone had gained weight, "*You're* looking prosperous."

"How are you feeling? Can I get you anything?"

She shook her head, but then, a few minutes later, she whispered,
urgently, "Basin."

I held the kidney-shaped pan for her while she retched, bringing up maybe a teaspoon of thin liquid. She groaned, her eyes
watering. I wanted to cry myself, to run away.

When she lay back, I sat there, not knowing what was next.
"Mom, do you want anything? Some water? Can I . . . ?" At this
moment, life seemed so thin and hard, with so little to look forward
to, that anything I could say would seem trivial, irrelevant, false. I
went and got a cold washcloth for her face. She nodded, but didn't
say anything.

I leaned against her arm, holding her as carefully as I could,
thinking that she was sixty-four years old, and this would be her last
year. I'd come home from D.C. for a few weeks after Dad's first heart
attack, then again, three months later, for his funeral. Was I going
to be doing that again? His mother's cross burned in my pocket; I
could feel it against my leg. I couldn't even imagine how to give it
back to her.

I inadvertently squeezed her. She pushed me away. She never had
wanted to be held—why should it be different now? Wiping the
moisture away from her dark eyes with a handkerchief, she whispered, the sound of it raw and painful, "If only there were some
other way. To be sick. Out the ears or eyes. Anything but the
throat."

After a few moments, she waved her hand at the glass of flat ginger ale on the bedside table. I held it for her, guiding the straw into
her mouth. She lay back and we were quiet. I put my hand on hers.
In about five minutes, she whispered, "Lizzie."

"You want me to get Lizzie?" The resentment roared up in me,
the sense that her habitual unfairness deserved the punishment of

illness. I muffled the thought and went out, escaping. I hadn't even been in the house for twelve hours and already I thought I'd suffocate if I didn't get out soon.

/   /   /

That night, I said to Lizzie the words I had been rehearsing for so long: "Sweetheart, I have met the man I want to spend my life with. I wrote to you about him when he and I were still just friendly. Jean-Pierre Bukimana, the government minister? But we've been *really* together for six months now, and I've never felt anything like this."

Her answers, in my head, when I imagined giving her my news, had been something like, "Oh, Annie, I always knew the right man was out there for you," and other kinds of romantic dreck. What she actually said was, "Six months? You've been with him six months, and you didn't even let me know?" Tears came into her eyes; she cupped her hands together over her mouth: a clasped fist of shock and abandonment.

"Oh, Lizzie." I touched her hands, but she pulled away. I wanted to say, *The phone is so difficult; I didn't trust a letter,* but I had been far away and self-absorbed, and I had let her down. Nothing I could say would hide that.

"*Where* do you want to spend your life with him?"

When I put my arm around her, she said, so quietly I almost couldn't hear the words, heard them inside my head as when we were children, "I always thought you would get this foreign stuff out of your system. And then you would come home."

I stroked her hair, but she held herself away from me, her body stiff and unforgiving.

/   /   /

California astonished me, as if I had never seen it before. What I couldn't get used to was how rich and smooth-surfaced everything was. *You're going to have to keep your mouth shut,* I said to myself. I made a resolution not to be obnoxious, but I broke it over and over.

The second day, we went to Long's for a refill of Mom's pain-killer. Margaret had her children; Aurora and Lizzie were at home with Mom. Though I was afraid to leave the house—Jean-Pierre still hadn't called and I was sure he would as soon as I wasn't there—I had to stock up on the things I'd need for Africa. Nasal spray, vitamins, eyeliner, ibuprofen. Two-pound chocolate bars for presents for everyone—they'd cost more than thirteen dollars each in Burundi. I had my list ready, but when we went inside I lost my mind.

Long's Drugs. My God. I'd been in drugstores thousands of times, growing up, but I'd never *seen* one. At first, I was overcome by delight, and went up and down, touching Midol bottles, twelve kinds of cold remedy that suppressed all symptoms, sixteen brands that worked on coughing only, suppositories, cans of chopped clams and salad dressings on sale, Disney dolls from movies I'd missed. *This is the nonsustainable society,* I said to myself, but I wanted to roll in it like a dog in carrion. I could buy any of this, could come back the next day and it would all still be here. I had a sense of being in free-fall.

By the pharmacy, decent, thin condoms lay in bright stacks by the dozens: Kimono, Trojan-Enz, twenty varieties. A dizzying display. But I wasn't using them anymore; I was on the pill instead. Suicide, Zoë would have said. Zoë was a nurse, big and blond and messy, full of wicked intelligence. A licensed helicopter pilot who tottered around on forties-style heels, accomplishing stunning amounts of work. We'd been a team for my first year in Burundi, before I took the human rights job. Together we'd done AIDS testing and condom demonstrations, while trying to reassure the appropriate officials that we weren't pushing birth control. The majority of Burundians were Catholic. The frustrations of our task brought us together, but what made the friendship was the intimacy of knowing all each other's secrets, troubles, and small boasts, of being similar creatures in a new country.

I could hear her voice saying, "And you're supposed to be an AIDS educator. I shudder." She would raise herself up on her reckless lizard-skin heels, and then suddenly become serious. "You know you must stop, darling. I want you to promise me." And sometimes I woke in the night, sweating. But with Jean-Pierre, I couldn't stand having anything between us.

The candy aisle held me for five minutes. Then I tried to take in the whole store at once and felt such a rush of nausea that I had to run outside, dropping onto a planter box, my head between my knees, teeth clenched. Susan followed me out, which doubled my determination not to be sick in the parking lot.

She said, "Aunt Annie?" So serious, so concerned.

I answered, my head still between my knees, "In Bujumbura, the capital, there are half a dozen pharmacies the size of one of those aisles in there, dusty, the shelves half empty. Closed much of the time. Old medicines, mostly for malaria, parasites, pain. And, even that, people can't afford. They have to take the ones that make them sick and deaf."

Margaret, holding Bobby's hand, came out of the store while I was talking. I lifted my head and said, "I'm trying to be good."

She said, "If you weren't so sure you were succeeding, it'd be easier to have you around." I was speechless. She went on, "A friend of mine from college went into the Peace Corps. Cameroon. When she came back, she was totally unbearable for the first month, unpleasant for three months, and it was six months before she could just go to the store like a person and get milk and pretzels without treating us all to lectures on advertising and world markets, the oppression of the Third World, and the voracious planet strip-mining of our consumer society. Fortunately, her condition turned out to be fully treatable with regular television and intravenous frozen yogurt."

Susan was watching both of us, waiting for my response. I stood up and said, "Do you know that apples in Burundi are imported from Europe and cost six to fifteen dollars a pound? I would give about five years of my life for one of the Gravensteins from our own orchards." I knew, of course, that she carried them with her.

Margaret grinned and brought a bag out of her fat purse, holding it out to me. I picked a gorgeous apple, deep green shot with red, and bit into it. So crisp and tart, mouth-puckering. Perfect. Bobby held out his hand and Margaret gave him one too, her eyes on me, watching me lick up the juices. She said, "Do you think we could go now?"

I said to her, "You have the car keys, Lieutenant. I can shop later."

/   /   /

The weekend came and went. Jean-Pierre didn't call. I was missing him, enough to talk Lizzie's ear off about him, despite the anxiety on her face, the way she would touch my arm, as if to reassure herself that I wasn't disappearing just yet. Monday night, Lizzie, Susan, and I were making dinner in the kitchen. Bobby and Aurora played going-to-the-hospital, piling Barbies onto fire engines too small to hold them.

Margaret, who had been with Mom, came in. "It's these twenty-four-hour days that do it," she said, dropping into a chair. And then she saw Susan, trimming green beans at the table, wearing a T-shirt with a cowboy smoking and the words, "Smoking kills." Her voice so sharp that we all looked up from our tasks, Margaret asked, "Where on earth did you get that T-shirt?"

"I won it." Susan was sullen, immediately defensive. She bent her head so that her shoulder-length brown hair fell forward over her face. "At the Family Life Expo. I guessed which plants were poisonous and which were safe. African violets are OK."

"Don't wear it upstairs. What are you thinking of? What if

your grandmother saw that?" Margaret began to cry, putting her head down on her arms as if she'd given up. Aurora and Bobby, frightened, began to cry with her, uncomprehendingly. But Susan's face showed a sudden, terrible understanding.

Lizzie said, "Your mother is just tired." She put her arms around Margaret's back and rubbed her cheek against Margaret's shoulder, Aurora hanging on to her leg. "You're scaring the offspring, Meg," she said, sounding both sad and angry. Bobby buried his face in his mother's lap. She gathered him into her arms, tears still running down her face.

Susan ran out of the room. Now we were in a position—we could lie, pretend this wasn't happening, or have serious talks about death. I thought to myself, *This isn't your decision,* and was ashamed of my cowardice.

Lizzie said, "We need to get out of here. Let's get one of Mom's friends to come in for the day—they're always offering."

Margaret, subdued, said, "I can't believe I did that." She'd been beautiful when younger—dark eyes, smooth deep-brown hair, oval face, long graceful body. Of all of us, she was the most like our mother. Full of the energy required by daily life. She'd left school at nineteen, after a brief bout with college, which had seemed to her to be full of classes where she was asked to take seriously the question of whether she actually existed and how she could prove that logically, or lectures based on slides of fragments of Minoan statues. So she'd dropped out, taken an accounting certificate, gone to work. Married. Started a family. Her whole face and body expressed practicality, hundreds of hard, small decisions about money and chores, years of getting up to look after everyone else, her body increasingly a thick armor.

Lizzie said, "Maybe it was meant to happen," and Margaret, the snap and energy gone out of her voice, said, "You always think everything was meant to happen. Maybe some things are just plain old irrevocable mistakes."

The phone rang twice, and Susan called, "It's for Aunt Annie. A man with an accent."

Even as I jumped to my feet to run out to the hall phone, I could see Lizzie trying to hide her unhappiness and Margaret noticing that Lizzie knew something she didn't.

I leaned against the wall, weak from the sound of his voice. He wanted to know how I was, about my mother. I told him, and then said, against my will, "I miss you."

"Me too." He paused for a moment. "Life without you, it's very flat." The richness of his voice, its own particular timbre. Our connection had that sound of oceans on the line, the annoying wait. I heard the echo of my voice, deep and strange, before his reply.

I asked, "What is happening?"

"Elections take place this week. The borders are still closed." The government was afraid of Hutu support from outside. If he were even willing to say this much on the monitored phone, the country must be at the edge of open civil war.

"Should I be worried about you?"

"No, UPRONA is doing well." A remark for the listeners, members of his own party. We couldn't discuss the possibility of the Tutsis rigging elections or the probability, if the Hutus did gain power, of the army refusing to allow President Major Pierre Buyoya, who'd taken power in 1987 in a bloodless coup, to step aside if he didn't win. But what if the army was really 90 percent HIV positive, and reassured about keeping their power for a few years, for whatever was left of their lives?

Jean-Pierre said, "Ah-na?" I couldn't ask any political questions. His family was Ganwa, the princely clan, originally above both Tutsis and Hutus in the hierarchy, and now either considered to be Tutsi or allied with them. To Jean-Pierre, the Hutus were the enemy. It was so confusing: everyone spoke Kirundi, intermarried, were— Hutus and Tutsis alike—about three-fourths Christian, the rest animist, and yet such bitter enemies.

And I couldn't express to him over the tapped phone how badly I wanted him, how I imagined him stretching his arms overhead and smiling at me in some golden morning, the long lines of his torso, the dark gleaming of his skin against the white sheets, the movement, as he stretched, of muscles across his chest and belly. Running my tongue over his collarbone, down his chest. His skin against my mouth, his happy sigh.

Instead, I asked, "How is your family?"

"Very well. I wish you could be here for Christine's marriage. We will have the ceremony at the cathedral and the reception here, at my house. Andre has given the family two bulls and twelve cows. A huge bride price. My sister is beside herself with pride."

She was his pet. Entrancing: high cheekbones, a turn of head as regal and graceful as the bust of Nefertiti, a clatter of bracelets. A way of dipping down her head in well-simulated shyness, while her grin gave her away. Mocking, a little arrogant.

The phone lines crackled. Jean-Pierre said, "I think of you every day," except that in French it was much more beautiful—something like, "I think of you all the days."

I was about to answer, but we lost our connection. The Parisian operator announced this, rudely (the line to and from Burundi went through France, then to the Midwest, and finally to me in California), and then the line went dead. It could be hours before he could get another line out of Burundi, if he were even going to try again.

I went back into the kitchen. Conversation stopped.

"So," said Margaret. "Give."

"Oh, did I not mention that I'm seeing someone?"

Lizzie turned a chair around and sat down, legs hooked around the sides, chin on her hands. "How serious is it?" Margaret gave her a look that said she wasn't deceived by Lizzie's pretense of ignorance.

Susan asked, "Is he *foreign*?"

"Not at home, he isn't. He would be here."

Margaret said, "He isn't a native, is he?"

"*African,* Margaret. Burundian. He's the smartest, most perceptive man I've ever known. Extremely passionate about the things he cares about, but open to reason. Reserved. But he can also be really funny. I want to spend my life with him." I would have eaten, raw, on a stick, the heart of anyone who tried to keep us away from each other. The happiness of the phone call faded. What had he said after all? He thought about me. Maybe the real, not imagined, me would be disappointing to him when we saw each other again. Or the real Jean-Pierre disappointing to me.

Margaret sat down at the table and took my hand. "Annie. It's wonderful to be in love. Congratulations. But think. Don't say to yourself, 'Margaret's never been anywhere, she can't help being a bigot.' Marriage is hard enough under any circumstances. And when you try to put together such different backgrounds, histories, cultures, expectations, even—especially—races . . . now don't stiffen up on me. I'm talking to you in our family kitchen and don't have to pretend. Do you want to walk down the street and have everyone stare at the two of you forever? You want your children to have to face racism their whole lives? What do you have in common with this guy? Can you really imagine being eighty with him?"

"The average life expectancy in Burundi is still just over forty. Of course, you have to average in infant mortality. . . ."

"Oh, for Christ's sakes, would you *shut up*?" said Margaret.

Susan said, "God, we have to get out of this house. You're all losing your minds."

"We have the psychic fair a week from Saturday," said Lizzie.

"*Really* great," said Susan. "That should help a *lot.*"

/   /   /

It seemed to me later that the whole three weeks, which went by terribly slowly, and then seemed to have lasted only five minutes, consisted of sitting with Mom or watching my family squabble in the kitchen. But of course everyone except me went to work, and we had to drive the children to and from school, lessons, and friends' houses.

I was in a dream world, trying to get news from the papers, the radio. On June 1, the presidential election went forward. Buyoya had only 32 percent of the votes in the election. His opponent, Melchior Ndadaye, a Hutu banker, not even a military man, but someone who had spent years in hiding in Rwanda, had received more than 64 percent of the votes. He appeared to be a pacifist, for reconciliation. It was over, and FRODEBU had won. Jean-Pierre wasn't answering his phone. I wasn't worried for his safety; there were no reports of violence. But I wished I were there in Burundi, where history was happening, that I could talk to Jean-Pierre, see his face. Meanwhile I sat in California, buying chocolate bars and getting ready to go to the fair with my family.

/   /   /

At the Health and Harmony Fair, the sun was already beating down at ten-thirty in the morning. A juggler on a unicycle lurched past. A mass of people swarmed around us, in tie-dye, feathers, gauze, long lacy skirts, huipils, embroidered vests, and caftans. I was amazed at how many, many *white* people there were. A sea of white faces, lost in soft daydreams of themselves and their lives.

Margaret's husband, Jerry, said, "It's going to be hell to keep this group together. Now, don't go wandering off. The place is full of freaks and losers and you want to be careful."

The fairground fields were full of booths for shoulder or foot massages, psychic healings, free chiropractic examinations, five-minute personality typings, paintings of unicorns and dragons, and velvet hats and capes. Lizzie was doing treatments somewhere. Aurora marched toward a cart covered with paintings of fruit ices. We chased her, passing a geodesic dome where people in matching T-shirts turned in circles, chanting. Jerry snapped at Margaret,

"Don't let her get lost." Another person, more guarded and malicious, seemed to be looking out from somewhere back behind Margaret's eyes, but she didn't say anything. It unnerved me, that look. Jerry may also have been unnerved; he shrugged in a kind of apology. Margaret raised her eyebrows at him, then picked up Aurora and slung her onto one hip. Aurora put her fair head down on Margaret's shoulder, snuggling.

The children wanted to start with waffles, ice cream, whipped cream, and nuts, which was, of course, out of the question, but the adults couldn't agree on what we did want—macrobiotic seafood wraps or Cajun gumbo, roast corn or gyros. We could eat anything; nothing there would give us dysentery or tapeworm, but I couldn't say this to the family. Jerry said, "Let's split up and meet in fifteen minutes in front of the center stage. Margaret can take the kids."

I bought Thai chicken-on-a-stick and noodles and walked to the lawn in front of the stage. A bluegrass band had the stage and people were dancing just in front. Belly dancers in full costume with consciously mysterious smiles threaded through the crowds. What would Jean-Pierre think of all this? Wouldn't my old, pre–Jean-Pierre self have been obsessing instead about whether Janvier Barantandikiye and Jacques Nahimana were going to rot in jail or whether the new government would make a difference to them?

I shut my eyes. I remembered being in the spare room, putting away some books; Jean-Pierre had come up behind me, unexpectedly. He put his arms around me, and, out of nowhere, though my mind had been full of little practical matters, I turned in his arms and then we were on the bed, locking into each other. The headboard banged against the wall, over and over, and a part of me was aware that Deo must be hearing it in the kitchen. Jean-Pierre must have known it too, but we couldn't stop or even move to the floor— we were consuming each other. His salty, delicious smell, his face buried in my neck, his urgent kisses. The exactness of his weight, the way he fit into me. How we drove each other on.

"Aunt *Annie*." Someone poked me in the side, and I looked around. Susan. I was Aunt Annie, sitting on a Santa Rosa lawn with a plateful of semi-Thai food on my lap.

"Your chicken is getting cold."

I began to eat it, and she said, "Grandma is dying." She spoke so softly that I had to lean forward to catch the end. Her voice came out flat, but she was asking me.

"No one can know that. People have cancer all the time and get over it, Susan."

She gave me a look of dislike. "One thing when I grow up. I don't know whether I'll get married or what kind of jobs I'll have. But I do know I won't *lie* all the time."

Behind us, Margaret's voice said, "After you finish your hot dogs, we'll see."

My face, neck, whole body had gone hot with shame. I said, "Yes, I'm sorry. She is."

"How soon?" She had such an adult look, an adult voice. Thirteen years old.

"Maybe a few months. Maybe a couple of years."

Family sat down all around us. Bobby said, "If I were a wolf, I'd eat like this." He crouched on all fours and began to gnaw at his hot dog, dribbling relish, smearing his chin with ketchup.

"Mom, are you going to let him do that?" Susan sounded like a child again. There were tears in her eyes; her face was red with anger.

Margaret said, "When you have your own children, you'll see. The first one you have energy to civilize. After that you abandon them to their own animal natures and a disintegrating society." Without much conviction, she said, "Bobby, why don't you sit up and eat with your hands. Like your cousin Aurora, like the rest of us, and like all the hundreds of people around us."

"You look like a *moron*," said Susan, and he sat up. She leaned over and wiped his chin with a paper napkin. She was trembling all over, and her lips moved, talking to herself, rehearsing some angry speech. After a moment, she got up and walked away.

"Where are you going?" shouted Margaret, and then when Susan didn't answer, "Be at the front gate at three! Don't make us wait!" To me, she said, "She was just a baby, about five minutes ago. Little cooing noises. Hanging on to the coffee table so she could stand up."

Jerry showed up. "I found Lizzie. She's sharing a booth with an aura reader."

The aura readers, a very high-tech group, were actually in an adjoining booth—one man ran the video camera and fixed the images on the screen, another did computer printouts, a woman up front handed out literature. The woman was saying, "When I was in Hong Kong, I was always getting red and yellow for some reason. That mental energy—chi—they're into it over there. I got tired of reading them."

Lizzie finished with her customer and picked up Aurora and gave her a kiss. "Mommy's hair," said Aurora, taking hold of her braid and blissfully wrapping it in one hand, pressing her cheek against it. Lizzie, in a long mirror-spangled skirt and two scarves tied together as a top, her face tired and peaceful from giving treatments, looked as otherworldly as Aurora.

Margaret said, "I thought I'd take the kids over to the bubble-jumping tent."

"I've got to eat. I've been doing treatments all morning, and I'm starved."

Aurora and Bobby shouted, "The bubble tent! The bubble tent!" and Margaret said to Lizzie, "You go, I'll take the kids," and Lizzie said, "Annie, come with me," and she and I headed back to the food aisle, she with her arm around my waist, nuzzling me in the shoulder. We bought food and walked, winding up under a tree near the AIDS clinic booth.

Lizzie held her hummus pita in her hand but didn't eat. "I have to talk money with you." I began to lick my lime ice. A procession went by: four huge figures that seemed to represent earth, air, fire, and water; fiercely smiling monstrous heads with long, flowing cloth bodies. Two sweating, shirtless men carried each figure. One looked embarrassed, but the others were grinning. Lizzie stayed silent, holding her pita.

I said, "Just say the word. I can probably lend you up to five grand."

She looked amazed. "Do they pay you so much?"

"I've been very thrifty. That's public health money. Human rights doesn't pay for shit, and when this job ends, I'm going to have to live on savings for quite some time." Women in robes danced among the papier-mâché figures, shaking tambourines. A boy of about twenty, in jester's motley, led the way, playing a recorder.

Lizzie said, "It's about *Mom's* money."

I wanted to pretend to myself that I'd never thought of the difference that a third of the price of the house and orchards could make. If I could make her live, wouldn't I? But I couldn't, and an ugliness seeped in around the edges: the thought of her money.

Lizzie touched me on the arm. "Margaret has her power of attorney. She's been paying the bills, household expenses, property tax. But Mom thinks that Margaret and Jerry may be running down the account, using it for their own things as well. She's afraid to say anything. She wants us to find out."

My first response was, Oh, this is too much. That we couldn't be expected to deal with this too. Not, I noticed, that it was impossible, though it would never have occurred to me not to trust Margaret. "It must be an accident. Sloppiness in the bookkeeping."

"Mom doesn't think so. She thinks they feel they've done more than their share. And Jerry's sales have been down. Bad times in the business world. His world. Mine is great—everyone wants a healing, but I still don't make what he does. I don't live at their level."

The juggler on his unicycle, or maybe another one, wobbled along the road, past the garbage pails. I put my hands over my eyes. *"Margaret."*

"She always had to have first pick in the games."

"Even if it's true, can we prove it? What would we say to her? And the children?" The thought of the family scene made me sweat. And why should it stop there? "Families end up in court, with life-long feuds—children taking sides, families never seeing each other again. Bobbie and Aurora separated, Lizzie."

She nodded—she had thought of it. "If it were my money, I might say, 'Let her. Don't break up the family over this.' But Mom is asking us for help."

Margaret, who we counted on for her solid, impatient practicality, the decisive one, with her scorn for what she called "weakness," or "people who read instead of living." She'd always patronized Lizzie and me, roughly, affectionately, and we counted on her even when she annoyed us. Could she be stealing from Mom? Now that it had been brought up, even the suspicion of it—maybe some drugged delusion of Mom's—would poison all of us.

My lime ice dripped over my wrist, but I'd lost interest. I felt cold and sick, removed from the sun and celebration all around me. "I'm leaving in two days. What am I supposed to do?"

"I've ordered copies of Mom's bank statements. I'll write you if they prove anything. You can back me up from there."

I nodded. "Lizzie, I keep thinking about Jean-Pierre. It's like a sickness. I mean, it's real, but also . . . is it real? Can you tell if it is or not?"

She struggled with herself, then said, "It sounds real to me. It's just you never had it bad before, and it hits you harder, late, like mumps. It feels like dying, like it never happened this way to anyone in the world, and like it will never get any less intense, but you know better."

"Some part of me knows better. Some part of me knows that our mother is really dying, that real, innocent men are being tortured in Burundian jails, that real Burundi itself is in a time of tremendous change. But some other part of me knows fuck-all, and that's the part running the show."

"Look," Lizzie said. "I traded for this." And she opened her bag, taking out a rosy glass wand filled with a thickly glittering liquid, the star on top hung with shining ribbons and hearts. She leaned forward and brushed my shoulders with it, as if she were knighting me. Across the way, a sign said, "The arisen JESUS walks the earth. He is HERE amongst you."

/   /   /

The night before I left, when I went upstairs, Mom wasn't lying down but making her way around the room. She'd been downstairs earlier, sitting out in the garden for a couple of hours. She'd said to me, "Since I start the treatments next week, this may be as good as I ever feel again." She appeared to be opening up somewhat, to be allowing herself to admit, at least to the adults among us, that her time was now limited.

When I came into the room, she stopped where she was, leaning with one hand on the dresser. Her face was grim with the effort not to show pain.

"You don't think you're overdoing it a little?"

She said, in her new gravelly whisper, "I can't stand the clutter."

"I'll deal with it. What are you trying to do, overwhelm me with guilt?"

A little smile came onto her face at that. She moved to the bed and stretched out, pulling up the covers, curling her cheek onto her hand and closing her eyes. Her face so pale and tired. I thought, *Please just die and get it over with,* and then, as shocked as if someone else had said it, *Live forever and don't leave me, Mommy.* The fear of being left behind.

I gathered up dropped tissues, rehung a shawl. The dresser

seemed oddly bare. In the wastebasket—a plastic-lined wicker, threaded along the edge with artificial roses—shards of glass and old family photos looked back up at me. I knelt beside the basket, fishing out the whole family in a formal studio portrait, my mother and father at Bodega Bay, my mother laughing and holding down the edges of her sun hat while the wind blew her dress to one side. I spread them out on the dresser, then went to sit in the chair beside her bed.

After a minute or two, she opened her eyes. She whispered, "We would have done better in cattle. If your father'd had a little gumption." And then, "I want a cigarette so badly. Even now. And why not, really?" And then, "When are you going back?"

"Mom, you know I leave tomorrow."

A thin whisper, "I thought you would be here for the chemotherapy."

That was as close as she ever got to asking for something. I took her hand. "I'm sorry," I said. "I'll call you. I'll write every week. You have Lizzie and Margaret. And I'll try to be home for Christmas."

She shut her eyes. "Maybe I'll still be here. Maybe not. But it's your choice, isn't it? I hope you won't regret it."

"I don't want to leave."

"But you don't want to stay." She took her hand away. I felt caught in a trap—any answer would be wrong. My body remembered Jean-Pierre, the feel of his skin on mine, the sound of the cicadas outside, the sense of being one animal together. My mother, her eyes still closed, was nodding, but I was feeling the urgent need to get *home* to Burundi, to leave my resentful, helpless child-self behind and go back to doing useful work. Visiting the jails, talking to people, reporting on human rights. Raising money. Bringing in outside experts. Trying to help with the great project of moving Burundi toward democracy.

Three

From San Francisco to Paris to Nairobi to Kampala, I had a book in my lap, which I hardly read, dozing off and on, dreaming of the family and Jean-Pierre. In Nairobi, most of the Europeans and Americans got off, and the plane filled up, a few tourists on their way from the animals in Kenya to the animals in Rwanda, but mostly Africans laughing and calling out to each other, stuffing impressive amounts of baggage into tiny spaces: bundles, duty-free bags, and VCRs still in their boxes. Despite all the people on the plane, I was in luck—the two seats beside me stayed empty, and from Kampala to Rwanda, I stretched out and slept. In Rwanda, all the seats in my section filled up again.

A tall, bony Swedish missionary and a woman who may have been his wife or sister got on with fifteen Rwandan orphans, all, I think, with AIDS. The missionaries each held a baby, and so did the two oldest children. All of the children were thin, a few skeletal, the lines of their strong skulls prominent under their skins. One of the girls, about five, in a ruffled dress and braids, squirmed constantly, wanted to be up and down the aisles, had to be continually told—in Kiswahili—to do her part. Some of the children were sick or having diarrhea. The flight attendants (tall, gorgeous, probably Tutsis, strong-smelling from the journey and with splendid arrangements of braids) and I were occupied from Rwanda to Burundi with assistance and cleanup. The missionaries were flying all the way to Sweden. I couldn't even bear to imagine it.

And then, finally, we landed in Burundi. Burundi! How is it that you can get onto a series of planes and be flung from one universe into another in just a couple of days?

I arrived in Bujumbura on Sunday afternoon, confused and exhausted. From the air, the central area of the capital city, with its two-story buildings and paved streets, made a patch of gray against the dusty brown streets of the *quartiers* and the lush green of the hills that hid the houses of the rich. The sun shone brightly onto the corrugated-steel rooftops in the *quartiers*. About three hundred thousand people, more or less, lived in Bujumbura, most of them in conditions unimaginable to those who had never seen the Third World.

Because I hadn't been able to get in touch with Jean-Pierre before I left, Jack met me at the airport. "Barantandikiye and Nahimana are both out," he said. "Free. You have a meeting with Nahimana next Tuesday. You probably won't be in shape to be much use tomorrow, so don't even bother coming in. Nahimana has some interesting information, some new names. A man with his smarts, his political organizing history, might go very far if Burundi is really opening up for the Hutus."

I wanted to hug him in delight, but with Jack that was impossible. He scanned the airport over my shoulder, his eyes darting here and there, as usual. Unless he were about to lie, in which case he looked you straight in the face with the utmost sincerity, and sometimes took hold of your hand, for emphasis. He was even taller and thinner than I remembered—he had the dried look some outsiders get after years in Africa, as if the water's been baked out of them.

"How did they get out?"

"The new government. This could be going to work. Things are tense, but the army seems to be settling down already. Unbelievable. The first couple of days we had demonstrations. The university students." Who were, of course, all Tutsis. He whispered into my ear, grinning, "Only the Burundians would demonstrate against the unfairness of an election in which the majority party won."

The porters, in red, half Jack's size, staggered under my suitcases. I'd traveled international rules to Burundi—piece, not weight. Jack and I greeted Greeks and Belgians we knew, Burundian lower-level government ministers, one of the American wives on her way home or to Europe, the American economic/political officer on her way to a conference in Kampala. I was trying to remain coherent, focused. Burundi—the gray light of almost-rain, the strong smells of human sweat, the reddish scent of the dust, the mango and papaya tropical smells, a haunting sense of human tension and of growing things and languorous, obstinate decay—had taken me over.

Jack said, "The demonstrations were peaceful. Quiet. The Burundians still haven't got used to the idea that they can talk out loud, even have opinions. There were a couple of small placards, but mostly just the students marching." He led us to the old Land Cruiser. The porters demanded some astonishing amount of money—two or three dollars each—because of the weight of the bags, and Jack was sharp with them, in Kiswahili. *"Utalii bei, bwana"*—That's the tourist price, mister. He wound up giving them more than usual, setting a bad precedent, but we had a guest coming in, a French human rights expert, the following month. We didn't want his bags damaged.

I counted over my bags once again—by some bizarre chance they had all made it—and Jack put the car into gear. He said, remembering, "How's your mother?"

"Dying."

He was silent, uncomfortable, shaking his head. My tears came up and spilled over then; I had a flash reversal of feeling, wondering how I could have been so stupid and heartless as to come back, not to wait with her until the end. It rose up and struck me in the face—my stupidity and self-righteous sentimentality in trumpeting about international human rights to myself when my mother was dying.

Jack, as if he were being goaded from the side by a stick, lurched toward me and patted my knee for a moment, clumsily. We don't always get on, Jack and I. I wouldn't sleep with him when I first began working for him, and he holds that against a woman.

I'd forgotten, in such a short time, how the cars jammed along, three and four abreast on the left and right sides of the roads, the dozens of people darting in between, the deep red of the dirt. We passed Old East, the Volkswagen dealership, swung around the roundabout, and moved into town along Premier Novembre, going by COTEBU, the cloth factory, and BRARUDI, which bottled soft drinks and Primus beer. An old man, peddling along on his Chinese bicycle, wavered under the weight of bunches of green bananas piled up behind him, the stack taller and wider than his thin body.

It was midday, all the shops closed for lunch and the streets thronged. We had to inch our way through the roundabout near the Novotel and onto Avenue de la Liberté. Jack was telling me stories, gossip of the ex-pat community, rumors about the government. Who was out, who was in. I asked about Marie-Claire, my friend at the clinic, who was recovering from the birth of her fifth and sixth children, twins. But I couldn't ask about Jean-Pierre. There was this look that came onto Jack's face when he saw us together. I don't suppose he could help it, or maybe even knew it was there. I'd heard him, more than once, make sneering remarks at the *boîtes*, the nightclubs—the Cadillac or the Black and White—watching Peace Corps volunteers dancing with Burundian men, about "cultural experiences" and "suburban babies on the loose." Or even, when he was feeling really nasty, about the spread of AIDS in action.

By this time in the long dry season, everything had gone to dust, the lush, moist, thick greens, brilliant oranges and purples and magentas of flamboyants, bougainvillea, jacaranda faded and dim. As we slammed on our brakes to avoid bicyclists, and ran the edges of the road to Kinindo, my *quartier*, avoiding the trucks and minibuses bearing down on us from the other direction, I was calculating how long it would take for Jack to drop me off, for me to express gratitude and get rid of him, to shower and change, greet and give presents to Deo, climb into my rattly little VW and drive up the hill to Vugizo, the *quartier* where Jean-Pierre lived.

/   /   /

But when I got to Jean-Pierre's, I found that half a dozen members of his family had shown up unexpectedly. I tried to conceal the physical shock of my disappointment, as if I'd been punched in the stomach. He greeted me at the door with a friendly handshake, for his family's eyes, and an agonized look they couldn't see—apology, frustration.

Jean-Pierre was the oldest of fifteen children; his father, a powerful man, had had two wives. Jean-Pierre's half-brother and sister, Bertrand and Françoise, as well as Christine and her new husband, Andre, were planning on staying the week in Buj. I had met all of them before, but only casually, at dinner parties. They now stood and greeted me politely, with huge Burundian smiles. A people so hidden, angry, frightened, reserved, and yet they have these smiles, as if giving you everything, an offering of piercing sweetness. Françoise's husband had stayed in Gitega, but she had her children with her. They were outside, their shouts and laughter drifting in through the windows. The smell of onions and peppers roasting in palm oil filled the room.

Jean-Pierre had a forty-foot living room: a grand, decaying salon, its uncomfortable furniture brocaded in a stiff French pattern of fruit and flowers, the ceiling twelve feet above the red-tiled floor.

The electricity and plumbing worked only sporadically, black and red ants marched across the floor, and geckos ran across the ceiling, but he had three bathrooms and six bedrooms. The house, splendid and ruined, sat grandly in the middle of a series of terraces of papaya and mango trees.

"Ah-na Copeland, how nice of you to come by," said my love, as if to a friendly acquaintance. "We were just discussing Western influences on Burundian society. Won't you join us for lunch?"

He hadn't told them while I was gone; did he think he could keep our love affair a secret forever? He could be so cowardly about what people thought of him. I wished he had acknowledged our situation, but it would get me nowhere to force the issue publicly.

I accepted a citron, bitter and too sweet, and sat down, smiling angrily. Wooden carvings, bas-reliefs of drummers and women with children on their backs, hung on the walls, and covered Burundian baskets, coming to fierce points at the top, sat like sentinels at the room's corners. Across from me hung a painting done by a Parisian friend from Jean-Pierre's Sorbonne days. Very tachisme, huge dripping paint strokes, black and red and white.

"Burundian society has been degraded by too much Western influence. I am afraid I think it is a very bad thing, this betrayal of our traditional culture," Bertrand said to his brother, as if he were apologetic, but favoring me with another enormous smile. No one would have taken Bertrand for Jean-Pierre's brother. Bertrand's mother had probably been quite plain. Bertrand's face was thicker, coarse, and he looked rumpled, as if he'd been slept in. Jean-Pierre had an intrinsic elegance. Like the Raouls and Lord Desmonds of my mother's books, his bone structure showed him as an aristocrat. All of his moves as graceful as a cat's, exquisite, even when he was asleep, drunk, or ill.

Françoise, who'd studied economics in Kenya and London, and who appeared to be speaking to a larger audience than the family in the room, said, "In some ways, yes, we have more than we would have had. Cars, radios, the dubious benefits of technology. Something resembling an international market, though with our dependency on coffee and tea and the rates set by the Europeans . . . still. But colonialism reinforced our society's divisions, and Western culture has destroyed our traditions. What we lost when we lost the king, the rule of the dynasties—we lost our *self* as a people. How can this be replaced by electronics?"

Although it was usually the Burundian upper-class men who were trained from just before adolescence in *imfura*, eloquent speeches, poems in celebration of one's own heroism, and other rhetorical skills, Françoise took pride in her abilities in these arts. She still traveled to Belgium and France every few years for vacations and shopping. She had a minor government post, but she lived on family money, and, perhaps, bribes, in Burundi the standard method of accomplishing business. Françoise, like Christine, had that Nefertiti look of high cheekbones and long jaw, but she had a distinct overbite, which gave her a particularly imperious, authoritative look.

She was pregnant again, and wore a protective bamboo amulet around her neck with a chunk of quartz inside, a symbol of the baby she carried. During the conversation, she would sometimes cover the amulet with one hand, reassuring herself that it was still there. In her brilliant two-piece dress of puffed sleeves, red and violet butterflies, she seemed to fill not only her chair but her whole corner of the room. Elaborate coils of braids. Shining eyes and lips. She said to Jean-Pierre, "Surely you can't disagree. The degradation is all around us." She was speaking French—they all were. A polite gesture toward me.

I shifted my weight from one side to the other on the very hard piece of furniture that passed for Jean-Pierre's couch. If the family hadn't been there, I would have been on a pillow on the floor, or in bed. Jean-Pierre on me, under me, bending me over from behind.

The hard lines of his belly and thigh. The particular shock when he entered me, never what I expected or remembered, an intensity of longing so unbearable that it disguised itself as pleasure. I said to myself, uselessly, *Stop thinking about it.*

Jean-Pierre crossed his arms, staring at his older sister, his beautiful face rigid and unfriendly. "Nonetheless, I, for one, am not prepared to return to the fourteenth century and a life of cattle herding and boasting over banana beer. Life in the fields."

Christine, amused, tolerant, put in, "Ninety percent of our peasants still spend their lives in the field. Ninety-eight. In any case, we were never in that position."

Jean-Pierre wasn't looking at me. None of them were, but light had begun to pierce through the fog of my jet lag and frustrated desire. I understood the purpose of this attack on the West, polite as it was. Stories about us had made their way upcountry to Gitega where the family lived, and this delegation might even be in town in order to interfere.

Bertrand showed all his teeth. "Democracy. An idea of the Americans, French, Belgians. The Belgians ran our country for forty years, treated us, *treat* us, like goats, worse than goats, and now? An alien political system forced upon us. Monarchy is a stable form of government. Military rule, perhaps, became necessary at a certain point, as a result of Western meddling. With democracy, there will be trouble."

Jean-Pierre asked, "When has there not been trouble in Burundi?" and Phillippe appeared in the doorway just then with his announcement that lunch was served. The family stood up and went to seat themselves. I went the opposite direction, into the hall bathroom, to wash my hands.

Jean-Pierre came in after me and took hold of me, pressing me up against the sink, covering my face with kisses. I thought I had remembered us together—what his body felt like, my ferocious desire for him, but my memory was nothing. Nonetheless, I was angry, and pushed him away, my bracelet clanking against the porcelain as I leaned back. "Are you ashamed of me?"

"Ah-na, there is so much you don't know about Burundi," he said in a whisper both sad and urgent. "We do not have time to discuss this. We are not in Paris. There you can live together three years and no one thinks anything. Here, a woman is one thing or another. If my family thinks of you as my concubine, that is the end of our possibilities. A concubine is only a concubine. Marriage is a quadrille—do you know quadrille in the United States?" I nodded dumbly. Neither of us had ever said the word *marriage* to each other before. "The steps are just so. There is no variation."

I whispered, "Jean-Pierre, are you proposing to me in the bathroom?" I couldn't sort out the happiness from the disappointment— I had hoped for something a little more scenic and moonlit.

"No," he said, moving away toward the door. "When I propose, my intermediary would approach your family. And she would need the permission of my *Sewabo*. He is the *Umukuru w'umuryango*. If we are too open now, he will know." And he went out before I could answer. *Sewabo* was an uncle on the father's side, *Umukuru w'umuryango* the chief of the family. This gave me information I hadn't had, about Jean-Pierre, as much as about the structure of his extended family. I waited two long minutes, then followed him back to the dining room.

During lunch, the talk was all of family matters—the illness of a child or a cousin, the birth of twins to another sister, the poor health of the twins' father. The children were terribly, enchantingly polite at the table, *pudique,* seen and not heard.

Watching the smallest of Françoise's daughters, who was about eighteen months of age, unsteady and adorable with her tiny braids and white dress, I had an almost physical need to take her into my arms.

When I propose, said Jean-Pierre's voice in my head. An attack of longing overtook me—to have his baby growing inside me, to hold my child in my arms, to watch Jean-Pierre, his face full of light, playing with her, then giving her back to me to nurse. The flow of food through my body, the ability to nourish my baby.

I said to myself, *What happened to work? What happened to life and health and the universal rights of humankind?* But some time-clock trick of my body and genetic conditioning had turned me into a female animal. Would our children have Jean-Pierre's beautiful cheek-bones or my family's solid, oval face? And would my children be born in the traditional Burundian way—at home, cleaned and protected with cold water and butter, the placenta buried beneath the birthplace, and the umbilical cord made into an amulet? On the whole, I thought I would rather fly to the U.S. for my final trimester and give birth in a hospital.

Bertrand said, "He was very sick last year at this time," and Christine answered, "The doctors in Gitega are no good."

We were having Phillippe's best dish: *Capitaine,* Nile perch, baked in rich orange palm oil with slices of tomato, onion, peppers. Phillippe was a superb ironer and much more interested in house-keeping than Deo, but not, in general, half the cook. Deo was always surprising me with new dishes he'd learned from previous employers, secrets he'd been holding in reserve. A mixed blessing—not only did I get heavier by the month, but it's difficult to say to some-one who has just made you an unsolicited cake that you really need the floors cleaned this week.

Phillippe and I smiled at each other as he served; the Hutus are more for democracy than the Tutsis, by and large. Unlike the family, he approved of me, not only as a person, but the idea of what I represented.

Still, despite myself, I felt a strong affection for Jean-Pierre's family. In the first place, I loved everything connected with him. His old shirts. His pillow. Literally the ground he walked on. But I also loved his family because they loved him. And I could see their point of view. Wouldn't he be better off with a soft-spoken, exquisite, pliable, and like-minded *Burundaise*? She would mother his children firmly, be swallowed into his family without a murmur. Her father would make his speeches at the wedding—she was not to come home, she had a new family now. How could Jean-Pierre's family have imagined me? How could he have imagined me?

/   /   /

Jean-Pierre and I had met eight months earlier, in my first week with *FreeAfrica!*

Jack had insisted on dragging me to a government reception while I was still scrambling, frantically trying to acquire the necessary knowledge, background, sense of how things worked, and to figure out how to inhabit my new role as human rights advocate. Eleven million people in a country the size of Maryland, institutionalized oppression, centuries of rage. A people dedicated to their secrets—you ask the meaning of a proverb, any custom, and the response is secretive, suspicious. "Why do you want to know? What do you plan to do with the information?" Where can an outsider begin?

The woman who'd held the position before me had been temperamental, abrasive. Jack had fired her on an impulse, in the middle of an argument, and been stuck afterward for someone to do the work. He was too stubborn to hire her back, which is what she was expecting, and he didn't have a wide field of applicants to choose from. Then he thought of me. He and I had met at a dinner-dance at one of the American embassy houses, and he'd noticed the way I listened, the way people told me things they perhaps hadn't meant to. In desperation, he'd offered me the job. Since the funding for my condom project had appeared to be on the verge of drying up altogether, and since I passionately wanted a change from public health work and AIDS testing, I'd accepted.

But then I had to prove myself. He was taking a risk; I had taken a bigger one. After all, he could always fire me as he had my predecessor, and where would I be then?

So when he told me we were going to this European Community reception, I went, though I knew my ignorance would show in every conversation. I debated coming down with some sudden illness, but instead put on my most serious dark-print dress and a professional manner. I'd read somewhere that quiet people are assumed to know much more than they're saying. My strategy would be sober and brief responses to questions, with an ironic, knowing smile and the occasional display of human rights data or obscure facts about Burundian history. But nothing about Hutu or Tutsi warfare, nothing about *Imana* (alternately luck, fortune, or God) or about the spirits of the dead who give out God's messages, nothing about family structure or private life. The facts had to be very obscure, very neutral, not to trespass on the Burundians' sense of privacy. I would be on stronger ground when we got onto matters covered by the *International Herald Tribune*.

An hour into the reception, I was standing by the EC representative's handsome swimming pool, drinking imported South African Cabernet to increase my bravery, and discussing the continuing economic implications of reunification with a junior assistant to the German ambassador, a very pale young man with a rabbit mustache and a way of pinching his lips together after making a point. We were boring each other and trying to conceal it. He said to me, switching the subject with relief, "Ah, there is a very useful man."

He gestured to a group of Burundians—he meant the Minister of Foreign Affairs, who was uncharacteristically sympathetic to the outside world. My eye, however, was caught by another man. Tall. Graceful. An air so serious and intent that it was as if he drew light into him where he stood, a magnetism that created his concentrated force. But then someone apparently said something funny. He

laughed, and the change was complete—an unself-conscious, abandoned delight.

"I don't know any of those men," I said to the German, who was
really so extremely dull, but I was about to get something from him,
so I felt a moment of affection.

He went around the group, naming them one by one: the For-
eign Minister, two professors at the university, an underling in the
Foreign Affairs Ministry, and the man I wanted to know about.
"Jean-Pierre Bukimana," said the German. "He does something in
Interior, but doesn't quite have minister rank yet. But I understand
he has a history with Buyoya, so you never know."

Jean-Pierre said, long afterward, that he didn't hear us discussing him, and I don't know, but I do know that he looked around
just then, straight at us. I may have been smiling at him; I had no
control over my face at all at that moment. I wouldn't say it was love
at first sight. I wouldn't say I even felt lust, not then. There was
something about him that made me happy, immediately, and I
couldn't keep from showing that.

He looked, gave a kind of smile, looked back at the minister,
who was holding forth and waving his glass for emphasis, then
looked at us again.

Twenty minutes later, in what I felt to be a painfully obvious
display (I was suddenly fifteen years old and convinced that everyone at the reception must be looking at me), I'd rejoined Jack and
maneuvered us into Jean-Pierre's group. There were introductions. I
was trying not to make a fool of myself. Jean-Pierre, standing next
to me, asked how long I'd been in Burundi, I said a year, he asked if
I liked it, I said I had never been anywhere more beautiful, and that
I'd found the people so kind.

"We are not kind to each other," he said in his beautiful French,
which I was hearing for the first time. I thought, *I am hearing this
man's voice for the first time,* and it seemed strange that we didn't already know each other. His eyes looked into mine from a place of

such depth and humor, such awareness of the world, that everyone around us seemed to be sleepwalking by comparison.

"We like Americans in Burundi," he said. His face, boyish and unguarded when he laughed, was now thoughtful, restrained, elegant. "I myself am a member of the Burundian-American Friendship Association. BAFA. We meet Thursday nights at Le Rendez-Vous. But we have many more Burundians than Americans—those who are members are usually from your embassy, your AID. You must come some evening. We would like to have the participation of more Americans."

"A splendid idea," said Jack, who was thinking *contacts*, while I was thinking *contact*. Standing next to Jean-Pierre, I could smell the faintly spicy scent of his skin, couldn't stop imagining my lips on his chest, neck, jaw, him leaning down to kiss me. I'd never felt anything so instant, never been so overwhelmed; at that point it was still only delicious, not yet in the realm of urgency and pain.

By the time, two months later, when I seemed to be having car trouble, and he followed me home from BAFA to make sure I arrived safely, I was eaten up with longing. Obsessed by him. I could be sitting in Le Rendez-Vous and know when he'd driven up outside, just from the response of my body. It was like being cut to bits all day long.

From time to time, I said to myself, during those two months, "What are you doing?" This was so far beyond the realm of anything I'd ever felt before, and it scared me a little, to be so out of control. But I was only pretending to consider the matter. I don't believe I could have stopped myself, even if I had wanted to.

The night he escorted me home from BAFA, I made some excuse to get him into the house. We had been talking, flirting for weeks, and it didn't take much. From there, matters progressed rapidly. That first time we made love, I found myself in a country I had never before even known about. I'd really come to think I'd die if I couldn't have him, and when he entered me it was as if he were, at that moment, saving my life.

/ / /

Really, I had only sympathy for his family and their position, though I couldn't help resenting their presence. I behaved myself at lunch and afterward, shook hands all around, and went into the hall to the bathroom. When I emerged, Christine was there. She said, quietly, with her self-sufficient smile, "We may all be having dinner at Napolitaine Thursday."

I said, "That's funny. I was just thinking about Napolitaine earlier today."

She said, "The role of coincidence in our lives is so extraordinary, don't you find?"

"Synchronicity."

"Ah, well. In Paris, of course, the students were wild about Jung. They were all for making friends with their shadows. Are you friends with your shadow, Anna?"

"I've never really thought about it, one way or the other," I said, and she laughed, not unkindly but affectionately.

Jean-Pierre, evidently uneasy, came into the hall then, saying, "Are you all well?" A reproach, not an expression of concern.

"Bring your friend to dinner Thursday," said Christine. "I find her extremely entertaining." Was this a gesture of friendship, a further test, an opening for me to make a fool of myself? I couldn't tell how she really felt.

Jean-Pierre, obviously irked by her interference, said, "That was my intention," but it wasn't clear whether he was telling the truth. This was what frustrated me most about Burundi then. The unwillingness to be straightforward, to explain anything. We said goodbye, and I went away without the kiss I longed for.

I drove down to the clinic to find Marie-Claire. The family lunch had unsettled me; the thought of the dinner at Napolitaine made me anxious. I had just sort of, but not really, been proposed to, and I had no one to talk to about it. I was missing Zoë again, wishing she were still in Burundi and not in Malaysia. There must be women who can do without their best friends, living on love and work, or perhaps satisfied by the complicated and painful love of their families, but not women I know. I wanted our daily phone calls, her wicked gossip, her tenderness toward her AIDS patients, the sense that I had an ally.

My friendship with Marie-Claire was more formal. The clinic I'd worked in for my first year in Burundi consisted of two rooms and a tiny bathroom on Avenue des non-alignés, a long, pitted, dirt street overhung with dusty flamboyants. We were only a short walk from Kapa's, which made the pastries for most of the ex-pat events, as well as the only real whole wheat bread in the country, though Pâtisserie Atlas sometimes came up with a good round, dark loaf on a Thursday. Marie-Claire, Zoë, and I had often had coffee and sweets at Kapa's before beginning our exhausting, gritty days. Now I occasionally met Marie-Claire there, but our discussions were edited: we didn't talk about Burundian politics or our emotional lives. She didn't read, and we no longer had the daily events of the clinic in common.

The clinic provided both treatment and education, including role-playing with women, teaching negotiation. Most HIV transmission was male to female, the men acquiring the virus, giving it to their wives, denying that they had it. And then there was the problem of maternal-child transference. If a mother were positive, her child might be born without the virus, but then acquire it through her milk. If we could get the mothers to stop nursing before the child was six months old, the child had a chance of escaping, but the mothers had so many good reasons to go on nursing, and we had such a long tradition to fight.

On the clinic steps, an old man, gray beard, one leg shriveled from polio, smiled, recognizing me, and held out his hand (my mind, playing a worn but inescapable tape, repeated, "Five bucks' worth of vaccine, five bucks' worth of vaccine, and his whole life would have been different"). I saluted him in Kiswahili and gave him a red twenty-franc bill so filthy it reeked, like most Burundian money, which stayed in circulation forever.

In return, he clasped his hands together, raised them up to me, the money cupped in between his palms, and gave me a brilliant smile, peaceful, delighted. I thought it would, in some ways, even be better to be an old Burundian polio survivor than part of a society ridden by to-do lists, five-year plans, goal visualizations, early withdrawal penalties, digital clocks, fax machines, and Federal Express. But that kind of thinking was exactly the sort of sick, false nostalgia that made me so crazy when I heard it from tourists—two weeks in Africa and they were experts on the true meaning of life.

The clinic door stuck, and I pushed it open with a crack, shaking loose some of the dust on that glass—everything wore a layer of dry, red-brown earth. A poster with a worried doctor, a skeletal, bedridden patient, and the words *"Tout le monde peut éviter le SIDA"* (Everyone can avoid AIDS) hung over the reception desk, peeling up at one corner where the tape had dried.

Evariste, the receptionist and messenger, lounging at his desk, broke into an immense smile, jumped up to shake hands, and we exchanged the long series of Burundian greetings. He told me that his brother's wife had disappeared, upcountry, but the rest of the family was fine, his children were fine, how was I? The exhausted mothers and joking men in the tiny, stuffed-to-capacity waiting room listened to us talk, many of them coughing or breathing painfully.

The examining door was closed. Marie-Claire, hearing our voices, left her microscope and came out from behind the counter. We clasped each other's hands, our eyes full of tears. She said, "Your mother?"

"Still alive, but I don't know for how long." Marie-Claire was thinner, older, something sunken about her face. She wore a pair of *bihume*, amulets to protect her against the malice of those who have been killed and who now look for revenge against the living. I asked her, "And how is your family? The babies?" They wouldn't be named yet, not till they had lived through infancy, though they might be referred to by some ugly nickname—Mouse Dung, Little Whore—to make them seem undesirable to the spirits who might otherwise snatch them away. Marie-Claire was a Catholic, but she also observed the older customs.

"The babies are well enough. But my second boy is gone—an accident. They strike us and drive on." She meant the Tutsis. "My fourth brother died. A cancer in the bones. And my youngest sister is sero-positive, diagnosed this week. We did the tests here."

I put my arms around her, and she allowed it, though it was odd for both of us. I don't know what I said; I was full of horror and sorrow.

She said, "They're in God's hands now. Each week that I'm still alive, I give thanks."

I felt myself hung all over with stupidities, like Christmas ornaments—my foolish lovesickness, my hysteria over the incipient death of my mother, already older than most Burundians would ever be, though by her age any woman who'd managed to survive would be shriveled, toothless, used up. And then all the imaginary problems on which I wasted most of the resources, such as they were, of my mind. My little career frets. Worries about my goddamn fucking weight. Day after day in some kind of stupid dream.

I said, "Do you need help?"

She rolled her eyes. "Is there a day when we don't?"

"I have a free afternoon," I said, and she wanted to at least demur, I could see that, but she was too tired. So she put me to work.

Four

Since I didn't have to go to work the next morning, Deo and I took a taxi to Nyakabiga market, since parking there was impossible. Now that Jean-Pierre had said the word *marriage*, the possibility of a lifetime in Burundi had suddenly become real for me. What would it be like to live here forever, where almost everyone around me was dramatically poorer than I was? Where there were so many terrible stories, histories? Where I was always marked as white, a foreigner, visible? Where nothing was private? Where I was understood, by the Burundians as well as the Europeans, to owe it to the Burundian economy to have servants: guards (male), a gardener (male), and, above all, a housekeeper (male)?

Deo's and my pleasure in seeing each other had temporarily melted the strains and irritations of employer/employee relationship—his refusal to iron until forced into it; my sharp tongue; the small disappearances of jewelry, liquor, foodstuffs; even his silent disapproval of my loose morals. A strong-minded fundamentalist, he put in his time in the kitchens and bathrooms of expatriate Americans while waiting for Judgment Day, which, by his calculation, couldn't be far off.

Often I felt I would rather do every lick of work myself. But on the ride to the market we joked in a combination of Kiswahili and French, with occasional words in English, and he told me stories about his nine children (although not his wife, who, according to custom, was never mentioned except in the context of childbirth or childhood illnesses), while I told him stories, thoroughly edited, about California. We were having a good time, although we didn't really understand each other. Deo had been to Zaire once, Rwanda twice, and had only the knowledge of the U.S. of someone who'd worked in the houses of Americans for years: we were rich, temperamental, bizarre; we paid better than the Europeans and were softer; we insisted on a lavish variety of foods and fussed over how they were cooked; we came and went, disappearing from Burundi into the void outside Africa. He could read and write, a little, but always the Bible or notes about household matters.

The taxi slid and honked through the streets. Our Zairian driver, considerably more sophisticated than Deo, made sly jokes which let me know *he* knew about Jean-Pierre. How fond I clearly was of Burundi and Burundians, how a woman finds her way to the top—all this with a wink in the rearview mirror. It still shocked me, how everyone in Burundi knew everyone else's secrets. His joking made me anxious; if a taxi driver I had never met knew about our affair, how could Jean-Pierre's family be in any doubt? The driver also denounced the alternating passivity and vengefulness of the Burundians, in a way that exacerbated my anxieties about the possibilities of the outbreak of trouble and that made Deo very quiet.

We were in Nyakabiga *quartier*. The dusty streets would turn to thick, car-catching mud in the rainy seasons, lined with little airless houses with flat sheets of corrugated steel on top, people lining up outside for water, children playing on a stoop. Cutout doorways and windows with rough wood for shutters, doors.

And then, as we approached the market, taxis, bicycles, livestock, beeping minibuses, even the occasional truck, struggled, honked, roared. A noisy, surging, dangerous throng of people and cars seethed at the market's edge. Children lounged alongside the occasional parked car, the one who'd been paid to guard it, and the others waiting for a chance to make off with rearview mirrors, antennas, bumpers. Always an accident or two, the crowds engaged and shouting.

Deo and I, clutching our big, woven baskets, got out, and I paid the driver the agreed-upon sum, though he wanted to jack it up. We were immediately enveloped by children. "Wait," I said to them in Kiswahili, "just wait." All around us were glorious piles of dark red tomatoes, huge stacks of pineapple and papaya, green bananas and tainted lettuce, the smells of dust and gasoline, the sight of endless lean-to stalls, the throngs of people. Long open sheds had counters piled with immense baskets of red or white or mottled greenish dried beans and, off ahead of us, meat and fresh-caught fish—huge Nile perch, their eyes not yet dim, gills still bright red, and heaps of tiny, sun-drying *ndagala*, sending out a strong fish smell, silvery, enticing.

The children were pulling at me. They needed money, they hadn't eaten, they would carry my things, sell me bags. "You must help us, madame, we are so poor," they called out in accomplished, pathetic French. Little smiles, sly, irrepressible, from my usual helpers. Urgent hand waving, begging, reproaches from those less sure of themselves.

Deo snapped at them in Kirundi, and I said, "Deo." Because some of my favorite market urchins were among them, grinning shamelessly, rubbing their bellies. They might even be hungry, but they were in luck today, and so they made a game or contest out of it. I couldn't take all of them, so the game had a desperate undertone. If I picked them, I'd buy a slew of plastic bags for ten francs apiece, and their week would be made. They would earn more in an hour than a day laborer would be paid for sweating all day in the streets. But if I didn't choose them and no other rich people came along, they would have nothing. Some of these were AIDS orphans, others from families too big to feed any of the children *enough*. I always bought ten times the number of bags I needed; my cupboards at home were now stuffed with them.

I picked six of the kids. Another three or four, determined and hopeful, trooped off with us, while my official companions scolded them, tried to chase them away. We pushed our way through the trampled cabbage leaves, dropped refuse (in the rains we'd be up to our ankles in black mud), dusty scraps. I had a good grip on my purse. A couple of my urchins were skilled thieves.

The thought reminded me of Margaret, but only for a moment. I had decisions to make—was I going to cook at home or let Deo do it, would I be eating at Jean-Pierre's much of the week, were the bigger children selling me more than their share of bags and the little ones getting pushed aside? And all the time, vendors shouted, "Madame! Madame!" at me from all sides, the children jostling and pulling. Was it perhaps more oppressive, less of an adventure, when I thought of shopping this way, or leaving it to Deo, for the rest of my life?

Men lounged together, sardonic, slow-moving, telling jokes. Staring at me. Everyone else here was African, except for one Frenchwoman, who stared straight ahead, snapping out orders to her housekeeper and his helper. Would I become like her in five years? In twenty? Most of the little stalls were run by a couple of men, or a woman with her baby and teenage daughter, or an old woman alone, and sold only a few items: garlic, onions, and potatoes, or mango and papaya. Other parts of the market had soap, bright rolls of cut cloth, cheap sandals, kerosene, mattresses.

Here everything was necessity, survival, no jugglers and psychic readers. Did I belong here or was I fooling myself, identifying with the urgent need of the Burundians when the real question for me was whether the self-indulgences of plenty were inevitable? Besides, what did I know about Nyakabiga? Maybe it was more like the Health and Harmony Fair than I understood. Maybe the place was full of aura readers, or soothsayers.

"Deo, are there people here who predict the future?"

"It is wrong to predict the future. Only God knows what will happen." He was withdrawn, sullen—he thought I wanted my fortune told.

We started with the long open shed where we bought lettuce. A bad idea, but I was stubborn and regularly risked not only the ordinary, everyday diarrhea but permanent intestinal damage. Was I never again to just eat salads without worrying? But I remembered Jean-Pierre's way of dipping his head and grinning after he made a joke. I pressed my hands over my eyes, trying to stop the chattering little worries of my mind.

Deo and I visited with the stall vendors. We pointed to green onions, a tiny cauliflower, peppers, a paper twist of green peas. The prices had shot up—Deo said it was because it was so late in the dry season, but it was also because I was there with him. We had to buy potatoes, onions, beans, palm oil. He had used most of what was in the house while I'd been gone, a four-month supply in a few weeks.

We bought tomatoes from our favorite, grinning women (who also succeeded in selling us unnecessary peanuts). Tomatoes like some strange dream, wild nightshade fruit in gleaming piles, an impossible size and color, some bursting already, spilling their juices. Tiny shriveled peanuts. And, across the way, great bunches of green bananas, still on their stalks. All beautiful, as vivid as if I had never seen any of it before. Who wouldn't trade comfort for aliveness, if she had the choice? The vendor wanted to know, was I married yet? She and the women for three stalls around burst out laughing. I said I was too young to be married, and they laughed again, though they looked disapproving, and I heard a word for "grandmother" in Kirundi. Which I felt as a blow, though I tried not to. It was true. A Burundian woman my age could have been a grandmother.

/   /   /

On the way home in the taxi, we were quiet. Deo looked out the window, humming a hymn. I was remembering a trip to the Source of the Nile and the falls at Karera with Jean-Pierre, Zoë, and two Peace Corps volunteers—Sally Chalders, Fisheries, and Patrick Riley, Forestry—whom I'd gotten to know on my visits to Kirundo province.

We drove along a clean main road, built by the Chinese in the failed hope of encouraging Communism, and then dusty, rutted backroads. People everywhere trudged along the sides of the roads, disappearing back into the *collines*, the hills. The achingly beautiful rolling landscape was covered with banana trees, rice, everything under cultivation. The best guess on Burundi's population was eleven million people, and we could see the signs of the growing erosion of the countryside.

The pyramid monument, on a hill with a panoramic sweep of countryside below, was satisfactory, but the Source of the Nile, one of about five in central Africa ("the southernmost source of the Nile," people said, though I think that *National Geographic* puts the actual source in Uganda, or maybe the Sudan), was a disappointing trickle. A small bubble of water rose from the earth, ran down into a puddle, then escaped underground again. I squatted beside it, letting it run over my fingers, trying to feel an appropriate emotion. I said to myself, *This is the source of the Nile,* but it seemed too dubious. Could that immense, famous, seductive, dangerous river really come from this puddle? Whose version of the truth could be trusted?

Jean-Pierre, his face knowing and ironic, watched me crouch

beside the water. After a few minutes, he said, "It's not what you thought it would be."

I stood up and held out my damp hand. He took it, smiling.

Immediately, a group of men crowded around, insisted on guiding us, selling us flowers, offering bracelets of Zairian malachite. Jean-Pierre, who usually was firm about beggars and touts, let them, laughing. After one or two questions in Kirundi, they treated him deferentially, with some distance, concentrating on me, and then on Sally and on Patrick, who bought a walking stick. Immediately, men converged from all over, offering other walking sticks.

"I have a stick," Patrick said to them in Kiswahili, laughing, waving it, but he was now perceived as an expanding market for walking sticks, and, in fact, back in Buj, within a week, word had got around and he was offered sticks for a year afterward, anytime he visited town.

We left then and drove for hours—singing, telling jokes, exchanging stories about the best and worst trips of our lives—over the pitted dirt roads to Karera, to the falls, stunning even in the dry season. Jean-Pierre and I left the others sitting below, photographing, and climbed the cliff to see the upper falls. The shape of his back through his shirt, the way his waist moved down into his trousers, a sudden, characteristic turn of his head, and I was desperate for him. I would have given five or so years of my life for just one real kiss, right then. I put a hand on his waist for a moment, but dropped it as useless. The word the Burundians use about themselves, often and with pride, is *pudique*. Prudish, we might say, but the connotation is of modesty, reserve. Self-restraint is the great virtue. Jean-Pierre would never touch me in public, even if no one else seemed to be nearby.

We clambered over rocks to the edge of the streambed, and he squatted beside it, examining the marks that showed its winter width. Sweat shone across his forehead; I wanted to lick it off. I don't know what I might not have done if Sally hadn't come up behind us, delighted with herself for having made the climb.

What I remembered, dying for him again, was that ache of desire, growing as we left the falls, then that night in our hotel room, the pain of wanting him all day and the glory of his body finally on and in mine, our becoming a single wild creature. And yet, within an hour, after talking and drifting off into a dream of movement, of driving, bouncing across winding roads, I was awakened again by my body's trembling. Desire that hollowed me out, left me helpless, paralyzed with need. I could not, ever, get enough of him. How many years would it take before that painful edge went, the sense of his presence, body and spirit, even *before* he entered a room, the long reveries of desire?

/ / /

The taxi pulled up in my driveway, and Deo and I got out, staggering under the weight of our baskets and bags. Before we had it all put away, Deo began to make small noises of apology and distress. It turned out that although he hadn't bought any food while I'd been gone, he'd somehow spent all the money I had left for emergencies. He hadn't paid the electrical company either; I was going to have to straighten that out. And then, from his stories, it became clear that he had spent his next month's salary, which I'd given him before leaving, and he wanted a loan. I almost never said no, and didn't this time. But I was annoyed, and guilty about my annoyance. Wasn't I exploiting Deo? He had come with the house; if I hadn't hired him, he would have had no place to go, but no matter how much higher his salary was than the money earned by most Burundians, it still wasn't enough. So wasn't he entitled to get whatever he could out of me? I believed this, with my mind, but my ridiculous feelings were hurt whenever he stole from me. The stealing seemed, though I knew better, a betrayal of our joking, the hours we had spent cooking together, our storytelling about our histories and families.

The phone rang. Jean-Pierre said, "I have gotten rid of them for the afternoon. Till after dinner. Can you come here? Shall I come there? Do you still want to see me?"

My crossness was gone at once. "I'll be there right away. Twenty minutes."

"A very long time," he said, laughing but serious, his voice thick with desire. I put down the phone and ran out the door.

/   /   /

But it's never simple to drive across town in Burundi: cattle in the road, stopped minivans, people trying to sell you flowers or food at stop signs. It was almost one before I pulled up to Jean-Pierre's gate, honking to wake Pero, his *zamu*, guard. By this time, it was as if I were running a fever, hot all over and so wet with desire that I'd pulled up my skirt in back while driving, so that I wasn't soaking it, though I kept myself visibly decent, my thighs still covered in front.

Phillippe, Jean-Pierre's housekeeper, had passed me on the hill, backpedaling his bicycle to slow down, his head tucked, not seeing me. When I honked my horn, Pero let me in through the gate, smiling, lascivious, mock-deferential. He found our love affair very entertaining; we were his television and movies. I know he habitually listened outside the bedroom window—once we heard him sneeze. He'd addressed me as *Bibi* (lady) until the first night Jean-Pierre and I had made love, and then the next time he saw me and forever afterward, he called me *Mama*. *"Jambo, Mama."* With that knowing grin.

Jean-Pierre's Suzuki was parked in the driveway. I ran up the steps and he came to the door. We stood looking at each other, grinning like idiots, before he reached out to pull me inside. Pero, a few feet away, watched us with interest.

As soon as the door had shut behind me, I put my hands up to Jean-Pierre's face, as if I were blind, running them over his wide forehead, strong cheeks, the bridge and nostrils of his nose, his lips and jaw. He caught hold of my hand and pressed his cheek into my palm, passionately, then held out his arms. I leapt up into them, catching him around the neck with my arms, my legs wrapped around his waist. We rocked back and forth like that, his face buried in my neck. Although I now, finally, had him, I was in a desperate state of missing him, all the accumulated longing choking me.

He carried me into the bedroom, dropping me down onto my back on the bed, pulling off all clothes that were in the way—his, mine. His face, so beautiful, so serious, so complicated, was killing me. I would have done anything in the world to have him right then, and it only seemed he was taking too long, so that when he did enter me I cried with relief. There was no barrier between us, no part of me that stood by, separate and thinking. I was so out of control that he had to hold me down to stay inside, and I know, from the marks I found later, that he bit me hard on the shoulder, raising a dark, purple bruise.

When he came, it was with a long, breathy, painful cry, his head back, teeth bared, his face almost frightening—I saw it only for a moment, thrashing underneath him, my own orgasms more violent with his abandonment, and then he was dropping forward, his head on my shoulder. After a long, still moment, he began to laugh, weakly, and I joined him.

He greeted me formally, in Kiswahili, as if we hadn't seen each other in weeks, as if the whole family lunch had never happened: a formal acknowledgment of time passed. *"Habari ya siku nyingi?"* (What is the news of many days?) Taking his cue, I responded in kind. My earlier questions and worries evaporated in the deliciousness of being with him. We were both giggling; we'd reached the stupid stage and now entered into our various little jokes, completely satisfying to us, very undignified.

We had to drink most of a liter of water, then we discovered ourselves to be hungry and put on enough clothing to go into the
kitchen (the thin curtains provided no real privacy against Pero) and
eat large amounts of the *ndagala* with green banana, the red beans,
the peas that Phillippe had left on the stove. I asked Jean-Pierre
if he had to go back to work, and he said, no, he had told them he
wasn't well and wouldn't be back today. Since he was extraordinarily
conscientious about his job, I felt proud of enticing him away from
it. We went back to bed, made love again—more slowly this time,
more elaborate variations—dozed, woke, made love.

It was only then that we began to be able to really catch up,
though, as usual, we didn't fully understand each other. Although
he explained the new atmosphere, the shifting of tensions among
Ndadaye's twenty-three ministers, I didn't quite follow the intricate
descriptions of who at the ministries had been transferred to a new
post, who had been given different responsibilities, who was new,
and how the changes affected family alliances.

I did follow him when he said, "Among the ministers, nine are
Tutsi or Ganwa, and many of the subordinates as well. He wants us
in place to show that he is not against us. He says that he believes
in an end to fighting, that Burundi must be a just and unified country with respect for all its people. I don't know what his plans are.
Does he mean real reform? Or does he mean to slowly replace the
army and then strike out? The Hutu are triumphant, but he has con-
trolled them, at least at the beginning." After a long pause, he went
on, "If we could have, at last, an end to revenge. If this could happen in Burundi . . ." His voice trailed off, as if he were afraid to say
any more, to let himself hope.

I did understand, or thought I understood, fear and vengeance.
I remembered reading about Hutus and Tutsis in the thirties. A
group of Hutu landholders, who had only a *rugo* each, not even a
colline, in Ngozi and environs, had been tricked by the Tutsis gov-
erning locally, who told the Hutus they could escape slaving for the

colonials by performing certain tasks for the Tutsis. Once they'd begun these tasks, however, the field work, water carrying, even personal service, the Tutsis had them declared *abagererwa* (serfs, sharecroppers) and confiscated their land. At which point some of them were kept on to work and others sent away, randomly or with malice, by their new landlords.

And Hutus I'd come in contact with through the human rights work had said to me, Imagine this: a brother-in-law is gone, inexplicably. A year later, you see someone walking down the street in the very clothes he was wearing when he disappeared, and you can't say a word. Or you work on an important Tutsi's house, you're a small-time carpenter, and when the work is done, you ask to be paid. He laughs at you and, when you persist, chases you with his car, runs over your arm when you fall down. You bind up your arm and go to the police station. They beat you and lock you up for a week for having the temerity to speak against someone so important.

The Hutus waited for the next outbreak of mass violence, in their dark houses with the rippled steel roofs, hot in the daytime, tormented by insects at night. Tensed against the possibility of terror, ready to fight or run at the first sign that it might be beginning again. And the Tutsis, after centuries of oppression, now had to hand over the reins—of course they were waiting for the Hutus' revenge. I couldn't say any of this to Jean-Pierre.

Instead I tried to convey the long, slow peace of Sonoma County. "It's a place where you can drive through miles of hills that turn dark gold for most of the year, narrow roads, trees, farms, and then a sudden turn might take you through eucalyptus trees to the ocean or into the redwoods."

"So it is a kind of paradise there where your family lives?" He was smiling at the idea, his hand in my hair, possessive and tender.

"It's not stunningly beautiful like the north counties or down around San Francisco. The thing about it is a kind of plainness. The everyday. You drive these winding roads past fields of cattle, and the air feels hot and still. Even the parts of the county that have car dealerships, malls, it seems as if they're suspended in time. Because it's so isolated."

"Do you realize, Ah-na, that your words say this is plain, it is isolated, it is not beautiful, but your tone is full of nostalgia? Do you wish you were back there?"

"I'd rather be here." I put my hand on his body, tracing the muscles of his stomach.

He sat up, putting his hand over mine, imprisoning it. "Because of being together?"

I had to think about this for a moment. Then I said, "I don't understand anything as clearly until we talk about it. Our points of reference are so different that we have to define everything for each other."

"So you like who you are when we are together." He was still sitting up, his legs crossed under the sheet.

"Yes, but it's also Burundi itself that makes me want to be here. Not just the beauty, or the way people actually interact with each other here instead of just getting down to business. The feeling that real life is happening here. It's not just some great, smooth machine." I started to laugh. "Maybe I like Burundi because it isn't a nation full of people watching television."

"Much better for us to be cultivating the fields all day," Jean-Pierre said, then stretched out beside me again, smoothing back and separating the strands of hair stuck to my face. "Do you remember I had a surprise for you?"

"A long time ago."

"Very long." He was quiet for a moment. "When we can, I want to take you upcountry for a few days. We never have enough time together."

I nodded, but I felt as if, in fact, I were drifting in a large, un-demanding pool of time, infinitely peaceful, my skin against his skin, my entire body and spirit focused on this moment, and it seemed to me I could shed my family troubles and take up my life again. *Home:* a few feet of skin, muscle, blood—the contact between us, the feeling that with him I was safe and could drop, for a little while, the guard that I kept up against the world.

/ / /

My family accompanied me now, in my head, whenever I took a walk or drove somewhere. I remembered trying to explain Burundi to them. The taxi drivers, idling in long rows in their blue and white cabs, driving down either side of the street or in the middle. The way everything is run by kinship networks and systems of patronage. The importance of the frighteningly thin cows. Driving past one herd, I relived a conversation I'd had with Mom the morning I left, when she was going on about cattle again, and how we should have raised them instead of growing apples.

I said, "In Burundi, cattle are the measure of wealth. *Inka.* Cow." My mother's mouth made the shape of the word, though she didn't say it aloud. I went on, "They're exchanged for land, taxes, as a marriage settlement, for political interactions, to buy favors. *Ibiturire,* what we might call bribes. You see these herds of terribly thin long-horned cows. There's not enough food for them all, but you wouldn't eat them, except under extraordinary circumstances, because it would be diminishing your wealth. People eat goats a lot. Goat brochettes, goat cheeses."

"The place I wanted to go was Japan. Armor and temples. A way of thinking so different." Her eyes watered, from grief or pain. She blotted them with a tissue.

"Do you want some more codeine? It's nearly time. Or I could read to you." She had us all reading to her from the pile of romances, almost every night, but this time she shook her head. I couldn't give her Japan; it was too late.

"Do you want me to tell you about cows in Burundi?" She nodded, just barely. I said, "I was at the wedding of a friend. A Peace Corps volunteer was marrying a Burundian." I looked to see how she responded to that, but her face was blank. "The receptions go on and on, and it's not like Zaire. Some chanting of wedding songs, but then afterward no music, no dancing. Everyone sits politely, crowded together, holding their Fantas and smiling. The bride's and groom's fathers, at some point, take turns making speeches. How he's responsible for her, and she has to look after him. How she'll be sad among strangers at first, but shouldn't think of coming home again; she belongs to her husband's family now. At one of these receptions, during one of the long pauses where you're trying to talk with people—and everyone stares at you when you're an outsider— I asked someone how you tell a good cow from a bad cow. The standards of judgment. What do you think, Mom?"

She gave a kind of a shrug, but she was a little interested. Coming from our territory. She whispered, "Amount of milk, amount of meat. Breeding stock."

"That's what we think. But the man I was talking to told me that there are three criteria by which the quality of a cow is judged. Number one is the cow's historical importance. That is, for how many of the family's major events has the cow been with the family? Number two is how good the cow is at guarding the house. And number three?"

She shook her head.

"Number three is the cow's leadership ability—do the other cows follow it, does it show leadership in the herd? And that's how cows are judged in Burundi."

She gave me a small smile then, shut her eyes, and said, "You'll do what you want to. You always did."

I didn't understand how that followed from what I had said, but this was as close as I could picture to her giving me her blessing.

/   /   /

In the office, I sorted through my piles of accumulated work as a way of avoiding what I really needed to do: to write fund-raising letters that our U.S. connection (to call him an office would be overstating the case) would send out for us.

Jack had gone out on a jail visit; Charles, our Burundian interpreter, secretary, and source of all information, sat at his desk retyping a list of names of our Burundian contacts, in a code that would protect them if our office were broken into. He whistled a little, a French tune current around town.

I asked, in French, "Charles, what year did Ruanda-Urundi become Rwanda and Burundi?"

"Nineteen sixty-two. The Republic of Rwanda and the Kingdom of Burundi. Our year of independence, after the tragic assassination of Prince Louis Rwagasore in 1961." His tone was cool. When we'd first begun working together, he'd been so friendly, so charming, that seeing him was a big part of my pleasure in the job. After a couple of months, though, he had changed. I must have done something to bitterly offend him, but I never knew what, and it was impossible to ask. I still grieved for our earlier friendly ease.

My attempt at a letter lay on the desk in front of me.

In the heart of Africa, right between Tanzania and Zaire, just below Rwanda, lies Burundi, a country embarking, for the first time in its history, on the adventure (wrong word?) of democracy.

During the centuries around 1000 AD, the Bahutu, Bantu farmers, settled the small (area? kingdom? No, not then—territory? Mention that the borders were about the same as today?) and lived a peaceful life of raising bananas, cassava, and beans until the arrival of the Batutsi, a Nilotic people who drove their cattle down from the north three or four hundred years after the Bahutu settled the

kingdom, and, during the seventeenth century, established a kingdom
where they ruled over the Bahutu. They shared a language, spiritual
beliefs, and customs, but the Batutsi had the political power, and the
seeds of future enmity were sown during this pastoral period.

This was full of problems, apart from the ridiculously long second sentence. And what about the power of the Ganwa (and could I
put that in a document? How could I not if it were true? But what
if Jean-Pierre somehow saw it?). Also, did they raise the same crops,
the bananas, cassavas, and beans that the subsistence farmers did
today? Would anyone be interested in all this? Surely not if I related
even the briefest version of a history of Burundi in relation to the
outside world. I had a batch of notes that read:

Late 17th C—reign of Ntare I, first mwami (king)
1850s—visits of Burton and Speke—first intrusion from Europe
19th C—Mwezi IV becomes mwami (mention alternating kingships
    of the four great Ganwa clans/houses/dynasties? Shakespearean
    dramas of betrayal and revenge?)
End of the 19th C, Stanley and Livingstone's explorations. Then
    Germans take over territory for "administration," colonialism,
    then England and Germany divvy up East Africa, resulting in
    German occupation of Ruanda-Urundi (also Catholic missionar-
    ies establish a presence).
1908—death of Mwezi IV (Gisabo), social unrest (German control
    slipping)
WWI—Belgian troops fighting, occupation.
Post-WWI—British & Belgians agree on Belgian administration,
    League of Nations confirms. King Leopold, Belgians start the
    Burundians growing coffee, Belgians destroying local adminis-
    trative & justice systems
Post-WWII—Belgium reprimanded etc at intervals, oppressing the

Burundians, pillaging not administering (too confrontational a statement? Use official language of trusteeship missions instead?)

October 13, 1961—the assassination of Prince Louis Rwagasore

July 1, 1962—Burundian independence

1966—with Mwami Mwambutsa (hiding?) in Europe, after a series of assassinations of high government officials, the heir, Prince Charles Ndizeye, asks Michel Micombero, the minister of defense, to help him take power, and then, five months later, Micombero seizes power for himself in a coup and declares that he is the first president of the brand-new Republic of Burundi

I had given up here—this was hopeless and getting worse by the entry. It also left out too much, including any explanation of what it all meant. Worse still, it gave no sense of the episodes of terrible violence between the Hutus and Tutsis, including the massacres of 1972 and 1988, the long, slow progression toward independence, and the details of the assassinations and military coups that had been the means of changing the government right up through Major Pierre Buyoya's bloodless 1987 coup. And then Buyoya's new constitution, the one that denounced violence and "tribalism," the constitution that, in March, had been ratified by the people in preparation for the presidential elections. In which Buyoya had lost to Ndadaye.

All this history was too much for a funding letter. Who would read to the end? I picked up my pen and started over.

Since you care about human rights, we are writing to offer you the chance to participate in a historical event, the transition of a tiny (no, then no one will give anything) of a country at the heart of Africa from military rule to democracy, a chance to help the Republic of Burundi escape its bloody past, no

This wasn't any better. I put the letter aside and went back to my sorting.

/   /   /

That night, alone in my bed, sleeping a painful, dream-ridden sleep, I woke to the sound of an engine, a car out front. Headlights flashed up my pale curtains, then switched off. My watch said 12:10. I was filled with an inordinate happiness. Jean-Pierre's steps sounded on my front stoop, his key in my lock, and then he was in my room, skinning off his clothes. Two minutes after the car had stopped, he slid, warm and naked and vividly alive, into my bed, pulling the covers over his shoulders. I held out my arms, my body already arching toward his. He whispered in my ear, his body a beautiful shock on mine (its weight, its sweetness), "I have to be gone before five." I nodded, my cheek rubbing against his. *"Mille vaches,"* he murmured. A thousand cows, one of our jokes. He'd once said this, recklessly, when I speculated on how many cows I would bring as a marriage price. From time to time, after that moment, he would say *mille vaches* and it melted me; I understood that he was saying how unreasonably precious I was to him. Outside, the cicadas buzzed, like electric wiring gone crazy, and the pinkish-gold security lights shone through the curtains, repeating the leaf-and-vine pattern onto the tiles of the floor.

Five

I parked down the block from Napolitaine, the pizzeria next to the French embassy, and was surrounded all the way to the restaurant by a crowd of begging children. Taxi drivers called out to me, reproaching me for walking. Feeling besieged, guilty, angry—and guilty about being angry—I went into Napolitaine to meet Jean-Pierre, Christine, Andre, Bertrand, and Renard Uwizeye (also from Interior) with his girlfriend.

Three or four waiters stood about aimlessly. Their white jackets hung on them, giving them a temporary, uninvolved air, as if the real waiters were elsewhere and these had borrowed their clothes for a joke. French and Belgian couples and groups we knew were at tables all around us, eating their pizzas or waiting, arguing, flirting.

At the other end of the restaurant, a group of official Americans, including a bunch of loud young Marines, one or two embassy officials with their wives, and a few Peace Corps volunteers, were laughing loudly. One of the Marines demonstrated how he could stick his knife into the table between his fingers without hurting himself. He'd been shouting at an embassy wife, in a raw boy's voice that came right out of rural Texas, "Well, d'ya believe in past lives? How 'bout ghosts? D'ya think it's over when we die? Or d'ya think there's somethin' else?" She was embarrassed, obviously suspecting a trap. She seemed to have an expression of permanent, polite misery. I didn't know any of the official Americans well. I saw them occasionally with their children at the ambassador's pool, at Fourth of July celebrations, or shopping at Dimitri's for something I couldn't find in the open-air markets.

We had made the rounds, greeting everyone we knew, and then sat down. We ordered, and then waited for an hour and forty minutes. Eventually, a waiter we summoned explained that the cooks had made our pizzas badly and had to start over. We had already drunk numerous giant bottles of Primus, the least acid of the two available beers, on stomachs empty except for *la salade*, tiny plates of cabbage and kidney beans swimming in oil. We began to make jokes, to speculate on what they'd have to do to remake our pizzas. Grinding wheat. Killing cows to make sausage. The sort of joke that seems funny when you're three-quarters drunk.

So we were all laughing, except for Bertrand, who was belligerent. He'd drunk more than two liters of Primus. First he'd argued with Jean-Pierre about differing memories of some incident from childhood. Now he was going to make a scene. He was saying, "The way you do things down here in the city—having to wait two hours for a meal!"

"And this isn't the case in the Interior?" Jean-Pierre asked. He had his hands folded on the table in front of him, very patient, very still.

"And your crime—the bandits in the streets, the thieves in the houses. No order. And the traffic. Too many people! Too many cars!" He shook a finger in Jean-Pierre's face, glaring, then looked around for the waiter.

Christine and I began doing a female thing: soothing remarks, little jokes. She was sitting directly across from me, and we caught each other's eyes with a small smile, ironic, comradely, acknowledging that we were on the same side. Then we began to giggle—we were on the near edge of drunkenness, hungry, slightly hysterical—and couldn't stop.

"Women," said Bertrand. "You might as well take the goats out to dinner with you. Put a dress on them and take them to dinner. Isn't there any pizza, madame goat? What a shame. Won't you have a little of the grass out front?" He stomped off to the bathroom.

Christine and I were helpless with laughter. Jean-Pierre, Andre, and Renard were half laughing, half bewildered. Renard's girl, a new one, whose name I hadn't caught, leaned forward. "Are there goats? I don't understand." Her French wasn't up to it. Renard, embarrassed, repeated the remark for her in a mixture of Kiswahili and Kirundi, and she laughed loudly.

Our pizzas arrived. Burundian pizza tends to have cumin or some other surprising herb, tiny slices of pepperoni dotted here and there, perhaps a few rounds of green pepper. Or bits of tuna over a blanket of heavy, yellow Zairian cheese. The waiters watched us eating—the price of one of the pizzas was about two weeks of any of their salaries. I looked down at my plate. Well, what was I going to do about it? Hand the money to the waiters and go across the street to the African place where I ate lunch most days? I pictured myself saying to my companions, "Let's go get some beans, green bananas, and *soambe*." The thought made me grin, despite myself. I wanted to just eat my dinner without having to think about it.

Christine said to me, quietly, "Pizza reminds me of student life. Of Paris."

"Finals."

"What I miss is talking all night with the other students. Proust, Kant, Kenyatta, Ousmane, the future of African self-determination. Immigration in France. The position of Africans—Northern and Sub-Saharan—in French society."

I said, "I miss the sense of expectancy, of unknown surprises ahead. My whole life looked like Christmas to me. Like the beginning of the rains when you've been waiting and waiting for the end of the dry season, when everything is covered with dust and the mountains completely obscured."

"You think you have no more surprises ahead?"

Jean-Pierre, maybe feeling left out by our concentration on each other, put in, "Somehow, I could be offended by this. Though I think I won't be." A hint to his family that he intended to be part of my future?

I said, "I'm happy. It's just that I think I know now what the shape of my life is, how it will be. Any surprises will probably be unpleasant ones."

Jean-Pierre said, "You're becoming a real Burundian."

Christine tapped his shoulder. "She says she's happy, but she's sad, *grandpère*. Why not comfort her?" She called him "grandfather" when she thought he needed loosening up.

He asked her, "What is it you want me to do?" They stared at each other with matching small smiles, lifted at one corner. Challenging each other.

"You could hold her hand."

"Is that so?" He looked away from her, at me, and what he saw on my face made him laugh. He reached out and took my right hand, looking down at it and turning it over to examine the palm, not looking at anyone's response, but not hiding what he was doing, which, apparently, was just within the bounds of acceptable behavior? Christine wore a cat smile. She nodded at me. I smiled at her in return and cupped my other hand under Jean-Pierre's.

There was a silence all around until Bertrand cried, "Is that it? Have we finished all the Primus?" He began waving for a waiter, who drifted obligingly in our direction, but didn't bring any more beer for another quarter of an hour.

Christine and I didn't talk particularly to each other again until we were leaving, when she said, softly, into my ear, "I had thought of going to the Cercle Nautique. Maybe tomorrow. Five-ish, to watch the Europeans watch the hippos. It's so amusing." Light from the restaurant's doorway shone onto her glossy skin, her regal and ironic smile.

I pulled my jacket around me. "I could show up about then."

"Good," she said, and gave me an insubstantial version of a Belgian good-night kiss—right cheek, left cheek, right cheek again—her lips brushing the air. Jean-Pierre, evidently uneasy about our exchange, put a hand on my shoulder, a light touch that turned me toward my car.

/ / /

The next day, two letters arrived in one mail delivery, a banner event. One was from Zoë and the other envelope was addressed in Margaret's round, firm, orderly handwriting. I tore into the letter from Zoë. She was self-deprecating about the end of a bad love affair and the disorder of her current AIDS prevention project, and then nastily amusing about some course she had to take from overseas for the renewal of her license. She was very enthusiastic about her new posting. "Malaysia is paradise, only just scrungy enough to make you feel how real it is. Just being a tourist here is *très fabuloso, ma chérie,* you cannot miss it. I promise that if you don't visit me—I'm only scheduled for three years, but I plan to extend, and I have *influence* here—you will regret it for the rest of your natural and unnatural life."

She'd included photos: of herself in front of the clinic, of women in brilliantly colored dance costumes displaying red and white fans, of buckets of fish at an open-air market, of people I didn't know posing together on a stunningly beautiful beach. Was I going to get to Malaysia while she was there? Probably not. To admit this made me a little sad. A closing down of possibilities. I was committed to Burundi now, never to be one of the stream of people who moved from place to place, dipping in and out of the world.

Putting down Zoë's exclamatory pages, I set aside Margaret's letter without opening it, keeping it on my desk all afternoon beside my computer, where I was typing up a report of my conversation with an aide to the Minister of Foreign Affairs. In which he denied, and I gently inquired, and he made speeches, pronouncements, justifications. I was typing up the record of the conversation, translating it into English. I had learned that the topic of the judicial system made him particularly nervous at this time.

Everyone has the right to an effective remedy by the competent national tribunals for acts violating the fundamental rights granted him by the constitution or by law (Article 8, Universal Declaration of Human Rights). Oh, that judicial system! Only seventeen lawyers for eleven million people, and about thirteen of those seventeen worked for the banks. It was such a despised and lowly profession that hardly anyone could be coaxed into the position of judge, and no wonder. Upcountry judges worked with 1978 law books from before the constitution had been suspended. Watching the Burundian legal system was enough to make anyone give up lawyer jokes for good.

Since this report was only for our internal use, and perhaps for sharing with our contacts at Amnesty, I was able to spend some paragraphs in speculation. But a part of my mind, seeing the envelope with its cheerful animal stamps, wondered why Margaret was writing. She wrote so seldom. Finally, just before leaving work, I opened it.

Dear Annie—

How are you? I am fine. So are the kids. Jerry had a cold, but he's better now. Since it was pretty much the first cold in the history of the world and required continual medical attention, that's good. And my job is the same as always. Same old Caswell's, same old routine. Selling lumber. Keeping after the clerks. We put in some new accounting software which has so many bugs they should sell it with a can of Raid.

So, I'm actually writing. Are you impressed? You should be. This is really hard. Guess I'm out of practice. Mom's between courses of chemo. She got too sick, and they had to quit. Lizzie took her to a homeopath. I was at work, and Mom was too weak to stop her. He gave her some ipecac or something—which seems to make her less sick. He says it's the dosage. Anyway, she's not upchucking so much and Lizzie thinks it's the remedy but I think it's because she hasn't had any treatments for two weeks. Boy, are you missing out. But hey, I guess you have servant *problems, right?*

Just kidding.

Mom was just telling a story about Grandma Eleanor. Did you know that her first house burned down? And that her oldest boy, Jackie, was killed in the fire? I just learned this yesterday—you could have drowned me in a bucket I was so surprised. He apparently left the oil lamp burning and fell asleep over his schoolwork. He was seventeen.

Mom woke up to voices and smoke and then shouting. Grandma Eleanor came in and pulled her out of bed, wrapped her in a blanket and carried her out, then went back for Uncle Bill and Aunt Susan. Mom says she doesn't remember very much, but that her own Aunt Kit told her, "Your mother just sat in a room for two months. Didn't talk. Hardly ate. Would hold a child if one came for comfort, but didn't talk to them, and mostly seemed to forget they existed." Great-aunt Kit told Mom that one day, out of nowhere, Grandma Eleanor stood up, went out, got the neighbors and Great-uncle Eddie, and began rebuilding the house. She worked on it all the time, the men couldn't keep up with her. But she never said a word about Jackie.

Great-aunt Kit said something to her about how strong she was, and Grandma Eleanor said, Great-aunt Kit remembered this forever, "What choice do I have?" and wouldn't talk about it. In a way, I think I understand her. But it beats the hell out of me that I never even knew this. Neither did Lizzie. Did you?

Yours truly, Margaret

I put the letter away, not in my bag, which could be snatched at any time, but in an inside pocket of my skirt. On my desk sat a windup toy, a fire-breathing Godzilla that I'd had for nearly a decade, from Santa Rosa to Washington, D.C. to Buj. I wound it up, and it marched across my papers. Tiny, harmless sparks shot out between the sharp teeth. I had no idea why Mom had never talked about her brother's death. What comforted me was the fantasy of myself in Jean-Pierre's arms, telling him the story, my imagining his wonder at the oddness of the concealment.

/   /   /

The Cercle Nautique sits at the very edge of the lake. There aren't many yacht owners in Burundi, but a dozen or so boats are tethered in the tiny yacht harbor there. Expatriate travelers—mostly arriving in large Overland trucks—camp on the grass. Random assortments of adventurers, German, French, and Belgian, occasionally British or American, collecting harrowing stories, interesting diseases, experiences of the real Africa, adventures not muffled by some plush package safari.

I arrived just after five. The sky hung grayish, hazy, over a thin white line at the horizon; the lake lapped in gunmetal-gray ripples against the concrete of the little harbor. Most of the tables and benches at the *Cercle*, bent and weathered, rust showing through the white paint, sat outside on a concrete deck at the water's edge. Christine wasn't there yet. I ordered a citron and took over an empty bench; the tables were full. When a batch of Belgian girls left, I moved to their table, pushing their leftover *frites*, cigarette butts, half-empty glasses to one side.

Various people I knew, and many I didn't know, sat and drank Primus or Amstel, or the bitter mineral water with slices of lime. The Europeans outnumbered the expensively dressed Africans, who clustered into bigger groups than the Europeans, surrounded by children in frilly dresses or good shirts and trousers, drinking Fantas. Citron, orange. Many people were eating piles of fried *ndagala* or *frites*, which tasted of beef fat and had thick dollops of yellowish mayonnaise over the top. A heavy Greek couple tore into brochettes of *Capitaine*, served with *frites* and salad.

Everyone had one eye on the water, waiting. For crocodiles, we had to go to the delta, the mouth of the Ruzizi where it poured into Lake Tanganyika. There we could look through binoculars at the embodied nightmares resting on a sandbar, motionless except for a widened mouth, the shifting of a foot, until they disappeared suddenly into brown, rushing water. At which everyone would unthinkingly move back from the edge of the bank, though where we stood was several feet above the surface of the river. But at the *Cercle*, sometimes hippos would surface just a few feet away, in the small harbor.

Down the beach, outside the fence that protected boats and customers, water seeped up into the reeds. Ragged men and boys wandered up and down or sat in the sand. It was the most dangerous place in town for anyone, African or expat, with any money at all.

Christine arrived fifteen or twenty minutes after me, while I was still waiting for my drink. She kissed me—right cheek, left cheek, right cheek again—in greeting and sat across from me. "So."

I said, "There are gendarmes everywhere today. And I saw a couple of tanks on my way in. I wonder if something is happening." My worries about Mom, the situation in Burundi, and even my funding letter had kept me awake much of the night. I was tired and on edge, anxious about the tanks and a little slow both in speaking and understanding French.

She shrugged. "It goes up and down. Of course, there is always the possibility of troubles."

By "troubles" the Burundians mean what we would call tragedy, disaster, genocide. She seemed removed, indifferent. I wondered if she were regretting her invitation.

The lake looked so flat, a dull shine, even with the afternoon choppiness of waves. So regular. I felt us to be in an enclosed country, thousands of miles from any ocean, thousands and thousands of miles from home. A sudden, sharp dislocation of my sense of gravity.

Christine said, "My brother is a very complicated man. I remember, as children, that he was fascinated by watching a black mamba in the garden, how it would eat, move. Anyone else would have called the guards or gardeners to have it killed instantly. And then, when someone did run shouting for the guards, and they attacked it with hoes, he would watch that too. The black mambas are the most deadly, more so than the green, even. You can die from a bite in seconds."

"Most children are interested in snakes," I said. I wanted her to tell me something less ordinary, something that would reveal Jean-Pierre's childhood to me.

She sounded impatient. "In Paris, we were at the Sorbonne together. I was a couple of years behind him, of course, and not doing as well. We shared a small flat. When I was tired, I would fall asleep over my books, sometimes on the couch, and wake at four or five to see him at the desk, still working. I asked, 'Don't you get tired? Are you immortal?' He was fierce with me. He said, 'A woman does not understand necessity. I will do whatever I have to. Of course I am tired. Of course I would like to sleep. But it's not important.' "

"He is admirable."

"Oh, well. He can be kind, funny, thoughtful. Like our mother. He's a good person to have on your side. I wouldn't want him for an enemy. He's my favorite brother, you know. Though I would never admit it."

Was this a sign of trust, a test? I wasn't sure how to answer.

The waiter brought my citron, and she ordered mineral water. They had a short, sharp conversation in Kirundi, and he took a few of the dirty plates away in a mournful shamble.

"My brother says that your mother is very ill."

Had they discussed me? What else had he said? Had he talked about our future? "She has cancer of the throat; she's dying."

"It must be hard to be away from her at this time." Her voice was disapproving.

On an impulse, I said, "Did you talk about reincarnation, in Paris?"

"Sometimes. Here also, many people believe that the spirits of our ancestors are always with us and are reborn into other bodies. *Ubuzimu.* I myself am a Christian, though I have failed to believe in heaven. It's insufficiently plausible to me, and in all the pictures, everyone is white. All those Roman bedsheets and golden harps. No drumming, you know." She allowed herself one of her small, ironic smiles. An Egyptian statue. "Do you think your mother will be reincarnated?"

"My sister does a thing with people—she takes them deep into their own minds. They seem to remember other lives. Of course, it could be a genetic memory or maybe something they've read and forgotten."

"Did she do this with you?"

"Once. It was oddly convincing."

Two adult hippos and a baby surfaced, suddenly, right in the tiny harbor, not six feet from our table. There was an outcry, laughter, cameras whipping out and going into action.

Christine said, "In fact, a hippo is a very ugly animal. Don't you find? And on land very dangerous. More people die from hippo attacks in Africa than from any other animal. Though nothing like the numbers that die in automobile accidents. Or wars."

The hippos *were* ugly, an obscene nakedness: their mouths yawned, a bellowing threat, blunt peg teeth, raw pink gullets. Their immense rears, when they dove, popped up like a bad joke. But the baby was adorable. I said so to Christine. She said that the young of any species had to be presumed to be enchanting; it was a survival mechanism. She said, "One assumes that they are also enchanting to the mothers."

And then she said, "And, after all, one must have some amusement in the intervals of one's charity work or profiteering."

I wanted to say, and didn't, that Burundi would be in trouble if we all disappeared.

She leaned forward and touched my hand. "I don't mean anything against you. I have a fondness for all the charity workers, escaping their bad love affairs into the exotic life of darkest Africa, and meanwhile so earnest and full of efforts on our behalf."

"Are you classing me with the charity workers, then?"

"Would you consider yourself a profiteer?"

I said dryly, "It could be argued that human rights is a question of self-interest in the end. That a world where rights are suppressed is unlivable."

"And there are no human rights violations in your own country."

"You might not deny that the situation is nothing like as urgent," I said. And then, to her silent waiting, "To fight for human rights in the U.S. takes either great patience for organizational work or considerable money, and I have neither. And, in fact, by the time a person has considerable money, he or she has usually talked himself out of the necessity. The world begins to seem very fine as it is, and preservation becomes the order of the day."

She laughed then, unexpectedly, and, switching to the familiar for the first time with me, said, *"Tu es assez sympa, mzungu"*—a slangy mixture of Parisian French and central African Kiswahili, which I would translate, very loosely, as "You're OK, white girl." Though the gender in *mzungu* isn't specified.

And from that time on, we were friends. She was often in Bujumbura, and we began to spend quite a lot of time together. Jean-Pierre wasn't as happy about our friendship as I would have thought he'd be, though he said he was delighted. I worked it out that he probably felt either a) somewhat jealous, b) nervous about the inter-section of his worlds, or c) shy, afraid that she would tell me boy-hood stories, revealing him in a less than heroic light. Or, perhaps, that I would tell her intimate things about the grown-up Jean-Pierre. But my friendship with Christine was no longer only about Jean-Pierre. I had found with her that sense of surprised kinship, which I'd never before had with a Burundian woman. Understand-ings, shared jokes. I missed her on days when I didn't talk to her.

/ / /

Jean-Pierre seemed to be relaxing. Maybe because the idea of mar-riage, though we didn't discuss it, was out there between us. Or maybe because of Christine's influence, her encouragement. Earlier, he had been reserved much of the time. Now he seemed more open. We were at my house one evening, eating my homemade pasta with garlic and *soambe*, manioc leaves ground with peanuts and oil. The pasta had a thick, chewy texture and fell into unnerving coils. We ate a lot of the salad and baguette. I was afraid Jean-Pierre would think I couldn't cook.

We sat at the table on the veranda, the vines on the railing heavy and sweet-smelling, the cicadas a wild buzzing all around us, the neighbor's dogs roaming up and down and barking behind the hedge that separated the yards. Jacques, the night guard, was play-ing his radio by the gate twenty feet away. I could feel him watch-ing us from his post in the dark.

As we were finishing dinner, I said to Jean-Pierre, "I'm sorry. My pasta is usually much better than this *paste*."

"This is more interesting than ordinary pasta. You can put what's left in a jar full of water in your living room, and tell every-one it is the brain of a former lover." He leaned back in his chair, putting his feet up on the opposite chair and crossing his arms like John Wayne.

"So you think I choose my lovers for their brains?"

"What did you choose me for?"

"Your kindness to puppies."

He laughed, but he sounded unhappy. "I have always been kind to animals. Sometimes you can be perceptive." He pushed aside his plate, and picked up his fork and my fork, and wiped them off. Then he stacked them on each other, the beginnings of a log cabin of silverware. "Do you have more of these? A whole pile."

I went and got the silverware drawer, emptied it onto the table, and we started to build a tower, listening to the cicadas, the tinny sound of the radio, cars honking and accelerating on the hill outside the enclosure of my hedge. My gold bracelet clanked against the forks and spoons as I worked.

Jean-Pierre said, after a couple of minutes, "Look, we can make a tunnel going this way and have two towers, one on either side."

"The spoons are too slippery." In the warm evening, my fingers were damp.

"Put it through the fork like this."

I slid my spoon into the fork he was holding, pushing the fork into his finger, stabbing him accidentally. We both began to laugh.

"How vicious women are." He held out a knife, as if to defend himself.

"Is that what you think?" But I was uncomfortable.

He saw this and put down the knife. "What I think about women—I struggle with myself. I have two minds, two sets of beliefs. The one I grew up with. And the one I acquired at the Sorbonne. My education tells me that women are not inferior to men, that the workers are not inferior to us. I read *Das Kapital*, you know, and John Stuart Mill and Simone de Beauvoir. All of that. But my *feelings* come from my childhood. I *feel* that you're inferior to me. And I also feel this about Phillippe, Deo, and so on."

"And Christine?" I thought, *So I'm jealous of her, am I?* I hadn't known it until that moment.

He looked at me more sharply. "You see? I underestimate you. No, not Christine. She *is* me, so how can she be inferior?"

I was silent. I hated what he was saying, but he was so earnestly beautiful, so full of light, trying to identify the truth. After a moment, I took up a pair of knives, adding them to the tunnel between our towers. "Maybe I will change your mind about women. Over time."

"Yes," he said. "I am hoping for this. At least, the part of me I prefer is hoping."

"There you go, Jean-Pierre. When you say that, I think, well, he has no intention of changing. And am I to encourage this?"

He ducked his head down, grinning sheepishly, so that I could see what he must have looked like as a small child in trouble.

I said, "Explain to me: what makes a woman inferior?"

His expression became serious, and he started and stopped once or twice. "If I say that a woman is more emotional, that she is not capable of the same bravery, you will point out to me the women who run countries, do scientific work, everything I know. So it is . . . it is about boldness. It is about making the decision that has to be made."

"I want to say that I have seen women be ruthless on behalf of their children, or their ambition, but then it seems to me that you're defining the terms of superiority. What about kindness, compassion, wisdom, humor, imagination? Why is bravery the ultimate value?"

"Do you believe that women are kinder and more compassionate?" He had a small grin of impending triumph.

"Well, I do," I said.

"Because they are mothers? Because they have the biology to nurture, the instincts selected for by tens of thousands of years of being patient with infants and children?" He was pressing home his point, and, even as I nodded, reluctantly, he said, "And you believe that these qualities are superior." We both began to laugh. He pointed a fork at me. "But if, at the beginning of our conversation,

I had said to you that you believe women to be superior, you would have denied it."

"I believe that either sex is capable of any emotion or behavior," I said, but Jean-Pierre was still laughing. "Too late," he said. "You have given yourself away."

S i x

I was at work by 7:30, my normal starting hour, because of the long lunches. My meeting with Jacques
Nahimana was at 10 A.M. and meanwhile I was trying
to make sense of the papers I'd left behind and those that had piled
up while I was gone. The implications of democracy in Burundi. No
one could agree on who the Hutu and Tutsi really were in relation
to each other; some people even could be both, depending on,
among other things, their family histories of intermarriage.

The whole question was actually legal and cultural, not really
ethnic or racial at all, and complicated by various clan and kinship
ties, differences of status within subgroups, the elaborate traditions
of patronage relationships. And then there were the royal princes
and princesses, the Ganwa, the four ruling dynasties—Bambutsa,
Batare, Bezi, and Bataga—who once upon a time had produced, in
turn, all of the country's kings, but who had lost most of their power
in the seventies and now were mostly linked with the Tutsi, even referred to as Tutsi sometimes. And the pygmies, the Twa, very much
a minority, were somehow part of this ethnic and social tangle,
though not usually in the public discourse.

I was frightened by how much I didn't understand, the infinite
possibilities for stamping my clumsy feet into the middle of some
situation that needed absolute tact and delicacy. I had thought that
human rights work was more urgent than passing out condoms and
giving health lectures, that it offered the opportunity to improve society on a wider scale, but that morning I was missing my life as a
public health worker, where the societal and economic challenges
sometimes seemed insuperable, but our goals were limited and clear.

I puzzled my way through a stack of human rights articles from
obscure newspapers, transcripts from BBC telecasts, reports on missing persons, formal denials from various ministries, and an analysis
by Paul Allen, who sometimes did independent contract work for
us. He was currently on vacation in Greece, meeting his girlfriend's
parents. They had retired to Corfu after forty years in Bujumbura,
leaving their son to manage the family store and boats. Charles was
at home with a bout of malaria. He had terrible stomach pains, and
the friend of his who brought the message said that he had been attacked by a *gikange*, a ghost or spirit—formerly human, now a kind
of evil naiad or dryad.

By 10:20, I hadn't even begun to make sense of my paperwork.
Jack, meanwhile, had seated himself on the edge of my desk, too
close, making remarks about how I'd have to really work to catch
up. His eyes were on my breasts. He said to me, "I hope you're
getting enough *sleep*. I hate to think of my employees wearing themselves out in their private lives." He drew out the word—"prah-ahi-
vate." A little leer. The Warner Brothers wolf, snappy suspenders,
tongue to his knees.

The sound of knuckles on glass from the outer office interrupted
this. I was very relieved to have Nahimana arrive, and went out front
to greet him, my face breaking into a huge smile. I had expended so
much work on his behalf that he'd entered into my imagination, as
if he were a friend. And here he was, free and in front of me, a man

who could change Burundian society. Didn't his release from prison show the value of what we were doing in Burundi?

He returned my smile, but cautiously. Though he had never seemed to trust me, I still found him enormously likable. He was fairly tall, which might have meant some Tutsi in his family background. Long face, bad teeth, smiling cynicism. Somewhat thin, still limping. Burundian prison is like some medieval nightmare—dungeons, the horrors of an ancient madhouse. We'd been told, though as usual we didn't know exactly who or what to believe, that the guards kept two-thirds of the small amount of beans and flour allotted for prisoners, that prisoners died every day of hunger, disease, torture, that families were rarely notified of these deaths, which were all listed as being from natural causes. We were allowed, on visits, only into an outer room. We had several times had the experience of sending food in over time for a prisoner, and then eventually hearing from someone else that the person had died. We could never find out what had happened to him.

Nahimana was guarded, shaking my hand, accepting coffee, making jokes about the dust and traffic. Affable, charming. But the real man was living somewhere far back behind his eyes. Talking to Jack, he relaxed, just perceptibly. Jack's French wasn't as good as mine, but he was a man. Maybe Nahimana felt a woman had no business inside prisons, at committee meetings, in government affairs.

"It's wonderful to see you on the outside," I said.

"We appreciate your efforts very much. *FreeAfrica!* and Amnesty have obtained the release of several of us. That outside pressure. Without it, even with the change in governments, nothing would have happened yet. Once a troublemaker, always a troublemaker. In Burundi, our troublemakers do not become heroes, either international or national. We are not South Africa here."

"Although Burundi has had a system very like apartheid."

"But the world does not know that Burundi exists. In any case, outside opinion would better know what to make of our troubles if the Tutsi were white." The guardedness was very evident. "Their position, of course, is also unfortunate. At this time." He offered me a placating smile—did he think I had Tutsi sympathies?

Jack said, "Officially, you understand, we can't take sides in any conflict. Our business is to report and try to correct human rights abuses on either side."

Nahimana gave me a sidelong glance. "This is understood between us. You have, of course, friends in the government as well."

My God. I said to him, "Surely you don't believe that our efforts on your behalf have been in any way compromised by our other friendships?"

He licked his lips and spread his hands before him. "As I said before, I am a grateful man."

Jack, oblivious, said, "Well. We do what we can. *FreeAfrica!* is a small organization, but very dedicated. Now if you could fill in Anne here on some of your new information, that would be extremely helpful."

Nahimana said, "I will tell you whatever I can," and I heard what he was saying, the danger he was putting himself in by telling us anything at all, the trust we were asking from him.

"Please," I said. "And we, in turn, will be grateful for your help."

/   /   /

Christine and I spent long weekend afternoons at the Club Lac Tanganyika, occasionally with Jean-Pierre, more often by ourselves. Her husband, Andre, never a lively companion, didn't like the beach, though he joined us sometimes for dinner afterward. The Club Lac Tanganyika was an enclave, which might have been a luxury hotel somewhere else. Here it was desolate, hardly used: a dozen or so people on the beach, mostly ex-pats and a few rich Africans, hardly ever any guests. A fenced beach, cabanas, a sweeping curve of buildings, a long turquoise pool, palms.

Americans had been forbidden by the ambassador, for safety reasons, to go in the lake. If we disobeyed, we would supposedly be ordered to leave the country. It was too near the delta at the mouth of the Ruzizi River, and not long before I arrived a Russian woman had been seized by a crocodile and carried away. She'd been standing knee deep in the water, her husband and children only a few feet away on the beach. So although, when no official Americans were around, I did swim in the darkish water, cloudy with sand, I never did it without thinking of her sudden disappearance. Swimming was probably safe during the daytime; crocodiles are most active in the late afternoon. Other people, Belgians, Africans, were windsurfing without apparent worries.

Christine and I would unpack our big woven baskets, oil ourselves, and lay out our towels. The waves were tiny—lake waves, a gray-brown lapping at the shore. As the afternoon went on, they stiffened, and we enjoyed watching the windsurfers and boats being tossed around and occasionally dumped into the water.

I felt I could spread out any topic for examination, and Christine, with her intelligence and common sense, would give it back to me, clarified, orderly, self-evident. I worried, often, that I was boring or annoying her. But she didn't give evidence of minding.

One Saturday afternoon in late July—not long after President Ndadaye had made a public decision to free five hundred political prisoners, both Hutu and Tutsi—we'd been reading on the sand. Christine fell asleep, stretched out on her back, eyes hidden under dark glasses, her Senegalese novel facedown on her rib cage. I lay on my stomach, propped up on my elbows, reading a book of life stories of African women. When she woke, I didn't know it at first, but then she turned her head toward me. She took off the glasses—in Burundi it's rude to talk to someone while wearing dark glasses. Her voice was sleepy. "I was dreaming of you."

"What were you dreaming?" I was flattered to have made it to the inner level of her mind.

"You were a little girl. We were in the market; you were trying to buy too much. Cloth, food, knives. More than you could carry, and so much of it so sharp. I wondered why no one helped you."

"What did you do?"

She was silent for a moment. Her skin shone with oil. She turned on her side, facing me, and shook aside her book. Her modest dark-gold tank suit showed her strong legs, flat stomach. I had been wanting to ask about her stomach—whether she did sit-ups. With an American friend I would have.

She tucked a hand under her head. "In Paris, I had the sense, all the time, of how much I didn't know about the world around me. No matter what I read, who I talked with. Like swimming in a dark sea. As you are now."

I said, "Sometimes I think it's as if I'm working from an ancient map of the world and don't even know the shape of the unknown countries."

"It's strange that I know so much more about Jean-Pierre than you do, but you know him in ways I never will."

A blond boy with a sail ran past us, shouting in French, scattering us with sand. His mother shouted at him from farther up the beach, telling him to be polite. I wanted to ask Christine why she helped me so much, what made her want to spend time with me, but I was afraid.

She seemed to answer my thought, which must have shown on my face. "I like that I can help choose for him. It is very bad that he has not married yet. The Burundian woman he could marry—to satisfy our *Sewabo*, our uncle, she would have to be a Ganwa princess. And my brother has said to me that they are not bearable, these princesses. Spoiled growing up. Waited on. Allowed to think themselves finer than gold. Sitting about in the evenings, playing the zither, singing laments. An insult to me, you see." She laughed.

"You, on the other hand—he says you know how to work. And you do not carry the history we all do. I wouldn't mind having you as a sister. Since I can't marry him myself." She laughed again, as if she had surprised herself, had said more than she meant to.

I didn't know how to answer this. After a minute I said, "I would like to be your sister, to have you in the family. If your sister were stealing, what would you do?"

"Are we back to Margaret again?"

"She has secrets, Christine."

"Everyone has secrets. Why must you do anything? One can sometimes simply wait. *Mirisha Mutumba ziramiye Muhama.*"

"Would you please spell it for me?"

She did, and I wrote it down in my proverbs-and-Burundian-ways notebook, then waited. Some Americans arrived, noisily, waving to us, and settled themselves in the sand. A big to-do with umbrellas, lotions, potato chips, balls, and Frisbees. People we could swim in front of—I'd seen members of this group do it themselves.

Eventually, sighing a little, she said, "It means that though the cows are peacefully chomping the grass in Mutumba today, tomorrow you will have to take them to Muhama. That you should not look ahead for trouble. Right now there is peace, but later on difficulties will find you, and you will have them on all sides."

"My mother says, 'Don't trouble trouble, till trouble troubles you.' " This was difficult to render into French. I didn't know if I had gotten it right.

Christine nodded. "You don't know the future."

"So I shouldn't make any five-year plans?"

She smiled. "When I first saw a day-planner in a French stationer's, I was amazed. The shopkeeper told me that he sold most of them to Americans living in Paris. So many lists—goals, things to do, things to buy, priority tasks—so many places for making decisions. For which one often doesn't have the necessary information."

"But we do get things done."

"Yes? And what do you think of these things, once they are done?"

I looked down at my book.

Christine reached out to touch my arm. Affectionately. "Do you want to go in the water? It's getting hot."

While we were swimming, Jean-Pierre arrived. He turned out to be in a pissy mood. He was hungry, and not pleased with my snacks. He didn't want to go into the water until we came out, and then he didn't want to go in by himself. He was so short with us, so uncommunicative that I said to him, "Well, then, why did you come if you didn't want to be with us?" Because it seemed to me that he was acting as if we had come along to bother him when he was engaged in some serious and vital action.

He said, "I suppose you want me to chatter like a woman." I had a flash of thinking, *I can't seriously want to marry this* testosterone *case. When there are a million sensitive Californians back home.* I could meet a man in a cafe, reading about meditation or the emotional capabilities of animals—fleshy, strong-nosed face, hair pulled back in a ponytail. He would be smiling, highly educated and full of theories about metaphysical matters. Respectful of my feelings. Humorous, gentle, peaceful to come home to—and, above all, familiar. I felt a rush of distaste for this imaginary man. *Jean-Pierre is the only man.*

I said, "Didn't you want me to help you redefine your ideas about women? The concept that talking equals chattering, for instance."

He turned away, showing displeasure at my tone of voice, waiting to be coaxed into a good mood. Christine lay on her back, holding her book up to shield her face from the sun. She appeared to be reading, but she had a little smile on her face. I stretched out on my stomach and picked up my own book. I was not going to baby him. I was thinking, just then, that on the whole I'd rather marry Christine or Zoë, and that it was inconvenient to prefer men to women, romantically and sexually.

But then Jean-Pierre's mood switched courses. He turned around, took my book away, and put the palm of his hand against my cheek, looking at me apologetically. Irresistible. I tried to hold out at first, wanting to punish him, but couldn't. I put my hand over his.

Christine, no longer pretending to read, was laughing at us. "Anna, *grand-père,* you are both absurd." This would have made him furious, coming from anyone else, but he smiled at her. She said, "We have been at home too long without a vacation. We should all go to Paris for a month."

"Why Paris?" He was indulging her. "Why not somewhere extraordinary?"

She said to me, "If you could go anywhere in the world?"

"Boating down the length of the Amazon."

"Too difficult, too dangerous. Let us go to Java and Bali, and lie on an island beach, eating fresh crab, with the blue sea around us."

"You are both soft. Women." He waited to see if we would respond to this provocation. "You want to be warm. I will leave you to your rivers and beaches, and I will go to Antarctica. To live in the snow, to carry out research, always fighting against the cold."

"In fact," said Christine, "we should all go to Paris together. Jean-Pierre, why don't you find out what we can do?"

"Impossible right now," he said. "Maybe at Christmas."

We went off to meet Andre for dinner, and I went back to spend the night at Jean-Pierre's house, our small quarrel forgotten.

/ / /

Zoë had sent me her new phone number, but she didn't expect me to use it—the difficulties of calling Asia from Burundi were mind-boggling. I wrote her a long letter, apologizing for my delay in responding, and describing in detail my mother's cancer, how things were with Jean-Pierre, what had been happening at the clinic.

Though I also needed to answer Margaret, I had no idea what to say. Finally, I sent a letter thanking her for the story about Grandma Eleanor and burbling about my new friendship with Christine, about some movie Jean-Pierre and I had seen at the Ciné Cameo, about my wish for the beginning of the long rains.

A couple of days after I mailed it, I had a letter from Lizzie.

Sweetie—Oh, how I miss you! Aurora misses you too. She said, "When is Aunt Annie coming?" and when I told her a long time, she said, "Tomorrow?"

Sometimes Mom seems to be doing better, and I get a kind of crazy hope, then I dream she's died and I wake up crying. I was thinking of Mom as a baby, having to start all over. I thought about that a lot with Aurora, who is such an old soul. Aurora would cry with frustration at each new thing she tried to do—it seemed to her that she should know how to do it all, but her body was tricking her.

Margaret keeps complaining about how poor they are and how they have to tighten their belts. Meanwhile, she has all these new dresses; Jerry has a brand-new set of golf clubs. I wish I could stop taking such an interest in everything they buy. I feel toxic about it.

Susan has a new boyfriend. Margaret and Jerry hate him, of course. So Susan is starting to act like a teenager. A little early, but maybe she had too many hormones in her milk? I try to keep Aurora on soy milk as much as possible.

I had a memory that I've never gotten in touch with before. This still happens to me, even though I think I know most of my past lives. I was a man in a Chinese prison, about two centuries ago. I'd been some kind of government official, and my warlord had fallen. I'd been expecting to go into exile, but someone imprisoned me instead. I remember the coldness and loneliness of prison life. I feel for that old man in prison, who was me. I remember writing this poem.

In my cell, I think of my family.
Outside, the willow leans into the river.

Inside these dark walls, only a little rice.

I don't miss banquets. But I wonder where my lord is now.

My wife, my children, do they weep for me as I do

for them?

At my house in the country, it is springtime.

Blossoms fall to the river, floating downstream.

Here it is always winter.

My cheeks grow old with my tears.

When once life is gone,

It can never return.

So, Annie, I wonder about this. What did I learn from that life?
Is it worth the memories of the pain? There are times when I love
what I do, but other days I feel so old, as if I were standing above
high water and could see all the way down. I remember so much, so
many lifetimes and people. And, sure, if you have karma together,
maybe you keep meeting each other, but what about the particularities
of each life that come and go and are lost forever? I have to keep
meditating, keep grounding myself, and even then there are moments
when I don't want to carry it all.

There are days when I think I can't even bear all I remember
about Jackson, and that was just a few short years in this current life.
A man who splits when you get pregnant isn't a person—he's a type.
I wonder how I could have fallen in love with a type. Do I need more
lessons? All those lifetimes, and I haven't learned enough? I shouldn't
write letters when I'm sad. How I wish you were here and we could
just go eat Chinese food and have a hot tub and talk about nothing
and everything. Aurora is waking up from her nap—I've got to go.

I love you. I miss you.

Lizzie

I read that letter about four times. I wished passionately that I
could talk with her, could put my arms around her and just hold her.

She would always be my baby, no matter how many lifetimes she'd lived or imagined. I didn't want her to have "lessons." I only wanted her to be happy.

I would not be able to describe this letter to either Jean-Pierre or Christine, any more than I could tell them what Lizzie really did. Ordinarily, her clients would come to her rented studio cottage in the woods of northwestern Sonoma County: hundreds of small panes of glass, with crystals and eagle feathers twirling down from the ceiling on colored cords. Extremely cold and damp in the winter, no insulation at all, the walls dripping with rain, the interior smoky from the woodstove that was its only heat. Rats in the ceiling. Lizzie had lived there with Jackson until she came home from shopping one day to find Jackson's stuff missing and a tender letter on the pillow telling her that he was setting her and the unborn child free. Of course she'd cried for weeks, had her friends in to do healings on the space, but when Aurora was born, she seemed to put Jackson out of her mind, to settle back into the cottage with her baby.

Now sometimes Lizzie went to her clients' homes. Occasionally she did her sessions at Mom's, in our faded white gazebo under a branching of oaks. I had thought of asking to try a session, but wasn't sure whether it was impolite to ask for her professional services. Of course she would offer them as a gift, would be insulted if I tried to pay, so I couldn't even ask. In the end, though, she suggested it herself.

We had been cleaning up from lunch while I told her a Burundian folktale. There are hundreds of these: long, rhythmic, repetitive tales of sly rats and helpful toads; jealous royal wives who set princes adrift in boxes of wood, only to be defeated later when the grown princes procure talking tobacco that gives away the women's crimes; or tales that explain how it is that mice and men come to live together. The stories teach craftiness, prudence, dignity, family responsibility, secretiveness.

The one I told Lizzie was the story of the old cow who was the king's favorite because she ran so fast. He visits her every day to bring her salt. When she becomes old, though, he abandons her. She's so furious that she refuses to graze. The cow herder asks what the trouble is, and she explains it all to him, how the king no longer loves her, how she wore herself out and grew old running for him. The herder says he will take her anger on himself, so she can calm down enough to graze. But the anger drives him wild, hurling him about, and everyone remarks on it and is terrified. On the way back to the palace, he meets the queen. She asks what troubles him, he tells her his story and the cow's story, she says that she will take on his anger to bring him ease, but it makes her go crazy in turn.

"And all the people watching are terrified and astonished and afraid to approach her," I said, and Lizzie said, "Yes, OK," in a get-on-with-it tone.

I said, "Burundian folktales are like this—they get their effects from dramatic repetition." But I went more quickly through the episode of the king, who takes on the queen's anger and is driven wild, much to the fear and astonishment of the spectators, and then the sheep, who says to the king that he will take the anger so that the king may be at ease. The sheep, of course, is driven crazy and flung all over by the anger.

"Finally a dog says to the sheep that since he's a dog, he's used to being angry, and so taking on the anger will make no difference. The king is known for keeping his cool, but a dog will always be angry and will always run around anyway, so who gives a damn? And he takes on the anger, and runs into the hills, but he can't stop running. And all the people remark that since he will never stop running, he can never get rid of the anger, and he will never be free of this anger which has already done such damage. And the moral of it is, the Burundians say, 'This kind of fate only happens to a dog that gets itself mixed up in powers it doesn't understand, one that tries to handle powers that are too strong for it.' "

"I don't get the point," Lizzie said, after a moment.

"I never get the point of Burundian tales. But they have a certain inexplicable beauty."

She mused on it. "It seems like it should end with the king, that he takes the anger back on himself and completes the circle."

"We'd think so."

"Or that the dog would take on the anger and just handle it, and everything would be OK. But who comes out well at the end of all this?" After a minute, she said, "It's like the story of a past life. Sometimes they make perfect sense, and sometimes they're very puzzling." And then, "Do you want to visit your past? I could do some Reiki and regression on you." I nodded, delighted, and she said, "Let's go outside then."

It was midafternoon by then. Mom was sleeping and the kids were watching a video, with Margaret nearby in case of trouble. Lizzie and I went out to the gazebo. We brushed the dirt and leaves off the picnic table inside so that I could stretch out on my back, arms at my sides. I could see around the house to the straggling rows of apple trees, their heavy branches propped up by boards, sagging under the weight of reddening Gravensteins. Light filtered down in diamond patterns onto us. Rainbow-colored lozenges of light, from the crystal amulet that Lizzie wore around her neck—"To balance and augment my own energy"—swam over the wood of the gazebo. I shut my eyes. I had no idea what to expect.

Lizzie stood very still for a few moments, doing something like humming, though it wasn't exactly that. Then she placed her hands on me, palms down, at various points on my body. I can't even say where she put her hands, what she did, but where there had been walls or lumps in me, patches of brick crumbled away and something blew through me. Not wind. Maybe light. Tears ran down my cheeks.

When I was weak and clear and ravaged, she sat beside me and, in her soft, sweet voice, encouraged me to relax, up and down my body, for a long time. I felt a combination of impatience, boredom, and acquiescence. Then she began encouraging me, in my floating, dark, almost-sleep state, to push backward in time. Under her guidance, I swam back through my childhood, into the womb and through, struggling through some dark and frightening place, until I came into another set of memories.

A dark little place, the walls in close, no windows. Some kind of hut. Then hot sun, stooping in the field, digging into the ground. Maybe planting something. I think I had a beard. Then I was eating dinner, a stew like lentils with sharp cheese and dark bread, and I reached out to give someone a slap in the head. I don't remember what he or she said or did, only my own sensation of anger, the clear, instant determination to put a stop to something that couldn't be allowed.

When Lizzie brought me back out again, I told her about the memory. She nodded her head. A pattern of shadow striped her down one side of the face, her body, across her gauze skirt with its fastening of tiny brass bells. She said, "Mostly they're like that. If I get Cleopatra or something, I encourage them to go in another direction."

"Do you ever get Cleopatra?"

"Not much. Not the way I do it. People regressing on their own are frequently Cleopatra. Or Merlin. They remember being king. Of course, hardly anyone ever was. Most lives are a lot more like the one you remembered."

I didn't want to be rude but couldn't help asking, "Then why do this?"

"Your own memories are always interesting. Your own dreams, interpretations. Even if they're inexplicable, like that story about the old cow. At least your previous lives shed light on your current karma. We just touched on it. We could go further back sometime, to other lives. When you understand the meaning of the past, of your own actions in the past, you know more about your tasks in this lifetime. What you're here to learn."

Susan came out of the house, looked around, hesitated, then came toward us.

I said, "Aunt Lizzie's been regressing me."

Susan's voice was very soft. "I was an eagle once. About five lives ago. I guess. At least I had those memories."

Lizzie put out a hand and touched her on the cheek. She didn't flinch, but I could see her remembering her separateness. So hard to be thirteen. Lizzie said, "It's difficult to remember the animal or plant lives. They're so different."

It was getting to be late afternoon. The ever-present guilt, with all those people, of doing anything besides the continual work of cooking, dishes, cleaning up, sitting with Mom, started to take hold of me. So I proposed we go back into the house, but all that evening and the next, the sensation persisted of my own heaviness and sureness of purpose, the weight of body and the darkness around me, then the moment of anger, the sense of something like satisfaction, a job well done, in delivering that slap.

S e v e n

A couple of days after I received Lizzie's letter, Jean-Pierre and I sat at a table between the bar and pool in the central courtyard of the Novotel, the big hotel at the hub of downtown Bujumbura. At 5:30 in the afternoon, the sky was a heavy, warm gray, the faded pool a pale, grayed blue. The air smelled of chlorine and frangipani. Light struck the surface of the water and reflected back into our eyes. Families swam in the pool and played on the porous concrete rims. Businessmen, government officials, and expatriates stood by the bar and packed the tables, eating *pain au chocolat* or *brioche* and drinking heavily.

I had been trying to describe the complications of my family to Jean-Pierre. "So then there's Lizzie. She's unimaginably good. I suppose I feel about her the way you do about Christine."

"She is a part of you."

"The best part of me." I smiled at him, and he nodded, acknowledging a hit. I went on, "She has a three-year-old daughter. Aurora. The two of them together are so graceful, so delightful that they're like creatures from another world. So when Lizzie takes you back into what seem to be memories of another life, it makes more sense than if someone else did it. As if she's taking you into that other world as well."

He said, a little formally, "I look forward to meeting them. And to seeing this other world in which I might not believe."

"Christine doesn't believe in reincarnation either." I used the Burundian word, *ubuzimu*.

"I keep an open mind. If only to convince myself that so many years of education were of some use." He touched the back of my hand, smiling, and winked. We looked into each other's eyes, a locking together of the inside selves in shared amusement.

In the pool, a small boy choked on some water, and his mother lifted him out onto the side, where he spat clear liquid, coughing.

From outside came a muffled roar of traffic, the honking of horns, shouting, the cries of men hawking necklaces, walking sticks, and carved statuettes in front of the hotel. I said, "You should try getting regressed, then you could see for yourself. Anyway, I'd like for you to meet Lizzie and Aurora. And my mother, before . . . I don't want you never to have met her." My voice trembled, and tears came into my eyes.

He looked at me, then down at the flats of his hands, pressed against the table. My heart pounded so fiercely that I could hear nothing else in my ears, as if I had stepped off a cliff. But Christine's encouragement had made me brave.

"Yes." He paused, thinking. "I have been thinking of our own time line. You and me. But perhaps *Imana* has another time line for us, a faster one than I have pictured." *Imana,* God or fate or soul, who manifested as a white lamb, but was more often the inner spirit in all objects and creatures, the essence of good, of delight, of fecundity: Giver, Creator, Fire-Lighter. At least, that's what I'd been told, but when I tried to confirm it, people had smiled, shaken their heads, shrugged. Even Jean-Pierre had said, "We don't explain *Imana.*" Frustrated, I had just nodded, but I'd wanted to say, "You don't explain anything in Burundi. What kind of country has to keep everything unspoken?"

A shadow fell across the table between us, and I looked up, shielding my eyes against the bright reflections from the water. A colleague of Jean-Pierre's from the Ministry bent over us, beaming. We stood up to shake his hand. He shook Jean-Pierre's, then clasped mine in both of his. I felt his gold rings imprinting themselves in my flesh from the strength of his grip. He said, "Let me just get my beer, and I will join you. What luck to find you here." He hurried away, a tall, heavy man in an expensive suit, sweating in the warm afternoon.

My voice came out a hiss, the sound of a spoiled child on the brink of tears. "We are *never alone*. Colleagues, family, the workers, beggars." Embarrassed, I shut up.

Jean-Pierre said, "If I hadn't lived in Paris, I wouldn't even know what you mean. It's not an African value, solitude." With a broad, welcoming smile, he waved at his colleague, who was watching us from the bar.

I nodded, looking back at the pool, where three small boys raced each other at the shallow end. After a moment, I whispered, "I'm sorry. I've got a grip. You can count on me."

"Yes," he said, as his colleague walked toward us, giving us a huge answering smile and holding up his beer in salute. "That is one of many things I like about you." His smile became mischievous. "Love," he said, very quietly, in English, just before his colleague joined us. I could feel myself going red. Although I was dismayed to be such a fifteen-year-old, a wild happiness had rushed up in me, my blood blooming just under the surface of my skin.

/ / /

Jack was particularly impossible at work that week. Almost certainly because I was so happy—he had an instinct for the happiness of others and wanted to stamp it out. A cynicism that at first I had thought was at least partially joking, but he disliked humans. Particularly, though not exclusively, Africans. The Burundian acceptance of fate—a kind of shoulder shrug toward disorder, disaster, decay—made him wild. He was a secret believer in progress and thought that certain Burundian traits, including a time sense that had more to do with the eternal than with clocks, were signs of stupidity.

I knew several people with this attitude. At first, I wanted to ask them, "Then why are you here?" But after watching them for a while, I understood they liked having servants, or they were scornful of people who lived in the U.S. and had "ordinary" lives, or they didn't know what else to do. Jack, I think, couldn't have survived in a life where he had to meet the daily demands of his own society.

He had been slamming around the office in a temper. Charles made an excuse and left to run an errand. It was hot, and the fumes of minivans and cars came through our screened windows. We had an air conditioner, a little one, but it had broken, and there was no money to fix it until the end of the month when our next grant payment came in. Instead we had an old fan, which made a loud whacking sound, a kind of "Veh, veh, veh, *whump,* veh, veh, veh, *whump,*" which got on my nerves incredibly.

We were working on a project designed to further our understanding of local decision making. We always had too many different projects going on at once. Jack was easily bored. I thought our scattered way of going at things reduced our effectiveness, and I had unwisely let him see this. He was at his desk, his feet up, reading a paper I'd written. He made me hang around, in theory to explain points that were unclear, in actuality so that he could insult my writing, thinking, and knowledge of Burundi.

What I was trying to describe were the various levels of local decision making or conflict resolution. The first is *Urubanza rwo mu muryange,* the decisions made by the head of the family and the elders, to resolve disputes within a family or between families. The head of the family can try a form of extended mediation, lecture, delivery of proverbs. He has to be consulted, even if they know he will be unhelpful; if the disputants go over his head, he's in a position to make real trouble.

The next stage is at the level of the hill, *Urubanza rwo kumagina*. When the family attempts at resolution fail, the hill elders all gather at what an American would think of as the scene of the crime, engaging in a ritual as formal as an Elizabethan court dance. If this doesn't work, the conflict moves up to the subchief level, another tribunal.

Sometimes people opt out of the negotiating system and resort to poison instead. In the city, during bad times, they're apt to denounce each other, to let the army kill their enemies. The conflict-resolution process is supposed to help prevent violence, to serve as a substitute.

Bribes, *ibiriture,* play a part in the ordinary procedure. Also the history of family obligations and who owes what to whom. But it's hard to get it laid out explicitly. It's hard to get any information out of Burundians; their history has made them secretive.

What we were trying to understand was how this traditional problem-solving method interacted with the odd, despised legal system imposed by the Belgians, a system that worked about as well as one of those old broken hydroelectric dams that dot Africa as monuments to early ideas about development. I had spent a couple of weeks talking to people, studying Warren Weinstein's historical research, and writing it all up.

Jack banged his heel on the desk. "God, you're pompous," he said. "Did they teach you that in graduate school?" And, later, "I wonder what your real native language is. Something they write on the moon, maybe."

I said to myself that he was angry that I knew so much more

about Burundi than he did when he'd been there so much longer. He was bound to feel that a woman and employee should know less in any case. Very old school, our Jack. In the U.S., we would have been political enemies, although the concept of an enemy in the States is so dilute compared with the energy and the seriousness given to enmity in Burundi. And he was envious, because he didn't have a girl just then. He wouldn't sleep with an African woman, and most of the ex-pats were on to him. Celibacy made him monstrous.

"Don't smirk," he said. "I hate that goddamn smirk of yours."

I said, *"Ibitgiye Inama Ntigegira Imana."* (God will not be present with/help the arguers.) I was being clever. This is an expression used in the sorts of cases we were discussing when the disputants wouldn't submit, or when the judges themselves got caught up in arguing. Jack had seen the proverb, but would have had to look it up to know what it meant. Or ask me, but of course he wasn't going to do that.

He looked at me, then jumped up and poured his cup of coffee out onto our suffering office palm. We'd endeavored to give our tiny office something of the dignity and authority of an American law office—files, bookcases with leather-bound books, plants, even leather chairs, though, unfortunately, rather ripped and scuffed. The place was dusty, though, and had the hopeless, decaying air of most Burundian offices. I was at least trying to keep the plants alive. At that moment, I was not able to remember one good thing about Jack.

He said to me, "You can do better than this. You go talk to some elders." He held out the paper, with a mean smile.

"Si, Mushebuja." I was calling him boss, patron, but implied in it was the sense of a protector. In return for my services, and perhaps the occasional female calf, Jack would defend me and my property against all comers.

"Don't push your luck, Anne."

I remembered, a little late, the fate of my predecessor, and said, "I'm sorry, Jack. I don't know what got into me."

Now he was pleased, and I felt like dirt. What I mind about earning a living is not working—I like to work. It's this kind of moment. Maybe the self I was giving up wasn't my best, a kind of twelve-year-old brattiness, but I didn't abandon it out of compassion, largeness of spirit, any motive I could have felt good about. Simple survival. He had me by the paycheck. I took the paper I'd worked so hard on and set about redoing it.

/ / /

Jean-Pierre arranged for the two of us to travel into the interior, the trip he'd once planned as a surprise, but now I knew about it ahead of time. We stayed in the hills above Muramvya, a long, steep, winding drive, up and up, as if we were driving into the sky. A Greek family had a series of bungalows and gardens on a hilltop, with a central restaurant, flower beds, a swing for the family's children, and lawns in the middle of the cultivated fields, which spread down the hills in all directions. We could stand at the edge of the gardens and look down over what seemed to be most of Burundi.

Dotted everywhere on the hills below were the round shapes of the *rugos*, clusters of round, thatched buildings that make up a homestead. The parents sleep in a central building where the family gathers for meals. The grandmother and the girls sleep in one hut (where the banana beer is kept), the grandfather, boys, and goats in another, and the cows in their own. Rippling banana trees and oil nut palms divided the green fields around the *rugos* into sections. The hills so green, so red, the sky so intensely gray. Glory.

There were no other guests that weekend, and our bungalow was well away from the house. We were finally completely alone. Our first night there, we let go, playing in ways we hadn't before, at first tracing patterns on each other's skins with a bar of chocolate (slower to dissolve than we'd expected, so that it was more funny than anything else), and then using bits of ice chips from our cooler. The beginning of the night was full of laughter and squirming, touch on touch, a game, but it carried us downriver so that we made love for hours, stopping, exploring, starting again, changing rhythms, moving to a place where the sensations were so intense that I was actually crying, and he was groaning. Most of the night was almost wordless, and conversation, when it occurred, was confined to about the level of, "Stop, stop, I can't stand it," "How about this, then?" "Oh, God, no, yes, *please*."

"What do you *do* to me?" he asked eventually, pretending to be angry, but not entirely joking, and I said, in response, "What do we do to each other?" By the time we fell asleep, it was nearly day, and I almost couldn't tell where my body ended and his began—we were one heavy, intertwined creature.

We slept late, breakfasted, took a short walk, went back to bed, slept. By then it was too late for lunch, so we unpacked our cooler and brought out dark bread, imported German mustard, tomatoes, thick yellow goat cheese from Zaire, and a fruit salad of ripe, sweet mango, papaya, and pineapple. We sat on a bench in the garden, our knees touching, no one else around. A bird sang somewhere above us, a rising arc of notes. I thought, *I have never been so happy in my life.* I looked around, wanting to fix the details of this moment in my mind: Jean-Pierre's smile, the faded wood of the bench, the swing set, the grass, the flower beds, the valley below us, and the taste of bread, cheese, tomato, and mustard.

"This view is much more beautiful in the wet season," said Jean-Pierre lazily. Neither of us had said anything for several minutes. "Perhaps we can come back in a few months."

"But we're going to Paris for Christmas." I was teasing him, but it was also a question.

"Everything is possible," he said. "Why not?"

In the late afternoon, he went for a walk by himself, and I read on a chair outside our room, sitting in the sun. Then we had dinner, alone on the restaurant's terrace. The Greek family and their two workers were uninterested in us, almost invisible.

We looked out over the still-dusty valleys below and ate a dry-ish, crackling roast chicken and peas. It wouldn't be dark for an hour, but the cicadas were already buzzing wildly in the trees along-side the restaurant. Thinking of Lizzie, I asked, "Can you have memories that don't seem to be your own? I think I did, of a past life. So what does that say about the memories we think we have, what we believe happened in our lives?"

Jean-Pierre set down his fork and rested his chin on his fists, considering. Then he said, "Maybe the memories we use to tell our life stories are not even the important ones. Maybe it has to do with our concept of what we have been. A man says, 'I was a brilliant leader,' and denies any memory that stands in the way of this idea. Maybe this man ran away in a battle; maybe he was invisible at meetings. But he doesn't remember these events. For him, they don't exist."

"So if we can forget so conveniently, why have painful memories at all?"

"Because some events have so much power that you cannot for-get them. Or you do forget them, you bury them alive, but some-thing brings them back to you. And then you cannot escape them." He spoke very slowly. It was dusk by then, and the lights in the restaurant eaves had been switched on, a pinkish-gold glow.

I was excited by this idea. "Memories might be made by the sheer intensity of an experience. Or maybe by repetition—the scenery along the drive to work during a certain period. You see it every day, and it burns itself into your brain. And that's what you remember of that time in your life."

He had pushed his plate away. "Did you want dessert?" He waved to our waiter, who was smoking at the far end of the terrace.

I went on, "So rather than choosing memories to construct a

story, it's more a question of framing our life story around our most insistent memories. And we can make them mean almost anything. They can't be eradicated, but they can be changed as necessary over the course of time."

Jean-Pierre pleated his napkin, frowning. Our *dames blanches*—white ladies—arrived, an ice cream sundae very popular with rich Africans and expats, and quite expensive, since the ice cream was usually flown in from Europe in big freezers. Here the ice cream tasted homemade, very sweet and cold in our mouths, lovely in the warm evening.

When we went back to our room, he caught me off guard, kissing me fiercely, wrestling me onto the bed. I tried to respond out of my lazy, reflective mood. Some subtle, prolonged play would have been fine with me, but we weren't having that. When he began to strip off my clothing, I said, "Yes, but go *slow*, Jean-Pierre," and he did, but he sped up again almost immediately. I thought it would be fine, once he was inside me, and so I helped him, though I wasn't really ready. Then, just as my body began to open up to him, he came. I wanted to slap him, my eyes filling with tears of frustration.

He lay on top of me, his face in my neck, for a long few minutes, and then he raised himself on his elbow, taking his weight, and looked down at me. I shut my eyes, not wanting him to see the tears. He kissed my eyelids. "I am sorry, Ah-na. Tell me what I can do for you. For your body." He touched one breast, lightly. "For your heart." He touched the center of my chest. I was melting toward him but attempting not to show it.

He struggled with himself, visibly. He rolled over and lay beside me, his arm across my stomach. "I want to say, we will have times in our years to come when we have to be patient with each other. And then I am afraid to say 'years.' In America, you make all kinds of promises, and they mean nothing. Your extraordinary divorce rate. You know how we feel about it."

I nodded. From time to time, Burundians would ask about divorce, why we in the U.S. and Europe divorced so often, what we meant by marriage if not that it must be a lifelong bond. And with the question, every time, came this tone of shocked censure.

"There's so much you don't see about Burundi. If you . . ." He shook his head. "But I love you, Ah-na. Sometimes it makes me happy. Sometimes it frightens me. Tonight, I am frightened. I am in very deep water with you, and I feel it closing over me."

When, half an hour later, we made love again, I found places in myself that had never been touched before—this wasn't the intense, delicious physicality of the previous night, but an emotional event, with its physical corollaries. I felt *myself* open up, level after level. An abandonment so far beyond orgasms that it made them almost irrelevant. And Jean-Pierre, falling into me, crying out in amazement at what was happening to us, was absolutely there with me. He was so fierce, so tender and exposed, that I would have done anything at all to protect him—from the world, from myself, from himself.

/ / /

The next morning, we went for a walk in the hills. The endless dry dust sifted across our feet, sticking to our clothes, hands, faces. We walked along a ridge, the hills falling away to each side of us, the sunlight brilliant all around us. *Rugos,* banana trees, an impossible richness of green trees, even at that season.

Jean-Pierre was explaining to me how it felt to have the expectation that you, or your family, could ascend to power: the maneuvering, the political enmities, how everything had changed with the end of the monarchy, what he felt now. "I cannot say to my family that I think the republic is, in fact, the best thing for Burundi. Bertrand, for example, hungers to be *mwami*. If the possibility existed that I, as his elder brother, could stand in his way, I think I would be in danger, although he is fond of me. And this is how the longing for power, the access to power by any means, ruled over us. An election, I think, is a better way. More orderly, more honorable, better for the country, better for the people. So I am not sorry that we no longer have the possibilities we once did, except that the *mwami* is the link between *Imana* and the people. What one doesn't escape is the sense that these are our people, to look after, to protect."

Children, laughing, came up to us, standing behind each other, one or two, suddenly bold, asking Jean-Pierre questions in Kirundi, giggling.

"They want to know if there's any possibility that you're a demon."

"I don't think so. Not that I'm aware of," I said to him and then, to the children, *"Hamjambo, watoto"*—Greetings, children. They scattered, screaming with laughter. *"Hujambo, mzungu!"* one of them answered, and that made the others laugh harder.

One of the children, a girl in blue with short braids, presented me with a flat rock. I thanked her formally. She had huge eyes in a thin face, anxious, wary, but with an extremely sweet smile. Leaning over my palm, she traced the edges of the rock, showed me how it was a face.

A snake slid across the path, not too close to us, but the children, shouting, ran away, waving their arms at us to show us that we should run too.

Jean-Pierre said, "I'm hungry. Shall we go back?"

He put his arm around me, extraordinary for him, in front of people, and we turned around, waving to the children, and walked back up the path. I couldn't remember ever feeling so utterly peaceful. I thought how often we worry ourselves sick over a situation, completely unnecessarily. I put my arm around him in return, and he smiled down at me.

/   /   /

One of my most vivid memories of that fall was the beginning of the rains. It had come to seem that they'd never start up again, that the world would go on drying, shriveling up, turning to dust, until Burundi looked like Mali. Desert. Every time I took a walk and saw the waste, the drying, I was reminded of the Burundian farming methods, their catastrophic erosion of all the "thousand hills." At the time I thought of it as my worst fear for Burundi.

All kinds of memories of that short, sweet early fall. I thought, at the time, that I was mildly unhappy. I had the fear that my mother would die at any time, and every day I woke up wondering if that would be the day I'd get the phone call I was dreading. My work didn't seem to be going well; I was restless and discontented, and increasingly annoyed with Jack.

But I also remember the rain crashing down onto my roof, pouring off the eaves, running in sheets over the edge of the porch while I sat on a chair, feeling the warm, wet air, watching the garden pool up below. The tremendous thunderstorms and pouring rain, Jean-Pierre and I making love inside—lunchtime, early evening, all night long. The light shining through our curtains. He grinning up at me from below, confident, wickedly teasing me, delighted by his effect on me.

I remember shopping for fabrics at Nyakabiga with Christine, getting dresses made by her tailor, laughing over some amazing Cameroonian novel we'd found—we were trading books back and forth. I remember interactions with the merchants and stall keepers in town, little ordinary jokes. I remember the red earth running in the streets and the red edges of Lake Tanganyika. How green everything became in only a couple of weeks. I remember a Burundi of jacaranda and the smell of wet earth, of smiling guards when I went to talk to someone I knew at the U.S. embassy.

I remember loving Bujumbura and its trees and sky, the red-dirt streets and African houses of the *quartiers*, the amazement of people in some tiny restaurant when I spoke Swahili, the children laughing and chanting *wazungu, wazungu* while Rebecca Price (a Peace Corps volunteer, down from the mountains) and I ate rice studded with tiny rocks, green bananas in palm oil, oily red beans.

Not one of these memories pure and clear, all of them overlaid and corrupted by what came afterward.

Eight

When it started, I was in the country's interior again, though not with Jean-Pierre this time. Jack, Charles, and I were in Cibitoke province, looking into the story of a Hutu worker's disappearance. We'd talked to the man's family, but it wasn't yet clear that this was political. Jack thought we might be looking at marital trouble, and that he'd disappeared to Bujumbura, or even to Rwanda, very much of his own volition. I thought Jack was preparing to slander an innocent victim; Jack thought the man in question might be about to make a fool of us, and that we should wait to see whether someone didn't spot our hero around town. Charles was being tactful, but I thought he agreed with me.

Even if Jack's Land Cruiser hadn't been more comfortable and tougher than my VW bug, I couldn't have driven. My generator had failed, and I'd been waiting for weeks for a part to be delivered from Zaire. So Jack was driving, I was beside him, Charles was in the back, and we were arguing about what to do with our report.

/ / /

It's hard to know how to start describing what came next. Because though it might well be the point of telling the story at all, all I can say is what happened to me, and what happened to me is trivial. I know that. And if all I do is add a little more misery, a few more ugly memories to the collective storehouse, well, any *Newsweek* or *Time* can do better on that score, printing photos of heaps of bloated bodies in the sun, so that we turn the page, thinking, *What can I do about it?*

I'm not leading up to any philosophical or moral points here. I haven't developed any answers. I just find myself reluctant to remember even as much as I can, wanting to gloss it over, to put down only the essentials as I remember them or have worked them out.

Because my memories of that drive, of that whole period—the days and weeks that followed—are very patchy. Ordinarily I remember everything; it was always a joke, sometimes an annoyed joke, in my family, the way I could remember interactions and conversations, word for word, for years. But great chunks of my memory of this time have disappeared entirely. Other parts of that drive, and the following nightmare, are so vivid that I have been possessed by them forever afterward, uncontrollably and constantly in the first months, but recurring with sudden force, sometimes out of nowhere, for years. I spent so much time learning *not to remember*, and now I'm back in it. But I have to tell it. I see no way out but through.

/ / /

October 22, 1993. Early in the morning, we began the drive home. We had camped out the night before, hadn't listened to the radio, and had no idea of what had happened, what was taking place. We were on our way home and had been driving for an hour when we saw soldiers, a roadblock, spiraling jagged wire across the road, just beside a small grouping of houses. Next to the road sat a hut with a charcoal grill out front, where goat brochettes were roasting, though no one seemed to be attending to them. The barbed wire had been wrapped around a banana tree on one side, a post on the other.

Roadblocks were nothing new—we didn't even speculate about it. But these soldiers waved us over, made us get out of the car. They seemed angry and afraid as they asked for our papers. They talked to each other in urgent Kirundi, huddling together, holding their guns. They wanted to know, and their French was so poor that Charles had to translate, what we were doing upcountry, where we had been. What were our purposes in Burundi? They searched the Land Cruiser. For weapons, I think now.

The soldiers took our residency cards, and that was when I began to be afraid.

One soldier, tall, in an olive beret, bayonet fixed, held on one hip, as if he were balancing a baby, said something to Charles in Kirundi. Charles responded. One of the other soldiers asked a harsh, demanding question. Charles answered it, meekly. He was rumpled—we all were, from the long, hot drive. All we had been thinking was that we had four or so hours more together before we could get home and get away. There were more questions, what sounded like accusations. One of the soldiers shouted at another, and they all looked over their shoulders, up the road, their grips tightening on their guns.

Charles was sweating through his shirt in patches. He began arguing, but in a humble tone I wasn't used to with him. He said to us, "They say you can go on, but I must stay."

Jack said, "Well, that's clearly impossible. Do they want money?"

It was very unusual at a Burundian roadblock to be shaken down for money, valuables.

"They say my papers are not in order."

"Tell them we have friends at the embassy. Make them give us their names."

Charles answered Jack, "I think not, in this case."

I said, "But, Charles, you aren't just going to stay?"

"I think if I do, I won't live a long time."

"Are they giving a reason?"

"They think perhaps I'm a spy. An agitator. My being with you makes me suspicious."

I said to them then, in Swahili—I don't know where the inspiration came from—using the bossy tone of a woman used to having her way, "What do you mean by this?"

They looked at me in surprise, as if the luggage had spoken.

"This man is my cook. I'm giving a dinner party tomorrow. I can't do without him." I talked to them the way I'd heard Belgian women with the shopkeepers, their housekeepers. Charles and Jack were stiff beside me, with fear, maybe anger.

One of the soldiers said something about the documents, that Charles wasn't a domestic, but I brushed that aside. He had worked for me in an office, but was more valuable to me in the house, and I hadn't gotten around to changing the papers.

One of the soldiers threw up his hands and said something, and then, without apologies, they were handing our papers back. They said something in Kirundi, and Charles said, "We can go. They say drive straight to Bujumbura and don't get off the road."

I nodded, still imperious, and we got into the Land Cruiser. We were all sweating. We drove off, the soldiers turning away from us to watch the road. I was too embarrassed to look at Charles, except out of the corner of my eye. I said, "I'm sorry. I couldn't think of anything else."

Charles had his hands pressed between his knees, trying to keep from shaking. He made some joke about making me a good dinner. Now that it was over, I was terrified. I thought that we all could have been killed, could still be killed, and yet it felt unreal. A nightmare.

Ten minutes later we came around a bend in the road and were in another world. Suddenly, there were bodies beside the road, bodies in the ditches, people running after us with their hands held out, some of them bleeding. We couldn't encompass it at first, couldn't believe what we were seeing. It had been such an *ordinary* day; we weren't prepared for it in any way. The panic set in before the accompanying understanding. Jack said, "Jesus God," and began to drive faster and faster.

The roadblocks we passed through had been abandoned, rolls of barbed wire and burned-out cooking fires marking where they had been. We saw more people running, shouting, and then there were actually piles of bodies, heaped up every which way, broken and unreal. Blood ran over the dirt in thick rivulets. I hunched over and wrapped my arms around my belly, as if I could protect it.

A young woman ran out of the cluster of houses, her arms over her head to protect herself, wailing. She couldn't have been more than three feet from the Land Cruiser. For a moment, she put out her hand to us, begging us to stop, to intervene. Our eyes met. She was tall and slender, with a heart-shaped face, a kerchief over her head, a gap between her teeth. A face for mischief, telling jokes, but now it was full of desperate refusal. The knowledge of death. I felt a shock of recognition; I didn't know her, but it seemed as if I did. I was up on my knees, leaning toward her, unable to speak. Then the man behind her sank his machete into her, and she just fell to the ground. Houses behind them were burning.

Jack put his foot all the way down on the accelerator to get past the soldiers. I was craning around to see what had happened. Charles had put his head down onto his knees and was moaning. I suppose he could take it in—he was Burundian—he understood what was happening. He whispered, "They're killing us," but I didn't know then whether he was identifying with the people outside, or if he thought he, Jack, and I were going to die.

I said something like, "Jack, that woman," and he just ignored me. Nauseated, terrified, I had the conviction that this woman, out of all of them, we should have saved. People were running after us, calling out to us, waving their hands in supplication. I was too afraid to see them clearly. But this woman, it was as if we knew each other—I couldn't escape the memory of her eyes, that look. She had known she was going to die. There had to have been something I could have done. Even now, I feel both these things: that it was impossible, that there was no way to stop it, and that I myself am guilty of her death.

Charles wrapped himself in a blanket and hid on the floor, in case we came to more manned roadblocks. What we saw, flashing past. Not a bad dream, too real. Children killed along with the adults. The running, shouting, flames, bodies.

Stretches where life seemed to be as normal. Houses, banana trees, goats, children. People who didn't know what was happening yet.

Then the killing again.

Toward town the roadblocks started again—at one, the soldiers took our money and watches, unusual for a Burundian roadblock, but nothing was usual—and I had the sense of how they could do whatever they wanted. That we could die right there and no one would ever know what had happened to us. Terrified that they would find Charles, take him away. Then kill us for hiding him. But I couldn't seem to feel the reality of what we saw; it was like struggling, and failing, to wake up. I couldn't get a full breath, my lungs were being squeezed shut.

There was a glass wall between me and the world, paralyzing me. A dry, mocking voice made comments in my head: this was the real life I'd come in search of; here we were, having a quintessential African experience. I wanted to strangle it. I was sick, then, though we weren't able to stop. It was impossible to take it in.

Just the one woman I could comprehend—the horrified feeling

of having failed her, and then a muffled desperation for the people who ran after us, their hands held out, pleading. Driving in Burundi, even under ordinary circumstances, means dozens of people waving, putting out their hands for rides. Sometimes you take them: the ride becomes crowded, intensely uncomfortable, dusty, strong-smelling, public; sometimes you ignore them (rationalizing to yourself that you couldn't have taken everyone anyway, but only a very few; even if you stuffed your car with a dozen, everyone crammed together the way they were on African buses), and then you carry guilt instead, the knowledge of your own selfishness.

That day, we would have risked our lives if we had taken up people we couldn't vouch for, but leaving them behind meant that dozens of them were certainly killed. So we became complicitous. The longer we drove, the more I felt like a killer.

Not far from town, someone had been chopped up—there was just a foot in the dirt. A foot and part of an ankle, bloody, a good ten feet away from the nearest bodies. Maybe someone had thrown it or kicked it, some sudden, bizarre game or impulse of triumph. The image would wake me up, heart pounding, sick and blind, for so long that I could never have imagined it, but at the time I hardly thought I was taking it in.

Everyone has the right to life, liberty and security of person. (Article 3)

There are hours of total blankness, funny gaps. Jack and Charles and I must have discussed the situation, but I don't remember one word, except for an argument over whether to take the main road, which we stuck to. I do remember Charles saying, from the floor, when Jack wanted to stop, "God, are you crazy? Do you know what is happening out there?"

The trip went on and on and on, horror and guilt and paralysis and fear. We came into the outskirts of Bujumbura, full of dread, but the streets at the edge of town looked strangely normal. By this time I was beside myself with fear for Jean-Pierre. I fought with

Jack to put me down at a street corner with a line of waiting taxis so I could go looking for him. I said, "Jack, I'm not messing around this time. I have to do this."

We were driving along the university road, a long, bare stretch, and I realized that things weren't as normal as I had thought at first—ordinarily there would have been cars, people walking along with loads balanced on their heads, children and goats. But the streets were almost deserted. And then we heard the sound of shots, screaming, off to our left. Jack sped up. "We're going to the embassy."

I hated him more than I ever had. *"I have to find Jean-Pierre."*

He didn't slow down. "I'm sure they'll let you use the telephone."

Charles was up in the backseat again, his face closed and ill. I think he was on Jack's side, but it was unnecessary for him to say anything, since Jack had the wheel. I turned away, my face against the seat. There was nothing I could say that would move him.

The embassy people had been snotty sometimes about small things in the past, but I have to say that they were very good at that time, well organized, generous with the information they had, willing to take surprising risks.

Just then, though, I was furious, because the consular officer, Bob Pierce, was adamant: I could not go roaming about. He said that President Ndadaye had been assassinated in an attempted coup, that the country seemed to be exploding. All Americans would have been immediately evacuated, but a newly formed Committee of National Salvation had closed every way out of the country: the airport, the port, the borders. They had even shut down phone service.

The embassy people were already in their own fortresslike houses, connected by some elaborate system of illegal CB radios which I'd always thought ridiculous. Bob Pierce told me, kindly, that my own house in Kinindo wasn't safe, but that they could put me up in one of the embassy residences. I resisted the idea of being trapped in an embassy house, thought of the Peace Corps instead. The staff had big houses, though not as shamefully grand as those of the embassy people. But when I asked, I was told that most of the volunteers who'd been in the interior had escaped in their old, shared cars, or on their motorcycles, and come to town. They would go to Dar es Salaam once they were allowed to leave and meanwhile were staying in big groups at the houses of the director and assistant director. So there was no room, except at an embassy house.

I could have defied the edict, but I was afraid to be alone. Burundi now appeared to me in a very different light. I had told Margaret and Lizzie stories, but it was a kind of bragging. This was different—to watch humans killing other humans had caused damage that I didn't, at that time, even begin to understand. I *wanted* to leave. And if we were leaving Burundi, I was not going to sit in Nairobi or Dar es Salaam with nothing to do while my mother was dying in California. If Jean-Pierre were all right, I was getting him out and taking him with me. I'd need the help of the embassy people for this, would need Bob Pierce to stamp that essential visa in Jean-Pierre's passport.

For that, I would do whatever I was told. So I said thank you, and accepted an offer to stay with one of the embassy secretaries, Charlene, a charming and socially adept career professional, nearing retirement, from Baton Rouge, whom I knew from her little formal dinners. She'd spent much of her time in EUR, the European bureau, and loathed Africa, but was always displaying her good sportsmanship. Staying with her was a decision I later regretted, because she was not one to allow me to bend the rules in any way.

Bob told me that I had one hour to pack one suitcase and a carry-on, all I'd be allowed to take when I left the country; an embassy car drove me to my house and waited for me. Deo wasn't there, and there was no note. I hoped he was safely at home in the hills, with his family.

I stripped off my skirt, blouse, underwear, bra, everything, and threw it into a pile in the corner. Not because it reeked of fear-sweat, though it did, but because I had the *sensation* of being covered in blood. I took a hot shower, scrubbing and scrubbing until my skin was red and scratched. I left my dirty clothes in their pile and dressed in clean ones; I didn't remember I had left Dad's cross in my skirt pocket until much later. During the drive home, I had forgotten all about it.

Forty minutes later, I was sitting in the middle of heaps of books and clothes, legs crossed, reading. For some reason, I had decided that the essential decision was what books to take with me. A state of shock and madness. I was doing everything to try not to think of Jean-Pierre and what might have happened to him.

It seemed to me that I had to have the book I'd been making my way through—*Popular Cultures of East Africa*—and something for plane trips or long evenings of waiting for the airport to open. I'd been planning on *The Mill on the Floss* for my next international flight. I read part of it: Maggie's determination to escape her family, to stain her face and run away to the gypsies, how she imagined they would welcome her. Then I put that down and picked up a book on crocodiles I'd been reading earlier.

> The anatomical configuration that results in the appearance of a smile may be part of the reason that crocodiles arouse such dread among the surrounding peoples. Another is certainly the crocodile's habit of disappearing with its victims under the surface of the water, where it will roll the body as it sinks and then wedge it under a rock, waiting until the flesh is soft enough to be good eating.

Lifting the book overhead, I threw it across the room. It bounced off the wall and fell to the ground, the pages crumpling underneath it. *Where was Jean-Pierre?* I could see him, in the dirt, covered in blood.

I jumped up and ran for the shower again, saying to myself, *Stop this, you're clean,* but the compulsion had hold of me. Then I had only fifteen minutes. I knelt on the floor, going through my things, trying to decide what to abandon, what to take. My favorite scarves, some jewelry, papers. Part of my brain was making what seemed like rational decisions, though all around me were objects, books, clothes, kitchen things: possessions that I grieved to leave behind, almost certainly forever. And even at the time I knew that was irrelevant, even despicable. I threw all my photos in an envelope and stuck them in my carry-on.

By this time, it was late afternoon, and the day's rains were pouring down, crashing onto the roof, falling from the gutters in sheets, pooling in the garden outside my window. What I was trying to keep my mind from was imagining it all over Burundi, soaking the bodies, turning the blood to washes of pinkish water. Would the killing have let up? For what? For the killers to have a break and some brochettes? Would they be inside a hut somewhere? Huddled together? Telling jokes? Still in a blindness of focused killing? What were they thinking about, those men?

And then I thought that it was fall at home, I'd need sweaters, but they were too bulky to pack. I could borrow some from Lizzie, or go to a thrift shop. I wanted this so badly, to be in calm, sunny Santa Rosa, trying on other people's clothes with the cars outside in the peaceful streets. To not know, to not ever think about it. *Not to have seen it.* Immediately, the image of the rain-soaked bodies took over my mind.

I took down my Japanese woodcut of the Spirits of the Dead, which I'd lugged with me from the U.S., trying to decide whether I'd miss it forever if I didn't pack it, or if I needed the space for practicalities. Then my door banged open, and before I could run away, but after I had pictured my death in detail, Jean-Pierre was in the room, wrapping his arms around me and kissing me all over my face. I burst into tears of relief and strained exhaustion.

He was trembling, damp from the rain. "I have been here three times," he said. "Last night, today. I didn't know what might have happened to you, upcountry. And your embassy is useless." He had tears in his eyes, but now that he knew I was safe, he started to become angry, a reaction. "Why didn't you come to me?"

"They wouldn't let me. Will you stay with me here?"

He said, "It is not safe for either of us. And I have responsibilities, Ah-na. The Hutu have gone mad. I have no news of my family. Rumor says people are dying everywhere. More than hundreds. Thousands. President Ndadaye is dead. And Karibwami and Bimazubute—the National Assembly has no leadership. So the Hutus are revenging themselves now, slaughtering us."

When he talked about the Tutsi, he said *us*. Could what he said be true? I'd seen soldiers at work with their bayonets and machetes. Tutsis. But not many—could he be right? What if the soldiers were only those who had been caught upcountry and were responding to the massacre around them? Either he was denying the truth, or I had been making a terrible assumption that, in any situation here, the Tutsis had to be the villains.

I just wanted to hold him, to feel his cheek on my shoulder and my cheek on his, his chest against my breasts, thigh against thigh. To smell the hot, acrid smell of his adrenaline-sweat. I could feel his heart beating against mine, and that was all I wanted, that he should be there, that his heart should still be beating.

The driver of the embassy car appeared in the open doorway, his eyes flickering away from us. "Madame, it is past time," he said.

Jean-Pierre gave him a sharp command in Kirundi, and the driver, looking offended, left.

I said, "Jean-Pierre, we need these people. We need their help."

"I will take you to my house, but I must leave you there. With the guards. I have to do what I can to preserve stability. And when I can, I must go find my family."

"There was this woman, Jean-Pierre. She put out her hand to me."

"They should be here, in town. If I hadn't wanted them to go." He let go of me and turned away, on his heel, walking back and forth to the door. I could tell now that he wasn't seeing anything in the room, wasn't actually with me.

I said, "It's too dangerous for you to go upcountry. You can't do anyone any good by risking your own life."

Then he did look at me for a moment—his face cold and removed—and I would have insisted, but I felt how cruel it would be. After a short silence, I said, "Bob Pierce wants me to stay with Charlene, the embassy secretary."

"And you want to do this?"

"I'm afraid they'll be angry if I don't. And if you can come see me there, if they get to know you, then they'll help us. And if your family comes to stay with you, and I'm also staying with you, won't that make a different kind of trouble?" I had both hands on his arms, propitiating him, but he was angry.

"Get ready, then. I will take you."

These weren't the terms I wanted to separate on. I didn't actually want to make love—I was still too sick and wild, but it might be our last chance for a long time. And maybe sex would anchor me inside myself again? I would have made an advance, but was stopped by the idea that he might be shocked or revolted. We had never yet turned each other down; I didn't want this to be the first time.

He helped me finish packing. I locked up my house and left it. Deo still wasn't back, but I left him a couple of months' wages in an envelope with a note. I didn't know whether I would see him anymore and had the sense, again, of unreality. That life should have been continuing on, with its petty irritations, hedonistic pleasures, the illusion of work, when all the time this had been waiting.

Jean-Pierre left me at Charlene's house without a kiss. I desperately needed more time with him, for comfort, to sort out what we were doing. His face had its blank, closed look—our common ground seemed to have disappeared.

Charlene stood at the gate, her lips smiling, but her arms folded and her eyes narrowed. She welcomed me, showing me inside, inspecting me avidly out of those watchful eyes in the plump, beaming face. I looked over my shoulder as we went up her steps, but Jean-Pierre's car had disappeared down the rutted dirt street, and all I could see was the bizarre innocence of lush flowering trees.

She said, "Of course, we won't be having visitors during this period." She said this politely, with that same smile, but the tone was a challenge.

"Surely our friends can come to visit us."

"If you don't feel able to live with the conditions we have to accept here . . ." A threat.

And where was I to go? I couldn't stay at my house. I couldn't walk to California. My reasons for not going to Jean-Pierre's still seemed valid, no matter how painful it was to be separated from him. I needed the embassy's help. I said, "I so appreciate your letting me stay here. It's wonderfully generous of you."

She smiled more broadly, inclining her head, with that look of real pleasure we get when imagining our own goodness. "After all my years in the service, dear, I've come to know when we have to pitch in and do our part."

Pitch in and do our part, pitch in and do our part sang in my ears, and I had an image of us setting up tents and starting fires with two sticks, singing camp songs, and then my imagination threw in front of my eyes the face of the woman, pleading, the machete chopping into her as she fell.

I stopped where I was and put my hands over my eyes, trying to press it away.

"You must be so tired," Charlene hummed at me. "Why don't you go into my room and rest before you meet everyone?" It was a kind of nightmare feeling, that inside was no better than outside, that I was headed into a different kind of trap. I thanked her again for being so kind, and we went into the lush, baroque living room where I'd only been for ex-pat dinners and ornament-making parties at Christmastime.

Nine

Almost immediately life settled into a new series of rituals, patterns, protections both against what we knew and what we didn't know, though we pretended, mostly, a kind of horrifying normality. Eating cookies. Playing *cards*.

Every surface of Charlene's house was crammed. Dozens of framed pieces of needlework, bits of art from all of her overseas tours, inspirational posters with soft-focus children holding hands in the woods, and photographs hung in rows from the ceiling down to the tops of the furniture. She collected salt and pepper shakers, hundreds of them: dancing chili peppers, little bathroom fixtures, cake slices, Eiffel Towers, Mickey and Minnie Mouse, Fred Astaire and Ginger Rogers. Embroidered and beribboned pillows covered every chair and both couches; lace antimacassars hung over the backs of everything. Floor-length sweeps of cloth flowed from the tables, printed with golden marigolds entwined with their leaves, rosy and spiked bouquets.

Etta, who was a "rover" and in Buj on TDY (temporary duty), filling in between the deputy chief of mission's secretaries, was staying in the house, as well as Charlene's unemployed daughter, Amy, and her six-year-old, Cyn, and two American tourists, backpackers who'd gotten stuck on their way to Gombe. Also Charlene's dogs.

Charlene's housekeeper, Jacques, was there, and his younger brother, Sylvestre, who'd come to Charlene and Jacques for training in how to be a housekeeper. Then there were the night and day guards, neither of whom felt safe going home to their own neighborhoods. Over the next several days, other Burundians came for shelter, staying out back, listening to the radio and conveying to us all the latest rumors. Someone said that it was true that the Hutus had begun by killing Tutsis, but that the Tutsis were now retaliating. Several thousand people were supposed to have died in a few days.

On the drive, I had been frightened, but it had been like a nightmare, unreal. Now I was afraid—and not only for the people outside our walls. Outsiders were usually immune, or had been in the past. But anything seemed possible. Every day I thought, This could be the last day of my life.

We spent hours every day "exchanging information," or talking over the rumors. The CB radio, on all the time then, squawked and chattered. Charlene's call sign was "Mississippi"—the call signs were all rivers, the names expressing homesickness, or a longing for the exotic, or a memory of some previous, vividly remembered posting. Amazon, Yangtze, Volga. "Congo, Congo, this is Rio Grande—how do you read me?" "I read you Lima Charley, Rio Grande." Checking to see that the others were still out there.

The workers huddled around their radio outside, in the back of the house, under the wide eaves, coming in from time to time to report that the lake had been poisoned, and we shouldn't drink the tapwater, even boiled and filtered, or that the government said that only a couple of hundred people had died. When we looked out over the city, we could see buzzards circling, kites and crows in greater numbers than we had ever seen.

Being there was a horrible mixture of fear and boredom. We couldn't get away from each other. Except that we all napped, or pretended to nap, sometimes in corners of the room. Naps, under certain circumstances, were allowed within the hinted rules of the house—a tacit acknowledgment of the situation, which we so often seemed to be pretending somehow *didn't exist*. The pretense of napping was our only privacy. And I wasn't sleeping at night, so was always tired during the day. But we were also overwhelmed by fear, not so much for ourselves as for all the people who we hadn't heard from. Fear that Buj would explode any day.

/   /   /

A handwritten, semi-indecipherable message to me arrived with one of the workers who came to take refuge with us. It was from Jack, in a kind of invented code that referred to events in our daily office life, full of sentences like "That time the German guy told the story at that embassy party, it was that, with our old friend, you remember Tuesday morning." Making my way through it, I figured out that Nahimana had been killed. He'd been bayoneted in his yard, and then the soldiers had gone in after his family.

I didn't take that in for a while, thinking that it had to be a mistake, that I had misinterpreted the note, that Nahimana couldn't have just ceased to exist. A man who could have done so much for Burundi. I remembered his wary, beautiful smile, and I stopped eating almost entirely. Most of the people in our household stuffed themselves all day long from Charlene's stockpiles, comfort, proof that they were still alive. I found food sickening, though I did my part of the general housework. We told ourselves that we couldn't make Jacques do it all, but really we needed to keep active, feel useful, not to suffocate each other. We had no idea when the airport would open, which didn't stop us from endless discussion and speculation about it.

/   /   /

When Jean-Pierre came by, three days later, I threw myself into his arms in the yard—I couldn't help myself, though I was aware of the presence of the other Americans, of the workers watching from the shadows. Charlene stood ostentatiously in the doorway, talking over her shoulder to someone, but also watching us and blocking the way in.

The sky was a fairly clear gray, almost blue, with bright, cheerful clouds. The grass and trees shone from the morning's rain, and water pooled in the reddish ditches beside the road.

Jean-Pierre embraced me, quickly, then stepped back, resting his hand on the bougainvillea-draped gate. I was trying to tell him about my nightmares when he began to talk about going into the interior to find his family. He said he'd be leaving as soon as he finished certain affairs for the Minister. This frightened me enough that I immediately stopped going on about my own dreams. I said to him, "It's not safe yet," and he said, "I have to know what's happening, if they need me." He asked if he could come in for a few minutes.

"I think it's impossible, right now." I wanted the comfort of his body so badly that I had half persuaded myself it was the only thing that could keep me sane. But that wasn't what he was asking for, and the terms of my being there had, in any case, been made subtly but definitely clear. Charlene's stance in the doorway reinforced them. The Africans at this house were workers; they were outside, and we were inside. If I hadn't still been in my state of shock, paralysis, I could have stood up to the unspoken assumptions, but my brain, failing me, said that if I followed the rules, we would be safe. And that I didn't know whose goodwill might not be needed, at any moment, to ensure our safe passage.

Jean-Pierre was evidently disappointed, maybe hurt, somewhat baffled. We nearly quarreled; he made some remark about how I had suddenly become more like the other Americans.

This made it a bad moment to ask what I had planned, but I needed to do it while I could. "Jean-Pierre, will you go with me to the embassy? If we get you a visa, you can come to see me in California."

"Why are you leaving Africa? Why do you think I can leave?" He frowned at me. I was speechless. He went on, "My family needs me, Ah-na. And I have a responsibility to my country."

"The embassy people will probably send me home soon. And I don't know when they'll let me back. This way, you can come for a visit, when things are a little calmer. Meet my family. You could apply on your own when you wanted to come, but it would be easier if we were together."

He uncrossed his arms, still frowning, but giving me a small nod.

I said, "If we can get you the right visa, it will be good for months. And it will be easier to get it right now, when I'm with you."

"Let us go quickly, then."

I ran up to the porch, said to Charlene, "I'll be back in a couple of hours," and patted her elbow, the propitiating gesture of a small child. Before she could muster herself to answer, I ran after Jean-Pierre, blushing over my public display, and worried about the consequences of offending Charlene.

In the car, Jean-Pierre said, "No news at all. Nothing is traveling up or down. There are no vegetables in the markets, and nothing comes in from upcountry."

"But, Jean-Pierre, that just means that we couldn't have had a chance to hear anything."

He didn't answer me. I had had dozens of conversations with him in my head, so many things I wanted to say or ask, but they'd dried up, and I couldn't think of anything which wasn't irrelevant or egotistical chatter. He wasn't in the mood to talk, so we drove almost in silence to the embassy.

It was afternoon, and Bob Pierce would ordinarily have been doing his visa interviews, but nothing was ordinary. The visa line was closed, and I had to get Bob to make an exception for us. Then it took a lot of arguing on my part to get Jean-Pierre a visa. Jean-Pierre's money, family connections, roots in Burundi were all nothing beside his presumptive desire to get out of Burundi and not come back. I think what clinched it, though Bob to a certain extent simply rolled his shoulders and shrugged, taking a chance on us, was Jean-Pierre saying to him, "Perhaps I don't need a visa. I don't know that I will actually be going to the U.S."

I said, "What are you *talking* about?" and he said, "I have to go to Gitega to find my family, Ah-na. I have to see whether my work requires me. I may come in a month or two, if I can, for a short while, but I cannot be certain that I can go, not right now."

I said, "But, Jean-Pierre," and Bob said, "I'll give you a three-month tourist visa, then," hastily, getting us out of his office.

We didn't go to his house. I was full of desire, but said nothing. He dropped me off at Charlene's, with a brief, embarrassed, but public, kiss on the cheek—astonishing from him—and said, "I will come back when I can. Do not go out. Be safe. Will you promise me?"

"Where would I go?" I asked him.

"Don't go anywhere," he said. "Not right now."

/   /   /

At Charlene's, we played more cards, dealt with Cyn's tantrums, got in the way of the workers, and tried not to be spiteful toward each other. Playing cards had become our chief visible occupation, apart from needlework, eating, and napping. The first night we'd sat around while people told stories of the most awful things they'd lived through overseas. A kind of competition. I tried to be understanding about everyone's questions, not to see my fellow prisoners in the house as vultures, circling avidly.

Of course they wanted to know what was actually happening outside our fortress house. But when I tried to say anything, the tears would start up. I'd never cried much (though I would have to get used to it—a useless, excessive empathy which now responds to anyone's troubles with an instant, easy leaking from the eyes). But at that time tears still came as a humiliating surprise to me, and I would struggle against them, while everyone looked away in embarrassment or patted me in a way I hated. And their own stories, of this or that coup, of fires and minor gun battles in Latin America, had been outdone by what was happening around us.

After a couple of hours, Charlene had said, "Well. Look how many of us there are. We might as well pass the time." And she got out her bridge set. So we came to an unspoken agreement not to dwell on it—that temporary household was exhaustingly full of agreements, almost all silent, so that they had to be guessed at.

The first two nights we'd played bridge—Charlene belonged to bridge clubs at every post—but the backpackers, Sylvia and Tommy, had never played, I wasn't much good, and Amy was a sloppy, impatient bidder who couldn't remember what cards had been played and ran out her trumps too early. This led to fighting with her mother.

Sylvia, twenty-two years old and already, despite her current uniform of loose batik dresses, nose ring, unshaven legs, and long straight hair, headed for a life of middle-class femininity, of tact and the smoothing over of difficult situations, said that it had been a long time since she played poker, and did we all know five-card draw? We'd been playing poker, fairly successfully, ever since.

The third evening after the day of the visa application, we were playing seven-card stud, with deuces wild. Amy spread out her cards—a full house with a pair of aces and three queens. We were playing for buttons; Charlene, who knitted sweaters and little suits for her granddaughter, and her grandnieces and nephews, had a huge button collection.

"You weren't bluffing!" Charlene smacked Amy's hand, playfully, but maybe a little harder than she had meant to. "I should have guessed. You look just like Cyn when she's getting away with something."

Six-year-old Cyn had already been put to bed. She didn't fully understand what was going on but was made restless and difficult by the atmosphere. She'd resumed tantrums, a stage she was said to have passed through long before, and I was longing to give Amy some tips on not being helpless and overwhelmed by her. Since I didn't have children, I was under the impression that I'd do much better if I had the chance.

Charlene said, "We've almost eaten this batch of oatmeal cookies." She had a freezer filled with consumables, including twenty big tubes of Quaker Oats. "Let's do these in, and Jacques can make more tomorrow. Before the eggs go bad." She passed the plate around, and everyone took another cookie or two.

Sylvia said, "I wonder if the airport will be open tomorrow."

Charlene said, "I'm just so thankful that I had Jacques stock up on beans and rice this month. Otherwise I don't know where we'd be." We all praised her foresight. I had my eyes on the table much of the time, tracing the pattern in the cloth, but I joined in the compliments. Charlene went on, "Of course they steal everything. It's impossible to keep the most basic supplies on hand."

Etta said, "Isn't it *awful?* In Egypt, I went through pounds of sugar every month. They stole it for their coffee, which they liked to have taste like sweet mud."

Amy said, "Do you remember that nanny in Korea?" and her mother said, "Oh, God, of all of them, she was the worst. Not just food. Toys, clothes, jewelry. And she would deny everything with the most *bland* face. Say that things were lost. Finally I fired her and got her base privileges revoked—we were living on Yongsan army base then."

Etta too was full of memories of her foreign service career. She appeared to be complaining, but her tone was one of nostalgia. "In Indonesia, they would take money out of our purses when we forgot to lock them up. One day I had to call all of them—cook, gardener, chauffeur, housemaids—in and say that if that money didn't reappear, I would be calling the police. And that night it did. But I still missed my favorite gold chain, which disappeared during pack-out."

Tommy, Sylvia's boyfriend, who was dealing, said, definitely, "I think everyone has a full hand now. Shall we play?"

Whenever I shut my eyes, the images of blood, the woman in the kerchief, the foot in the dirt, swarmed over me. It took all my resources not to jump up and head for the shower—we could not afford to waste the water. And two or three times a day I had to give in anyway, rinsing myself down, scrubbing and scrubbing with the water off, then turning the water on just long enough to get rid of the soap and whatever I'd scratched away. Sometimes I scrubbed myself hard enough to break the skin, even to draw a little blood. And maybe that was part of the point.

/   /   /

Early one evening, I decided to write a letter to Jean-Pierre. I had to get him to California, to introduce him to the paradise that was my home ground. He could marry me and become a citizen, could teach at the local university. French, maybe, or African history. They'd fall over themselves to get him—an African who'd done his advanced studies in history and politics at the Sorbonne? *Sans doute. Pas de question.* In like Flynn. We could take the children to France for a few years to keep them from becoming insular or provincial, visit Burundi perhaps every three years or so, during calm periods. I wasn't going to mention any of this, just to write about life at home for him.

Paris, with its big-city problems, overwhelming artistic and political life, snobberies, was one thing, had given him ideas about life outside, but it had nothing to do with my home. Jean-Pierre needed to get to Sonoma County, to breathe the clear air. Away from Burundi and its heavy gray skies, the almost visible poisons of fear and hatred. The blood in the dirt.

I wrote, *In central Sonoma County, we have a Mediterranean climate: warm, dry, perfect for apple orchards, vineyards, and farms rich in fat, lazy cattle. To the north, you can find redwood forests along the deep green Russian River. If you follow the river to the sea, it becomes wild, a rocky and amazing coast, often mysterious with fog. People are more relaxed in Sonoma County than they are in the urban areas around San Francisco, an hour away.*

I couldn't think how to make it personal, vivid, not with Charlene waiting outside the bedroom where I was trying to write. And it wasn't "my" room—I shared the living room with the tourists, which made my insomnia worse. Charlene, Etta, and Amy and Cyn each had a bedroom; the only unoccupied room was the storeroom, which was kept at an air-conditioned fifty degrees, almost a refrigerator. Even the bathrooms had a certain protocol. Not possible to spend too long in either of them. So I left the bedroom and said to everyone in the living room, "I might just go outside to the garden." They all watched me, their eyes diagnosing, evaluating.

Charlene said, "Watch out for the mosquitoes, dear. You'd better use your repellent and light a coil. Remember, it's still Africa."

"I hadn't forgotten," I said. And then, cravenly, "But thanks. I appreciate the reminder." I went out back, not too close to where the Burundians were hanging out under the eaves, boiling speckled yellow beans on their old outside stove and listening to the radio. They nodded at me. Jacques greeted me in French, and I responded in that language.

It had been raining but had stopped. Out behind Charlene's house, a papaya tree dripped water on the scraggly lettuce patch below. I went to the edge of the terrace and sat on a wet lawn chair, my knees drawn up against my chest, face on my knees.

One of the guards asked another, in Swahili, something that I'd translate as "What's with the Tutsi Captain's woman?"

Another said something about my morals, about softness and corruption. I didn't entirely take it in. My head had snapped up to look at them—I was trying to make sense of what the first man had said.

Jacques said to them, in a sharp undertone, "Fools, she speaks Swahili, don't you know that?"

Jacques stood by the stove, stirring the pot. Sylvestre, squatting on the ground, was polishing Charlene's shoes. One of the guards had been lounging in a chair and the other squatting on the ground facing him. The various Africans I didn't know were sitting on old lawn chairs or the ground, leaning against the pillars of the house.

The only way Jean-Pierre could have a military title was if he had been in the army. I remembered, or rather really heard various key remarks for the first time. Christine's *I wouldn't want him as an enemy*. Nahimana's guarded hints.

In front of all these men, most of whom I didn't know at all, I couldn't ask for an explanation. At first I thought perhaps I'd misheard, but it was clear from their expressions that I hadn't. Surely I must have misunderstood. But all kinds of small events and interactions could be perceived in this light and made a horrible sense. The way the soldiers bowed to him. Christine's account of his fascination with the black mamba, which I had thought just an ordinary story about childhood, but now perceived as a warning. His moments of ferocity. I said to myself, *You're in a nightmare state, you would believe anything.*

Was there an officer of any rank in the Burundian army who was not, in his own person, responsible for the deaths of hundreds, probably thousands, of people? Who had not only given orders, but had killed and killed and killed?

I said, aloud, without having meant to, "It's simply not possible." My voice trembled.

Jacques was looking at me with pity. One or two of the others were grinning in angry contempt or embarrassment, but most of the men were staring at the ground. I don't know what they were thinking, but my state must have been evident.

I went back into the house and got into my sleeping bag, curling up in a corner of the living room. Which, of course, seemed to be full of people. Sylvia was saying, "But it's so perfect. I can't get over how you do this," and Charlene was answering, "I do a diagram on graph paper before I start, so I know exactly which color of yarn to use on each square. Then I pull it up from behind and over like this, do you see?"

I wrapped a pillow over my head and pretended to go to sleep. Christine's stories. And Jean-Pierre himself, hinting at all I didn't know, about him, about Burundi. "Sometimes you can be perceptive," he had said. Then I had heard *perceptive*. Now I heard *sometimes*. He and Christine wanted me to know/didn't want me to know. Both could be true at once. Or else I was paranoid. Could I ask either of them? If it weren't true, what would my suspicions do to our relationships? What if I made it a joke? "You'll never guess what I heard these men call you." He knew me too well for that.

I wrestled with these thoughts for hours, including over the dinner which I didn't eat, though I got up for it, and through the evening card games and speculations on the latest rumors. I lay awake most of the night, going over them again in my mind. The responses of soldiers at checkpoints, their deference to Jean-Pierre. Nahimana's wariness. Nahimana, who was now dead. I repeated that to myself, but it didn't make it any more real.

Over and over, I said to the invisible Jean-Pierre, "Please don't be angry. You know I never really doubted you. But you see that I did have to ask?" Sometimes, during these imaginary conversations, he forgave me at once, almost laughing. Sometimes he was stiff and unbelieving, and I had to talk him into relenting toward me. Sometimes he walked away and never came back. Finally I fell into a hard, thick sleep.

It was the first thing I remembered when I awoke, and I thought, *I don't have to ask him. Someone will have the real story. Jean-Pierre doesn't ever have to know what I heard.* Barantandikiye—but I didn't know where he lived. Other contacts, from the Red Cross, from FRODEBU? And then it came to me—Charles, apt to be home in Buyenzi *quartier*, hiding with his family. Charles, who had been so friendly at first, and then seemed to be my enemy. Because of Jean-Pierre?

Charlene, of course, tried to keep me in the house, but I was past caring about her help, or her possible malice. Ignoring everyone's warnings, I went out in the street, walked until I found a taxi, and took it to his house. The very few Burundians out and around stared at me in amazement. The streets were weirdly calm, deserted, a ghost version of the Bujumbura I had known.

The taxi driver didn't want to drive to Buyenzi, and when we got there, he didn't want to wait, but I wouldn't pay him, and I told him that if he stayed for me, he'd get four times the usual rate. He kept looking over his shoulder at the deserted streets; I was not at all sure that the lure of money would be strong enough.

Charles lived in a one-room house, cutouts for windows, corrugated steel roof, his children crowding behind him at the door, until he spoke to them sharply in Kirundi. He didn't invite me in, very strange in Burundi, and at first he wouldn't even talk to me. "You shouldn't be here."

But I persisted. I asked after his family, his own safety, what he had heard about Nahimana. Then I said, "Charles, did you know that Jean-Pierre had been in the military? That he was a captain? Is it true?"

He stood on his step, in his doorway. "Have you asked him?"

"You're saying it is. You're confirming it."

One of the children was crying in the house. Charles was silent. An upended metal bucket on the stoop spilled a trickle of water across the steps and into the dirt.

"Please, Charles."

"Why do you come to me? Is he not your friend? Is this news to you?"

"Who would have told me? When you and every other Burundian I knew kept this a *secret*." The size of the betrayal made me speechless. I was trying not to cry.

He was silent again, then, almost apologetic. His voice softer with me than I had heard it since those first couple of months, he said, at last, "I thought you knew."

I couldn't even respond—my thought at that moment was, Could people have thought I'd known and that I'd loved Jean-Pierre anyway? That I could have somehow *overlooked* it? I said, "Please tell me what he's done. Please tell me what he's responsible for."

More hedging. At last he said, almost inaudibly, "That I cannot do. In our country—you must see that you cannot ask this."

"I'm sorry," I said. I was hating him, and myself. "Thank you. Be careful and look after your family, Charles. Stay out of trouble."

He said, "It is in God's hands," and that was the last time I ever talked to him. I don't know what became of him. He's not one of the ones I heard about.

I thought he was lying about Jean-Pierre's past—no, not that, exactly, but that the Burundian rumor mill had falsely indicted Jean-Pierre. Charles had heard the same stories as the workers, and it was all about as plausible as the poisoning of Lake Tanganyika. I had to talk to Jean-Pierre. I gave the taxi driver Jean-Pierre's address, had to raise the promised rate again, and finally he drove me there, at top speed, whipping around corners so that I had to cling, nauseated and frightened, to the seat in front of me. Once I paid him, he gunned the engine and jerked the car forward, disappearing from sight. I went into Jean-Pierre's house, which was entirely deserted—no workers, no family. I sat down in his living room. And waited.

He came home at 10:15 P.M., exhausted beyond politeness. "What are you doing here?"

I said to him, "I love you." I put my hands on his strong and beautiful arms. His face made me sure that everything I'd heard was a lie.

He touched my hair. "I love you too." He still sounded annoyed. Then he bent down to kiss me, and our bodies flared up, instantly, so that in another minute we were on the carpet, biting each other and groaning. Our long abstinence, and my sense of danger, of not being sure who or what he was any longer, made my desire more violent, my body reckless. He responded by instinct, pounding into me as if he wanted to punish me, to leave me permanently marked or torn.

Afterward, we lay on the carpet, touching down our sides, half dressed. The lights from outside gave me a view of his profile, his eyes.

I said, "Charlene's guards called you 'the Captain.' "

There was a long silence. He asked, "Is that what you came here for?"

"I had to see you."

Another silence. I would have thought that he'd gone to sleep except that I could see the shine of his eyes in the half-dark. I rolled onto my side, semen leaking down my thighs.

"The state has a body. We say *le corps*." The sense of a living body, not, as in English, a corpse. "The heart moves blood. The ears listen. The cells divide. Food is taken in at the mouth. The legs carry the body where it must go. When the body is threatened, it does what it has to in order to survive."

I whispered, "What do you do all day?"

"Now I am a part of the head. When I was young, it was the arms, the hands."

"Can you tell me what happened?"

Another silence. "Why do you need to know?" Then, after a while, "There was a struggle. In 1966, after the army had to take over. Or the struggle began before. Who can say when it started? The National Assembly was rotten and needed to be abolished. The dangerous had to be executed. We had to let the country know what the Hutus had done. Then, in 1972, you know, the Hutus took up arms and began to kill. They had organized a genocide for us. All our efforts were spent to overcome that."

I knew that the Tutsis claimed this. Also that in putting down the uprising, the Tutsis had slaughtered between a hundred thousand and two hundred thousand Hutus, including anyone with any influence—government workers, teachers, students.

"I was in Bururi, then Bujumbura. I was twenty-one, and I had to command trucks." The trucks which had rounded up thousands and thousands of Hutus to be shot. "My family had ties to the National Revolutionary Council. I worked with the *jeunesses*." The young. Another long silence, and then he said, "I do not talk about it. I do not forgive the Hutu for what they have done to us. For what they have also forced us to do. Then. In 1988. Now."

I wanted to get up and run, but my body had frozen to the floor, my heart pounding, stomach sick. I thought, *I am having a nightmare. This is not my real life. He's not saying these things.*

The sense of dream had hold of me. Though I couldn't think, I had the feeling that my actions now mattered, that in front of me was a doorway I couldn't see. I got to my knees, shakily, as if I were drunk, then fumbled my way into my clothes. He said nothing. I walked a long time through the streets before I found a taxi; nothing happened to me, though I think I hoped it would, that I would be killed, and it would be over. I know I was wishing I had died on the drive home from the interior, before I had learned about Jean-Pierre.

Charlene let me into the house, scolding, minatory, but I just looked at her blankly. I went to my spot in the living room, and still in my clothes, stinking of sweat and sex, I curled up into a ball and went to sleep.

/   /   /

In the morning, Charlene made a huge fuss. I apologized many times, without minding—I was feeling free. Not caring what she thought, feeling myself getting over Jean-Pierre already. Obviously I hadn't been as ferociously in love as I'd thought. And I remembered Jean-Pierre's weaknesses, bad habits, attitudes about women. I was ashamed of myself for having been so stupid, for missing all the signs, for not *paying attention* to the world around me.

I didn't know what would happen to Burundi. I had been fooling myself into thinking that everything was better now, that 1972 and 1988 were as far away as the fourteenth century. Maybe I wasn't helping to bring a new world. Maybe no one could. Or maybe this was temporary, and Burundi was still on the road to democracy and peace. I would go home, help look after Mom, and have time to understand what to do next.

But by eleven, I was remembering Jean-Pierre's laugh, the feeling of his arm thrown across me at night, the look in his eyes just before he kissed me. The way he knew exactly what to say, his pleasure in his nieces and nephews, his constant perceptiveness about people and his interest in the world. The ways we could talk.

By noon, I was thinking again that there had to be a mistake, that he had been there, but he hadn't really *participated*. If I talked to him in more detail, I'd find out he'd been testing me, maybe, or he'd been compelled into whatever he'd done and was too proud to admit it. If he were an American war veteran, maybe with post-traumatic stress disorder, wouldn't I be there for him? And he hadn't actually said that he'd killed anyone. He had been there, which was bad enough, but who knows whether I would have done any better in his place?

I felt both resistance to the love that had come back full force and a relief in surrendering to it. I had to talk to him, to get it straightened out. Despite Charlene's raised eyebrows and small, irritated sighs, I stopped playing cards, and concentrated on writing letters, covering pages with exhortations, pleading, ripping them up, trying again. I knew I wasn't behaving well, that it was, in fact, kind of her to have me there, and that I was an irritating and unhelpful companion, but sorting things out seemed like an emergency. I wrote to Jean-Pierre that I had made a mistake, I couldn't bear life without him, I loved him with my whole body, heart, spirit.

I went out one more time, got a taxi, and went to Jean-Pierre's. I had to pay heavily again, but this driver seemed pleased by the windfall. "In Burundi," he said, "we always have troubles. I am content to be weak and insulted, to suffer hardship and persecution for Christ. My weakness is my strength. Paul said this." He waited for my response. If I had let myself say to him that this suffering was for no one and nothing, that it was a huge fucking waste, would he have put me out of the taxi?

I didn't take the chance. I folded my hands and listened. He added, kindly, "I am a Catholic. My faith is in God." He began to whistle, a hymn that I remembered as one Deo had liked.

Jean-Pierre wasn't home, but Phillippe had come back. I greeted him, asked after his family, told him I was leaving a letter, then added to the folded sheets of paper more explanations, more questions. *Please, please come to see me.* By this time I was crying. Phillippe watched me with sympathetic interest. I gave him my watch as a present and said, "Please make sure he gets this letter."

He clasped it between his hands and raised it, as if in prayer. "God protect you, *Bibi*."

"And you, *Bwana*."

We shook hands, formally, and I went back to Charlene's to wait, not afraid of her anymore. And because I wasn't afraid of her, she seemed to be of me, so she didn't challenge me, and we all waited together, uneasily, a few more days.

/   /   /

Then the airport was reopened.

It was a wretched trip home. I don't even want to remember it. I was beside myself with fear and regrets, and ill and light-headed from not eating. When I closed my eyes, I saw blood, bodies. Jean-Pierre, in my dreams, became unrecognizable—I would look by the side of the road and see him, unaware of me, hacking at some un-known woman. It seemed that I had to keep my eyelids open, be-cause when they closed, the images assaulted me.

What had happened to Marie-Claire, Deo, Christine? Where were they? And what was Jean-Pierre thinking? Did he have my letter? What hadn't I seen, or heard, at the time? His cheerful cal-lousness in some situations. The occasional frightening look. *Who was he?*

From time to time I slept, and it all followed me into my dreams; I was helpless against it. I wanted Dad's cross, suddenly, like a child who's lost her security blanket. I cried over it. How could I have been so reckless, abandoning it to whoever went through my things? All that racing around in taxis—why not one trip to my own house? How dangerous could it have been? I tried holding Jean-Pierre's gold bracelet, but it didn't fit my hand the same way, and it reminded me of my nightmares.

We were routed all over the place because of the last-minute

scheduling. Airport personnel were sympathetic about my impossible, inaccurate tickets, but they were also full of a minimally restrained curiosity. Sometimes I said too much and regretted it.
Sometimes I kept quiet, resenting people's curiosity, the vampire
avidity for blood and war stories. In all, it took me six flights and
seven airports to get back to San Francisco.

Ten

Lizzie was waiting at the gate at SF International. When she saw me, she ran forward, hesitated, then threw her arms around me. I hadn't called until Frankfurt, thinking they wouldn't know what was happening, that, as usual, Burundian events would be ignored in the U.S., but we'd made all the papers. My family had been trying to reach me in Burundi for weeks. Someone at the State Department had "assured" them that "all nonessential personnel will be evacuated as soon as possible." They had been imagining the worst.

Lizzie asked, "What happened over there?" and I said, "It's still happening." Then I couldn't talk any more, and she said, "Let's get your bags and go to the car. I'm a fool; of course you can't tell me in the airport." All around us, business travelers and tourists trotted busily in and out of their gates, rummaged in their carry-ons, ate fast food in paper wrappings, and stood at the white courtesy telephones, their luggage clutched between their legs for safekeeping. A small girl in a pinafore held a set of balloons which read, "Congratulations." A man in his thirties stood beside her with an armload of roses.

On the way to the baggage claim, Lizzie's arm around me, I started to pull myself together. I blew my nose and asked, "How is Mom doing?"

"She's been pretty bad. They haven't been sure whether she'd make it to the end of this round of chemo or whether they'd have to stop it and wait."

"Is this what you'd want at the end of your life? So cruel to put her through this when they already know . . . why, Lizzie?"

"I suppose they have to take any chance they can. Like keeping patients in comas on life support."

"My impression from the magazines is that doesn't happen anymore."

"I don't know what you're reading," said Lizzie. We were at the carousel. My bag was already winding around in a pile of others. I hadn't really expected to see it again. I seized it in both hands, swinging it to the ground and staggering. As I started to walk toward the carts, Lizzie said, "What about the rest of it?"

"This is what I have left. And you know what? I don't even care. Stuff. Set decoration. But this is the wrong fucking movie. Wrong life. Wrong planet. Could you tell me, please, where is the world a person could stand to live in?"

"I think let's get you out of here," Lizzie said. We fed a dollar into a machine and took a cart. On the way through the underground passages to the garage, she was quiet, her arm around my waist. We got into the elevator with a couple of glossy business travelers, who edged away from me, nostrils pinched, exchanging glances with each other.

In the car, she asked, "Can you talk about it? Do you want to?" She'd parked next to a concrete pillar. Outside the sky was overcast, thick, black-centered clouds threatening rain.

I said, "Not yet."

She put the car in gear and backed out. "OK. Then I have to tell you about Susan. So you have a little time to get used to it."

"What's happened to Susan?" This was the nightmare dread—to run and run and then lock the door behind you and feel, behind your back, that what you'd been running from was waiting behind you, in your own house.

Lizzie braked and put a hand on my arm. "She's *all right*, Annie. In one sense."

A car behind us honked, long and hard, the man leaning on his horn and shaking his open hand at us, pointing to the exit and elaborately rolling his eyes. Lizzie made the sign of a blessing over him, two fingers held out like a medieval Madonna, and gestured him through. He shot around us, giving us the finger. "May you get what you deserve," said Lizzie peaceably. She said to me, "That's either a curse or a blessing, depending. Maybe he's on his way to the deathbed of his best friend. Or else he's just an asshole."

Then she said, "Susan. Well. She was caught by a teacher's aide last week with her boyfriend and some other kids, doing mushrooms. The teacher made some elaborate agreement with them and didn't call the police but called us instead. She was still high when we went down to get her, there was a huge fight, and she told Margaret she was pregnant."

"Pregnant. Can't be. She's twelve, for God's sake."

Lizzie paid the parking attendant and then pulled out into a lane that emptied straight onto the freeway. "Thirteen. Turned out she was just a couple of days late and imagining things. But there's been nothing but scenes ever since. She hates us for not having told her the truth about Mom. She says we lie to her constantly and should expect her to model her behavior on our own. Her boyfriend is nineteen. He takes drugs, rides a motorcycle. Margaret thinks he's a dealer and a child molester. Susan sees him as a misunderstood knight. So they scream at each other all the time. When she's home."

"They scream at each other in Mom's house?"

"She came downstairs in the middle of one of these things, and now she's down as much as possible, lying on various pieces of furniture with her hand clutched to her chest saying that it's better to go now and she should have died years ago."

To my dismay, I started to laugh. Lizzie joined me. "It's too much," I said. "Sorry. Not funny." We were laughing in great, agonizing gusts. "It's not possible. Stop the car, let me out, I'm not going back there."

"This is your *vacation*, just relax and enjoy." Tears were running down her face, and she said, "Stop, I'm going to wet my pants."

"I want my real life." And then, without any warning, I began to cry. I whispered, "Lizzie, my best friends—I have no idea where they are, what's happened. Jean-Pierre went right into it. And he, maybe he . . ." but I couldn't tell her. What came out of my mouth was "There was all this *blood*. And a woman. She had her hand out to us. She looked into my eyes and then she died." I put my head down on my knees. I had abandoned Burundi. I had lived, while Nahimana, and thousands of others, had died. Inexcusable. Lizzie drove with one hand on my back, silently. There's this about my sister—she's the only one in my family who can be counted on not to talk when there's nothing to say.

/   /   /

Had I really wanted to describe it to them? To see in my own family that unpleasant mixture of avid curiosity and a strange admiration, almost envy? I don't know, because, incredibly, we hardly discussed it. I walked straight into the middle of a scene.

Susan was in the hallway, her back against the post at the bottom of the stairs. A black leather jacket covered with political buttons hung on her. She had dyed her hair purple and pulled it up into an elaborate, braided topknot. Margaret, out of control, slammed her fist against the doorframe, her face red. "You are *grounded*."

"Are you going to call the police if I go out? Have me locked away as incorrigible?"

Margaret turned her face toward us as we opened the door, her eyes wet with rage and fear. A parent's nightmare—what happens if they finally reject your authority?

Susan also looked to us, her face full of appeal. At her age I'd wanted nothing so badly as a set of molds I'd seen at a cake store, for making castles from multicolored sugar. She took a step toward us. She had her eyes on me, the newcomer; I was being asked to take sides, to knock sense into the enemy's head.

Margaret shouted, as if Susan were deaf, or as if she could penetrate the barrier between them if she were only loud enough, "Danny is a *criminal*!" And then, to me, "This child is running around with a criminal! She can't see it—she doesn't know her ass from a teacup yet, and she's screwing herself for life."

Susan shouted back, as if they were across a canyon from each other, "I love him. If you'd ever loved anyone but yourself you might understand that. He makes me happy, OK? Does that make him a criminal?" She said, pleading, "Aunt Annie, *you're* in love. Talk to her." And then, the threatening, tough voice and posture reasserting itself, "I don't have to put up with this. He and I can get a place. I can go where I'm wanted."

I moved toward her, my hand out, as if to a feral cat that might scratch or bolt. The jet lag had hit. I felt as if I were at the bottom of the ocean. My ears roared. Out of my mouth came, "Sue, sweetie, at least be using condoms for your own sake if not for ours. You don't know how heartbreaking it would be if you actually got pregnant. And you can't know what else this boy has done, is doing. You risk becoming sterile if you get chlamydia. You could get herpes and never be free of it again. If you don't protect yourself, you could *die*. AIDS is a bad, bad death. The worst." In my mind, the woman fell under the machete. Nahimana collapsed forward, bayoneted in his own garden while his family hid in the house. Uselessly—the soldiers went in after them.

Susan drew herself up, glared at me, hissed, "Danny would
never . . ." and ran past me and out the door.

Margaret threw the spoon on the floor. "That was just great, Annie. You should really have some kids of your own, you have such a
gift with them." Then she walked out.

Trying not to cry, I whispered to Lizzie, "I feel so helpless."

"What you need is a shower and a nap. It's not your fault, Annie. It's just a mess."

At the top of the stairs, in the shadows, stood my mother. When
she saw me looking at her, she moved away, back into her room. She
would be furious if I didn't come straight up to see her, would mention it again and again, to all of us, for days, but I was not prepared
to deal with this. I said to Lizzie, "I have to make some phone calls."

"Annie." She pointed to Mom's closed door.

"I can't."

"This isn't a can-or-can't type of situation. You know that."

I said to myself, *You've done harder things,* but I couldn't think
of any.

/   /   /

Mom had crawled under her covers again, fully dressed. She wore a
white mohair sweater with small blue beads, the hairs of the mohair
standing up and waving like cilia.

I went and knelt beside the bed, putting a hand on her back.
"Mom." The windows were shut because of the rain; the room stank
of dying flowers, a rotting, sick smell.

"I suppose it's too much to ask that every one of you should not
do her best to poison my last days with worry." She was holding me
accountable for the massacres in Burundi; I had obviously arranged
them to make her anxious.

Since she had, as so often, taken my breath away, I couldn't
answer.

"Susan, Margaret, you. At least I have Lizzie. Thank God there's one person I can rely on."

"I think Margaret has done a great deal for you, Mom." I wanted to hit her. Which, of course, made me ashamed of myself. Mother dying of cancer and I want to belt her one. I said to myself, *Suffering has evidently ennobled you.*

"Lizzie always had a quality of sweetness. There aren't many like her. I wonder, how can this be my daughter? Like having given birth to an angel. It makes me think cloning is a good idea, after all. I wish I could clone her."

I thought, *I hate you.* My guilt was making me sick to my stomach. I said, with so much restraint that to this day I am proud of myself, "Mom, if you think about that remark, you might see that it could be considered insulting to your other children."

"No, I don't see it. There aren't many like her, that's all. She's a real asset to the community."

Community meant something very particular to Mom. She'd grown up in a tiny town in northeast Missouri with a passionate sense of enclosed neighborliness: VFW auctions, fund-raisers for the sick or injured, pancake breakfasts at church, Christmas fairs where neighbors sold each other crocheted toilet-paper-cover dolls, thirty kinds of homemade fudge, Rice Krispies squares with caramel filling, and lacy wreaths. Not one person in that town who didn't know everyone else's business, everything discussed by the neighbors, slowly, endlessly.

Mom had been twenty years old, not long after "the end of the War"—as she said—when she came west. She'd had an *idea* of California, a warm, golden haze of sunshine, movies, new starts, but had been oppressed and frightened by L.A. She took a bus to San Francisco, and then, moving farther north, found herself in sunshine, if not in glamour, working as a night clerk in one of the first of the big hotels in the Napa Valley, long before "the wine country" became a tourist industry.

She roomed with the Copelands, a farm family. Cattle, and a couple of apple orchards out to the west. Brisk mother, father with a temper, four big boys, Midwesterners at heart—solid, hard-rind practical, physical with their affections and humor. The youngest wasn't much of a farmer, but had silky brown hair, a sly, if gawky, sense of humor, an attractive, slow-moving, deep-voiced laziness. She was married to him for thirty-seven years, and, somewhere in there, he had turned into my quiet, defeated father. Because of her? Because of life?

I said, "Do you want me to read to you?"

"What I would like is a little rest."

"OK, Mom. I'll talk to you later." I went out into the hallway and shut the door quietly behind me, making my way downstairs, holding the rail, taking deep breaths of air.

The whole house looked unreal to me. The kitchen had an air of discombobulating normality. A few dishes in the sink, cartoons taped to the refrigerator, a jar of jam still on the table. On the floor by the sink lay two or three smashed Cheerios that a quick sweeping had missed. A wreath of dried baby's breath and some kind of grayish fern hung beside the refrigerator. So *ordinary*. Rain poured down outside the window. Like a stage set for some earnest, dreary play.

I tried calling Burundi. The phones were working, but Jean-Pierre wasn't home, and no one at the embassy knew anything further about him, about Christine, or about Marie-Claire. Someone had seen Deo, which made me light-headed with relief, though also guilty. All I could do for Deo was send money, a reference, nothing in the face of what he and his family needed.

/ / /

In my dream that night, there was a fort which was also my mother's house, located in Burundi. This seemed to be in the Sierras, the location of a cabin we'd borrowed a few times for winter

vacations when I was a child—icicles, walks in the snow. Tobog-
ganing. I was out hiking in the pines and found myself surrounded
by Hutus and Tutsis, dressed in military khaki, grinning, wielding
machetes.

A horror and refusal came up in me, the product of so many
dreams where I'd watched the violence again. I did and didn't know
I was dreaming—I had the sense that it had happened before, also
that I *could not* watch it again.

But everyone was laughing, using their machetes to cut grass.
Tears of relief ran down my face, and I laughed too, saying to myself, *You see, peace is possible after all. And you thought they were going to
kill each other.*

Somehow, though, the violence started up. Then I was inside the
fort, but I looked out a window and saw that Susan and Bobby were
outside, in the middle of the killing—Bobby walking along the top
of a wall, his face serious and remote, Susan apparently oblivious. I
believed Aurora to be out there with them. On the ground, just beyond the window, lay a single foot, and I understood that it meant
everyone would die.

I had blithely locked myself into the fort, abandoning them all.
Desperate with fear and self-reproach, I tore open the door and
bolted outside. I ran and ran, not fast enough, calling out, knowing
I was not going to be able to save them.

Although my room was cold, I woke in a sweat. The image
of their innocent lack of awareness imprinted itself on me for the
rest of the day, no matter what I did. Aurora and Bobby, at least, I
could hold on my lap, against my heart, like a poultice. Reassuring
myself of their safety. Susan I hardly saw, and I couldn't treat her
like a child, could no longer gather her onto my lap and just
rock her.

/   /   /

Mom had decided that she couldn't bear the noise of television, so she lay in a nauseated fog while we made our way through romantic adventures. Innocent girls and big, sardonic, commanding men. In exotic locales—these books had to be set in Greece or Argentina, Malaysia or Brazil. Only the exotica of tourism: slightly risky new foods, moonlit walks, quaint local customs, hibiscus blossoms in the hair. Some pounding foreign sea against the white sands of a strange beach.

I remembered my mother, years before, laughing with satisfaction when reading Sei Shonagon's *Pillow Book*; she had some fantasy of herself as a lady of the court in Heian Japan. She particularly liked Shonagon's lists. "Things That Give a Clean Feeling." "Pleasing Things." "Unsuitable Things." "Things That Give a Hot Feeling." Or the list of "Surprising and Depressing Things":

While one is cleaning a decorative comb, something catches in the teeth and the comb breaks.

A carriage overturns. One would have imagined that such a solid, bulky object would remain forever on its wheels. It all seems like a dream—astonishing and senseless.

A child or grown-up blurts out something that is bound to make people uncomfortable.

All night long one has been waiting for a man who one thought was sure to arrive. At dawn, just when one has forgotten about him for a moment and dozed off, a crow caws loudly. One wakes up with a start and sees that it is daytime—most astonishing.

One of the bowmen in an archery contest stands trembling for a long time before shooting; when finally he does release his arrow, it goes in the wrong direction.

Now I found myself reading to her, at her express wish, from *Love's Racing Heart*:

Adriana bowed her chestnut head, her large violet eyes filling
with tears. But she wouldn't let him see. She would never let
him see!

Raoul, striding across the room, sneered at her. "I suppose
you fancy yourself an expert," he snapped.

She jumped to her feet. "I grew up at the races!" she cried
out. "My father trained thoroughbreds!"

Raoul caught her by her shoulders, his stormy gaze raking
hers. She wanted to look away, but she couldn't! She was trapped
like a little bird, her heart pounding. Did he know what his
touch did to her? He bent and kissed her, bruising her lips, setting her head reeling. When he let her go, her soul was on fire.
"That should teach you to meddle in affairs that are over your
head," he spat, and left her alone, dissolving into angry, helpless
tears.

"Read it again," my mother said in a whisper, and I did. Once
again, I'd been, unfortunately, reminded of Jean-Pierre. These sod-
den romances made me want him to rake my glance with his, bruise
my lips, and set my head reeling. Also, though the books were never
explicit, they were amazingly arousing. They brought up a flood of
images—Jean-Pierre on me, grinning, pinning one arm above my
head, his tongue slowly exploring my skin, or me kneeling in front
of him on the cool tiles of his floor, my feverish desire, the longing
to swallow him altogether, he with his head thrown back, groaning,
pushing, losing control. And then, somehow, Adriana and Raoul in
a whole variety of moods and positions. Every time these fantasies
took hold of me, my anxiety about Jean-Pierre grew. I couldn't admit it to anyone—my fascination with the romances, their effect on
me. My sisters and I, downstairs, made little jokes about them. Very
small jokes, avoiding outright disloyalty.

All the while, my mother lay in bed, sicker by the day. The room
smelled of vomit and fear-sweat, no matter how we tried to air it or

put out little china bowls of rose petals and cloves, while she watched us, a small, terrible, ironic smile on her face. We were trying to pretend this was for her; she knew better.

/   /   /

I escaped when she dozed off. On my way downstairs, the sensation came over me of being covered in blood and muck. I wanted to throw up. A rational part of my brain said to me, *Post-traumatic stress, stay and fight it,* but my arms felt the blood running down, my back itched, the blood seemed to be oozing over my thighs. I could imagine it entering me like some foul demon lover. At that, I could not contain myself. I bolted for the bathroom, turned on the shower and stood in it until the hot water began to run out, soaping and soaping and soaping myself, shampooing my hair three times, scrubbing until my skin was bright red. Streaks where I'd scratched myself ran up and down my arms and belly.

When I came out, the mucky sensation was gone, but I couldn't breathe. I wanted to jump right out of my skin. I understood suicide then, as a violent flight from this claustrophobic entrapment. I could not bear to be what I was, feel what I felt for one minute longer. I put on jeans and a sweatshirt and jacket and went outside, sitting on the front steps, under the eaves.

The whole world was obscured by a dark, late-afternoon drizzle. Not the warm, drenching rains of Burundi (the pink blood diluted, running down the dirt, a foot by itself, droplets of mud and thin blood running down the ragged half-ankle—I said to myself, *Stop it, stop it*), but a cold, thin, liquid fog. The trees were dark with it, water puddled into dark mud on the lawn, the dandelions and skunk grass bent down, flattened.

Perhaps Jean-Pierre hadn't gotten my letter, and I wouldn't be able to reach him. I felt both despair and hope. If I didn't see him, maybe the addiction would gradually relinquish its hold. I could get over him, on with my life. Or maybe I was being a coward, running away from what was most real, hiding in my safe little backwater where no one felt the reality of the world outside, with its wars, its terrible needs.

How did that world become real for me? One day, when I was nine, I was humiliated because someone said something about the Bahamas, and I had never heard of those islands. I went to my third-grade teacher—Miss Jenson, who was pretty, which we cared about, and kind, which mattered more, though we took advantage of her. She knew we were wild about her; she didn't know why she couldn't get us to behave. She was always delighted and relieved by any sign of interest in learning, so she hunted up a *National Geographic* for me, full of photographs of the Caribbean: brilliant skies and seas, grinning people, hillsides exploding with flowers, baskets of beans in the marketplace, bright cloth, astonishing paintings. I kept the magazine for a month, guiltily, going over and over the pictures every night, drawing unsatisfactory scenes with my crayons, daydreaming about the people who didn't look like anyone I knew, their colorful clothes, generous smiles. They spoke another language. What did they think about? Could you think the same things in Creole that you did in English? What did they do all day? Swim? Sit in the marketplace? Did they have to go to school? When I grew up, I was going to be either a zoologist, a lawyer, a mother, or an actress. Maybe two or three of these at once. What did these people plan? If I had been born as one of them, but with my own mind, would I be the same person?

So other places now began to exist for me, at first as the dreamy locales of vacation brochures and romances, but that changed too. After college, I got my master's in public health and then wound up in Washington, D.C., living in a continually changing household of students and poverty workers. First I worked for the public health department, then I had a job with Food for All, whose motto, "There can be no peace without justice," didn't exactly match what we were doing, but sounded wonderful.

We went into the inner city daily with our pamphlets and counseling and our supplies of donated canned goods and powdered milk, supposed to be teaching nutrition, first aid, and tobacco, alcohol, and drug prevention. Some of the nurses had experience, knew how to be helpful and unobtrusive, but I learned painful lessons from every family we worked with. After a year, I was feeling that a fifteen-year-old willing to pass out the donated food would be at least as useful as I was, and then a friend of a friend staying in my household talked enthusiastically about opportunities in development, about AIDS prevention in Africa as a way to make a difference in the lives of thousands of people. He gave me an address.

Eight months later, after applications and background checks, language and cultural training, courses in cross-cultural health education and the politics of birth control and condom use in a largely Catholic country, I was on my way to Bujumbura. And now I would not ever again be free of knowing what it was like.

Was I going back to public health, or would I try to stay in human rights? Couldn't I just get a job where I worked with my hands and came home tired at night? Making wedding cakes. Working behind the counter of a bookstore. Cutting hair and listening to people's life stories, the small worries of weight gain, difficult teenagers, the grief over individual deaths, one at a time, from natural causes.

I took a scrap of paper and pencil out of my pocket and wrote, *Who is useful? What does it mean,* useful? *What I owe. The world? Mom? Who could answer?* The sensation of being covered with blood slid over me again, so I had to jump up and run for the shower.

/ / /

Afterward, I went to find Lizzie, who was on the sunporch in back, sitting on a cushion on the floor, her huge sweater stretched out to take in the warmth of the space heater in front of her. As if she were a monster, engulfing it.

I said, gripped by the nightmare that pursued me, "Lizzie, I understand what the tale of the old cow and the king means. That *anger*." And then I said, "Please distract me. I'm feeling disgustingly sorry for myself because I have witnessed other people's troubles. It kills me that I thought I could be useful. And I think I won't get an actual deep breath until I talk to Jean-Pierre and know he's OK."

She said, "You want distraction? Look at these bank statements. Eight or nine thousand dollars missing. Depending on whether some of it went for the furnace repair."

I lay on the old couch, picking at cotton batting through a split in the chintz. Lizzie lay propped on the floor beside me, both of us cold at our backs, hot where the heater blasted our faces and hands.

"You know," I said to Lizzie, "they might mean to put it back."

She leaned forward, lifted a lock of my hair, checked underneath. "Inflate to thirty-two pounds."

"Why not? People do—borrow without saying anything. And then, when Jerry's business is better, they'd quietly restore it. Have you thought of what we'd do if Margaret walked out on us?"

"What makes you think they're in it together?"

"Who, then? Margaret?"

"Or Jerry."

"She'd know. She'd know to the penny."

Lizzie lay on her back on the braided rag rug, her long skirt over her knees, blowing up with warm air, then pointed the heater at me, a blast of artificial summer. She pressed her palms over her eyes. "So, Margaret, saving for her old age. Maybe the marriage is in trouble and she's socking it away."

"If it were Jerry, I'd say a girl. Blond gymnastics instructor in her twenties. Plays Brahms on the piano. From a moneyed family, but acting out."

"But it couldn't be Jerry. Not the money, I mean. Maybe the gymnastics instructor."

"Well, can you imagine Margaret if he did?" We both laughed, and she said, "Oh, hush, what bitches we are."

The heater made my face too hot; I was sweating, though my back was still chilled. I blew at my hair, which was sticking to my damp cheeks, and said, "Mom needs her. So do we. I'm not going to bring it up. What if we put her into a rage?"

"What we could do is a little detection? Try to find out what's going on, why she might need the money?"

"And what are we going to tell Mom?"

"Tell her it's not clear yet. Tell her we're investigating what might be a bank error."

I said, "Lizzie, I have been so wrong about practically everything in my life. How do I know that we're not wrong about this too?"

"Let's not act right away. Maybe we could spend some girl time with her, see what she lets slip. Mom's friend Jean could come in for the afternoon, the kids could go to day care or friends, and the three of us could take a sisterly breath of air. Let's just have a good time, and see what we learn."

Eleven

Friday morning, Margaret, Lizzie, and I drove downtown. All the pressures we were under, our fears, desperations, conflicts, now lifted us right up in the air like a fistful of helium balloons. I had a weirdly manic feeling, as if I were about to explode.

We parked on the roof of the Third Street garage, in the cool early November sun. Margaret, who was driving, made a note on her checkbook of the parking space number. We descended the stairs and went into Books & More to buy adventures for Mom, shiny new books with glossy-haired girls and men with raking glances.

"I've got the Civil War." Lizzie waved a fat paperback called *Graycoat* in the air. She wore a floating dress with a multilayered hem, and she'd had her hair done in dozens of tiny braids with rainbow beads at the ends.

Margaret took the novel, looked it over, and shook her head. "No history."

"I've got Greece," I said. *"Aegean Nights."*

Lizzie approved. "Greece is good."

"The cradle of civilization," said Margaret.

"Actually," I said, "doesn't current thought have it in Africa?"

Lizzie took *Aegean Nights* out of my hands, fanning herself. She had hold of the edge of her skirt and did a little step, a sort of Greek-inspired version of a samba. "Moonlit adventures at the Acropolis. Octopus and retsina in seaside cafes. Greek fishermen jumping lightly from rock to rock. Sun and sand and love."

Tears came into my eyes, and I whispered, "It is so good to breathe again. In Burundi, it's like you're choking on poison gas all the time." I blew my nose and wiped my eyes, trying not to lose it in the store. Lizzie put her head on my shoulder.

Margaret said, "You're not going to think about it today. You're not breathing any poison gas now. That's half a world away, and you're right here, buying books for Mom." She was, as usual, tidy. Green visor, polo shirt and trousers, back straight, chin up. She wore a photo button pinned to the collar of her shirt: Susan with her arms around Bobby, who was sprawled across her lap. "We've got nearly a dozen romances. Surely that should do it?"

Behind us, a thin boy in round wire glasses smirked. He had a copy of *Gödel, Escher, Bach* in his hands, was holding it, as if accidentally, so that the cover could be read.

I said to my sisters, "Aren't you *hungry?*" and we went out into the sunlight, putting on dark glasses. The drivers, honking, sped around each other. In Burundi, people drove in whichever direction they pleased, including sideways, and you had to be on the lookout for flocks of goats, a minibus stopped dead in the middle of the road, streams of pedestrians.

My sisters and I debated Chinese versus Thai, organic health food versus Indonesian, coffee shop versus a sixty-foot salad bar, and decided on Harry Chang's.

"I shouldn't eat Chinese," Margaret said. "I'm too fat."

"You're not as fat as I am." I had been gaining even more weight

in the U.S., though several times I'd made vows to eat nothing but
salad for dinner, or had started the day with chalky protein-powder
diet milk shakes.

Lizzie, who stayed slender without effort, said, "Harry Chang's
is never oily."

We walked closer together, Margaret and I, giving her bad
looks, united, for the moment, against her thinness. Four teenage
boys, up a side alley, were playing some kind of soccer, using a rub-
ber ball with a map of the world printed on it. One kicked it up in
the air, where the blues of the oceans flashed. Africa presented itself,
then Asia, as the globe spun around, dropped, bounced off the
ground. Another boy, in dark cutoffs, a sleeveless undershirt, and a
cap turned backward, kicked the globe against the brick wall of a
software shop.

Lizzie shook her head one way, then the other, tossing her long,
soft braids back over her shoulder so that the beads clanked together.
"I had a client last week who remembered a perfect love. Brazil in
the eighteen hundreds. She was forced into an arranged marriage,
but her husband was killed by thieves ten years later, and she and
her love were united, living together into old age. She says she still
hasn't gotten over him; she can't commit to any other man. I said he
might not be on earth right now, he might not be a man, he might
not be the right age. She said it doesn't matter—she learned in
Brazil how to wait for him, and she will, no matter how many lifetimes it takes. I can't decide what I think. Maybe it's truly romantic. Maybe it's drugged, ridiculous."

Margaret said, "I saw Tony the other day. Do you remember
Tony?"

Lizzie said, "Tony! He had that duck cut!"

"He was beautiful to me," Margaret said, defending herself.
"Tall, thin. Elegant hands. Of course I loved him—he was my first."

We all had to stop in the middle of the sidewalk for this. I
said, "You *slept* with him?"

Lizzie echoed me. "You fucked Tony DiAngelo?"

Passersby turned their heads to listen. Margaret began walking again. We were almost to Harry Chang's, and she lowered her voice as we entered the tall, hushed grays, the painted screens, into the smells of ginger, garlic, sesame oil, fresh hot meat and vegetables.

"He has a wife, his second, a daughter from this marriage, a daughter and a son from his first marriage. He studied philosophy, dropped out of school to become a tree surgeon, ran a landscaping business for a decade, fell out of a tree and hurt his back, went to school in computers but hated them and now is selling real estate in Napa. Big estates, vineyards, those little Victorians in the center of town. He has a pinkie ring. One ebony oval and small diamonds on either side. You never think anyone you once loved will have a pinkie ring."

"But you were only fourteen. You were so severe with us. Did Mom know? Where did you go?" We were whispering, indignant, amazed, our imaginations fired up. Tony and Margaret writhing in the backseat of his old Plymouth with the daisy decals. Or maybe they'd snuck out to the orchards, spread a blanket over decaying rattlesnake grass.

Beautiful waitresses, waiters, handsome Harry Chang himself, surrounded us. We weren't so much seated as incorporated into the decor. Soon we had hot and sour soup.

Lizzie insisted. "But we none of us *knew*. I thought we knew everything about you."

There was a short but painful pause. Margaret said, with something intended to be a laugh, "Well, you were only fifteen when you were running around with Sandy Matthews."

"I didn't sleep with him."

I said, "You didn't? I was sure you were having sex."

"He came on my *sweater*. I *would* have had sex with him, but he could never wait long enough. I wrote poems, made lists of names for our children. I would have *died* for him."

We hadn't been that much older than Susan when we started our sex lives. Although no one said her name, she was on our minds. Our memories reassured us in one way—we had been a little wild ourselves—but the thought of her also ratcheted up the tension. Now we were dissolving in giggles, holding our heavy cloth napkins over our faces. I couldn't look at the people on either side of us.

Margaret said, "So, Annie, what *I* want to know is, is it different with an African?"

Lizzie said, "Oh, hush, Margaret." But Margaret had a stubborn look. She said, "I'm not asking what you think I am. After all, it's a whole other country."

At that moment I had what seemed to me an inspiration. I said to her, "OK, I'll tell you the real truth if you'll trade me. Like when we used to play Truth or Dare, but no dare. I answer this and then you answer one question for me."

"Fair enough," she said. She wasn't quite meeting my eyes. Lizzie had gone very still.

I lowered my voice so that they had to lean forward to hear me. "All right. The thing is, you know it's always different. Remember Ty?"

Lizzie said, "The Aquarius, that guy who did the tapestry rugs, sold them at fairs."

"Every time, it was magical—as if we were building something. Air castles. We heard things. I had visions. White peacocks in the snow, whirling trees. Fainted a few times."

Margaret crossed her arms. "I wouldn't have let *him* go. Whirling trees. Did you also get orgasms, or just the trees?"

Plates arrived: prawns, chicken, tofu nestled in vegetables, a great dish of fried rice and a little one of steamed for Lizzie, since the fried rice had some kind of meat or chicken, each dish adorned with crackling wonton skins.

I paused until the servers had set everything out and gone again. Then I said, "Oh, orgasms. Is that an *issue?*" My sisters, now united against me, gave me a bad look. I went on, quickly, "Anyway, there was Bob, and with him it was always sweet. Like animals in a burrow. Or Phillip with his fantasy games, mirrors, costumes and props. Continual surprises."

I was almost whispering now. "What it is about Jean-Pierre, it's hard for me to describe, that's all. I'm giving some context. Because Bob, for example, was magical with his tongue and hands, and Jean-Pierre is even clumsy. Except that when he just touches me, just puts the flat of his hand on my skin, I go liquid. I never wanted anyone the way I want him. We're like wild animals, tearing each other to pieces. And when he's inside me, it's as if everything is in complete harmony, that there is nothing else I could ever desire again. That this is the most perfect moment in the history of the world."

They were both quiet a moment. I blinked away tears.

Margaret said, "So, should I be dumping Jerry and getting a plane ticket to Senegal or Kenya?"

"That's another thing. You ask about *with an African*. I don't know about an African. I only know about Jean-Pierre. Maybe, for me, he's the only man on earth."

Margaret said, "Sex wears off."

"He'd be a great father. A great companion."

Margaret had a way of locking her hands together, elbows out, as if she were about to begin a prayer. "What does he *do*, Annie?"

"In bed?" It amazed me to have her ask, even in this conversation.

"For a *living*, dear."

"Oh. I thought I'd told you. He's in the Ministry of the Interior. Not religious, government. Like a cabinet member. Not quite that high-ranking. Yet. But people say."

"So this guy's big stuff, is he? We shouldn't be picturing him in a loincloth?"

"Try a coat and tie. Presiding at meetings." Unfortunately, I got boastful, convincing myself. "His family is one of the royal clans. Although the monarchy is probably finished."

Lizzie said, "A *prince*. Annie's found herself a *prince*."

That was when I opened my mouth and said to Margaret, "Your turn. What happened to the money?" It just came out. And I had been rehearsing tactful, loving, tricky, subtle, open-ended or devious questions, comments, conversational beginnings, or secret traps for days. I turned immediately, horribly red.

The first expression that came into her face was relief and surprise, followed almost instantly by craftiness, a wall of reserve. But *relief*. Lizzie's face, dumbfounded, confirmed that she was seeing what I was.

Margaret said, "What are you talking about? What money?"

Lizzie crossed her arms, staring at the table, clearly angry with me for my clumsiness. I said, stumbling, "Several thousand dollars is missing from Mom's checking account. The one you've been managing."

"How do you know?"

"Mom called the bank for a balance. It's down about nine thousand dollars."

"Well, I've been too busy to look at the statements. They obviously screwed up their records." She was red and blinking, but her words came out smoothly and a little too forcefully, as if she'd rehearsed this moment ahead of time. "Why are you asking me in that tone of voice?"

I said, still clumsily, silently cursing myself, "I just thought you might know something." I was careful not to implicate Lizzie—I had already done enough damage.

Margaret said, "Or perhaps Mom spent it and just forgot. She's not thinking too clearly these days." Her tone was one of indignant innocence, evidently faked.

"I didn't think of that. I'll have to check with her."

Margaret smiled, lips only. "Ask me any time you're having trouble figuring out what Mom might have done."

Lizzie said, "Does anyone have room for dessert? I was thinking of some ginger ice cream." She and Margaret looked together at the menu. I was wondering about that look of relief. Had she just been waiting, all this time, for the other shoe to drop? Had she been afraid of a confrontation with Mom? Or was there some other reason that she wanted us to ask her about the money?

/ / /

The hospital where Mom went for her treatments had been built in the early sixties and still looked like something from a distant future. Hard, shining glass and steel. Concrete blocks. A Martian fountain. Where the Jetsons would go for chemotherapy. I thought about, but didn't describe, the downtown clinic/hospital in Buj with its grimy floors, peeling walls, piles of bloody, used dressings and unsterilized instruments.

Margaret and I sat outside in the pale November sun, two days after the lunch at Harry Chang's, watching Bobby splash his hands in the fountain. Mom wanted us to be there before and after her treatments, but wouldn't let any of us in farther than the waiting room. Margaret and I were still shy with each other. We perched silently on the fountain's concrete edge, the rough man-made stone cold through our clothes. Bobby leaned over, fishing for the change people had thrown in. To make wishes? *"Let us take her home this week." "Please let it not be malignant."* And ordinary, daily wishes too. *"Let him love me the way I love him." "Please don't let the business go under."* Prayers, in fact, but with the tossing of a penny or quarter. Bargaining with God or the fates.

Margaret had tried to keep Bobby dry for the first few minutes, but had now given up, and just held on to the back of his pants to keep him from going under altogether. Light struck out from the hospital's windows, from the metal rods piled on the fountain's central set of blocks, from the rows and rows of cars.

"So," she said. "You think you might be going to settle down and get a real job, now you're back?"

I said to her, "Tens of thousands of people disappear every year. Millions grow up illiterate and underfed. *Documented* torture, killings, arbitrary imprisonment in 142 countries last year."

"Watch this," she said to Bobby. "If I argue with your aunt Annie on this, I magically become one of the bad guys." Bobby went on fishing. He had a fair handful of coins. A woman inching by on a walker gave us a disapproving look.

"A man I know—knew—a Hutu, had soldiers come to his house, sure he was a supporter of one of the illegal political parties. They tore half his guts out and left him for dead in the bushes beside his house. Friends got him to what passes for a hospital, and somehow he didn't die. A week later soldiers came through the hospital and slit his throat. He wasn't even particularly political. He was feuding with a neighbor, and the man turned him in. He had seven children. The oldest three, all boys, were killed at the same time."

Bobby had begun paying attention. He said, "*Super*man will get them. *Sharp*tooth will tear them to pieces." He climbed down on the ground and made *Tyrannosaurus rex* motions, curving his first fingers into two claws, still gripping his coins in both palms. He opened his boy-mouth to show teeth, tipping his head back in a roaring hiss.

Margaret said to me, "Little pitchers, Annie," and then, "I never could talk to you when you got like this. And now you *of course* have suffering credentials that make you an authority on everything. I've never seen anything worse than someone getting a ticket for running a red light. This makes me utterly ineligible to mention that you're over your head for some guy you can't possibly be happy with and getting old enough to be in danger of missing your shot at the best thing in life. You can't save the whole world, Annie."

"So what am I to do, Meg? You want me to give up, come home, get a nice car and condo, start making payments? Go to the county fair on weekends?"

"Boy, you really despise us, don't you?"

"Is that what you think?" I was appalled.

"You think you've learned so much over there."

A little girl, about four, blond curls, dimples, patent shoes, a dress with pink roses and a bow at the lace collar, wandered up, head on one side, smiling at Bobby. He turned around and opened his hands, wordlessly showing her his coins. Her mother looked us over, smiled in an exhausted, abstract fashion, and sat on a bench.

The little girl said to Bobby, "All that money is mine." She nudged him with her arm. Margaret and I, helplessly, looked at each other, and then at the ground. Out of the corner of my eye, I could see her turning red.

Bobby examined the girl, then gave her a shove. She shoved him back, hard enough that he was rocked back against the fountain. Then she burst into tears and ran to the bench, burying her head in her mother's lap.

This was an opportunity to probe Margaret for information on her relationship with Jerry, her money situation, but I didn't have any appetite for it. At that moment, I liked her noticeably better than I liked myself. She was saying to Bobby, "You go right over there and apologize."

I said, "I'm sorry. Of course I don't despise you. How could I?"

She gave me a look, stood up, and marched Bobby over to the bench by the back of his shirt. He was wailing, "She pushed me *first*!"

Gathering myself together, putting one hand on Margaret's hot, damp back, I said, "I'll just go in and see if Mom is ready." In my voice, I tried to put all the love I felt for her, my regret at our current position, a blanket apology for whatever I would be compelled to do to her in the future. Still holding Bobby's shirt, she turned to look at me, a long, straight look of judgment withheld, private suffering, something like defiance. Her face had the dignity of its painful aging, the veins in her cheeks, pockets of fat, lines around eyes and mouth, uneven coloring. I understood that I didn't know anything about her life, that sometimes I forgot that suffering is suffering, even in the U.S., and without statistics assembled by the World Bank, Red Cross, Amnesty.

I found it, after all, very difficult to look her in the eye. She was the one who turned away from me, went back to the task of civilizing Bobby, while I fumbled away toward the hospital, Mom, and my next bungled encounter.

/ / /

The days took on a certain outward routine. Looking after Mom. Driving carpools, taking kids to school, Scouts, lessons, birthday parties, and soccer games. We didn't know what to do with Susan. When she was home, she was on the phone much of the time. I heard her say, "I'm living in a consumer society. I'm just a product myself, you know?" and, another day, "I think about you all the time." If she saw us anywhere in the neighborhood, she would glare at us, vaporizing us with her laser stare.

Margaret had tried to get the whole family into counseling, but Susan said that if they made her do it, she would run away and not come back. Jerry wanted to put Danny in jail. We all discouraged any action against him, afraid of losing her completely. We were at a loss, and talked to each other about it all the time, uselessly.

Since Susan had some interest in my overseas life, I tried to use that as a lever to talk to her about the problems inherent in seeing someone so much older than she was. But she was instantly on the defensive, saying, "You think I can't trust Danny because he doesn't buy the straight world's belief that booze and cigarettes are fine, and anything else is evil and dangerous? At least what we do is natural and doesn't hurt the body." The speech had a borrowed quality. "The big companies hate any use of plants—they don't turn the kind of profits that *your* drugs do."

"But we don't know what kind of effects this might have on your developing reproductive system."

"Oh, Aunt Annie." She burst out laughing. The first time I had seen her laugh in days. "Did they teach you that crap in school?" She grabbed her sweater and winked. "I'm getting my belly button pierced today," she said, and danced off up the stairs.

/   /   /

Sometimes I wished that I hadn't left Burundi, or that I'd gone off with the Peace Corps to participate in a holding-pattern life of hanging out in Dar: cafes, shared nightmares, maybe cynical, unfunny jokes. In Africa, it would have still seemed real, have been in context. Not as if I had just stepped through a doorway and left an entire universe behind, still suffering, while I fretted over whether pork chops at dinner would upset Lizzie more than they would make Jerry happy enough to keep him from grumbling, how serious matters were with Susan and what we should be doing to intervene. I'd gone back to stuffing myself, trying to feel something definite, solid. I felt *elsewhere*, in a painful, dragging way. I had to fight all the time against irritation over being interrupted. As if I were concentrating. But on what? I wasn't *doing* anything.

After about two weeks of this, I was reading to my mother one afternoon. We were in the living room, and the TV was also on. She'd stopped saying that she wanted to die and get it over with, but she still didn't want to be in her room unless she had to.

We were about three-quarters of the way through *Love's Wildest Temptation*. I hadn't exactly figured out what Violet's temptation was, unless it was falling in love with her rapist. I had serious reservations about this opus, and was debating bringing them up with Mom, who lay there like a ghost who hadn't decided whether or not to fully materialize.

Violet fell, gasping, into the back of the hansom cab. Her escape had been so narrow! Had Trefusis seen her? He must not know she was there! But even as she began to congratulate herself on her luck in eluding him, a voice came from the box, mocking her, "Is Milady in such a hurry then?"

He had seen her, pursued her, he had even managed to convince the cabby to let him ride on the box! A bribe, no doubt. As the hansom came to a blockage in the road—a man shouting at a child, who'd run in front of his horse, street peddlers joining in the fray—Trefusis climbed down from the box and entered her cab.

"Why so eager to escape, my love?" he murmured. Ah, he was cruel, taunting her! He still believed she had been unfaithful to him, had betrayed him with Randall. If only she could explain! But he was taking her in his arms. "Light women must learn to take advantage of these opportunities," he murmured.

She wanted to protest. Who had made her a light woman, if not he? Who had stolen her innocence? But he would never believe her. Her body helplessly responded to his strength as he crushed her against him, her lips as soft as his were hard and demanding.

My mother was going to want this read again. I didn't want to read it the first time. Watching her drug herself with these made me think that Lizzie and I had done the same all through our teens, that we had willingly corrupted our own imaginations. *Romance,* said these books, *is the most important thing in life.* How much of my addiction to Jean-Pierre—tall, dark, handsome, secretive, ironic, and impossible as any of the romance heroes—was a result of the ways I had mistrained my mind? What about Lizzie and her own unfortunate romantic history?

I felt there was something deeply kinky about reading aloud to Mom what was essentially pornography. I said to her, "What about some P. G. Wodehouse?"

She narrowed her eyes, her lips pinched together. She whispered,

"I don't feel that cheerful. I like these. Makes me feel I'm not missing anything."

Susan called out, "Telephone for Aunt Annie. From Africa. A man."

I was in the living room and then I was in the kitchen, holding the telephone, with no memory of getting there. "*Yes!* Hello?"

Jack's voice said, "Anne?" and I could have cried with disappointment.

"Jack, where are you?"

"Dar. With the Peace Corps. Drinking too much. Having a remarkably good time, plus there's no corpses. A few dozen muggers, and it's about a hundred and twenty degrees, but at least it's not goddamn Ramadan. Small blessings."

I wished, right then, that I were there, surrounded by people who'd seen what I'd seen, who had the news. "Do you know how people are, what's happened?"

"Well, Anne, that's what I called about. I could have written, but you know me."

I sank down onto the floor, on my knees. "Go." A prayer inhabited me totally: *Let it be anyone but Jean-Pierre. Even Marie-Claire. Charles. Deo.* A moment of the most desperate and terrible bargaining.

"Nahimana and Barantandikiye are both dead. With their families."

"Nahimana I knew." Tears were pouring down my face, but they were tears of relief, shock; the sadness came later. I was thinking *thank You, thank You.* It doesn't matter that I was ashamed of myself for this prayer, for the gratitude—it came right out of me, involuntary and absolute.

Jack said, "The fucking waste of it. Incredible. A pair of heroes, the kind of guys who should have been running the country in an actual democracy. What burns me up is that I thought anything could change. But that's Burundi. Coup followed by slaughter followed by coup. And then more slaughter. You might as well pour yourself down the fucking toilet as try to do anything for a place like that."

I was trying to think. "What do we do now?"

"I don't know what *FreeAfrica!* does, but I'm to the teeth with it. Let it slide into the pit now before it takes the rest of the planet with it."

"Are you talking about the entire continent?" Jack had spent more than twenty-five years of his professional life in Africa. Development and human rights work.

"I finally came to my senses. Save your own self, Anne. That's as much as anybody can do. As for me, I'm through wasting my life on this shit. I'm going to Zanzibar on the helo with a couple of Peace Corps chicks. Sand, lobster, and Indian ocean sunsets. And then I'm going home and getting me a teaching job. I'll be only too glad to correct fucking term papers."

"Why don't you just go to Zanzibar and think it over?"

"Zanzibar, *oui*. Thinking, *absolument non*. I'm a free man now, and a free man doesn't have to think."

I thanked him for calling and he said, "A fucking *waste*. Stay cool, Anne, and don't try to be a hero. There's no percentage in it." Then he hung up. For a few minutes, we'd been together; now he was back in Africa and I was left behind in Sonoma County, in my mother's gray house in the middle of her apple orchards, with the news only just starting to sink in.

Lizzie hovered over me, and Aurora put her hands on my cheeks. "Don't cry, Aunt Annie," she said, patting me with her little hands. This, naturally, doubled me up, on my knees, sobbing with a painful mixture of relief, gratitude, fear, regret.

When I had calmed myself enough to reassure them, I went off to Margaret's room. I knew Jean-Pierre would be home, and he was. Lizzie would have had an explanation.

I said to him, *"Jean-Pierre,"* overcome, and he said, "Ah-na." His voice was hoarse, exhausted; he'd been crying too. I found that the ruling part of me didn't give a damn about what he'd done. I wished to be someone who would not utterly betray all of her own principles. But much more feverishly, I wished that I were there to hold him.

I was so taken up with this that I wasn't thinking about the causes of his grief. So it took me completely by surprise when he said, "I don't know how to say it sweetly, so I will just say it. Christine is dead. Françoise is missing, with two children. Alexis, Candide. And my sister Regine, who you never met, is gone. Dead. Christine . . ." His voice broke, and he got out, "she wanted to go to Paris. We would have been there, but I was *too busy*." And then he began to make sounds I have never heard from another human, a private, terrible howling.

I said, "Jean-Pierre, oh, I'm so sorry," and then I shut up. I was crying too, in fear. After a couple of minutes, he began to pull himself together. "I must go."

"Jean-Pierre, are you coming here?"

There was a long silence, then he said, "I might, Ah-na. After the funerals. For a little while only, because I must support my *Umukuru w'umuryango* in looking after those of my family who are still alive."

And then, it astonishes me that I said this, but my mouth came out with, "Jean-Pierre, you never . . . in 1972 and then . . . you didn't yourself. You only gave the orders, right?"

He was silent again. Then he said, softly, and in a way that shut me out absolutely, "You think that would have made some difference. You don't understand how it is with us. If you think you do, it is only speculation. You cannot, ever, know the real Burundi."

I was afraid to say more. Afraid of what he'd done, afraid of so offending him that he would disappear altogether. When I saw him, then we could talk.

He said, "I must go. I will call you." And he hung up.

/ / /

I cried until I was sick, the sobs ripping out of me. Lizzie canceled her appointments to stay with me. I told her about Christine, all that intelligence, humor, grace, disappeared off the planet forever, and Françoise and her children—I didn't say a word about Jean-Pierre and his past. It wasn't possible that Christine was gone; it wasn't possible that Jean-Pierre was a killer. I had gone out of the country of nightmare and into someplace unimaginably worse.

Lizzie knelt down, wrapping her arms around my knees on one side and my back on the other. Lizzie the angel. Mom had a point. I didn't forgive Mom, but I also didn't hold it against Lizzie. Being the youngest is no joke; she carried too much weight from the beginning. Baby talk from the adults until she was eight.

When I was calm enough, she said, "We have to do something for you right away."

"Amputate my memory? Drug me on serotonin reuptake inhibitors?"

"I'm afraid for you, Annie."

"Counseling? I should discuss how I feel about massacres and then I won't mind so much?"

"Maybe an exorcism. Or, yes, therapy. A specialist in trauma."

Somewhere not too far away, a dog, probably chained up, was barking wildly, a ferocious, betrayed sound. "No, I don't think so. You feel bad, you talk to someone, you feel better. But maybe you could talk to the cat and get the same effects if the cat is a good listener. And I don't want to feel better. It would be obscene."

Margaret was in the doorway. "Oh, excuse me. If I'm interrupting." She moved as if to disappear before she could be sent away. Her face shuttered up, proud and uninterested, against the possibility of being rejected. Her hurt over Lizzie's and my closeness was on display. I felt love, guilt, and apprehension.

We moved over, making room for her on the porch swing, and she came and sat down beside me, hands in her lap, feet over the edge, just touching the floor. She pushed with one foot, swinging us back and forth. Why didn't someone shut up the dog?

Margaret asked, "What is it this time?"

"People I know were killed. Maybe people I know were killers." My throat closed up. What was Jean-Pierre doing at that very moment?

Margaret shook her head in sympathy, but it was clear it wasn't real to her.

I said to her, "Imagine if it happened in Oakland. In Marin. To people you know."

She said, "I can't. Why try to torture us with it? We're sorry for you, but we don't want to think about it. If this were the newspaper, I'd turn the page. People are killing each other all over the world. I guess you wanted to see that. You went and found it."

Lizzie said, *"Margaret."*

"Well, isn't it true? Haven't they been killing each other in Burundi for decades?"

I said, "The world is *out there*, Margaret, with its deaths, wars, disasters. The choice we have is to pretend it isn't happening and to sit about on our velvet couches drinking Long Island ice teas, or to go try to do something about it. If . . ." But I thought of Jack's remarks, and it seemed to me there was nothing to be done. I was crying again. Helplessly—I felt like its prisoner. There was no relief in it.

"I do a whole lot for other people," she said coldly. "I might sit on the couch and have a drink sometimes. I might *buy* a velvet couch, or a velvet living room suite, if I want to. Why not? I've earned it. Which is more than I might say about anyone else in this room. Who took the brunt of looking after Mom all this time while you two were flouncing around having exotic adventures and past-life regressions? Who cleaned her house, paid her bills, and listened to her stories over and over when we didn't know she was sick, when there was no glory in looking after her?"

Lizzie and I stared at her.

"Jerry was always saying we'd never have any fun again, that my involvement with Mom wrecked our life together. We could never just relax anymore. He said if I didn't spend more time with him, he'd leave. I had to do something; I had no choice. So we began going out some, buying things, trying to have a little fun for once. We only got some new clothes at first, went down to San Francisco for a dinner cruise. I borrowed money from Mom's account, not that much, a few hundred. Nothing for all the work she expects us to do around here. Then the refrigerator was making noise, and we thought we might as well get a decent one. Jerry wanted some fishing gear. It wasn't even that much stuff. But now . . ." She was silent, staring into space, her lips working in and out. "I say to him that I'm afraid he'll leave now that Mom's sick, and he says, 'She had just better get well, then.' "

We were shocked into silence ourselves. She said, "What does he expect? Does he think I can abandon her?" She rounded on us. "Happy, girl detectives? Ready to tell the assembled suspects how it was done, hand the culprit over to the police? And *Susan*. Oh, God, I wish I were dead." She put her face in her hands and began to wail.

Lizzie and I looked at each other, not knowing what to do. I felt, *Why didn't she dump all this before, when I could have coped?* Though I was ashamed of myself for being so selfish, I wanted to lie down and forget everything, to go to the movies like a normal person, not to be confronted by endless rushing nightmare.

Lizzie put out her hand and then pulled it back, as if it might be slapped away. "But why didn't you ask for help, Meg? I didn't know how much you were doing for Mom. I could have done some of it."

Margaret went on crying. I wanted to say that she should take a vacation, but I was also furious. She had been taking and taking, and it had only left her angrily dissatisfied. There was a kind of recklessness to the way she had told us, a satisfaction in making an exhibition of the hidden, and I understood the relief she'd shown when we first brought it up. She had *wanted* us to know, had wanted to confess to us, to tell us off.

But now she'd lost the power of her secret. I remembered Christine's story about Jean-Pierre and the black mamba; she had been saying that not calling the guards, being alone with the snake, gave him the power of *knowing* what no one else did. I could picture Margaret then, a man in another society, giving the orders to load up the trucks, gripped by her need to be in charge, to direct and control the secret, and by her belief that whatever she was doing was dictated by necessity.

Mom's bell sounded from upstairs, and Margaret stood up and blew her nose. "I'll *go*," she said, defying us both.

Twelve

I appeared to be helping to care for my dying mother, a very serious category of activity, but I rarely felt what I thought I should be feeling. Instead, too often, I was guiltily wishing that I could be somewhere else. And I couldn't fully enter into the family's feelings, the sense of drama. I secretly thought that we would be sad when we lost her, but that her death wouldn't *matter*. Not in comparison to tens of thousands of Burundian dead. What was one individual cancer in a woman who'd had a long (by Third World standards) and extraordinarily fortunate (by these same standards) life? But this was not something I could say even to Lizzie.

Margaret went on Zoloft and almost immediately began urging me to join her. I said to her, "If I'm having an emotion, I want to know what it is. If I look at an apple tree and love the shape of the branches, I don't want to wonder, is this me or the chemical? I'm willing to trade some sadness for knowing that my happiness is my own."

She said, "All emotions are chemical. What difference does it make where they come from? It's no more improper than taking vitamin C because you don't get enough from your diet. You just think your sadness is more legitimate than anyone else's, Annie. You're making a little shrine out of your emotions. God forbid anything should interfere with that."

For the next two days, we hardly spoke to each other.

Meanwhile, we were making endless preparations for Thanksgiving: debating traditional versus healthy menus; stocking up on cranberry sauce, frozen peas and onions, and olives before they disappeared from the stores; buying regular and gluten turkeys. I was mixing up the ingredients for stuffing one afternoon when Lizzie came in to say that Mom wanted me. "She wants to show you something. She's in the living room."

I dried my hands and went to see her; she was curled up on the couch, wrapped in a knitted afghan, as small and thin as some fragile, burrowing animal. On the wall beside her hung hand-turkeys in the shape of Aurora and Bobby's perfect little hands, decorated with felt pen and glittered-over puddles of glue. She patted the sofa, and I sat beside her. The TV showed some well-dressed people flinging themselves around a stagy kitchen in a transparent misunderstanding. Tinny laughter came from the screen.

"Did you want to talk to me?" I asked my mother. She put a finger to her lips. We were waiting for a commercial. This annoyed me, but then she took my hand in hers. I put my other hand over her thin, blue-veined fingers—how had she gotten so old? I was full of tenderness, all my anger disappearing. *I love you,* I thought, but she would have raised an eyebrow or shushed me if I'd said it aloud. My little mother. I was several inches taller than she, and though I probably only outweighed her by thirty-five pounds, it seemed to me that I was twice her size.

When the commercial for canned spaghetti began dancing across the screen, she took a black-and-white photograph out of her pocket. "Your grandma Eleanor. You remind me of her sometimes."

An ambiguous remark, but I thought it might be the greatest

compliment she'd ever paid me. I leaned over to say thank you, and to kiss her cheek, which she allowed, though she shrank just perceptibly.

Grandma Eleanor stood on a porch (the one she'd rebuilt?), wearing a flowered hat and driving coat, with an expression of grim satisfaction. I wanted to be like her; I wanted to be that strong, that sure of what I should be doing.

Mom whispered, "I have bad dreams. Drowning." She looked straight ahead at the TV screen, disassociating herself from her words. She wanted to tell me, but not to have any conversation about it.

I said to her, "So do I. Bad dreams."

She squeezed my hand.

/   /   /

Two weeks after we'd talked on the phone, a formal letter arrived from Jean-Pierre—written in the French style: elaborate, restrained. He began by saying that he would arrive in San Francisco on December fifth; he didn't mention our conversation. He wrote about his sisters as children: Françoise had loved to build small *rugos* by the banana trees in back of the house; Regine had made bread once for the family, and when it collapsed, she cut it into heart and diamond shapes and called it wheat puddings. He said he was being ridden by nightmares: *Every day, I plan to tell Christine what happened at the Ministry or what I saw on the street. Each time I realize that I will never tell her these things, it is as if I have gotten the news all over again.*

I felt a flicker of jealousy, but also kinship: I too kept thinking of things to tell her, was brought up short by the shock of her death. The reports from the news organizations—which had finally found reason to be briefly interested in Burundi—was that over 50,000 were thought to have been killed. I could not comprehend it. Not those who died then. Not the more than 200,000 who've died since. The number 50,000 had no weight or substance; it was another bad

dream. And yet, night and day, my mind spent most of its time trying to wrap itself around the meaning of that number.

I wrote down a few of these nightmares, thinking to drain them
of some of their power, but it only made them remain in my
memory in more detail as my desperate mind tried to incorporate
memories and knowledge it wasn't big enough to hold.

Running through a strange city, having to find someone, knowing something unbearable, not wanting to remember it. Afraid of
alleyways, neon signs, strangers. Then Christine, on the other side of
a wide thoroughfare. Screaming her name. Crying, "I thought she
was dead, but it wasn't true." Needing to reach her, but no way
across the street, no break in the traffic. People pushing against me.
An unknown language. A hole in the ground—me crawling down
into the earth, a long, cold crawl, then, finally, a cave. Stalactites and
stalagmites. Pools of water. For a moment, happiness—"This is the
place I was always trying to find."

Around the edge of a large pool, turning a corner: Susan's body.
Dumped across an outcropping of rock, blood running across the
rock floor of the cave in rivulets. Jean-Pierre standing over her,
holding a machete. His eyes meeting mine steadily, no apology,
instead an expectation that I should finally understand my own
complicity. Me calling, "Susan, Susan," as if she could hear me,
could get up at any moment. Jean-Pierre watching me, waiting for
my comprehension.

/   /   /

It was a long and painful month before he arrived. There were no
scenes at Thanksgiving, except that Bobby screamed for a third
piece of pie, was forbidden it, and was sick later anyway. That weekend, Mom asked us about the money, again, and Lizzie and I told her
it had been a bank error. That it had been transferred to another account. We hadn't yet decided—should we insist that Margaret pay
it back? How could we enforce that? Was she right that she had

done so much more for Mom? Maybe Lizzie and I should repay the
money. But though we didn't discuss this, we could see each other
noticing when Margaret had new clothes or the family bought new
gadgets, how freely they spent money.

My mind was so fuzzy; there had to be a course of action both
compassionate and fair, but I couldn't think of it. I was preoccupied
with my other griefs, and with Jean-Pierre's upcoming visit. Sometimes I thought I was dying without him. More than once I wished
I had never met him.

At the airport, finally, at 5:00 P.M. on December fifth, a clear,
bright Friday evening, my stomach hurt so much that I couldn't
stand still. I had to walk up and down, heart pounding, body pac-
ing out a circuit of the octagonal area by his gate. I went into the
bathrooms and came out again half a dozen times. Thick and foggy
with the leftover turkey, potatoes, dressing, pie. I'd meant not to eat
so much before he came, to be elegant and slim for him, but the
family situation had overcome me.

His flight was only forty minutes late—I suppose I'd been hoping it would be later. People streamed off the plane: families lug-
ging tagged strollers and piles of packages in bright red and green
paper, business people demonstrating by their walks and attitudes
that being in the air, on the ground, in New York or London or San
Francisco was all the same to them. A worldly wise superiority to
those traveling simply for pleasure.

Waiting for Jean-Pierre to step out of the gate, I scanned each
man. Most of them—self-absorbed, dramatic, sad and worn down by
daily life, full of rage, chunky, red-faced, or gaunt—were loved by
someone. Some woman, or some other man, waited with impatience
for the arrival of these men. In their alertness or apathy, humor, sly-
ness or nobility, they looked like animals: lion, chipmunk, orang-
utan, lizard, vulture, sheepdog. Many of them were being met,
women greeting them with short pecks on the cheek or long desperate or exhibitionistic kisses. It amazed me how much I was glad

none of the men, not even the ones who looked smart, funny, wide awake, belonged to me.

And then Jean-Pierre came out of the ramp into the gate area, looking around. His face looked thinner, long jaw and cheekbones standing out under his skin, purple shadows under his eyes. And he had an expression so infinitely sad I couldn't bear it. Depth. Substance. A terrible awareness, as if he inhabited two or three more dimensions than anyone around him. He had a fair amount of carry-on baggage, though not by African standards—one bag in each hand, another slung over his shoulder. When he saw me, his face eased and he almost smiled. He was so clearly the one, of all of them, that I wanted to be mine.

We swam toward each other through the crowd. He dropped the bags he was carrying, and I put my arms around his neck. A sign of the state he was in: he put his arms around my waist in return and dropped his face onto my shoulder. Or maybe he thought it didn't count, how he acted here in this foreign country. He looked like no one else at the gate. Even the American blacks looked more like the American whites than they did like him, because of his walk, his carriage, his expression.

We stood there, clinging to each other. He whispered something in Swahili, and then, said, in French, "Until I touched you, I thought you had to be dead too. At first I didn't believe they were dead. Now I no longer believe anyone to be alive. We're all ghosts."

I said, "Don't. Not yet." And then, despite myself, "I dream about her every night."

We kept our arms around each other on the way to the baggage claim, two ancient and frail creatures holding each other up. We got his luggage and went out to my car. It was hard to talk—our conversation was strained, our silences uncomfortable. He asked about the layout of the airport; I found out how his flights had been.

I drove us out onto the highway. What I'd rehearsed, over and over, was how it would be when we actually talked about his past, but I couldn't ask. Partially because of his look of terrible awareness, the purple shadows of grief, partially because he was so infinitely familiar and beloved, partially because I was simply embarrassed, afraid. And I couldn't put the two men together—couldn't reconcile my tired lover in the passenger seat of Lizzie's Volvo, leaning back and taking in the industrial sights of Highway 101, with the killing demon of my imagination and dreams, bayonet in hand, teeth bared, covered in blood.

He was looking away from me, out the window. "It is different than I imagined. No sense of history. All these giant hotels, warehouses—they look as if they were built last week. In Europe . . ." he didn't finish his sentence.

"This isn't San Francisco yet, not really. Highway 101 is famous for its ugliness. But there are some handsome houses at the southern edge of the city. We could drive along the waterfront, but I want to show you something else."

"One always has some image in mind. From the movies, perhaps, and then it is never what one expected." He sounded disappointed, already.

I said to him, "Just wait. You haven't seen anything yet. It could take days to show you this city. Don't draw any conclusions."

He shut his eyes for a moment. "Even in Burundi, the sky looks different; the trees look different. I am seeing through a ghost's eyes. The colors are gone. Nothing is interesting anymore. It is too much effort."

I put a hand on his knee. He wasn't as shocked by the mere fact of killing as I was—how could he be? But when I thought of my own grief, I couldn't imagine what he must feel. There was nothing to say. I squeezed his leg, to convey that I knew this. He covered my hand with his and opened his eyes again, looking around without interest.

I cut over to the rolling green hills of Highway 280, which led up to Nineteenth Avenue, the exquisite Mission two-story houses, the paint-flaking churches with signs in Chinese and Korean, the orange and white trolley lines. I took on the role of tour guide, saying things like, "In the 1980s, the Chinese replaced the Italians as the single largest group in San Francisco. The Italians really created North Beach—we'll see that tomorrow. This area is the Sunset district." Or, "All of this stretch is Golden Gate Park, part of San Francisco's national recreation area. Museums, lagoons, gardens."

Beside me sat the man over whom I'd been tearing my guts out for months, who had admitted he was a mass murderer (by my standards, not his own), and I was saying, "All through California you'll find entire neighborhoods of Spanish architecture. The Russians came to California to trap otter, but it was the Spanish who built the missions." I felt the old desire for him, but now it was mixed with fear, resistance, shame.

"Like the Catholics in Burundi. Missionaries in the U.S. How amazing. Preaching to Rambo." He leaned back, shutting his eyes. "You can even make me smile, a little."

I'd taken a room at The Glass Swan in San Francisco for a couple of nights. My idea was that he could rest up, and we could reconnect, before he had to meet my family, so we might as well do some sight-seeing. A European or American tourist would have been most interested in Fisherman's Wharf, the Golden Gate Bridge, the curving bricks and bright flower beds of Lombard Street, but Jean-Pierre wouldn't necessarily have the same stereotypes.

Instead, I'd take him for a boat ride in Golden Gate Park, walks through the Haight and into the Sunset district, down Market Street and the Tenderloin, with its homeless shelters and porn theaters. The beauties and dangers of my city, its heart-stopping cypresses and botanical gardens, its vivid, distinct neighborhoods and sad underbelly.

The Glass Swan wasn't far from the plush neighborhoods of

Russian Hill and the Marina, but it had its doors right on the noisy thoroughfare of Van Ness, which made it affordable. A small tree decorated with a few colored balls and some tinsel—a half-hearted concession to the season—sat in the lobby. A daughter of the house, somewhere in her early twenties, exquisite in a green T-shirt and sari, her forehead marked in red, turned the pages of the guest register and pushed it over to us to sign. "Checkout time is eleven A.M. If you need to keep the room longer, you will pay for an extra day." She handed us the key, on its huge red plastic marker. Before we left the room, she'd already turned back to her book, a paperback with a pirate and a swooning redhead on the cover.

About to be alone with Jean-Pierre, I messed around with the car, locking up, hiding things, taking in bags. Jean-Pierre carried in his big suitcase and collapsed backward on the bed. I took a long time to lock the door behind me. He watched me, his face unreadable.

I said, in a tone which sounded brightly, falsely social even to me, "I think I'll have a shower. Doesn't that sound like a good idea?"

He said, "Come here," and held out his arms. I went forward slowly. He pulled me down on top of him, and then rolled me over, onto my back, his weight on me, his lips on mine. I felt both desire and a sense of being suffocated. It wasn't clear to me how much of that had to do with his sour breath and the dried sweat of his long plane trip, how much from a moral loathing.

I kissed him back, not wanting him to know how removed I felt, hoping to get carried away. My sense of perspective was lost; it felt as horrifying to think that I might never again feel what I'd felt, that absolute, devouring desire and abandonment, as to think of the people he had killed. Tears leaked out of my eyes. His own eyes were closed—he tore open our clothes, pushing his way into me, painfully, because I was still dry. But he was desperate, hanging on with a grip that would leave bruises.

This brought me out of my self-centered preoccupation enough to understand that this was just as difficult for him. He was coming to me for comfort, for protection from himself and his emotions.

In response to this, I had another switch, a surge of protectiveness, of violent, ambivalent love, perhaps like the sexual response some women have at the moment of giving birth, following on all that pain. I had never felt this way about anyone before; if I trusted my instincts at all, then I had to begin to understand him, his life. Wasn't there some merit, at least from his point of view, in his belief that he was protecting his people?

Then I was horrified with myself. But if I weren't considering the possibility of his point of view having some validity, what was I doing with him?

He lay with his face in the pillow afterward, his arm flung across my belly. From the liquid sound of his breathing, I realized he was crying. He said, finally, "She was my heart. One can go on without anything else." I put my hand on his arm, almost afraid to bring myself to his attention. Was it possible that he would never again love anyone or anything better than her memory?

He went on, "What I think of, again and again, is that *I did this*. They had been staying with me. I was busy—I wanted them to go. If they'd stayed one more week, they would be alive now. Playing with the children, eating dinner, arguing, sitting in the sun. And we, *she,* should have been in Paris. Now she is a ghost. And so am I."

My own tears started again. I wanted to say, *It is inevitable that a survivor blames himself. You were not at fault. There's no way you could have known.* Even, *Maybe you will meet them in heaven or another life.* I thought of Christine saying, dryly, with her own particular smile, "I have failed to believe in heaven." I turned toward Jean-Pierre and opened my arms.

He crawled into them and put his forehead against my

breastbone. He whispered, "I am hurting you too. I can't stop, but I am sorry for it."

"I wish I could do something for you."

He said, "We cannot replace them," as if he were arguing with himself. Then, "What do you take to prevent children?"

"I'm on the pill."

"How soon can you stop?" His face showed a fierce, suffering hope, and I wondered if he were just picturing a continuation of the family line, or if he believed that Christine and Françoise could actually be reborn into our children.

I was saying, "You can't go straight from the pill into pregnancy," but he was on his own track, saying, "We couldn't have a family wedding. Not now. And there's my uncle." He was silent, thinking it over. "The worst he can be is angry. He needs my support, as I need his. So we could marry here, secretly."

"Las Vegas." He didn't understand, of course, and I said, "We can talk about this later." It was too soon to think again about marriage; my emotions were exhausted from the switches back and forth. But I was already picturing a real wedding, in the family gazebo. Not midwinter. Late June. Carved watermelons full of fruit salad. My friends in wide-brimmed hats and pastel dresses. I might go for a long off-white lace dress and flowers in my hair. But would summer be too late for Mom? Maybe we should have it sooner, after all. A Christmas wedding. Poinsettias and evergreens. White velvet.

Jean-Pierre, turning, let out a great sigh, and I blushed in the dark, ashamed of having left the real world for a fantasy of wedding-land. After a while we slept, painfully.

Then it was nine o'clock, and we were hungry enough to have Chinese food delivered. By eleven, we had gone back to bed. At some point, maybe around three, I became aware that we were both awake, lying side by side, only our legs touching. In the semidark, in this neutral room, it seemed possible to broach the subject. I whispered, "Jean-Pierre, there are things I have to . . . before our marriage. To know. Because I don't understand killing. I don't understand how a person can look into someone else's eyes and put an end to that other's life."

He was silent for quite a while. I wondered if he were pretending to be asleep, but then he turned his head to look at me, his eyes gleaming. Several times I almost broke the silence out of nervousness. At last he said, softly, "Your life has not taught you to understand that there are things that must be done. Your mother is vilely ill from her cancer. The treatments seem to make her worse. But, in fact, they are an attack on that element in her body which would otherwise destroy her. No matter how bad the symptoms of treatment may be, they are better than the destruction of the whole."

"How can you compare a human to a cancer cell?" I didn't say that I disagreed with the decision to give her chemo, which seemed a heartless way of ruining her last months.

"Ah-na, you do not think logically. It is essential to have perspective, or you lose yourself in a kind of weak pity and then the whole country may be lost."

The Hutus thought of the ruling Tutsis as the cancer, but I couldn't say so. "But to be able to actually do it."

His silence this time was even longer. Then, "I will only say, you do not see in the normal way at these times, you are not in an ordinary state. It astonishes me that you don't understand this—am I talking to a sophisticated, professional woman or to a child? To do what it must, the human has evolved mechanisms, including a kind of eagerness for battle. I don't want to talk any longer tonight, Ah-na. I am too tired."

So I left it alone, but when I went back to sleep, I dreamed of him as a child, his fascinated pleasure in watching the guards kill the black mamba.

I woke up again, my heart slamming inside me, and touched his arm. His face went from its peaceful relaxation to the waking

Jean-Pierre, the man I didn't know, but was going to marry? I shut my eyes, hoping he'd think it was an accident, that I was asleep.

/   /   /

When we awoke in the morning, we were entwined and having sex almost before we were awake, a sleepy, sweaty, side-by-side encounter, with him behind me. Our bodies had been adjusting to each other while we slept, and we were hungry for each other.

About noon, we got up, showered, ate the leftover Hunan pork and lemon chicken, and went out sight-seeing. Putting off meeting the family, buying privacy to work things out. But what? I hadn't even settled the question of whether I owed it to my family to tell them what I'd learned. It wasn't as if he were going to go amok and kill everyone over breakfast. I noticed that I had somehow *incorporated* my new knowledge of him.

We walked through the Outer Haight and went into two bookstores, then a third, coming out with poetry, history, novels, an English-language dictionary. "Let us look at rings," he said. So we went into jewelry stores, and I tried on diamonds, sapphires, and rubies, emerald-cut, brilliant, pear-shaped, set alone or flanked by other stones. I felt a little as if I were dreaming, floating along down a river and admiring the wild trees along the banks.

He liked a one-carat brilliant-cut diamond in bright yellow gold, a clawlike setting with four tiny diamonds around it, but it seemed gaudy to me. I couldn't imagine wearing it. I liked a cabochon ruby that lay in its platinum band like a pool of deep red water, but he said it reminded him of blood. I hadn't thought of that, but as soon as he said it, I pulled off the ring and handed it back to the politely disapproving jeweler.

I said, "Let's leave the ring question for a while and go back to sight-seeing, shall we?"

Boutiques, bead shops, novelty stores. In one bead shop, I found a basket full of charms against the evil eye in all different sizes, ankhs, women's symbols, Stars of David, Ethiopian and Western crosses, but I didn't buy any of it. I did buy Jean-Pierre a maroon pullover sweater for the cold winter nights. Despite anything I'd said, he'd been picturing a California of palm trees and bright blue swimming pools, girls in Malibu, Hollywood stars. He had a raincoat, some Belgian equivalent of Brooks Brothers, with him, but it wouldn't be warm enough, so he bought, at my insistence, a U.S. Navy pea jacket from a surplus store, in which he was so gorgeous that I wanted to ravish him right there.

We stood on Parnassus, looking down at the city, and he said, as if he had been listening to my thoughts, "Either this is a dream, or my real life is a dream."

"My sister Lizzie, my younger sister—"

"Aurora's mother."

I loved that he'd paid such close attention to my stories about my family. "Aurora's mother. Who does the past-life regressions. She'd say we were working off karma. That buried memories of all the pain will emerge in future lives, in dreams or bodily sensations that we won't understand, but which will gradually, over time, remove all of the poison."

He shaded his eyes, looking toward the ocean. The city lay neatly spread out in every direction: steep streets full of Victorians rolled down to the park below us—dark green trees, lakes and ponds, hills and meadows. "A part of me would like to believe that, to curl up in it and be comforted, but another part, my real self, resists it. It makes me angry, in fact. It trivializes life and diminishes their deaths."

"Do you think I want to diminish their deaths?"

"No." He put his arms around me again and I leaned against him, eyes shut, smelling his warm familiar skin, feeling my heart unclench. After a few minutes, he said, "I never imagined marrying anywhere but Burundi." My heart jumped, but he went on, "When you come home for good, though, it would be better if you were already my wife."

Although I wanted to say, "I *am* home for good," California was too new to him. How could he imagine settling down in a place he had only been for a day?

I took him over into the Haight for dinner, and we stuffed ourselves with tapas at ChaChaCha. All around us, the tables and booths were filled with artistic types. Elaborate Caribbean altars covered the walls. We didn't exactly fit in with the crowd, but we didn't exactly stand out either.

Jean-Pierre put his hands over his eyes. He said, "It does and doesn't remind me of Paris. I feel like a man from another planet." And then, "I think I've eaten too much. Let's go somewhere with very loud music where we will be unable to think for the rest of the night."

/   /   /

The next morning, I woke to Jean-Pierre running his hand slowly over my shoulders, nipples, belly, thighs—the lightest touch, which brought my nerves alive as it passed. The movements of that knowing, authoritative hand on my skin triggered waves of small, fierce orgasms, and I turned onto my side, facing him, bringing my hand to his chest, matching his movements. A picture rose in my mind— the hand that touched me holding a bayonet, stabbing forward, the ripping of flesh, spatter of blood. I shut my eyes, swallowing, trying to think of Jean-Pierre himself, of our lovemaking in Africa.

He put his lips on mine. The worry that I'd taste sour from sleep brought me back to the present. Jean-Pierre, still kissing me, rolled me onto my back, and I wrapped my arms and legs around him, bringing him closer, pressing him into me with the flats of my hands.

Afterward, I lay on his shoulder. I said, "I think I've lost something I might never get back, the sense that I could made a decision to carry out some work, and that my work would then help people, would matter to the world. And I don't know what or where I am without it." He lay beside me, watching me with his beautiful, serious eyes.

I put out a hand to touch his cheek. "I know how trivial this problem is, one woman, in no danger, worrying about whether she is useful. And yet, that's part of the problem too, that nothing I do or feel seems to matter, not compared to their deaths." I stopped, afraid of hurting him, raw with the fear of what I was putting into words. Jean-Pierre began to stroke my hair, listening, the steadiness of his touch indicating that he was listening to me, no matter what I had to say.

"In Washington, D.C., the people I took food to?"

"After you finished graduate school."

"Yes. We never acknowledged it, but they and I were always aware that what I had, what I knew, I had never earned. Some people were resentful, and I thought they were right to be. But I was quite sure I could and should help. And yet, I always felt stupid with them because of what they knew about the world and I didn't, the huge holes in my understanding." I whispered, "I think some of the blank areas have been filled in. But the price was too high."

/   /   /

We went out and rented a boat in Golden Gate Park, in the morning fog, and pedaled around the artificial lagoon with its ducks and waterfalls, cypresses and turtles. Jean-Pierre had the air of merely going through the motions; this inspired me to greater efforts as a guide. We ate our picnic lunch in the park, watching the couples necking in the grass; by then the fog had burned off, and the winter sun was out.

Jean-Pierre said, "They feel very free. Or perhaps invisible."

"This is a large country. Full of strangers who don't notice you, one way or the other. You can do whatever you please. San Francisco, particularly, is famous for this."

"They feel no obligation to the social structure." He indicated the couples around us with one disapproving hand.

Stretching out on the ground, I propped myself up on my elbows. I was wishing that he would stop talking, would roll me onto my back and kiss me, as if we were teenagers—though many of the couples were in their twenties or thirties. A man with a long gray ponytail, bandanna headband, and earrings kissed a blond boy in his twenties. A pair of women with matching magenta haircuts and silver nose rings tickled each other, laughing.

I said, "There are obligations. Mostly financial. If you want to eat and live under a roof. Or parental—children imposing structure by their helplessness, their needs. Still, people have some choice about how they arrange their personal lives. The triumph of the imagination. We submit less to necessity here than anywhere." I left it at that, not wanting to pound too hard, letting him think it over for himself.

We walked through the park, along the paths of the botanical gardens, into the conservatory, entering its warm, misty air and admiring the orchid show under the white dome, then out into the inner Sunset, where we bought bags full of dim sum, croissants, and piroshki. Students, old people, secretaries, and UCSF professors waited on corners for streetcars. The street lamps shone with tinsel; the store windows were full of holiday displays. One eyeless ebony mannequin in a red hat and fur boots leaned forward, hand posed at the mouth to blow a kiss to passersby.

We walked down Haight, examining sex shops, record stores, antiques, nightclubs, fabric stores, clothing boutiques of leather and lace. Spiked leather collars. Bustiers dripping with white ostrich feathers. In one store, an altar to Cher filled an alcove over a mirror, but the effect was somewhat lost on Jean-Pierre, who didn't know who she was. That surprised me. But he only read those sections of the newspaper that had to do with politics, business, agriculture, world prices of coffee and copper, shifts in economic climate. As far as our culture went, he knew some classic novels, mostly French, and then those icons pushed in his face even back in Africa: Rambo, Mickey Mouse, Clint Eastwood, Michael Jackson.

"What about this store?" he asked. Ravenna Fine Jewelry. The rings were arranged by stones—diamonds, emeralds, rubies, sapphires. We walked around, examining the cases. By now we had developed an eagle eye, though neither of us actually knew much about jewelry.

"That sapphire," I said. A star sapphire set in platinum, another cabochon, very beautiful, very expensive.

"Yes," said Jean-Pierre, and when it went onto my hand, it looked as if it belonged there, as if I had been weirdly naked without it all these years. I couldn't bear to take it off. The jeweler said they would size it for us; we could have it back in three days. Jean-Pierre said he would buy it only if we could take it at once. The jeweler, looking both annoyed and resigned, went into the back of the store, where we could hear him arguing. He said to us when he emerged that we could take it if we would wait half an hour.

We went outside and walked up and down the block. I wanted to ask, Are we engaged? We had never exactly had either a proposal or an acceptance. When our children asked . . . but would our children ask? Had I ever asked Mom? What would I tell my family? I could say that it had happened in San Francisco, which was true enough.

It was getting on toward rush hour. We collected the ring, and, to make up for all the sights we hadn't seen, I drove the long way, over to the financial district, past the TransAmerica Pyramid, around Union Square, then through Chinatown, both of us eating pastry and goodies from our bags while I inched us through the traffic, and out again, down Lombard Street, and out to the bridge, just in time for another amazing sunset.

We sat in a long line of cars crawling toward the toll gate. At every moment, I was conscious of the ring on my hand. I said, "You wouldn't be getting the California experience without commute traffic." This was almost the first negative thing I'd said, in a day of pointing out beauties, advantages, calling his attention to our wonders. I had become a real estate agent, not for any one house, but for a whole life.

"Will you think me very rude if I sleep through it?" His eyes were already closing.

I said, "You've done brilliantly for a man with jet lag," but he didn't hear me. I looked at his beautiful face, now uninhabited, as if he'd gone a long way off, and wondered if he himself had any idea how many people he'd killed.

My mouth filled with acid-tasting liquid. I swallowed and looked out the window at the BMW next to me, the frowning driver talking into his car phone. Just ahead of me, a pickup truck with three teenagers—a boy driving, his girlfriend nuzzled into his shoulder, another friend—shot into the space between two cars, then nipped forward a few feet, tailgating. This left me behind an old VW van with bumper stickers which read, "Another Mother for Peace," and "My Other Car Is a Broom." The whole back engine compartment was covered with Green Party stickers from the last election.

Beside me, Jean-Pierre sighed and shifted, turning, resting his cheek on his hand like a child. I took deep breaths, counting, in and out. *And one, and two, and three, and four.* The man in the BMW was shouting into the car phone, pounding his wheel for emphasis.

Jean-Pierre, waking briefly, gave me a tender, serious look that dispelled all the nightmare images. I put my hand on his knee, feeling the comfort of his body, even through his clothes. My other hand, with its star sapphire, rested on the steering wheel. Jean-

Pierre said, sleepily, "My Ahna," as if solving a mathematical problem to his own satisfaction, but almost at once the terrible, shadowed expression returned, and he slid back all the way into sleep while I silently rehearsed how I was going to introduce him to my family.

Thirteen

We got to Mom's house just after eight. Lizzie ran out to the porch, drying her hands on her skirt. The children followed her. Susan crossed her arms, leaning against a pillar. Aurora and Bobby let the screen door bang behind them, peering at us from behind Susan's legs.

Jean-Pierre got out, steady and polite, and leaned against the car, determined in the face of his jet lag. Just ten minutes before, I'd reluctantly awakened him, saying, "I'm sorry, love, but we're getting close." Without complaint, he'd straightened his clothes, buttoned up his shirt collar, and washed his face with bottled water. Now he was his most friendly official self—the man I'd first seen at the reception where we met.

I was worrying about what my family might say or do to embarrass me. I made myself open my door and stand up, smiling for their benefit, but they were all looking at Jean-Pierre. Lizzie came down the steps, holding out her hand. "You must be Jean-Pierre. Welcome to California. I'm Annie's sister Lizzie." She had a certain shy dignity, the hostess. I'd warned him about first names, but he was used to Americans.

"Where's his crown?" Bobby asked, audibly, before Susan shushed him. I was hoping Jean-Pierre hadn't heard. At that moment it seemed to me that I'd hardly ever done or said anything that wasn't inadvisable at best and recklessly stupid at worst. And, oh, God, why had I said a single word to my sisters about our sex life? What if someone made a joke?

Jean-Pierre said, "It is very kind of you to have me." His English sounded slow and rich, complicated in tone, as if he were offering secrets, but didn't want them fully understood. "And here are the children."

"More or less." She turned and said to them, "Why don't you come down and meet Aunt Annie's friend?" They edged down the steps, and she introduced them.

Susan, in an outfit it was much too cold for—sandals, a black tank-dress and semitransparent overshirt—had goose bumps on her arms and legs. She put out her hand, her eyes unblinking, as if memorizing him. "I am *so* glad to meet you. It's really boring around here, but I hope you'll like it anyway." Then she turned red, the family blush.

Bobby said to Jean-Pierre, who was squatting to shake his hand, "I thought you would have a crown and grass skirt like the king at the museum."

"You have a king in your museum?"

Lizzie said, "Oh, Bobby," and then, to Jean-Pierre, "An exhibit of African culture in San Francisco. I'm afraid we're very far from the rest of the world here."

"We are very far from each other," he said. Bobby was waiting. Jean-Pierre said to him, "But I'm not a king, you know, and even the king would dress in another manner now. As Western kings do. You also are not dressed as I expected. Where are your cowboy boots and hat? Where is your bronco?"

I said to him, "Wow, what have you been reading?" Bobby ducked his head, rolling his eyes and clucking with a mixture of pleasure, exasperation, and embarrassment. A certain resignation to the stupidity of adults.

Lizzie said, "It's cold out here, and you must be exhausted. Why don't we go in?"

Everyone had something to carry—baggage, packages and bags of food, parcels of books. When I handed Lizzie Jean-Pierre's carry-on, she saw my left hand for the first time. She looked as if she had been slapped. "What is *that*?" she whispered.

"What it looks like," I whispered back.

Her eyes filled with tears, and she kissed my cheek. "Congratulations, I'm very happy for you," she said, giving her best imitation of happiness before turning to go into the house.

We trooped inside behind her. I was seeing the house as if through the eyes of a critical stranger. Jean-Pierre's own house was so much bigger, and though it was shabby in the way that most Burundian houses are—cracked plaster, broken plumbing (amazing, in Burundi, to have plumbing at all)—it had such grandeur, with its fine paintings, architectural sweep, the twelve-foot ceilings. Even with geckos running up the walls, across the ceilings, even with four kinds of ants marching up and down the halls.

My mother's house looked dusty, cluttered, full of mismatched furniture, the walls hung with framed photographs of family and prints of calendar-style landscapes, the tables covered with knick-knacks from trips to Yosemite or L.A., weddings or births—a family code, indecipherable to outsiders. I thought, sometimes, of how much work it was going to be to sort through all Mom's stuff. The Christmas tree was up already, not yet decorated, oddly naked and out of place in the fussy room.

We filed into the kitchen. We used the living room for television or sulking; the kitchen was the room we lived in. Margaret, at the dish rack, turned around and put down her towel. She did what no one else had been able to—she walked straight up to Jean-Pierre, took his hand in hers, and, looking him in the eye, said slowly, with both restraint and feeling, "I'm Margaret. Annie told us about your family. I am so very sorry."

He covered her hand with his other hand, saying only, "Thank you," but with such dignity and sadness that my eyes filled again. The two of them had a *bruised* look, and they held on to each other's hands as if they recognized something in each other.

She said, "If there's anything we can do."

"There is nothing anyone can do. But I am grateful for your kindness."

"Just let us know. We're plain people, not very sophisticated, so we don't know your ways. If we do something that offends, it's not on purpose. And if we can make you more comfortable here, that's what we want to do." She was dealing with this better than any of us. She was *like* him, in her essential self, and I could see him acknowledging this.

He said, "I see that it is not only in Burundi that the Americans are very kinder than the French." He'd said to me, once, that Americans were more badly educated than the French or Belgians, but on the whole much kinder. Margaret was getting the edited version. I could see that he was prepared to be a hero, to sit and talk in English, which was failing him in his exhaustion.

I was worried about her response to the ring, but she didn't appear to notice it. I said, "Jean-Pierre's had a long plane ride"—I was going to say, "and a short night," but, for once, thought before I spoke. "And I've been dragging him all over the city. Let's let him meet Mom and then rest up."

Margaret said, "Mom's gone to bed. You can see her in the morning."

Susan said, "I'll help carry your things." She'd been trying, and failing, not to stare at Jean-Pierre. He seemed to take it in stride. On the way to the room he and I would be sharing, she said to him, "Were you ever in the U.S. before?"

"Never. Does that surprise you?" He spoke to her as if she were an adult. Despite his exhaustion and grief, he could still focus on her with his own particular awareness.

"It must be so weird, seeing all this for the first time." Her intensity made me uncomfortable. Swinging from right to left, she spotted my ring, picked up my hand, and said, "Whoa. That's so pretty. Is that a real sapphire?" I nodded. "You didn't have that before, did you? Is that . . . ?" She appeared to be on the point of asking whether we were engaged, but stopped short. Perhaps our faces gave her the answer. She kept looking from one to the other of us, speculatively, evaluating us as a couple. It was inevitable that the family would, but it still made me feel naked. I wished this could have happened earlier, before I knew so much about him, before he had become inhabited by grief.

"So, I have to go *talk* to some people," she said, and took off. When we were alone, Jean-Pierre said, in French and Swahili, "Your family seems very nice. Very welcoming."

"An introduction to the peasantry of the United States."

He gave me an odd look, and I was ashamed of my disloyalty. I was also feeling how far out of my league he was. My whole exposure to aristocracy, before Burundi, had been old paintings, British novels. His life was another world. Could he get used to the U.S.? I had to show him what peace could be like. I also wanted to say something about my mother, but her dying now seemed such a natural event. I felt a mix of emotions, including anger at being robbed of the chance to feel the genuine weight of her incipient death. Burundi had made all of our lives irrelevant.

We shut the door behind us and began stowing his luggage in the closet, under the bed, in dressers. I had noticed it before—how well we worked together. How our rhythms matched. I thought, *Is this what's important?* In Africa, you married someone selected for you by your family, though even that was changing. I thought it was too much responsibility to choose your own mate. Why else are book-

stores full of instructional manuals on love and what it means and
how to make it work and why it's gone wrong?

As if he'd read my mind, he said, "I do think it would be better
to marry now. While I am here. Is this possible?"

"And then separate?"

"Only until we have calm again in Burundi. And, as my wife,
you can return much earlier than the other Americans."

I sat on the bed and put my knees up under my chin. "Did you
like San Francisco?"

Jean-Pierre said, "I liked paddling. In the park. The ducks under the waterfall. Those black trees. Like a Japanese painting." And
then, "No, I didn't enjoy it, not enough. I'm sorry I can't be better
company, Ah-na." He sat down beside me and took my hand.

I wrapped my arms around him. "You don't have to be my en-
tertainment committee. But, Jean-Pierre, I want a real wedding.
This isn't the time for a celebration."

"No. The marriage we could have now. Quietly. But a celebration? I don't know. Maybe much later. I can't think of it. I don't even
want to enjoy anything. Since they can't."

I rubbed the sides of my cheeks against him, like a cat marking
its territory. His shirt was starchy against my face. He said, "I am
dead of fatigue." Then his face changed, and we both pretended not
to notice. He undressed slowly and got into bed. "Your sister Margaret is a very strong woman, isn't she? Very admirable. You are
lucky."

I don't think my hesitation was noticeable. I said, "I have always
looked up to her."

"A little like Françoise." And then, turning toward the wall,
"Oh, God."

I stretched out behind him, putting my arms around him and
stroking his shoulder and arm. "Does anyone know what happened
to her?"

"When the Hutus want revenge, nothing stops them."

There was a short silence. Then I whispered, "Do you want revenge?"

He turned around, so fast I felt him as a blur of motion, and then he was on top of me, pinning my arms to my sides with his elbows, looking down into my face. I could only just see the light of his eyes, the outline of his head. He said, very low, "You want to know. Well, then. Yes. I want revenge. I want to tear out their livers and make them eat the raw meat, piece by piece. To force it down their throats. That's what I *want*. What I will do, what I have always done, is what is necessitated by the best interests of Burundi."

My heart beat louder, my breathing tightening, but my body, shifting under him, began to press against him, opening up. The bodies had their own conversation—his growing erection pushed painfully into my hip.

"You have always acted only rationally." I said it flatly.

He took hold of my hair and pulled it back, tipping my throat up. I didn't resist. He whispered into my ear, "What is rational? Was I afraid? Have I taken pleasure in what I've done? Is there a moment when you strike your enemy and you feel his blood on you and you want to howl with glee?" He slid inside me, and my body convulsed so strongly that, for a moment, I couldn't hear him. "What is it you want to know, Ah-na? Is it the pleasure? Is it your imagining of what happened? Do you want me to take you with me?"

"No," I said. I was hanging on to him, in the grip of a terrible arousal.

"You want to know if it is sensible to marry me? Or do you want to know what a human feels in some moment you have always been too protected to know? Is that it? Am I your teacher?"

I said, *"Jean-Pierre."*

"You think you care about honesty? You don't care. You want to know what intestines look like as they spill on the ground. Gray and

slick, like great snakes of brain." He moved slowly, full of purpose—
I was mad with it. Tears of shame, anger, and sensation leaked out
of my eyes. I couldn't distinguish pleasure from pain.

His breathing thickened. "No, I have never talked about it."

I couldn't move my arms, but I pressed my face against his in
tenderness and wild triumph. I was seeing his naked self—he had finally given himself to me. I bit his shoulder to keep from groaning.

He pushed faster and faster, his head thrown back, teeth bared,
and then he gave a cry and collapsed forward. I felt his tears on my
neck. Very soon, he pulled out, turned to the wall, and put his arms
over his head, crooking his elbows, stopping his ears. When I said
his name, he refused to respond.

/ / /

In the morning, we were awkward together, not wanting to talk
even about small things, unable to meet each other's eyes. His dis-
comfort infected me, leaving me alone with my struggle with fear
and self-hatred, my understanding that I loved him at least partially
because of the raw violence in him. The dark creature in me had oblit-
erated the righteous, clear-headed one.

We went down to breakfast in silence. The family had planned
a party to go to the beach. My sisters discussed it over breakfast; we
tried to join in. Our strain must have shown, but maybe they assumed we'd had an ordinary fight or that Jean-Pierre was shy.

"It'll be good to get out of the house," said Margaret, and we all
nodded. When we first came into the room, she had looked at my
hand, shook her head briefly, but said nothing. Either Lizzie or Susan, probably Lizzie, must have said something.

I asked, "How's Mom?"

"Not too lousy. She wants to go to the beach with us. She's missing the ocean. And she wants to see both of you this morning." To
Jean-Pierre, her tone full of meaning, she said, "She's looking forward to meeting you."

He hadn't been following exactly, but he smiled and said, "Yes, very much." I put my hand under the table, on his knee, to let him know he wasn't alone here. He didn't move away. Right after breakfast, we went up to Mom's room for a formal audience. She was restless, still hurting, but a little more energetic and clear-headed. The doctor had changed her pain medication, which helped. She lay against her pillows, holding a Kleenex with one hand, shredding it with the other. Her face was sharper, thinner than ever before, the bones standing out under her pale skin. She'd lost more than twenty-five pounds since the chemo had started, and she hadn't had it to lose. Margaret had taken her to the beauty parlor two days earlier; her gray hair now fell onto her cheeks and forehead in strange little poodle curls.

She said to Jean-Pierre, "What do you think of the United States?"

I said, "Mom, he's only been here one day. Are you asking for an inclusive opinion? Should he tell you about Wyoming, New York, Missouri, North Carolina?"

Jean-Pierre said, "I find the people very kind."

When I'd first gotten to Burundi and was still in shock over the depth of the poverty and illness around me, the restrictions of life, the palpable tensions between Hutu and Tutsi, I'd said, when asked what I thought of Burundi, that I found the people very kind.

My mother said, "We have some good cows here. Annie here says your people value cattle. We also grow apples, did Annie tell you that?"

"We had your daughter Margaret's cooked apples this morning."

"Applesauce," I said. He smiled briefly, accepting the correction, not meeting my eyes. The room still smelled of illness, though we'd filled it with bouquets of flowers. It looked like a funeral to me. I remembered Christine saying, about a mutual acquaintance, "Don't you think he is so *morbid*?"

My mother had had Margaret's applesauce, along with some

toast and cottage cheese, on a tray in her room; the remains of it sat off to one side. "She's a pretty good cook, the best of any of you." She frowned when she thought of Margaret. But surely she wouldn't get into it in front of Jean-Pierre? After a moment, she went on, with a spark of malice, "Lizzie was more musical. Liked to tap-dance, as a child." And then, to Jean-Pierre, "Louis Armstrong. Maybe you dance yourself?"

Lizzie had never tap-danced to Louis Armstrong. She'd had this Fred Astaire record. I was in pain, even though, of course, Jean-Pierre had no idea who Louis Armstrong was. He was looking puzzled. I said, "We're only half an hour from the beach, but it's been months since we went."

Jean-Pierre, feeling, with his quick perception of situations, that I needed help, joined me. "Ah-na tells me that your beach is very different. She says I will find it cold."

Mom said, "Maybe not in the summer. If you come back." She gave him a sharp little look. "But I expect you'll be visiting somewhere else next year. Maybe you like variety."

I stood up, weak-legged with rage, and took Jean-Pierre's hand. "Mom, we're going to go get ready for the beach now."

She shrugged. "It's a funny thing about death. When you get close enough, things don't matter so much. You wonder what you spent your life making a fuss over." She waved one thin hand. "It's only for the living that death is a problem." Her tone changed, became brisker. "Go away, you two. Someone wake me when it's time to go."

On the way down the stairs, I thought, for the first time, about returning to Burundi. I was an outsider, a foreigner there, but no one had any particular enmity toward Americans. Bringing Jean-Pierre here meant plunging him into a ready-made network of traps, ugliness, racism. Which he would know about from Paris. But it was worse here, in many ways. Maybe I had no right to try to get him to move here. Could I go back to Burundi? Unimaginable.

Jean-Pierre said to me, "She reminds me of you, your mother."
I hated that. "How?"

"She is right there with you. You don't get away with anything."
Since she had uttered almost nothing but banalities, I wondered
how he had arrived at this. He went on, "I think she is an extremely
complicated woman."

This opened up for me the whole of the night before. I said, after a few moments, "So, what do you think of the 49ers' chances at
the Super Bowl this year?"

He wrinkled his brow at me. "Very good," he said. "Excellent."
Then he waited to see if I would give a hint as to what we were talking about.

/   /   /

Downstairs, there was, of course, a fight going on. In our family, it
takes a good three hours to get ready to go on a picnic. I have friends
who can get ready for two weeks in London or Istanbul, Bogotá or
Nairobi, in less time. When Jean-Pierre and I came into the kitchen,
we found Lizzie saying, in tones as cross as she ever used, "Oh, let's
eat nothing but beer and potato chips, then. Pesticide sandwiches."
She wore tie-dyed leggings and a huge pullover sweater with black
terriers marching across the front. She had her sleeves pushed up and
was chopping at a pile of broccoli and cauliflower with energy. Her
silver earrings swung down to her neck.

Margaret's face was pinched together, puffy. "If you think that I
have the slightest interest in sand-flavored tofu sandwiches with
those damn organic radish sprouts . . ."

Jean-Pierre was watching with interest. They both stopped
when they saw him, smiling brightly. Did he seem arrogant to
them? I wished that they could have met him before—I wanted to
ask them all to remember to make allowances.

We seated ourselves at the kitchen table, and Jean-Pierre said,
"Please don't worry yourselves." He sat patiently, one hand crossed

over the other, shivering a little, despite his sweater. His blood not yet thick enough for the change in weather.

Bobby was playing with a truck on the floor, vrooming it into the wall and then making a siren noise for it as it flipped over. He didn't have an ambulance, but he did have a fire truck, which rushed repeatedly to the scene of the accident. Accidents. "Fire!" he shouted, and Aurora echoed him. She then bound up the victims, her Barbies, which had once been Susan's, and sang to them, rocking them, "Rock-a-bye, rock-a-bye." Jerry blew through the room with an armful of towels, a portable radio, parkas.

Lizzie went to the cupboard and began getting out pickles. She said to Jean-Pierre, "Oh, we weren't saying anything important." She waggled her eyebrows at me, getting me off into a passageway. Jean-Pierre watched us go.

When she had me alone, she asked, "Will he eat a sandwich?"

I don't know what I'd been expecting. I said, "He's not a picky eater."

"I'd like to give him something he'd be comfortable with."

"Comfort's not a Burundian concept."

She gave me a look, as if I were being difficult, and stalked back into the kitchen. I followed. I hadn't seen Susan all morning, and didn't want to inflame anyone by asking.

Jerry came stamping into the kitchen. "It is *cold* out there." I was furious with Jerry, who'd said at breakfast, in front of everyone but Jean-Pierre, who'd gone back to the room for his sweater, "Of course she's going to marry an African. It figures. Count yourselves lucky the guy doesn't have a bone in his nose." Now Jerry was packing the car. His procedure was to put everything in, then take it all out again at least once, making an ordeal of fitting it together just so. "Other people go to the beach in the summer."

"It's more of an experience in the winter," Margaret said, and Lizzie said, "We're going to be at one with nature, except for seven layers of sweaters and coats."

Jerry said to Jean-Pierre, "You going to be warm enough?"

"Not, perhaps, before I must leave," said Jean-Pierre. "In Paris I passed months before habituating myself, but I had arrived in autumn. It was very cold, also inside. The French do not allow themselves heat until the proper time. They are very regulated."

"I guess it's about a hundred and ten degrees in Africa right now."

Jean-Pierre was working out the conversion to centigrade. I said, "Parts of Africa. In Bujumbura, it's probably about seventy. It's on the equator, but fairly cool because of the altitude. It's also the rainy season now." I'd told Jerry about Burundi's climate, but he was evidently imagining Kenyan plains full of lions and zebra. Or else some kind of jungle.

Margaret was making two piles of sandwiches, one with chicken, the other vegetarian. Lizzie had an eye to see that not too much mayonnaise got into those. She was doing peanut butter swirls for the kids. I said to Margaret, "We'll have to go in two cars. Maybe you guys should take Mom. Jean-Pierre and I'll go with Lizzie and Aurora."

Bobby ran the truck into the wall and cried out, "Fire! Everyone is dead!" Aurora waved her Barbie in the air, shouting after him, "Fire! Fire!"

Margaret said to them, "Go watch some television. Educate your young minds. And no sound on the commercials." Bobby was very good with a remote control, but the children were forbidden to watch commercials, and so found them desperately attractive.

Jerry said, "What are you guys *doing* with that lunch? I swear this is going to be a summer trip after all. Or maybe we'll just spend Christmas at the beach."

Lizzie was now bagging up organic baby carrots, sacks of organic prunes, raisins, dates. Margaret, cutting the sandwiches into triangles, said, "Maybe you have some dentist appointment at the beach? What are you so worried about? We'll get there before dark. Annie, go and get Mom up. Tell her we're leaving in fifteen minutes."

/ / /

It took another hour to get out the door, everyone trying to avoid a major fight in front of a guest. Susan, counting on the family desire to appear civilized, had casually appeared with Danny at the front door, announcing that they were meeting us at the beach and which one were we going to? Danny wasn't what I'd expected. Tall, pale, slightly hunched, hair falling over one eye, a vulnerable and transparent aggression. His motorcycle jacket hung on him, and he dangled a helmet with lightning bolts in the other hand. I wanted to poke Margaret, to ask how bad it could be if he wore a helmet. After they left, Margaret had to fight tears of rage.

I said to her, "This is a good thing. She wants to have him included in the family. Wouldn't you prefer this to her disappearing altogether? Be careful. This may be a limited time offer."

Jerry said, "If there is any *sign* of drugs, I'm going to beat the little bastard to death."

Jean-Pierre was silent through all of this. I thought he hadn't picked up on it, but in the car, with Lizzie concentrating on the road and me pointing out apple orchards, gorgeous, fat cattle eating in placid abundance, and stands of eucalyptus, he spoke up. "Is your brother going to beat this boy? Do you agree with this?" Lizzie and I exchanged glances in the rearview mirror. Aurora had gone to sleep in her seat.

I said, in French, to make life easier, "Not my brother. My sister's husband. He thinks, we think, Susan is too young to have a lover, and Danny is a bad influence. They were caught doing illegal drugs."

"How old is she?"

"Thirteen."

Jean-Pierre thought this over. I said to Lizzie, "I told him about the drugs."

"We should syndicate. *Love and Death in the Apple Orchards.*" As soon as she said it, she grimaced at herself, shaking her head. Jean-Pierre was looking out the window. He said, as if he hadn't heard, "So much uncultivated land."

/   /   /

The beach surprised him too, the wildness of it. The sheer length of the sand as it stretched out under the cliffs, the cold, gray-green water whipping up and crashing against the shore, the wind blowing the dune grass flat. He turned in all directions, wrapping himself more tightly in his jacket, his face amazed. I was suffering, though I didn't say anything. The sand, the water—these were going to remind me forever of Christine. I had begun to suspect just how long she would be with me. I remembered her in the sand, stretching, her smile both contented and ironic. *Christine me manque.* Christine is missing from me. And from the whole rest of the world, which, apparently, doesn't give a damn about what it's lost. Except for Jean-Pierre.

I wiped my face with my arm—the family either didn't notice, assumed that the wind was making my eyes water, or chose to let it alone. We lumbered under our burdens of ice chest, blankets, baskets and bags of food, staggering against the wind like an inept and overloaded bunch of nomads. We had a particular hollow, halfway behind a dune, from which we could see the ocean but be protected against the worst of the wind. The beach was almost empty, except for an old couple walking into the wind, two or three pairs of lovers snuggled into dune hollows.

Mom lay down first, on her own blanket; we helped her wrap up well. Her face was gray from the walk between the car and our spot, and her breathing sounded harsh, painful. Susan and Danny arrived while we were still spreading out blankets and towels, anchoring them against the wind with the weight of drinks, paper bags full of vegetables, chips and cookies.

"Hi," he said, sitting cross-legged on the sand, not in the charmed circle of our blankets. "Hey, sour cream and onion, cool." He began tearing into one of the bags of chips. Susan, raising her eyebrows at us, belligerent, sat beside him, taking a handful of potato chips herself. But she looked annoyed, almost wifely: embarrassed, resentful, defensive all at once.

"*Potato* chips!" cried Bobby, and Margaret came in right away with, "After your sandwich." She handed around plastic plates and sandwiches, while Lizzie poured out drinks into red plastic cups, scratched from years of reuse. Jerry lay down, hands behind his head, and then, after a moment, so did Jean-Pierre.

Bobby watched Jean-Pierre, humming to himself. When Jean-Pierre's eyes were closed, Bobby laid one quick finger on Jean-Pierre's hand, and then so did Aurora. Jean-Pierre opened his eyes and smiled at them. They both drew back, giggling. Once, in the airport in Buj, a tiny Burundian in a lacy dress and pigtails had touched my sandaled foot, to see if it were as cold as it looked. It was a rainy day and my skin was, in fact, clammy; I thought that forever afterward she would think of *wazungu* as having this texture. A bunch of salamanders.

Margaret was trying not to stare at Danny, but her face was red and her mouth muttered at the sandwiches as she pulled them out of their plastic bags. Susan had cuddled up against Danny's leg, as if he were a fire and she were warming herself. He had one hand on her thigh, proprietary, defiant, very young.

Mom refused a sandwich. Her breathing had stabilized, though, so she was able to sit up eventually and look at the ocean. All around her, we were tearing into our sandwiches, crunching on pickles and olives, talking about the chips. There was an argument about MSG, whether it was inherently bad for you or only if you were allergic.

Mom said, "When I was little, I never pictured God as having a beard. I couldn't picture Him at all. And then I got to California and saw the ocean, and I thought that if He were like anything, it would be that."

Dead silence for a moment. Jean-Pierre was trying to follow the rapid sentences. He asked, "A beard?" *"Un barbe,"* I said. *"Une barbe,"* he answered, one corner of his mouth turning up. I must have been correcting his English a little too often.

No one else knew what to say. Lizzie, in a soft voice, said, "It's hard to conceive of an omniscient being who sees everything and would still allow the suffering and horrors." Everyone looked at their food, away from Jean-Pierre.

Jerry said, "The whole free will thing has always been a problem for me."

Mom said, "Now I think of death as being like the ocean."

Margaret jerked up her head. Susan was transfixed: she clearly hoped to hear the whole, real, vital truth. Margaret said, "Mom," and Lizzie said, "Let her be. Why shouldn't she, if she wants to?"

I wanted people not to further hurt Jean-Pierre, but I could not think of how to avert this discussion. I began noisily ripping open whatever bags of chips and pretzels had not yet been breached and passing them around. "Lizzie, did you want some of the cheese twists? Jerry? Shall I give them to the kids or do you think they've had enough?"

Lizzie said, kindly, "Shut up, Annie."

Jean-Pierre asked Mom, "Do you mean that you disappear under the . . . ? Or stay above? Outside, the water looks calm, but it is full of . . . full of animals and plants. Rocks. Very movement. The same as here. *Ah-na.*" This last was a plea to me to help him out.

I said, reluctantly, "The surface we see is smooth, but the life of the ocean is as turbulent, aggressive, whatever you like, as life up here. It's just entering into another state, not really escaping the speed and ferocity of life." Jean-Pierre nodded agreement.

Mom brought her eyebrows together. "I mean peaceful. I mean never-ending. I mean *not personal*."

Danny said, "Well I think it all sucks. Like, this is a bunch of stuff everybody says to themselves. It's *peaceful*. Or it's *heaven*. Or you get *reborn*. Because you can't face up to it, that this is the whole thing and when it's over, it's over."

Jerry was up on his hands and knees, face a foot away from Danny's. "You think you might want to take your little Zen philosopher self off somewhere? You need to be shown some respect?"

Susan said, *"Daddy,"* and Danny said, "Whoa. Some people can't handle the truth," but his body was edging away, pressing back down into itself. Jerry must have outweighed him by eighty pounds. Jerry, satisfied, sat down and bit into his sandwich.

Danny, when he saw Jerry absorbed in his food, whispered to Susan, with a little smirk, *"Over."*

In one quick move, Jean-Pierre was up on his knees, looking dangerous. He said to Danny, roughly, "What do you mean, *over*? What do you think you know about this?" My family, who had only seen Jean-Pierre at his blandest and most courteous, were staring at him. But his face was sharp, absorbed in its suffering.

Margaret put out a hand to touch his arm. "I think Danny means that none of us can really know what happens." She had meant it as reassurance, but he drew back, angrily. Susan, who had been staring at the ground and poking her finger into the sand, gave her mother a quick look of surprised affection.

Danny said, "No, I mean it's *all shit*." His face had gone pale, the rosy acne standing out against his white skin.

Jean-Pierre and Margaret had their eyes locked together, frowning, in a brief struggle for dominance, but then she looked down, and it was over.

Lizzie, clearing her throat, asked, "Does anyone want to build a sand castle?"

I said yes almost before Bobby and Aurora. Danny and Susan

were on their feet at once, and I handed them sand toys. It's hard to make a scene when you're holding a yellow and red plastic bucket and red shovel.

Jean-Pierre said, "I think I would like some sleep more than anything." He had those purple shadows again, under his eyes, which made me want to protect him, though I was also embarrassed, alarmed. A memory of the sensations of the night before aroused me, then made me queasy. I got to my feet, shaking my head. My family were exchanging looks.

Bobby said, "But we're going to make a *castle*."

"Yes?" Jean-Pierre was puzzled but agreeable. The other Jean-Pierre had disappeared completely, and I could see my family making allowances.

"We've never made a castle with a real king before. It could be *your* castle."

Jean-Pierre looked to me for explanation, and I said, in French, "I tried to explain something about your family to my family, and obviously failed miserably. Now the children think you're a king. They're very impressed."

Jean-Pierre grinned, which brought me close to weeping. It had been so long since I'd seen that grin. He answered me in French, relaxing into the language, talking so fast that it was a moment before I caught his meaning. "The last thing I can bring myself to do is to disappoint the expectations of the young of the species. Shall I be regal?"

"It would be better if you'd remembered your leopard-skin robes."

"*Mille vaches,* I am amazed by your family." The first time I'd heard that name in a very long time. The family was looking shut out by our French. They suspected us of secrets. Jean-Pierre looked at Danny, then gave an almost invisible shrug and got to his feet. He had a guilty look, as if he were punishing himself either for his display of temper or for his momentary lapse into cheerfulness. He held out a hand. Bobby, shyly, stood up and took it, and then Aurora immediately caught hold of the other.

The three of them, and Lizzie, Danny, Susan, and I, set off down the beach. Danny had looked as if he might refuse, but he was already holding a shovel, and Susan tugged at his hand. Jean-Pierre, ahead of us, bent over to listen to whatever Aurora was chattering about, his face kind, attentive. While we were digging the sand castle, something he'd never done before, but which he entered into with energy, I thought that he had been a man of his time and place, formed by Burundian society. His actions hadn't been his fault, hadn't arisen from any deep flaw in his nature. Although they could never be excused, they could be explained and put behind him. Here in the U.S. he was a man who would play with his children, contribute to the community. I could help him with his damage, bring him back into the daylight world. Or, if we went back to Burundi . . . but I couldn't think about that, not yet. We could marry at City Hall, then arrange the rest of it later.

Bobby showed him how to drip the wet sand, piling up the lumpy, primitive heaps. Jean-Pierre, catching on quickly, built a series of towers to protect the central castle. Susan and Aurora, beside him, pressed bits of seashell and kelp into the castle walls, while I gathered seagull feathers for the castle top. Knee-deep in sandy water, with an energy that said he was proving himself, Danny furiously dug a huge moat.

F o u r t e e n

That night, as we lay in bed, Jean-Pierre began talking, his voice so quiet that at first I thought I had gone to sleep and was dreaming his low tones. Very different from the punishing, triumphant malice of our last lovemaking: now he was a man describing a nightmare, in the grip of the images.

"There was one boy. About eleven. His older brothers had gone into the truck already. He knelt down and held my legs. If I hadn't looked at his eyes." Jean-Pierre lay on his stomach, chin on the pillow, looking straight ahead, but then he tipped his head sideways, to see if I were with him. I put my arm across his shoulder. "Sometimes they struggled against us. But usually they thought it was fate, or they hoped obeying would keep them from being shot, so they climbed in. This boy was too young. Why did we take him? I say to myself that he was one of a dangerous family, and he would have wanted revenge very soon. When you kill the serpents, you must also destroy the eggs."

There was a long silence. Then, "If I could show you his face— very serious. Well behaved. He was crying but without begging. I didn't *see* this at the time. I was doing what I had to—I hit him in the head with the butt of my gun, and he went into the truck. I might have shot him then. Sometimes we had to. And then it was over so fast. So many of them." He was silent again. "And then later, in my dreams, I did see him. His eyes."

He turned away from me. "I don't allow myself to ask if it was worth it, if I had some other choice. Another people, with a different history, might have. For us, there was a terrible price. You make me remember, Ah-na. I wish I could stop."

"I'm so sorry, Jean-Pierre." My voice shook. The sense of being in a bad dream. "I won't ask any more." What he had done *could not* be justified. But then, I had no idea what I, or anyone else, would have done in his place, with his background and upbringing. Feeling him against me, his innocent skin, I asked myself, Was I God, to judge him?

/   /   /

Who else could rescue him from the past in which he was now drowning? Putting aside, for the moment, my ambivalence about bringing him here, I entered into my program of showing off my home: we went to bookstores and cafes, walked in the redwoods, went to concerts, little theater, and out to dinner, with and without my family.

We spent an extended afternoon at West County Hot Tub & Sauna. Before our massages, we sat in a private hot tub in a small, cedar-lined room, the floor and tubs faintly white and mossy with age, the water very hot, smelling strongly of chemicals. We had been floating for several minutes when Jean-Pierre asked me, "What was the basis for your hopes before? When you thought, 'I am a person who can help other people.' Did you have successes in helping people that made you so confident?"

"You've been thinking about this." Dizzy from the heat, I got out and sat on the edge of the tub, trailing one foot in the water.

Jean-Pierre sat back, his arms draped over the barrel's edge, feet disappearing down into the water. "I think about you much of the time." He gave me a small, wry smile. "Did you not know this?"

"The reason I thought I could be useful was . . . maybe it was that I never had thought about it. What I thought was, 'X needs to be done. Therefore I will do X.' When I ran into trouble, I didn't think that nothing could be done, but that *I* hadn't yet found what suited my talents best, that I needed to try doing a different thing. In the AIDS clinic, in Buj, there I think I was a tiny bit useful. But that might be the only time."

"Do you think about going back to your clinic? It would be acceptable to me if you wished to go on working."

This was actually a large concession, no matter how it sounded to an American. I smiled and shrugged. In case I changed my mind, I thought it might be better not to let him know that I was thinking of just having children, sitting on the beach (Which beach? In Burundi, where I had sat with Christine? In California, where we had picnicked with the family?), taking up hobbies. I couldn't stand to think of how self-important I had been, deluding myself about public health, human rights, my own ability to affect events.

"Do we want to invite my family to the wedding?" I asked. "They could come to City Hall with us."

"Will they want it to be elaborate?"

"Not if we don't tell them until the night before." He was thinking, and I said, "I'd like them there, Jean-Pierre. We could get married the Friday before you leave, and not say anything until Thursday night." After a moment he nodded. He picked up my hand, formally, and kissed it.

/   /   /

Jean-Pierre came with me when it was my turn to take Mom for chemo; I hoped he was noting the cleanliness, professionalism of the hospital. Since he hadn't responded to her malice, Mom had begun to take to him. Although she would joke about how he was a stranger she might never see again, she would ask for him to read to her. She liked his voice, his accent. And maybe he found some respite in helping to look after her. He read to her from *Love's Brightest Beginning*, stumbling a little over the words, frowning, his forehead creased. She lay in bed, eyes closed, a small smile on her face. His voice was as rich in English as in French; the book could not have sounded better.

I hoped he found it incomprehensible, but he said, later, "These books, what is their purpose?"

"For people to escape their own lives for a few hours, to live out a fantasy where things turn out just as they wish them to."

"They seem to me very wrong, somehow. Very dangerous."

"Well, they aren't written for men."

"For men they would be less dangerous."

I said, "Men have their own fantasies. And I would resist any proposition that says that men's fantasies are less dangerous than women's." He gave me a long, reproachful look. "I'm sorry," I said, and we let it alone.

Mom said to me, another time, when he was downstairs sleeping, "You're having a little adventure; well, good for you. I like him. Not as a son-in-law, of course." And she gave me one of her sharp, diagnostic looks.

I just nodded. She had never said a word about my ring. Had she even noticed it? Since it wasn't a diamond, she could pretend to herself, if she liked, that it meant nothing. My family is given to interfering in things—they think they can improve any and all situations. It still seemed to me that I had some time to get them used to the idea before we took any action, though Jean-Pierre's visit would be coming to an end soon.

/ / /

Less than two weeks before Christmas, downtown Santa Rosa was strung with white lights that glittered through all the trees. We had been to get a marriage license, which was now rolled inside my purse. I thought about how hard it would be to separate immediately after our wedding.

The enormous tree in the downtown plaza had more than three hundred brilliantly colored lights. Frenetic shoppers, some abnormally cheerful, others snappish and overwhelmed, crowded all the streets and stores. The radio and newspapers offered concerned stories about holiday overload. In fact, it was the dark of the year—we felt it in our animal selves. Even those who weren't grieving had a tired, lost look. Jean-Pierre and I, memory-ridden, felt increasingly alien from the piped-in carols, the tinsel, the endless beautiful lights. When we left off our raw confessing, or our arguing about what form our wedding would take, and tried to be tourists, it made us sadder than ever.

We were walking down Fourth Street, looking at the window displays, when he said, "Sometimes I was very, very frightened." He didn't look at me, but at an inflatable plastic Rudolph teetering in the middle of a pile of books on healing and food combining. "They aren't in the mind, the emotions. They come from and take over the body."

"Like love."

His shoulder, as if by itself, gave an impatient twitch. I knew I couldn't think of the right response to what he'd said, and it froze my tongue. I tried, "They say that bravery is acting when you're afraid."

He said, "It's late, Ah-na, I am cold." He looked at me, judging, irritable, then turned away. We walked briskly toward the car, and I tried to think of how I could not have failed him, what would have been the right thing to say.

Finally, he burst out, "For such a bright woman, you can be relentlessly stupid. Even now, you don't see what it means. They want to eradicate us. Look at Rwanda, where they have the power. Don't you know our history? Do you think it's some accident, the way they slaughter us? They want a world with no Tutsis in it."

I stood in the middle of the sidewalk, shocked breathless, and not only because I was wounded by his insult. I had been assuming, all along, that the Hutus were in the right. Because the Tutsis had the power.

I was trying to imagine what it would be like to feel that every one of my own kind was threatened, that we could be wiped off the planet, when he said, his voice softer, "I believe what I just said. But I also owe you an apology. For my hardness toward you. I think I'm punishing you for being alive, for not being her. Do you understand that?"

I did, I said so, and we looked into each other's eyes for a long minute or two, in exact, accurate communication.

"You do," he said. "Thank you."

/ / /

We went home and ate dinner with the family: Lizzie's *seitan* winter stew, full of carrots, garlic, and yams, served with pork chops for everyone but Lizzie, Susan, and Aurora, and rice pilaf and salad for everyone. Jean-Pierre's mood appeared at first to have changed, and he even joked with the children, though he was still subdued and hard to read. The children took him for granted. It surprised me, how well he seemed to fit. Some mysterious point of intersection. I didn't eat much, and I kept my head down; whenever I looked up and saw him, I heard, *For such a bright woman, you can be relentlessly stupid.* Maybe it was so unforgettably awful because it was true. I had my hands under the table, turning my ring, pulling it half off, then sliding it back on. Imagining my hand without it.

So I wasn't paying proper attention to the conversation and

missed how they got onto the topic of children. Jean-Pierre said something mildly disapproving about the wildness of American children—taking drugs, carrying guns—how hard it was for a Burundian to understand. Susan had her arms crossed, looking sullen.

Margaret snapped, "You find violence hard to understand?" Everyone around the table went very still.

"I find uncontrolled children difficult to understand," said Jean-Pierre, after a short silence, his voice polite, his face furious. "It is the job of the parents, of the mother, to be the responsible one. If children are allowed to run wild, they will."

At this, Susan sat up in anticipation, one corner of her mouth turning up in pleasure. Margaret's face had gone dark red. She looked at Jerry, who was staring silently at his plate, then back at Jean-Pierre.

As Margaret opened her mouth, Lizzie put an arm around her shoulder and leaned forward, saying, "Oh, I *know*. We have a Rousseauian ideal of childhood, and it can be so disastrous in practice. Aurora does just as she likes with me. But the old rules have changed. Jean-Pierre, I think if you keep watching you'll see the good side. How kids believe in themselves more. How their self-reliance makes them better able to cope with life at its most overwhelming."

"Divorce, traffic, floods of mail, two-career, three-career families, television," I said. "The world coming at you twenty-four hours a day, no matter how responsible and concerned the mother is."

Jean-Pierre, looking at Margaret, said, "If I have offended, please accept my apologies."

Her color was returning to normal. She gave a nod, but a stiff one; he had won another battle in their subterranean war. Jerry said, "Television is the worst invention of the twentieth century," and we were off onto a relieved discussion of TV, for and against.

After dinner, Jerry and Jean-Pierre, in the dining room, discussed the meaning of elections in America—to what extent the government of the U.S. was or was not in fact an oligarchy. Lizzie and I went into the kitchen to do dishes. Margaret was upstairs, reading to Mom; the younger children had been put to bed; Susan sulked ostentatiously in front of the television.

Lizzie, putting away leftover pilaf and winter stew, said, "I like your Jean-Pierre. He's very gentle with the kids. I asked Aurora if she liked him, and she said, 'He's a *good* man.' Jean-Pierre's rather foreign to me, and some of his ideas make me a little nervous. I can see he's grieving and under strain, and I don't entirely understand him, but I think you're right for each other."

I wiped a damp hair off my brow with one forearm and began mopping up a pan of pork grease with a paper towel. I smiled but didn't answer her. She said, "You're still in that totally lovesick state, but that makes a foundation for the irritable years. And together you and he seem complete—as if part of each of you was missing before."

"Lovesick."

"You practically fall over chairs and tables when he's in the room. You're only about half present with the rest of us. But we're happy if you're happy. I know he's sad, and that you're worried about him. In the end, though, this may strengthen you two."

"It's not quite that simple, Lizzie. We have some issues to work out."

"That's part of an engagement, isn't it? It brings everything to the surface for a couple. The 'I-need-more-space' and the 'if-you-really-loved-me-you'd' and the making up after. Drama and scenes are just an energy exchange. He's from another culture, which is always more complicated. But I'm starting to be excited for you, Annie. He *is* a prince."

"He has a temper."

"All the best men do."

Without having planned to, I whispered, "Lizzie, can you keep a secret?" She nodded. "We're getting married Friday afternoon at

City Hall, and then taking the family down to Marin for a serious dinner at Lark Creek Inn."

"Why is this a secret?"

"So no one will make a big to-do about it. He doesn't want that. We'll tell people Thursday night."

"Wow," she said. She silently dried a dish, over and over, wiping the towel in slow circles. "I'm glad you told me, at least. Can I help you buy a dress, or did you do that too?"

I put my arm around her shoulder and gave her a kiss on the cheek. " 'The family is the natural and fundamental group unit of society and is entitled to protection by society and the State.' Article 16, Universal Declaration."

"Could you stop? Everyone here already believes in human rights, Annie. You don't have to talk us into it." But she was smiling as she rested her head on my encircling arm.

/   /   /

In bed that night, reaching over Jean-Pierre to turn off the light, I knocked over a picture of Françoise. Jean-Pierre had photographs of his sisters, his nieces and nephews, propped up beside the lamp on our bedside table. As if, somehow, without this, he might already be beginning to forget. Or as if to keep them with him at all times. I straightened the photo, left the light on, and began moving my lips over Jean-Pierre's collarbone, chest, then up his neck to his ear. He didn't respond. I whispered, "Tell me where you are."

"I'm a little tired."

"You're not. You're holding out on me." I was still whispering, not arguing, seducing.

If he'd said he was thinking of his sisters, I would have left him alone, but he said, "I am thinking of a family we had to dispose of."

I threw one leg over his and slid onto him, looking down into his face. Jean-Pierre met my eyes and gave a nod of acquiescence, then put his arms around my back, pulling me down to him. I remembered Christine saying, "In Paris, the students were all for making friends with their shadows." Reality had its jaws open, and I was looking straight into them.

"The father was a troublemaker. There were eight children, six of them boys."

I moved my hips up and down, slowly, and when his body responded, I shifted to get him inside of me. "And how many of you?"

"More than twenty. But we had most of a hillside to deal with. Not the only one."

"Did the whole family die?"

"Everyone dies." He pushed up into me, showing me his teeth. I had hold of the short hair over his ears. I wanted to hear it all, to cure him, to know it, to get *inside* him.

He said, fiercely, "I will take you with me," and then he sank his teeth into my shoulder. I responded in kind. We pinched and bit each other all over, using our fingernails, mirroring the other's painful inventions. When he came, he put his face into my neck to muffle his yell, and I had a sudden, irrational fear that the family would hear us, even run down the hall, bursting into the room. The thought slapped me back to myself.

A long minute later, I asked, "What are we *doing*?"

He didn't answer, but only gave me a smile I still don't want to remember. Exhausted, my skin stinging from the bites and pinches, I put my head on his shoulder. I whispered, "Maybe I'm punishing you too. Because I want you to be with me, not longing for your ghosts." He stroked my hair with one hand, his face remote, withdrawn.

/   /   /

His plane ticket back to Burundi was for Saturday morning. Thursday morning, Lizzie and I went shopping. In the third antique store, we found a white tea-length dress from the twenties, with delicate opalescent beading, and in the fourth antique store, a pearly tiara-thing to wear with it. The shoes were easier; we found a pair in under an hour. We bought white roses, which cost a fortune in December, fir branches to go with them, and Lizzie bought a new camera battery, along with two rolls of black-and-white and three rolls of color film. She took me out to lunch, saying, a little sadly, "I guess this is your bridal shower." But she had been very good until then, so I refrained from pointing out how much more we had lost than the chance to have a big celebration.

/　　/　　/

Thursday evening, the whole family was together in the living room, in front of the fire. Mom had come downstairs and sat huddled in an armchair, wrapped in a blanket. She'd mustered herself to be sharp-tongued to Margaret, which was encouraging, and before dinner she'd even sneaked a cigarette in the bathroom. Margaret, Lizzie, and I had had an argument about it afterward, Margaret saying, "It's her right—why shouldn't she if she wants to? It's not like she has anything to lose," and Lizzie asking, "Then why put us all through the hell of chemo?"

"It's her hell," Margaret had said. "For us it's just unpleasantness."

I secretly agreed with Lizzie, but wasn't brave enough to say so. I said, "Who plans to tell her not to? Who's willing to say to her that she can't have the little she still wants?" and that seemed to end it.

Mom looked worse that evening, though. I couldn't tell if the cigarette (cigarettes?) had made her sicker. She was drinking hot mulled cider, like the children; the rest of the adults had mulled red wine with cinnamon sticks and bits of dark orange peel floating in the mugs. We'd put out plates of Christmas cookies on all the tables: gingerbread men, Russian tea cakes, bourbon balls, chocolate chip and walnut cookies, scotch shortbread, and an old family recipe involving cornflakes, sticky melted marshmallows, and green food coloring. They looked like piles of little leaves with a red cinnamon candy center, and they turned lips and tongues a bright, electric green. The children adored them.

Margaret had on a sweater I'd never seen before, new-looking and expensive: dark green and black checks on white with tiny vermilion lines. She saw me looking at it and raised her eyebrows at me, her lips drawing together angrily, her face going red.

Bobby and Aurora knelt in front of the tree. Shaking presents, holding them up to each other, grinning. "Nintendo!" said Bobby. "This one *is* Nintendo." Aurora held up a box and shook it. She didn't really understand the game, but she entered into it with glee. Bobby wasn't much good at guessing either, though he'd learned something from Susan, who pretended to be too old for this but had given the presents a thorough going-over when she thought no one was looking. The story had passed around among the adults, who took hope from this evidence that, in some ways, she was still a child. I remember Lizzie, when Aurora was a baby, squirting her with an imaginary can of spray fixative. "Spray, spray, spray," she would say, several times a day, looking at Aurora's perfect, premoral face, years away from any sense of the implications of good, evil, self-doubt.

Bobby and Aurora had roped in Jean-Pierre. They had adopted him; he'd said to me that playing with them was at once very painful and the only thing that helped.

Bobby said to him, "Guess what this is."

Jean-Pierre knelt by the fireplace, under the golden ropes of tinsel, felt-covered bells, and bright plastic wreaths. He shook the packages very gently, listening to each as if to a seashell at his ear. "Charcoal for the fire," he'd say. "Gold coins." "A Greek dictionary." "Cow . . ." and he looked at me across the room for help.

"Cow dung," I supplied, inspired by the nature of his smile, the mischief I saw there.

"Yes, it is cow dung."

"Cow *manure*," said my mother, in her new thin voice, but smiling a little.

Bobby, and then Aurora, in imitation, shrieked with laughter. "Cow manure! He thinks it's cow manure!" Bobby got up and danced an impromptu manure-jig of delight, and Aurora, over-excited, ran back and forth, her cheeks red, eyes too bright. It would be impossible to get them to sleep. Too much Christmas, too many cookies. She ran up to her mother, over to her grandmother, then back to where Jean-Pierre sat cross-legged on the floor, and dropped into his lap. His arms went around her without hesitation, and he bent his face down, pressing it against her hair while she snuggled into him.

My eyes filled with tears. I'd had three or four mugs of wine. I got up and went out of the room, taking some mugs with me for more mulled wine and cider. I wanted to wait to announce the marriage until the children were in bed, just in case it got tricky.

When I went back into the living room, it was Jean-Pierre who was looking sad, withdrawn. The family had begun a game of Monopoly, though it was much too late, even for the adults. As we bought property and landed in jail and won our second prizes in beauty contests, Jean-Pierre stared into the fire, his face painful, his shoulders down. Thousands of miles away, watching horrors.

I said to Jerry, "Do you still want to buy Marvin Gardens from me?" and he groaned with cautious desire.

"Depends," he said. "What do I have to give you?"

I said to him, "Take a look at the rent with just one hotel. This would give you a monopoly on yellows, and everyone always lands there."

Margaret said, "Don't. Annie's so greedy, she'll bleed you white." This got Jean-Pierre's attention—he looked at Jerry curiously as if to see how he could be more white than he already was.

"*I'm* greedy?" I said to her, and Lizzie said, "*Annie,*" making it worse. I was already blushing. I said, fast, "Oh, Margaret is the fiercest Monopoly player. She always wins."

"You could win too, if you played with your head and didn't throw away all your chances on sentimental gestures."

"At least I have generous urges toward other players."

The children stared at the ground, their bodies tense, their faces showing the strains we put them under.

Margaret said, "Sometimes you open your mouth and a little devil comes out."

My tipsiness made me incautious. I was both worried and angry. "Margaret, are you taking your Zoloft?"

"You *drunken* bitch." She said it so emphatically that two flecks of spit shot onto the pool of Free Parking money in the center of the board, making small dark spots on a golden $100 bill.

Mom, from her chair, said, *"Girls."*

Jean-Pierre, his arms folded, was regarding Margaret from the center of what felt to me like a halo of disapproval. His face was impassive, but cold judgment emanated from him. I was almost in tears because of how wrong the evening was going.

She looked at him, then took a deep breath, as if inflating herself. Her color was high, her eyes crafty. "You," she said to me. And to Jean-Pierre, "You went to the Sorbonne, you're some kind of prince. But I think you're trouble. And my idiot sister's so obsessed with you that she doesn't even use the brain she's got. She says living in Burundi is like breathing poison gas all the time. Human nature at its worst. So there's a logical conclusion to be drawn there."

Jean-Pierre turned to me, his face shocked and suspicious. I jumped to my feet. "She's making it up. Jean-Pierre, how can you believe her?" Then I turned to Margaret. "Thank you very much."

"The same to you, I'm sure." Her face was tight with an ugly satisfaction, the opposite of the crisply affectionate sister with whom

I'd bought books and eaten Chinese food, the sister who had reassured me that Burundi and its poisons were half a world away.

I said to Jean-Pierre, "Please get your coat. Come out with me. We need a walk—we need some air. Please." After a moment, he nodded and got to his feet, but he didn't touch me as we went out the door.

/ / /

Our closest neighbors had spelled out "Noel" in red and blue, with strings of blinking lights outlining rooftops, windows, trees, bushes, and fences. The houses along the road had set up elaborate mangers or tableaux of Rudolph and Frosty.

I said to him, talking urgently, "Margaret is making things up. But it is true that life is very difficult in Burundi. Very sad. We could go anywhere. Paris." He flinched at that, and, cursing myself for having mentioned the place Christine would have been safe, I said, "Though I think it would be better if you were here. Because France is so hard for foreigners. Just the paperwork. But here, we'd be with the family. You could get a job at the university, learn to live again." My earlier thoughts of returning to Burundi seemed absurd to me. I shivered, my breath forming a white cloud in the dark air.

"Are you suggesting I not go home?"

"Only to settle things, prepare to leave the Ministry. I would have to find a place for us, find a job myself." He put the palms of his hands over his eyes. I said, "We could stop wrecking each other. You could get some help. You don't have to stand there and watch Burundi eat itself alive. The history of the world has everything, more and more, to do with immigration. Eritreans, Vietnamese, Salvadorians. They all had lives in their own countries. They made the *choice* to step outside their own painful histories."

We had to stand at a street corner and let a string of cars go by, our feet and hands going numb. The house behind us had its garage doors outlined in colored lights, like a giant mouth.

"Do you know how many people want to become Americans? We can invent any kind of life we can imagine for ourselves here. Live in a tree house, sell self-hypnosis tapes by mail order, teach history at the university, have seven children or none. Just let yourself picture having so much freedom."

The light changed, and we were able to cross. I had my hands inside my coat, against my sides, warming them up.

He said, "Freedom. A house with no walls is nothing but wind."

"Just think it over. Where and how do you want your children to grow up? Imagine that you could *expect* them not to be killed. They wouldn't have to live with the memories that you do. They could be anything, if they could summon up enough energy or imagination."

We stopped at a house reinvented in light—its cornices, chimney, grape arbor, and bushes all shimmering white. He said, "This reminds me of Françoise, how she dressed for celebrations. With her it was not white, but every single color and texture—layers, jewelry, braids. A whole carnival, all by herself. She could be bossy. She was not a sensitive woman. But she was so loyal, such a strong mother. And there has never been anyone like her before. Will never be again." A tear sat on his eye's red rim, then fell down and ran alongside his nose. He wiped his eyes and blew his nose. "In Burundi we are always saying that it's God's will. If we don't die, we go to church at the end of the week and give thanks for the miracle of survival. I think of Françoise, of Christine dancing. I do not accept their deaths. I think I was spoiled by living in the West. I am not grateful to be alive. I am not grateful for the time they had."

We turned to walk on. He said, "Everything I say or do reminds me of them, and it eats at me. If we'd gone to Paris. If I'd kept them in town. I wake up in the morning, and the first thing I remember is that I'm here. I feel you against me. The second thing I remember is my impatience that sent them home to be killed."

"You must know, with some part of you, that it wasn't your fault."

"I am afraid that Burundi will tear itself to pieces forever. The Hutus will never be satisfied until there are no Tutsis left." He said, "You said that to her, that being in Burundi is like breathing poison gas?"

"No, but I did say that life in Burundi was too hard."

I could see from his face that he knew I was lying. We walked in silence for a while. Eventually, he said, "It's strange to me that you talk to people about our private matters."

"Just my sisters, Jean-Pierre." He nodded, his face remembering talking to a sister. I put my arm around his waist, trying to comfort him.

/   /   /

Everyone had gone to bed by the time we got home. Without saying anything, we went to my room, took off our clothes, and made love in the lamplight, very simply, full of kindness toward each other. He stroked my cheeks and kissed my eyelids from above. He had such a look of suffering on his face, almost of nostalgia. And he came almost immediately, very rare for him. He was embarrassed, but I held his face between my hands, whispering, "We have all the time in the world. Don't you feel that?"

He put his face into my shoulder, and just from the way he was touching me, it began to sink in. He was always very absolute— once he had made up his mind, there was no changing it. I pulled away, and he let me go, rolling off to the side.

I said, "You're going to Burundi, and you're not coming back."

He said, "My home is there. Yours is here. Burundi can never be your home. Tonight has shown me this." I could see tears on his cheeks, but I didn't cry myself. I didn't believe this was happening. He went on, "When I tell you that parts of me are missing, I think you don't listen. You hear what you want to believe. You see with your mind a man who used to exist. A man who was able to consider changes and adventures. But that man is now dead. As they are."

His leg lay against mine, the bodies still in perfect communication. I said, "You're just . . . your mind is making obstacles. We have been . . . what we have been doing together is too strange. And you've been too sad to really see California." I was so angry, so helpless, that I did begin to cry. It seemed clear to me that going back to Burundi was absolutely not an option, and also that he was being obdurate, thwarting not only me but his own best good. He'd lost all perspective, was seeing his desperate grief as a lifelong state.

When I could speak again, I said, "What is there to go back for? A lifetime of waiting for more death? Are you determined to turn yourself into a tombstone for them?"

In the lamplight the dampness across his cheeks and brow glistened. He smelled better than anything, ever—I wanted to bury my face in his skin. He said, "I have work at home. I cannot walk away from my family, my uncle, from my country when it is in such trouble. To be a Ganwa is to have responsibility. The monarchy is at an end, but we still have our duty to Burundi. Here I would be only amusing myself. All this sensualism, self-indulgence. But you can't spend your whole life in a bathtub."

"Are you going to let yourself be so constricted by the limits of your imagination? To throw something like this away?" I was furious for having lost my principles, for talking myself into trying to understand his past, imagining going back to Burundi. Was he going home to marry some *Burundaise* who would bore him? More predictable, less of a challenge, less of a playmate and companion. Not meeting him in his dark places. But maybe that was what he wanted.

We were no longer touching at all, had moved almost three feet apart. I didn't understand how we had turned, so fast, from two people about to be married into enemies. I had a wild sense of the irrevocable.

Jean-Pierre glared at me, his lips drawn slightly back from his teeth. Almost snarling. "In the end, like any American, you patronize Burundi. And, therefore, me. Because I am Burundi. You can't imagine I would see your big playground and not piss myself to get here on any terms. You want a plaything. Not me—some image of me, a cardboard cutout to watch TV and send the children to bed. You still don't know me. You still don't take any account of Burundi. Burundi is as real as America. Not as big, not as powerful, but it is one actual and essential little country on this big planet, and it is my own." And then he said, scornfully, "Did you really think I would be so overcome by your world? Yes, I love you. No, I will not marry you and come live your life."

I got out of bed and put on a robe. I suppose I had a confused thought that I was dying and needed to be covered, in case.

He said to me, still angry, but with his voice softening as he went on, "When I told you the story of the death of Ntare I, I left out something very important. Because I thought you would not understand, because I thought it did not matter that you would not understand, because I wanted you to think only of the king and his duty. But Ntare I is said to have had a very dear friend, a man he asked to die with him, a man he trusted. If his friend would stay by him for this ordeal, at a later time, in another incarnation, he would help his friend when his friend was in need.

"The friend agreed, but he was afraid. When the fire began to consume their room, while the king slept so deeply, the friend got up and ran from the palace. But the loyal retainers saw him and called out, over and over, that he was a traitor. They ran after him, cornered him, and killed him with their spears. When this story is told, it is not told as the story of Ntare I. It is told as the story of his friend, Barera."

When he spoke again, his voice was intimate, sad, the voice of my lover. "If we imagined that we could be together in one place, that was a dream. I didn't see it before. I do now."

"We would never see each other again?"

"We could." His eyes were red. "See each other sometimes. Write."

I wanted to take him on any terms at all. I had to turn away, to avoid the look on his face. "I am not going to let myself be torn apart slowly." I cleared my throat. "Continuing to be your lover, seeing you maybe once a year, waiting until you find the woman you really want and then abandon me for her." I stared at the rug, its red and yellow braiding, the flecks of blue. A piece of black thread had gotten stuck in the weave. "No life," I said. "No children." Waiting for his letters, reading them over and over, fantasizing about him. My life, like his, would become a ghost story. About the person who *wasn't there.* "If we can't be together, then I can't stand to know you at all."

I was quiet then. Waiting for him to get out of bed and sweep me into his arms, saying the things men said at the ends of Mom's romances. That he couldn't live without me. That he had always known we were meant to be together. That he now understood how his destiny had brought him here to live with me.

From the corner of my eye, I could see the motion as he put his hands over his eyes, silently. I waited a long time, maybe twenty minutes, before I took off my ring and dropped it beside him on the pillow. He shuddered, but didn't look at it, or at me. I stumbled out of the room and made my way to Lizzie on her sleeping porch.

The long, bleak landscape of my future stretched out before me. But I hoped he would change his mind, once he got back to Bujumbura, felt again the terrible atmosphere of suspicion and grief, began to miss me. Part of me clung to the idea that he was not going away for good, that I would not be forever without his irony, mystery, the richness of his company and observations. Another part of me believed any thought of a future together to be a lie. We were not going to see each other again, once he left to go back to Burundi.

Two days later, he was gone.

Fifteen

Christmas came and went, like watching an old TV: colorless, bad reception. People had to say things to me two or three times before I heard them. It had been a wet fall. By late December it rained and rained and rained. The tree trunks had gone soft and dank; rivers of brown water ran alongside the roads. Walking anywhere meant stepping over bloated, drowned worms: obscene-looking, pink and vulnerable against the mud. The sound of rain pounding against the roof made me wild with claustrophobia.

Nothing suited my mother—no book, no food, no small comfort—and she complained constantly, fretfully, retreating to her bedroom as much as possible. Life downstairs was just as bad. Margaret and I weren't speaking to each other. The children ran out of control. Cabin fever.

In early January, while waiting for Mom at the hospital, I bumped into my old friend Jeanine, from graduate school, where we'd formed a temporary alliance because we were the only two from Sonoma County. Now we stood in the corridor of the hospital, the electric doors sliding open and closed with a noise like a rush of water. Rain fell heavily onto the walkway and parking lot outside.

She described her children, her work with the county public health department, and then she asked me what I'd been doing. I told her, briefly, about doing AIDS work in Burundi, about moving back to Sonoma County to look after my mother.

Jeanine said, "You still know people in this county, Anne. Maybe you could give lectures in the high schools on safer sex. And we need an educational counseling component in the clinics. What do you say?"

Jeanine had an earnest face, all of her thrown forward toward the world, fine jaw, glasses and haircut that said she couldn't be bothered with lesser matters. Talking to her, even for fifteen minutes, exhausted me. I said, "I don't know, Jeanine."

"Think what a difference you could make to those high school students. Someone who knows what it's like to live in a place with a thirty percent sero-positive rate in the adult population. I mean, what a *deterrent*."

A man in his late seventies or early eighties stumped past us, lifting his walker and thumping it down again, an expression of profound determination on his face.

I found myself saying, "I don't think I can take on a professional job, at this point. I need to be free to look after Mom," and she pressed my hand, sympathetically, which made me feel like the fraud I was. Because I was thinking that maybe Margaret had some kind of point, however twisted her methods were in carrying it out. Why not look after myself for a change?

The idea I'd had, of a life of freedom and pleasure, was back, persistently. Why not find some fun job, where there was no miserable suffering followed by inevitable death? No clinics. No high school students ignoring the advice about condoms that I hadn't even been following myself. I could go every day to a place where people got their hair done or ate sweets in a charming room full of Victorian furniture.

At the temp agency, the woman looked over the résumé I'd done on a copy shop computer. "Most of this experience is in foreign countries," she said disapprovingly. She was in her forties, with sleek blond hair in a bun and the look of a pageant queen who'd been laminated some years earlier.

I smiled at her, professionally. I felt no fear. I had on a black jacket and skirt with a very contemporary beige blouse, my new heels crossed at the ankles.

"Still, IBM in Paris." She looked me over. I was wearing a color of lipstick called "Pecan Treat," and goddamnit, I *felt* like an administrative assistant. "And you managed an office of fifteen."

"Mostly French girls. But very experienced at what they did—they'd gone to work straight out of *lycée*. What I did most was arrange workloads, plan our shipments, manage customer relations." I felt a rush of freedom, as if I were dreaming and knew it. No controls over me, no need to behave.

"And just why is it you're interested in temporary work?"

"My mother is very ill," I said, softly, looking right at her. "Cancer. I need to be available. . . ."

Her eyes filled at once. She pressed a finger against her thick, black lower lashes on one side, then the other, to blot them. After a moment, she said, "I understand. Last year, my own . . ." She stood up and went to some filing cabinets, taking out a set of papers, standing with her back to me for a long time, blowing her nose.

I sat in my chair, the feeling of freedom gone, fighting tears myself. I had been parading Mom's impending death as a way of *not believing* in it. I concentrated, very hard, on thinking of myself running that imaginary office in Paris, the girls giggling with each other, falling silent as I approached.

Then the woman came back, under control, and handed me a set

of papers. "These are the instructions for your tests on Word and Ex-
cel. You can use the second computer." She pointed to a line of computers on the opposite wall. "Good luck."

/   /   /

As soon as I had a placement—three weeks in the office of a firm of
architects who were building shopping malls and bidding on library
and city hall renovations—I bought a ten-year-old Honda Civic,
which ran just fine, though someone had slammed into the rear
right fender, which I had to keep in mind. The car still angled
slightly when braking, despite subsequent body work. I was all set
up to begin a life.

Whether I cried at night was nobody's business but Lizzie's.
During the day I was a glossy, professional sailing ship. The architects, whose last temp had been a nineteen-year-old design student
on winter break, praised me constantly, my efficiency, my proactive
approach, my grasp of situations. The praise did not mean one thing
to me, just a faint warming around the frozen edges.

/   /   /

It rained, hard, for thirty of January's thirty-one days. In February
it went on raining. The Russian River flooded from Healdsburg
to Guerneville and out to the coast. People's basements filled
with mud; they had to be rowed out in small boats. A few people
died. The public health department was kept busy with press releases about tetanus shots and water quality. Highways 12 and 101
flooded, and the drive into Santa Rosa became a two-hour nightmare
of inching along wet back roads, through six-inch-deep puddles, the
dark rain pounding down, lines of cars backed up for miles and
miles, their headlights pale in the rain.

Everywhere I went, people said, "It's a tragedy. What a terrible
thing to have happen. Did you hear about the old man in Healdsburg?" They remembered other years when flooding had damaged

houses up and down the river flats. They commiserated with each other in low, shocked tones. My great accomplishment of those months was keeping my mouth shut; I never screamed at anyone, much as I longed to shout, *You insulated, stupid, provincial . . .* but to them it *was* a tragedy and what made them so lucky was not to understand their own luck.

I proposed to Mom and Lizzie that, since Mom seemed to have stabilized for the moment, we could take turns spending the night with her, and not all have to stay together constantly. This plan came to me out of desperation—I wanted some time to crawl into bed, by myself, and I was sick of the silence and avoidances of being around Margaret. Jerry was all for my proposal. And Lizzie wanted to return with Aurora to their cluttered fairy cottage in the woods. She was sick of living away from home, and of being caught in the middle between Margaret and me.

When I suggested the idea of taking turns, though, Mom was furious. This took me by surprise. She said, "Why not just put me in a home?" and, "It's not as if I have much time left with any of you," and, most unfairly, or perhaps most accurately, and therefore painfully, "I suppose you can't wait for me to die before getting on with your lives."

We said, "Oh, Mom," and "That isn't it at all," and "We're going to be with you, just not all at once." She lay on her back, lips pressed together, rims of her eyes reddening. No one else would have persisted, in the face of her misery, but I thought I had to be alone or die myself. We spent days talking to her about it. Finally, she said, "Do whatever you want, then," and, after an extended family meeting downstairs, during which Margaret and I never once addressed each other directly, we were in agreement.

It took me three days to find an apartment in downtown Santa Rosa. I wasn't picky. An anonymous little American box with straightforwardly superb plumbing, electricity, water supply. Up to code, though there were no laws or customs mandating aesthetics. I didn't know my neighbors on either side, and they smiled at me in an avoiding manner when we accidentally saw each other on our way to our cars at 7:30 A.M.

During the days, I did my job and made acquaintances. I put on outfits, styled my hair, and drove through the rain, careful about my braking, listening to the endless flood reports on all the radio stations. During the nights, when I wasn't taking my turn with Mom, I set about enduring. All those years I'd spent learning to think, and now I was becoming a champ at *not thinking about it*. Which turned out to be the primary survival skill. It all felt as if it were all taking place in a dream. I *was* the ice princess. This made me violently attractive to men. I hadn't suddenly become beautiful, though I'd stopped eating and had dropped down to my smallest size. But they swarmed around me at the grocery store, on the street, drawn by my complete lack of availability.

Because, of course, I was waiting for Jean-Pierre to change his mind and call. Lizzie said to me, "Annie, sweetie, did he sound like he had any doubts?" But it seemed impossible that he wouldn't come to his senses, wasn't finding his life colorless, empty, devoid of meaning.

My family kept asking me about him. What had happened? Had we broken it off for good? I felt a grinding, furious humiliation, as if I had dragged myself, half dressed, through the mud in front of them. Sometimes I remembered him only as brutal, secretive, moody. My stupid longing for him had transformed him into a heroic figure—his bullying into masterfulness, his inability to be open with me into depth of soul. And then my feelings would reverse themselves. No one would ever again look into my eyes with his level of understanding; I'd never again feel that fierce and absolute pitch of desire. I had been ruined by knowing him, had stepped into a country which I could never leave.

On my breaks at work, I often stood near my desk and looked out a window above the street, not far from the junior college. The rain fell; the sidewalks streamed with water; people pushed ahead of each other, their umbrellas black, purple, covered in hopeful designs.

One gray-but-not-raining afternoon, right below my window, a pair of lovers kissed lingeringly, then wheeled around, laughing, so light and full of energy that they were almost on tiptoe, the man with his arm around the girl's waist, energy crackling between them. My brisk practicality deserted me, and it seemed that nothing in any possible future was worth going on for. The whole climate I lived in was so heavy, so unrelenting, that I didn't believe I would ever again have an appetite for things. It seemed that Burundi, and Jean-Pierre, had broken me in some fundamental way; I understood the beaten look most people had.

/ / /

Susan was helping me decorate my apartment. I took a half day off (unpaid, of course, since I was a temp), and we went all over town. Afterward, we sat in the Victorian cafe I had pictured working in—Sweet Reveries—eating our flourless chocolate torte, which had a layer of chocolate ganache between the torte and the almond crust. We had piled our packages all around us. The trunk of the car was already full.

Susan said to me, around a mouthful of chocolate torte, "What most people don't understand about roller-blading is that it's an art form. If you become a roller-blading champion, it's not like Ping-Pong or something, and *way* not like roller-skating. It's more like you're a dancer."

"A really fast dancer," I said.

She swallowed, grinning. "A *really* fast dancer. A flying dancer."

I'd bought the two of us blouses, sweaters, and two pair of baroque pearl earrings while we were at it. My whole first month's pay and a piece of my savings. The newest Cuisinart, copper-lined steel pans, Japanese pillows and futon cover, handmade lamp shades with imprints of leaves, an artisan clock, hand-painted with brilliantly colored flying cats and clichés/proverbs. "A stitch in time saves nine." "Haste makes waste." "Time flies when you're having fun."

Although Susan had been delighted by the chance to go shopping and was very pleased with her earrings, we were both exhausted. I was trying not to show that I wasn't sure I'd bought the right things. Would they go together? Were they even my taste? What was that, anyway, my taste? And I thought we'd probably be a little ill from the intense torte.

Susan said, "It's not so bad, being single, is it, Aunt Annie? Because you can do what you like." She was scraping her cake plate with her fork, mashing the crumbs between the tines and then licking them. I wanted to hold her on my lap.

"Are you single, then?"

"Oh, well. I'm a little young for commitments." She said this in the tone of a twenty-five-year-old explaining why she won't marry her boyfriend.

I pushed away the rest of my torte.

"If you're not going to eat that," she said.

"You want more?" I asked. She blushed, but put her hand out for it. "Go ahead, then, if you're up to it. It's all yours." I slid it across the table toward her, and she tucked in. All around us, people free in the late afternoon—didn't they have jobs?—drank their cappuccinos and espressos, ate their lemon and pecan squares, chocolate cakes and tortes, slices of pie with whipped cream. I shut my eyes, wishing I had stopped eating a few bites earlier.

/   /   /

My sisters and I soon fell into the pattern of spending a couple of nights a week each with Mom, and one day taking a long lunch so that we could accompany her to the hospital for chemo, to the doctor's. In late March she had only one course of chemo left, for which we were all grateful, because it was making her sicker and sicker. The third Thursday in March, I sat in Dr. Hanson's soothing waiting room, reading an old issue of *People*, stories of collapsing marriages and movie triumphs. After ten minutes, it all seemed pretty much the same.

Dr. Hanson's plush office was full of soft beige and brown furniture, thick carpeting, a few discreet toys in one corner. Prints of woodsy landscapes in handsome wooden frames. Ducks floating on serene ponds, deer cropping grass. I picked up a fashion magazine and began reading an article called "What You Will Wear for Fall," which bored and annoyed me. I flipped through the pages. "Ten Ways to Get Him to Commit." "The *Real* Truth About Carbohydrates." On the table beside me lay a *Newsweek* with a cover story about the rise of AIDS in Thailand, but I refused to even look at it.

A woman came in, maybe only in her seventies, but ancient-looking, her face lined bone. Her walk was painfully slow—she thumped her silver-headed cane down in front of her and then had to lean into it to move forward. She had a high, bare forehead under a bright turban in oranges and greens. She couldn't have weighed more than a hundred pounds. Even after all my AIDS work, the hours in an oncologist's office, in the hospital waiting rooms, I had to work not to stare at her.

Christy, Dr. Hanson's cheerful young receptionist, got her settled, then said to me, "Oh, I'm afraid there's just a little more paperwork for you here, Annie." I went up to the window to try to straighten out the latest insurance tangle. While I was clarifying information on the forms, she said, "Another month."

I was abstracted and didn't answer. She said, "Your mother's been very brave," and I said something like yes, she had been.

Then Christy said, "Well, the worst of it's almost over, and in six months it will all start to feel like a bad dream. Some people won't do the whole course, but I don't understand that. It's nasty, but then it's over and you can get on with it. In a few years, it will all be just another memory."

I raised my head to stare at her. Christy was about twenty-two: round cheeks, light brown hair in a ponytail, her name in gold on the heart-shaped pendant in her cleavage. At that moment, she was giving me the bright, peppy smile for which she'd probably been hired. She said, in a rousingly encouraging tone, "In six months, your mother will be running her orchards herself and giving us all hell."

I said to her, softly, but full of anger, "My mother is terminal. On her charts, if you'd take a look. In six months she'll be . . ." but I couldn't finish the sentence. I thought of going straight to Dr. Hanson, wanting Christy punished for her stupidity, insensitivity.

Christy was looking at me in wonder. "Your mother's cancer is gone. The treatments are to make sure that there are no free-floating cells. They got the cancer in her surgery."

I whispered, "You're thinking of someone else."

Christy said, "We don't put terminal patients through chemo." And then her voice got brisk. She said to me, lecturing, pointing a red-tipped fingernail, "It's extremely important for our patients to have the support of their families. These negative attitudes and fears are very depressing for them. It can even slow their recovery. Maybe cancer used to be a death sentence, but it certainly isn't now. I don't know why people don't learn that. It's such a scare word that people just stop thinking."

"My mother's not dying?"

"Of course, no one can predict long-term futures—there's always the *possibility* of recurrences, but your mother's just sick from the chemo. As soon as that wears off, she should be fine. As long as she stays off cigarettes." Christy shook her finger at me. "And as for *you*. Your part is not to get in the way of her recovery. No more gloom." She smiled again, radiantly.

I said, "Why didn't you say something before?"

"Well, I certainly would have if I'd known you were having these worries. But your mom is one who doesn't complain about her family."

I went back to my chair and fell into it, the magazine open on my lap. I couldn't read. I couldn't think clearly. Could it be true? Why the hell hadn't anyone said anything? But Mom had kept us from talking with Dr. Hanson, saying she wouldn't be discussed, that it made her feel like a child. And with Christy, we talked about the weather, her cats, Aurora and Bobby's newest feats. We had taken Mom's word for absolutely everything, and it seemed she had been completely mistaken.

When she came out to the waiting room, I took her arm, helping her out to the car, scanning her face. She was thinner than she had been, but I could see, now, that she didn't have the bone-wasting look of the woman in the turban, of other patients I'd seen. I settled her in the car and said, "I left something in the office."

She said, "You're no better than when you were ten. We never took one road trip that you didn't leave your stuffed cat or felt pens somewhere."

I ran into the office, knocked on Dr. Hanson's door, flung it open. He looked up at me in surprise. He was at his desk, writing something. I said, "My mother's not dying?"

He said, and the look on his face told me everything I needed to know, "Dying?"

"Why have you let her think so?"

In a voice both offended and avuncular, he said, "I *beg* your pardon. Your mother knows very well that she's recovering. We talk about her plans for the future at every visit. What is this?"

I tried to summon myself, to respond in a way that wouldn't leave me embarrassed to see him ever again, but I was so angry, with all of us, that I was afraid to open my mouth. I turned and went back out to the car. My mother slumped in her seat, frail and helpless.

She didn't open her eyes when I started the car, which was just as well, because I was raging. The things I thought of to say to her. What kind of game was she playing? Why was she putting us all through this?

It was raining, though not at flood level. Drivers jammed the streets, cutting in front of each other, turning without warning, frantically using their hour between noon and one for eating, errands, shopping. Honking at each other, taking stupid chances. I thought how I hated the time-fret that had a clamp on all of our hearts.

In my confusion, I'd gone down Fourth Street, a mistake. I had to pay attention—people shot in and out of parking spaces, all the lights were against me, and I had to watch for drivers making dangerous left turns with only feet to spare.

If my mother were not dying, I could not think of one reason to stay in Sonoma County, sleeping through my life. In a few weeks it would all be sunny and predictable again. Life was peaceful, ordinary, unvarying. The people on the sidewalks went about their business. Thinking of their lunches, their dentist appointments, their diets, their afternoon meetings, their children's grades. Here, AIDS prevention information was in books, every magazine, on the news, distributed in leaflets and newsletters.

I remembered sitting in the clinic in Buj, role playing with a young woman who had thought of her body as belonging to her husband. At first, when I talked to her, she would only giggle and look down. I said, in a mixture of Swahili and French, "Suppose I am your husband, just back from my truck route into Rwanda, and I am saying we should go to bed together now. Suppose I say I do not want to wear a *préservatif*." I held out the condom to her. She shrugged.

I said to her, "You are still negative. A great piece of fortune from God. If you become positive, if you *die*, Léonie, what happens to the children?"

She looked at me then, her face hardening into comprehension. It was a moment I had let myself forget, but I was remembering it now. She took the condom from my hand and held it in front of her. "I say to him, 'With this, pleasure. Without it, nothing.' "

"And what if I say, 'Then I will go down the street and find pleasure elsewhere'?"

She looked doubtful. Then she said, "If I say, she will not know you as I do? I am your wife, and I know the things you like."

"You can tell him," I said, "that you'll put it on for him. You can make it a game." She giggled again and put her hand over her mouth, shaking her head. I reached behind me and pulled out the wooden model. "Practice on this."

My mother sighed, adjusting her seat belt, an unspoken comment on my driving that brought me back to Sonoma County. The longer I waited, the more impossible it seemed to say anything at all to her. Her puckered lips, her silences and sharp remarks—and maybe, too, the sense of myself as clumsy, Annie the cow, always smashing into places where I didn't belong—stopped me. In the end, we drove home in silence.

I helped her upstairs to her bed and went back down to make lunch, stayed with her through the long afternoon, then, at last, when Margaret came to silently relieve me, went home to my apartment to do what I'd been meaning to for some weeks, make some kind of order, sort through my tangles of papers and books, undone accounts, half-unpacked clothes. I'd given away the wedding dress, tiara, and shoes, but hadn't touched anything else. I thought of calling Lizzie to tell her about Mom, but this was news she should get in person, and I was too exhausted to drive up to her cottage.

The apartment was full of the delightful, elegant junk I'd wasted so much money on, and I was full of a bitter, heavy regret. Coming up on my thirty-eighth birthday, and what had I done in my life? Stupidly thrown it away.

I then knelt on the closet floor, trying to match up sandals—I could find one each of three pair. I said to myself, *I am not going to let things pile up and get disorderly next time I move.* But I'd *had* a system; it's just that it had failed me, or I had failed it, entropy triumphing in record time.

Should I have tried to go to more prestigious schools, studied public policy and gone into the political side of changing public health? Instead of struggling with individual behaviors, perhaps I could have affected some larger stream of events? Oh, what *difference* did it make, with fifty thousand Burundians dead? I put my hands over my eyes and curled up among my shoes.

/ / /

I picture myself reentering my earlier life right here, a ghost observer, shouting. A frustrated desire to tell that younger Anne how aggressively the self will re-form itself and go on, the regeneration of nerve and tissue over the scars. How much we change, in whatever direction we need to, away from what we think we can't get over.

And, yes, I would never not have been *changed*, all the way down, but there would be a time when being happy did not bring guilt, when I no longer felt that the least I could give to the dead was my endless grief. But just then I wouldn't have *wanted* to get over Jean-Pierre, to give up my rage against the way my life was turning out.

I thought, *What is left for me? What shall I do?* Immediately, as if it had been waiting for me to ask, a voice in my head said, calmly, clearly, *Call Zoë tonight.* Surprised, I tested it out again. *Call Zoë tonight.*

Slightly comforted by the thought, and sick of my self-pity, I stood up, took yet another hot shower, and drove downtown through the rain. Halfway up the block from Harry Chang's sat the Dragon's Lair, a bead shop I'd walked past dozens of times. Crystal balls, some with pewter dragons or wizards holding them; faceted crystals hanging from the ceiling; cards and games; and one wall with bin after bin of jewelry fastenings, semiprecious stones, and beads. I went inside.

They carried both new and used jewelry, with a case full of old, stopped watches, and trays of rings, brooches, and pendants, including Stars of David and crosses. In among all the other crosses was an old silver cross, tarnished, with some beading. It was bigger than the one that had belonged to my father's mother, and the beading was less fine, but it looked quite a bit like it. This one I paid for. It cost less than five dollars, including tax. I dropped it into my pocket and went back out into the rain.

Sixteen

It took me a couple of calls to track down Zoë, but I eventually found her at her clinic. She came to the phone, shrieking, "Cow-eyed Annie!"

"My dear Man o'War!"

"Are you OK? What I read in the *Trib*—my *God*."

"It was bad. Quick, change the subject." I wanted to remain coherent.

"And your mother. I'm so sorry, Anne."

I said to her, "Look, here's the rundown. Burundi, I'll tell you in person. I can't even begin. My mother is up and running for the next few decades. Jean-Pierre is history."

"Ancient?"

"Recent and bloody."

"I'd hoped that was going to work."

"So did I, dear." I had to stop for a moment to get a grip on myself.

A short silence between us, worth the money it was costing. Zoë knew Burundi and what it would have been like. She had seen, as no one in my family had, what Jean-Pierre and I were like as a couple, before the bloodshed. She and I had done AIDS work together; because of that the bond between us went all the way down to bone level.

Then she said, "You'll tell me in *person*? When are you coming?"

"Darling, I like how you know your lines. How's your prevention component? Are you looking for health educators with HIV/AIDS-specific experience?"

Another silence, very different in quality. Then she said, "Do you know, it's not impossible. But you have to know that your salary would just about cover nothing. Our money is a joke. My word as a gentleman: the program secretary moonlights teaching English, and the other nurse—I'm not shitting you, dear—gives the occasional weekend tour to visiting Japanese."

"She's Japanese?"

"Not she, he. Tad. American, but he worked in Japan quite a while. Knows the lingo, has a feeling for their many and determined preferences. You wouldn't happen to know Japanese, would you? Or to have taken up some charming form of needlework?"

"I'm good at the whole living-cheap thing. And I have some money saved."

Zoë laughed. "How anal of you. Listen, dear, give me a week. I have to use my ever-forceful charm on some people."

/ / /

That night, I dreamed of a place both Burundi and Santa Rosa. I had to cross the Ruzizi River—I said to Christine, "I just want to walk *into* the river. Isn't that ridiculous?"

The surface of the water had a silky, impenetrable look, sheets of intertwined cloth, smoothly braided. The lumps underneath showed the crocodiles. I fought a powerful desire to wade in, let myself be hauled underwater, drowned and left under a rock until I was good eating. The crocodile brain in action: impulses before speech, before emotion, before thought.

In places, the water stretched very wide. In others, it appeared to be narrow, but when we jumped across, we realized the deceptiveness of the illusion—the cloth that had seemed to be the bank on the other side actually covered more water. The crocodiles had been waiting for us. They emerged, mouths open in terrible crocodile display, teeth showing. We had to run uphill, struggling not to slip into the water. Christine tried to jump and landed in the water, halfway across.

I shouted, from the hilltop, "Swim, swim," and she swam as fast as she could, the crocodiles converging on her. I had the feeling she would be safe, but also that our troubles hadn't even begun to be over. We would have to cross and recross that tricky water again and again before we were done.

/   /   /

The next day at work I felt like I was being throttled—same old, same old concerns. I spent most of the morning wrestling through the architects' files; they were about to be audited for the state portion of their funding on a school renovation and had to demonstrate that they'd done something or other in the scope of work which hadn't been properly documented in the semiannual report. Then I had to take minutes at an endless meeting. A demonstration of the power of various local governmental or community-based organizational players—people puffing off their agendas, jockeying for position, concerned about the erosion of their profits or defining the conditions for their neighborhood, wanting to stop the incursions of the malls.

At 11:30, I drove across town to Caswell's Lumber and went up the bare wooden stairs to the top-floor offices. These offices overlooked the store below, only a half railing separating them. The noise of the PA system reverberated constantly through the building, but the office staff ignored it. They knew me and just nodded as I went back to Margaret's cubicle. She looked up in dismay, her shoulders drawing together in self-defense.

"Margaret, have you had lunch? Can you come outside?"

She shrugged and came, not looking at me. Perhaps she was afraid I'd embarrass her. I had been rehearsing speeches all across town: how I had thought of the different ways of losing a sister and couldn't bear it; how glad I was that she was alive; how sorry I was for not having been more supportive along the way with Mom. But I had forgotten the actual Margaret—obdurate, practical, a brick wall. You didn't make speeches to her.

We went outside to the parking lot and began to make our way up the sidewalk, dodging men carrying two-by-eights over their shoulders, decorative displays of concrete bird baths, abandoned shopping carts. I said, "Margaret, I'm sorry."

"You always are, sooner or later, aren't you?"

"I don't want us to part on bad terms. I'm moving to Malaysia almost immediately." I knew Zoë would come through. Once I had asked her for a job, that job was as good as mine.

Margaret said, with a short, hard laugh, "Yes, that too. Not a surprise. Why *not* go off and leave us with Mom?"

"I won't go until the chemo is done." I was getting ready to tell her about Mom, but she said, "Will you be back for the funeral, or shall we send you pictures?"

My temper flared up, and I burst out, "Why is it you always put the worst possible interpretation on everything I do?"

She put her hands on her hips. We stood at the edge of the lot, arousing some interest from customers. "And you give me the benefit of the doubt?"

"You're right. I'm sorry. You're right."

"You talk about being *sisters*. What exactly does that mean to you? You and Lizzie are sisters. I'm like the family dog that has to be chased off the sofa." Tears sprang into her eyes, and she pressed one finger over each lid. "You have each other. Who do I have?"

Why hadn't I seen how alone she was? Jerry was a creature of temper and demands. The children had their own furious needs. Margaret, working full-time, raising three children, looking after Jerry and Mom hadn't much time for friends. And she wasn't an easy person to get on with. Too blunt, too uncompromising. She saw Mom often, but Mom was not someone who gave to you, except materially, sometimes.

I put my arms around Margaret, and she stood inside them stiffly. Would I love Jean-Pierre if I didn't desire him so fiercely? Could I love Margaret for what she actually was? I said, "I love you, Meg. I've been a bad sister." She was crying. I persisted. "Do you think it's too late? Don't you think we could be friends?"

After a while, still crying, she got out, "How could that be? You won't even be here."

"We could write each other. We could try not judging the other's failures."

She gave a kind of laugh. "You mean, you wouldn't hold it against me that I'm a bitchy thief, and I wouldn't hold it against you that you're a self-involved, self-righteous dreamer who runs away from responsibility?"

"Something like that." I was trying not to get angry again; there was a fair amount of truth in her description of me.

She put her arms around me in return, finally. "I don't think it will work," she said, but she sounded a little cheered.

I could picture us growing closer, helping each other overcome our weaknesses, writing to each other what we couldn't say to anyone in our daily lives. But how likely was it that we would become confidantes? I wasn't even going to tell her about Mom. What if she went on a tear against Mom? Or abandoned her? Margaret could wreck all of us, if she really lost control. I said, "I think we can be real friends. And who knows in life? Mom could get well. Doctors are wrong quite often. Actually, I'm full of hope."

"Oh, Annie," she said. "That's just like you."

/ / /

In the afternoon, I had a bout of nightmarish images of Burundi, followed by an attack of weeping in the bathroom. And then a "hunch" that I would come home to a message on my machine from Jean-Pierre. I had these hunches at least three times a week.

From time to time, I'd think I was getting over him, and then an hour later the longing crashed in on me again. I tried, desperately, not to imagine/remember making love with him, or driving in the countryside, or the two of us joking with Christine over Indian food at the Shama Chinese Palace. Not to remember the feel of his arms wrapped hard around me in the night, the ways he challenged me to think about the world. Not to remember Christine's sly jokes, my stupid belief that I would know her forever.

After work, I drove "home" to my little apartment box, full of the conviction that I'd been thinking of Jean-Pierre because he was thinking of me. But my call indicator showed a red zero, so I left for Mom's without ever having taken off my coat.

I brought French vanilla ice cream and big Mendocino Cookie Company cookies, full of bits of white chocolate and macadamia nuts. It was Lizzie's turn to look after Mom. By the time I arrived at Oak Street, Mom had already gone upstairs. When I went up to see if she'd fallen asleep, she was sitting up in bed, talking to herself, though she stopped as soon as I came in the room.

It seemed time to tell her that I knew. "How are you feeling?"

"Sick." Her voice said that this was evident, that it was stupid of me to have asked. But if I hadn't, she'd have been annoyed at my thoughtlessness.

I sat down beside her. "Do you want to talk, Mom?"

"My throat hurts. You can talk."

"Bobby did something so enchanting yesterday. He came and got into my lap, and he was just talking about the other children at school. You know how thoughtful he is, for a little man of action. Yesterday he was cuddling up against me, naming his schoolmates, talking aloud about them, one by one. Who they are, what they like to eat and play, how he feels about them. Then he said, 'And there's Johnny. No one likes him because he's fat. He doesn't have any friends. But *I'm* his friend.' It was his indignation, Mom. His sense of fairness. Maybe he will fight injustice, somehow. Do something in human service. Don't you wonder who they'll be as adults, what they'll do in the world?"

She glared at me. Indicating that I was heartless and appalling for mentioning a future she could be expected to miss. Except for Christy, I would have fallen for it, would have been blushing violently.

I said, "In retrospect, we'll think naturally they would do X. But looking forward through time, it's such a mystery."

My mother lay back against her pillows. "Dizzy," she said.

This short-circuited my subtle attempts to lead into the subjects of fate, mortality, and her own particular condition. "Can I get you anything? Water, your pan?"

She shook her head. The expression of nausea and misery on her face conquered me. What did I know about why she did what she did, what she needed?

I thought, *But if I don't bring it up now, I never will.* I opened my mouth, and was just not able—what came out was, "Would you like me to read to you?"

She nodded. I picked up *The Pirate's Lady.* We were never going to discuss it, and that was that. I had the sense that she'd won, though I wasn't sure if she knew it.

/   /   /

When she fell asleep, I went downstairs, where Lizzie and Aurora were snuggled up together in a blanket on the couch, watching Aurora's favorite dinosaur cartoon, one which made the point that a baby dinosaur was lucky to be able to eat vegetables. Possibly the source of its popularity with parents. Aurora mumbled along with the naive and gung-ho dialogue, one thumb in her mouth, the other holding on to Lizzie's braid: "Mommy's hair."

I sat down on the other end of the couch, my feet against Lizzie's. She moved the blanket so that it also covered my legs. She'd looked at me when I came in, a quick diagnostic exam, and had evidently reassured herself that I wasn't in a crisis state.

We ate our ice cream from the carton, passing it back and forth and holding it down to the height where Aurora could get some. The cookies were soft with butter and pulled apart in a slow, satisfying stretch. The little brontosaurus on screen got in an argument with its triceratops friend, who ran into stones and trees in her stubborn fury to have her own way. The room was almost dark, the only light the shifting TV colors that gave Lizzie, Aurora—the entire room—an underwater cast. As if we were sitting in a giant, warm aquarium. The heater came on with a thump.

I said, "I've been wondering whether to tell you this." Lizzie held the spoon against her teeth, head tipped to one side, which made Aurora take a tighter grip on her braid. "At first I thought I might not. Because, frankly, I don't have any good explanation for it, and it makes someone we love look extremely bad. But it's our business too, and I'm sick of secrets."

She said, "The other sibling?" We called this kind of talk "circumlocuting." It was no good anymore in front of Susan, but it still worked with Bobby and Aurora.

"The matriarchal figure."

"She's done something?"

"It's what she's not doing." I felt both silly and portentous, an embarrassed sense of taking a small-minded revenge against my sick mother. "As in not preparing to quit this mortal plane."

"Annie?"

"Not readying herself for the next in her string of lives. Not even close to biting it."

"Source of info for this grave allegation." She was sitting up straight now. Aurora gave an annoyed murmur and settled against her more firmly.

"Dr. Hanson and Christy."

Lizzie let out a long, low whistle. Neither of us said anything for several minutes.

Finally, tears began to run down Lizzie's cheeks. She snuffled them away. "I don't know whether I'm happy or furious. The old *cow*. What does she think she's doing?"

"*Aucune idée.* I'm clueless. Maybe we should go up and put a pillow on her face?"

Lizzie laughed, a shocked sound. Because for her, emotionally, Mom was still dying, was the heroic, doomed, precious figure. For me, she'd come back to life, and I was mostly angry. Glad she was going to live, and also furious at her. And not as delighted by the prospect of her continuing existence as I would have expected; I'd rearranged my mind and future to do without her.

I said, "My best guess is, she likes being royalty."

"But, Annie, she's so sick."

"According to medical sources, she won't be once she's recovered from the chemo."

Lizzie thought some more. "Margaret?"

"I haven't told her."

"Would explain matriarchal figure's upset over the money." Lizzie put the lid on the ice cream and set the carton on the floor. "But why is she doing this? Does she think we wouldn't have taken care of her otherwise?"

"Would we have dropped everything else?"

"I would have."

"Gathered by her bedside day and night to do her bidding?"

"She doesn't trust us."

"The other sibling would be absolutely enraged if she knew."

"Would confront the matriarchal figure full force. Tempestuous scenes no one has the strength for, possible accusations of betrayal back and forth, possible breakdowns."

Aurora, absorbed in the show, put a finger to her lips. "Shhhh."

We lowered our voices. I said, "We could let the sibling figure it out over time. Or perhaps the star of the show would eventually make an announcement. Ta-dah! Miracle of medical science! Resurrection! The troops being entertained fall to their knees in gratitude." An image of Margaret's bruised-looking, dignified face reproached me.

Lizzie said, "I'm not at all sure it would be good for the sibling to know. At this stage."

I was ashamed of us, the way we patronized Margaret behind her back. "Well, think it over. Do whatever you decide."

"Me. What about you?"

"I won't be here. When the last course of chemo is over, I'm gone. To Malaysia." Her face began to gear up for a protest, and I said, "It's too late, Lizzie."

"I thought you would be home for good, after all this." She pulled away from me, crossing her arms over her chest.

"I'm sorry." I was thinking of how much more I had to be sorry about than she had any idea of, how much I had kept from her. How much I was going to go on keeping from her.

"You're glad," she said. An accusation. "You can't wait."

"Lizzie, I was thinking. About the sibling. She can't pay back the money. And I'm leaving you with all . . . I thought I would pay it. About three thousand now, and the rest over time. Let Mom think the sibling is doing it."

"Does the sib know you're planning to do this?"

"Maybe I'd like her to know, maybe I hope someone will tell her after I'm gone. So she'll know I mean her well. And also because I have a bad character, like everyone else, as it turns out. Except you." A nightmare thought possessed me, and I said, "You really are as good as I believe you to be, aren't you? You don't have any awful secrets?"

"I'm not all that good." Her voice was dry. "But I'm the way you see me. Maybe a few secrets. I ate a hamburger last week. I don't know what came over me. And then I was too ashamed to tell anyone."

She leaned over to put her head on my shoulder, disarranging Aurora, who resettled herself, sleepily, between us. I bent my head down to where Lizzie's rested on my shoulder, my angel sister, feeling her silky hair against my cheek, smelling her skin and hair along with Aurora's: warm, sweet, slightly animal scents. Rosewater, something musky. In my mind, I was planning my departure.

/   /   /

It was only four days before Zoë called back. Life in Sonoma County seemed much more vivid now that I was going to escape, calling up in me an affectionate nostalgia. I had absolute faith in Zoë. I have never seen such a champ at getting her own way. In the international field, your network is all.

My faith proved to be fully justified.

"Listen, dear," she said, calling me at 1:30 in the morning. "How are you at administration?"

I was fuzzy. "Talk."

"We have this project director with pull, but he hates doing any work. So we're horribly disorganized. He can find the money for a laughable salary for you in our publications budget, if you can combine education with administration. As in, basically running the program but with no authority or credit. And occasionally he'll screw you over and reverse some necessary decision. Mostly, though, you'll get your way, because he's out banging gorgeous locals and playing golf. Say yes," she instructed. "I worked hard for this, and we in fact need you."

"Yes," I said. "It'll take me about three weeks to get packed and out of here. Thanks, Zoë."

"Oh, you'll be cursing me, soon enough. It's abysmally selfish of me, because you're going to have a hellish job, but I'm dying to see you. There is such *divine gossip* here."

I said, "I could use a little divine gossip round about now."

"And you can do me another favor. I want you to flirt with Tad, the other nurse, the one who gives Japanese tours? I think he's interested in me, and I've got other fish to fry."

"I'm not flirting with anyone right now, Zoë."

"Nothing serious, sweetie. Just a little friendly conversation. He's a lovely boy. Smart, funny, simply transparent with goodness. Light shining through clear spring water. I promise you, he cannot lie. If he tries, he goes beet red right down to his collar. But I have found myself a devastating and twisted Frenchman. Much more my type."

"Sure," I said. "What difference does it make? I'll be happy to talk to Tad for you. But I can't go out with him or anything."

"That's my girl. Just distract him for me."

So that was it, my first introduction to Tad, a favor I would do for Zoë, an offhanded hello to the future I wasn't yet ready for. We would be married within two years. Marriage to Tad has taught me that "domestic bliss" does not have to be an oxymoron. It's easy to be friends with him. We get irritable, but don't really fight. Oh, I've always been annoyed at how most of the diapers were mine, the refrigerator defrosting and toilets. And he gets silent and sullen when I leave lights on or throw out something that could have been recycled; he said to me once, the height of protest, "I sometimes wonder whether you can *really call yourself an environmentalist*."

But I'm happy with him 96 percent of the time, much more

than enough to make a solid marriage, the edifice or carapace Tad and I live inside, small, soft creatures in a hard public shell. More than anything, he's my partner in the most urgent and delicious job of looking after Chris and Timmy. It's our best joke, to remember how, because we were so naively afraid we could never love anyone the way we loved Chris, we actually considered not having a second child. When we look at the two of them, we think we should keep going. But, fortunately or unfortunately, I'm too old for that now.

I never have found out what became of Jean-Pierre—I cut my ties with Burundi absolutely. From time to time I would read that the violence hadn't stopped, but I didn't try to find out more. As the country went into free fall, I didn't want to know who had lived and who died: no one who hasn't lived through it is in a position to judge this. But I can't help speculating sometimes—is he married? Dead?

Zoë said, "Then that's settled. I'll fax you the info about arrangements for the job. Oh, *how* I'm looking forward to seeing you. It's been such a desert without you."

Zoë and her hyperbole, her feuds, her 3:00 A.M. phone calls, her romantic crises. It was coming back to me, how exhausting she was. "I've missed you every day," I said.

/   /   /

I gave notice at my job and apartment, then completely lost my balance. Crying in the bathroom at work. Accessing my answering machine four times a day to see if Jean-Pierre had called. I began to imagine Jean-Pierre with some gorgeous Burundian, looking into her eyes with the smile which should be mine, imagined him calling her "*mille vaches*." A white-hot pain, as if my insides were fusing together.

Lizzie, Margaret, and Susan helped me repack my not-even-fully-unpacked possessions. I wrapped the gold bracelet Jean-Pierre had given me in tissue, and put it in a box for storage. A moment of panic squeezed my chest together, as if I were underground and the air had started to run out. I'd made a mistake. The grief and memories would keep chasing me. All I was doing was leaving comfort, familiarity, people I loved to go chasing off after—what? The idea that I could somehow help people, change things, make any difference at all. An idiot presumption of usefulness. The exact fantasy that had gotten me into Burundi in the first place. I said, not too loud, "I'm too old to keep starting over."

Neither Margaret nor Lizzie responded. I knew, and they knew I knew, various possible responses. Thirty-seven was still young. I wasn't really starting over, since I had all my previous knowledge and experience. Or either of them could have asked, "What choice do you have?"

/ / /

Late at night, exhausted from packing but not able to sleep, I wrote a letter.

My love—

There are moments when it seems clear that I'm better off without you. Did I know you? Or was what I thought I saw my own invention? But I wake up, every single morning, and you're not there. How thin and dry life seems. I go to work, see the family, cook for myself, do the laundry. Because I've been sold on the whole independence lie, I think that I would be morally superior if I preferred to be alone, in a cottage with a cat or two and a garden, or whatever Malaysian equivalent I will find, than to be longing for you. But what animal, including ourselves, is designed to be alone?

Here's something I picture: I'm here in this apartment ("new" apartment, I was going to say, but I'm already leaving), damp from a shower, wearing only a T-shirt, wet hair on my neck, packing for Malaysia ("Malaysia?" you ask me, listening to this, and I say, in my imagination, "Never mind.") when the doorbell rings. I haven't been expecting anyone, but somehow I know at once that it's you. The feeling of you at the door is like no one else. You have decided to come to the U.S.—you are surprising me. Someone in my family gave you my address. Lizzie, probably. Wanting to help us out.

I'm so weak, with happiness, with desire, that I have to lean against the wall for a moment. I'm already wet, my body alive only for you. I look through the peephole, but it's a formality—you're there, as I knew you would be, grinning. (I imagine that you smile the way you used to—I feel as wholehearted as I used to—everything is as it used to be. Happiness is completely possible, and I don't feel it as a betrayal of anyone or anything at all. You have left Christine and Françoise in Burundi happily planning for the births of their children; they are not only alive, but pregnant. You have never killed anyone in your life, never been associated with war, darkness, revenge.)

When I open the door, your arms are already going around me. I jump up into them. You close and lock the door behind you—my face is buried in your neck, and I can feel you getting hard. We don't even make it into the bedroom, but fall down on the living room floor next to my mother's old rocking chair. The first moment of kissing you, your lips on mine, is so sweet, so unbearable, that I could stay like that forever. But of course we don't. You are tearing our clothes away, and you're not even all the way inside me before I'm crying out while you groan. This is beyond making love—this is making life—there is no way this can miss. When you let go into me, I know that we have begun what will be our baby. We go to bed afterward, and I lie on your shoulder, feeling your skin, your breathing, your heartbeat, so sweet, so strong, so real. We make love again and again, all night long, but it was that first time, that reconnection, that made the child.

This is madness—to write this makes me cry. I want to talk to you all night again. I want to watch you rocking this baby, giving her mashed papaya from a spoon. I want to come home to you every evening for the rest of my life.

But the truth is, I will never, never, never see you again.

yours always,

Anna

I didn't, of course, send it. I tore it up and threw it in the trash, under my coffee grounds and banana peels, so that no one who might be going through the Dumpster would be tempted to try to piece it together.

/   /   /

The next day, I went to the bookstore, bought guidebooks and histories, and then went to the state university library, where I sat for hours at one of the microfiche readers, scanning the flickering texts of articles from the library's archives. I read that the prevalence of AIDS was high, and worsening, in Malaysia, though not yet as bad as in Thailand. Malaysia had a couple of hundred thousand registered heroin users, and a government unwilling to engage in needle exchanges or distribution. Kuala Lumpur and Penang also had problems with "schoolgirl" prostitution. More than three-quarters of those with HIV/AIDS were between the ages of twenty and forty, but a noticeable minority of teenagers, including those as young as thirteen, had contracted the virus. Oil-based lubricants were said to be popular among sex workers.

At the microfiche reader next to me, a girl with wildly curly hair and a serious expression was scanning graduate school catalogs. She had two or three boxes, from different states, and she made diligent notes of phone numbers and key information.

She could talk to her peers in a way I couldn't—they would listen to her. Wouldn't this be true in Malaysia? What if we could get teams of peer counselors among the young sex workers? Was there any possibility that the government might support this? If we started a pilot program . . . or perhaps this was already being carried out. What languages did the young speak? Should I be trying to learn Chinese as well as Malay? Even if most people still spoke English, it seemed to be a somewhat different English. Was there a place I could take lessons, or was that a ridiculous idea? Could Zoë herself teach me? I started a folder of newcomer questions and carried it home to pack in my carry-on.

Stopped at a red light, I bent over to look at my Malay phrase book.

Selamat Pagi. Good morning.
Selamat Petang. Good afternoon.
Terimah Kasih. Thank you.
Maafkan saya. I am sorry.

When I went to say good-bye to Mom, she was upstairs in her room. Still sick, though her chemotherapy had been over for two weeks. What a miserable business chemo is. In a hundred years they'll regard it with the horror we reserve for the endless, nearly casual amputations of the nineteenth century.

She said, without opening her eyes, "So you're off."

I sat beside the bed. Susan had embroidered a little heart-shaped pillow for her for Valentine's Day. Lace around the edges, a ribbon of red velvet, scraggly writing: "Love's Leading Grandma." I thought about how Susan would change as she grew up. When she'd been five, I'd pictured her, with all that confident energy, running major corporations.

My mother was giving a splendid performance, understated irony and hidden wounds. "I may not see you again."

I said, "I have faith that we'll see each other in the next world." She opened her eyes to look at me. "Or in subsequent lives. Maybe you'll be the child and I'll be the mother. Or friends, feeling, from the moment we meet, a deep and inexplicable bond." But then I had a reversal of feeling, a sudden tenderness toward the level of need hinted at by her long, high-caliber performance. A Tony—definitely live theater. Best actress in a dramatic role. I took her hand in mine, a little remorsefully. She was really so extremely miserable.

With the other hand, I went back to fingering Susan's cushion. Mom said, "She's not around much."

"Susan? It's not bad news, you know—she got tired of Mr. Wrong. After the picnic. I suppose seeing him with the family took some of the thrill off."

My mother said, with her small, sly grin, "His table manners."

"I think it might have been. Now she wants to be a roller-blading champ. Margaret says she's going to break a leg, it'll be badly reset, and she'll never walk properly again."

"You wait till you're a mother," my own mother said. A threat. "You think everything's so funny."

My throat closed. What would I do, be, if I never had children? No one could push my buttons like Mom; in seconds she could be all the way under my skin. I leaned over to kiss her soft, sour-smelling cheek. "Let's pretend I'm coming back tomorrow. See you tomorrow!"

At first I thought she wasn't going to answer, but then she rolled her eyes. "If wishes were horses," she said. *Then we would all ride.*

I said to her, "I'll send you a souvenir. Whatever they make in Malaysia." An image of blood seeping through dirt came into my mind, but I immediately began counting. I'd learned to focus on the images of the numbers as they marched across my mind.

It was the moment when I might have said to her, *I know you're not dying.*

She looked out the window. "If you girls knew what it had been like." But it was a mutter, more to herself. Although I was meant to overhear it.

I reached into my pocket, pulled out the cross, and dropped it onto her bedside table. It slid against a half-empty glass of water, clinking, coming to rest in the used tissues beside her pile of romances and the kidney-shaped hospital pan.

She turned back toward me, alerted by the noise, started to reach for the cross, then clasped her hands over her belly, looking at me with an unreadable face.

I said, "I could tell you the story of how I have that, how it got here. Maybe the truth, maybe not. But I don't think you want to know."

She fussed with her hands at the coverlet, straightening it out, arranging the sheet just so underneath. She hadn't seen the cross for years. Did she know it wasn't the same one? I couldn't tell. She said, "No, I don't believe I do."

"Yes." I sat for a moment, my hands in my lap. "Well then." I leaned forward, picked up the cross, and held it out to her. Her eyes met mine, the nameless creature inside peering out: crafty, self-protective, reptilian, heartbreaking. After a moment, Mom opened her right palm in acceptance. She examined the cross for a long time, then, looking straight at me, she closed her hand around it, an assertion, a statement of ownership, a reply.

Acknowledgments

For information on Burundian culture, history, proverbs, and society, I am grateful for assistance from Burundians I knew and friends in the Peace Corps, State Department, and various nongovernmental organizations. I am also deeply indebted to Warren Weinstein's *Historical Dictionary of Burundi: African Historical Dictionaries No. 8* (Metuchen, NJ: The Scarecrow Press, Inc., 1976), as well as to Ellen K. Eggers's *Historical Dictionary of Burundi, Second Edition* (Lanham, MD: The Scarecrow Press, Inc., 1997).

Additional information comes from René Lemarchand's *Burundi: Ethnic Conflict and Genocide* (New York, Cambridge, and Melbourne: Woodrow Wilson Center Press and the Press Syndicate of the University of Cambridge, 1994); Jens Robbert's *Le Droit de la Famille Au Burundi: De l'organisation familiale traditionelle au Code des personnes et de la famille* (Tervuren: Musée Royal de L'Afrique Centrale, 1996); Juan Navas' *Famille et Fecondité au Burundi: Enquête Sociologique* (Bujumbura: le Centre de Recherches Socio-religieuses de l'Episcopat du Burundi et la Faculté des Sciences économiques et administratives de l'Université du Burundi, 1977); and Marc

Barengayabo's *La Dot Matrimoniale au Burundi* (Rome: Pontificia Universitas Lateranensis, 1975).

The information on folktales comes from *Contes du Burundi*, collected and translated from Kirundi into French by F. Rodegam (Paris: Conseil international de la langue française, 1993). The story of the old cow and the king is loosely based on a version in this collection; the paraphrase, a few of the details, and the English translation are my own. The story of the king, his friend, and the end of the drought can be found in a different form in *Legendes historiques du Burundi*, collected by Claude Guillet and Pascal Ndayishinguje (Paris: Éditions Karthala, 1987). The paraphrase, translation, and some details are my own.

The text of the Universal Declaration of Human Rights, which I have quoted from several times, can be found on-line at http://www.un.org/Overview/rights.html.

/ / /

I am more grateful than I can possibly say for Ron: my first reader, my other half.

And I am thankful to, and for, my beloved family: Hannah, George, Zan, Marion, Peter, Melanie, Lisa, David, Edy, Laura, Steve, Matt, Kay, Taylor, Graham, Amy, Mia, Megan, and Alex. And to Laurence Kent Jones, Margot Livesey, Karla McLaren, Noelle Oxenhandler, Genoa Shepley, John Thomas Waddell, and Johnna Wenburg, who have all, in their different ways, been supportive and inspirational. My teachers—at the University of Michigan and elsewhere—have been brilliant, generous, and admirable both as writers and as human beings. I am very grateful to them. And to my fellow workshoppers and students in Ann Arbor, as well as my colleagues and students at the University of California, Berkeley.

The Colby and Roy W. Cowden Fellowships and the Avery Hopwood and Jule Hopwood Awards gave me time to work on this book.

Candice Fuhrman and Elsa Hurley are a writer's dream, in their criticism and in their support. And so is Deb Futter: I am grateful for her insight, her sense of humor, and her pitch-perfect ear. Everyone at Doubleday has been welcoming, patient, and a total pleasure to work with. I want to express my appreciation for their help.

Andrea Barrett took me in out of the wilderness, taught me what a book was, and kept me going. This novel is for her.

/ / /

No attempt to understand what happened and what it means, what provokes and continues the cycles of killing, is useful for the dead. But it is a human urge to cut a gravestone, out of whatever materials we have.